THE

TRANSFORMATION

OF

BARTHOLOMEW

THE
TRANSFORMATION
OF
BARTHOLOMEW
FORTUNO

A Love Story

ELLEN BRYSON

PICADOR

First published 2010 by Henry Holt and Company, LLC, New York

First published in Great Britain 2011 by Picador
an imprint of Pan Macmillan, a division of Macmillan Publishers Limited
Pan Macmillan, 20 New Wharf Road, London N1 9RR
Basingstoke and Oxford
Associated companies throughout the world
www.panmacmillan.com

ISBN 978-0-330-53381-2

1 3 5 7 9 8 6 4 2

A CIP catalogue record for this book is available from
the British Library.

Printed in the UK by CPI Mackays, Chatham ME5 8TD

Visit **www.picador.com** to read more about all our books
and to buy them. You will also find features, author interviews and
news of any author events, and you can sign up for e-newsletters
so that you're always first to hear about our new releases.

An empty belly hears nothing.

—English proverb

THE

TRANSFORMATION

OF

BARTHOLOMEW

FORTUNO

*L*IGHT FROM APRIL'S FULL MOON SWEPT OVER the Museum's façade and down the building's marble veneer. It illuminated the man-sized letters that hung high and large enough for a person as far uptown as Canal Street to see, spelling out BARNUM'S AMERICAN MUSEUM. From where I sat in my fourth-floor window, nearly all of Manhattan's sky was visible.

I pressed my back against the window frame and watched the moonlight dissolve a fistful of clouds. Its glow rolled across Broadway to cover the spires of St. Paul's and the front of City Hall, the mourning flag for Lincoln still listlessly hanging there, then spilled across the stables and roofs of houses abandoned to haberdashers and tailors. Most of higher society had stampeded uptown toward Fifth Avenue years ago, sticking to the highest part of the island and avoiding the land that sloped down toward the rivers on either side.

A bum staggered to a halt below me on a Broadway emptied by the encroaching night. He bellowed something indistinguishable, then tipped back on his heels to gawk, open-mouthed, up, up, up along the high Museum walls. He gazed in awe at the oval paintings of exotic tigers, whales, and a white-horned rhinoceros that were strung between each story of windows like pendants across the bosom of a well-endowed harlot. Who could blame the poor man for staring? Thousands before him had fallen for the gussied up old place, everyone from the city's poorest paupers to the families of its Upper Ten—and once even a prince. They, too, had all been enticed by the Museum's glitter. And why not? The place was irresistible. Banners and fluttering flags beckoned from the roof like welcoming hands, and a pied-piper band spewed out terrible music from the balcony twelve hours a day, every day except Sunday. "I take great pains to hire the poorest musicians I can find," Barnum liked to say. "They play so badly that the crowd moves into the Museum just to get out of earshot." Colossal gas lamps flanked the front doors, and just inside stood a huge golden statue of Apollo, his horses rearing, a lyre dangling from his naked shoulder. The great illuminator's index finger pointed toward the ticket window, just in case a visitor failed to see its shiny plaque.

The truth was, even I still found the place impressive after living here for nearly a decade. I'd been one of Phineas Taylor Barnum's Human Curiosities (viewed thrice daily under the moniker Bartholomew Fortuno, the World's Thinnest Man) since 1855, and, all in all, I could not complain about the way my life had unfolded. Few talents managed to make their way as far in the business as I had—Barnum's Museum was the pinnacle of our trade—and I made a good living off the gifts nature had given me. I had found a comfortable home.

So it was with a great sense of satisfaction that I sat on my windowsill that chilly spring night, just after the end of the War of the Rebellion, unaware that change twisted its way to me through the darkened New York streets. Mindlessly, I ran a hand lovingly across my right shoulder, never tiring of the intricacies of socket and bone, then lit a cheroot in defense against the fetid air; the local breweries, tanneries, slaughterhouses, and fat-melting establishments smoldered away even in the middle of the night. Looking north I could make out Five Points, the Bowery, and the mean area around Greenwich Street that was jammed with immigrants and other unsavory folks. So many Irishmen, Italians, and Germans had crammed themselves below Houston Street that I could all but hear the clang of their knife fights. I avoided visiting that part of town. In fact, whenever possible, I avoided leaving Barnum's Museum at all. A man like me had no business in the wider world. Let the outside world come to me and pay to do it.

Catching a whiff of spring blossoms from the West Side orchards, I couldn't help but turn to Matina, who sat on my divan, tatting a lace doily to replace the one she'd stained with lamb gravy the week before. Next to her rested a tray of empty dishes from her evening snack and a pillow she'd embroidered for me years ago with the words *He Who Stands with the Devil Does Himself Harm.*

"I told you it was possible to smell the orchards from here, my dear. Come and sniff for yourself."

"All I smell is garbage," Matina answered, from her seat. "Come away from the window, Barthy. I've something I want to show you before I leave for the night."

Matina, my friend and frequent companion, had spent the evening with me as she often did, and I was glad to have her company. She'd been a permanent fixture at the Museum for four years that spring, having come from Doc Spaulding's *Floating Palace*, the great boat circus that barged up and down the Mississippi. Her stage name back then was Annie Angel the Fat Girl, and although she no longer performed under that sobriquet, it suited her well. Matina was as charming as a beautiful child. With her blond finger curls, alabaster skin, and great blue eyes that gazed out at the world as if she were seeing it for the first time, she resembled a great big porcelain doll.

Flip sides of the same coin, we'd taken to each other the first time we met, and our friendship had only grown over the years, in spite of constant taunts from Ricardo the Rubber Man. "The woman weighs over three hundred pounds, Fortuno! And look at you. A stick figure! I'll bet it slips in like a needle in the haystack." I was mortified by such crass observations, especially when they were made in front of my lady friend, but everyone knew that Ricardo's taunts had little truth to them. Matina had understood from the beginning that my body was not built for pleasure, and we'd both accepted the limitations of our relationship a long time ago. I liked to think our friendship was stronger because of it.

Earlier this evening, I'd spent an hour or so reading aloud from the current installment of *Our Mutual Friend* in *Harper's*. Dickens's fine wit made Matina smile, and she giggled like a girl as she put away her lace and then plumped up the pillow on the sofa and tapped the seat next to her.

"Come look at my new discovery," she said, digging into her bag and hauling out an oversized book. She flung it onto the low table in front of her, jangling the lamp as it landed. "It's by the same man who wrote *Peter Parley's Tales of America*. But this one is about people like us. I hear it goes back hundreds of years."

The book, bound in black cloth and covered with fine embossing and gold letters, was titled *Curiosities of Human Nature*.

"He illustrates quite well, I think. Wouldn't it be marvelous if someday we wound up in a book like this?"

The leaves of the book crackled as I thumbed through the pages. Matina was right; the woodcuts were of excellent quality. Although I vastly preferred my own books on congenital anomalies—Willem Vrolik's *Handbook of Pathological Anatomy* or his more dramatic *Tabulae ad illustrandam embryogenesin hominis et mammaliam tam naturalem quam abnormem*—Matina's new book was not a bad alternative. Her taste usually tended toward the pictorial—like most New York ladies, Matina kept an extensive collection of *cartes* not only of Prodigies and Wunderkinds but of famous New York families like the Schermerhorns and the Joneses—but at least she was literate.

Matina flipped through the pages of her new treasure one by one. "It's quite comprehensive. Look here. He's done a whole section on dwarfs. Jeffery Hudson, born in 1619, only three feet nine." She furrowed her eyebrows and read out loud. "'Midgets and dwarfs have generally one trait in common with children, a high opinion of their own little persons and great vanity.' Ha!" She looked up, bright-eyed. "Well. *We* could have told him that!"

She was quite right. Over the years at least a dozen midgets had cursed us with their presence, and—with the exception of Tom Thumb and his lovely wife, Miss Lavinia—not one of them was tolerable. Dwarfs could be even worse—testy, arrogant, and impossible to please—but fortunately, Barnum rarely hired dwarfs. He thought them too misshapen for the delicate sensibilities of his feminine clientele.

"And here's a story about a young boy, six years old, who did impossible calculations in his head. You see here?" Matina used her finger like a teacher's baton, poking at the page. "Zerah Colburn calculated in his head the number of seconds in two thousand years. In less than a heartbeat he answered, Sixty-three billion seventy million." She looked at me with a touch of irony. "They say he had a very large head."

"Any good phrenologist would tell you that head size and intelligence are closely correlated," I observed.

Matina laughed. "What if I were to knock my forehead and develop a big bump right here?" She poked a finger into the front part of her brow. "Would that make me smarter than you?"

I let the comment pass.

Around midnight, Matina complained of heartburn and said she was ready for bed. I thought she would soon leave for her own quarters, but she surprised me by walking toward my bedroom.

"Do you mind if I rest here a minute or two? My stomach is bothering me something terrible. I won't stay long." As she passed, I caught a whiff of the sweet smell that always hovered about her. Tonight: a potpourri of pork shanks, braised leeks, and apples mixed with her usual lavender perfume.

Down went Matina's massive body on my bed, the wood frame groaning in protest, and within minutes she fell into a snoring sleep. Much as I would have preferred her to go to her own rooms, I could hardly have said no. It was my duty as a friend to accommodate Matina's physical problems. She suffered from a number of ailments, ranging from sleep difficulty to the swelling of her legs and, most recently, a racing of her heart even at rest, but anyone with gifts like ours knows to take a philosophical view of such complaints. I myself often suffered from swollen joints, the pain of bony knees knocking together, the bumps of exposed elbows, a lightheadedness appearing at inopportune moments, or an unpadded chair torturing my hips and spine. Every gift has its price.

I laid my comforter over Matina's bare arms—her off-the-shoulder gown was charming but not very sensible—and left to tidy up my parlor. After lowering the gas lamps, I swallowed a nip of tonic for my aching joints and shimmied back out onto my bedroom window ledge to watch the evening pass.

The clatter of a carriage in the street soon caught my attention. Gripping the window's frame, I tilted out to find the source. At first I saw nothing, only street shadows and lamplight and a gray dog darting between the sycamores across the road. And then there it was, a grand carriage appearing at the far end of Broadway, the clop-clop of its horses drawing it toward the Museum. How curious. One might expect to see a two-seater at such an hour, carrying someone's mistress home or taking a gentleman from the fancy brothels like Flora's or the Black Crook down to the scruffier waterfront ballrooms, but this was a landau coach, posh and stylish, its top latched down and its lacquered sides glinting in the moonlight.

Rather than turn west toward the more pleasant Church Street, the coach continued straight, passing the twin gas lamps that stood guard before the Museum's entrance. I leaned a bit farther out the window, straining to keep the carriage in sight. It came to a stop a few paces later. One of the horses whinnied as the driver jumped from his perch and drew open a cushioned door, ceremoniously rolling out the steps. A glimpse inside the cab attested to its luxuriousness: its walls were plush with padded fabric, its seats were covered with fine leather, and its floor was elegantly tiled. It was much finer than any coach I'd ever had the pleasure of riding in. I considered waking Matina, who took great delight in mysterious happenings, but the next thing I saw kept me riveted to my place.

Out of the coach, a tiny foot emerged, followed by a gloved hand reaching delicately toward the extended arm of the driver. An apparition appeared. She wore a full veil of white attached to a fashionable bonnet, and her traveling coat was of unquestionable excellence. This was a woman of quality if ever I saw one. She faltered on the stair, and the driver took her by the waist to assist her. She brushed aside his hands and gently stepped onto the wooden planks of the walk in front of the Museum.

"How dare you manhandle this woman, sir?"

A booming voice that could only belong to Barnum rang out from inside the carriage. Most intriguing. Had the great Phineas T. returned early from his scouting trip? Barnum often left us to chase down rumors and ferret out new talent, and usually he stayed on the road for months at a time, scouring the traveling circuses, the carnivals, and the other grand cities for the unnatural, the exotic, and the new. According to the Museum manager, Benjamin Fish, Barnum was not due back from his current trip until mid-June. That was still nearly two months away, but here he was, forcing his bearlike body out of the carriage door and stomping across the dirty planks of the walkway, sending the rats below scurrying into the street. I gazed down at the great man. Barnum's receding hairline hinted at his age, but his eyebrows—as bushy and wild as ever—spoke to how vital he still remained.

Barnum puffed out his chest, his belly protruding above his satin waistband, and approached the driver, who looked around the abandoned street as if Barnum were addressing someone else.

"Have you heard me, man?"

"I ain't done nothin,' sir," the driver yelped. "Tried to help her down is all."

"You've acted beyond your position," Barnum said. "You've forgotten your place."

I realized that I'd lost sight of Barnum's mysterious companion, but then I spotted her resting against a post. She straightened her veil with a small gloved hand as the driver shifted back on his heels. Barnum advanced. The driver clenched his fists in what looked like an acceptance of Barnum's challenge, but then he scuttled back and hopped onto his coach, barreling away in a storm of scattered stones and dust.

Barnum and the veiled woman, alone now, lingered in the gaslight below. I could make out only the muffled rise and fall of Barnum's voice against the soft murmurings of the woman's responses. Moments later, the great front doors opened and they disappeared into the Atrium. I retreated from the window back into the bedroom, calmed by the sound of Matina's rhythmic breathing.

In my parlor, I picked up the tray full of Matina's empty plates and glasses and set it outside in the hall for the chambermaid to fetch. The veiled woman must be a new act. But, if so, why would Barnum slip her in under cover of night? It made no sense at all. Barnum was the consummate showman. No one in the world knew how to create drama and interest the way he did, and every new act was an opportunity for him to step into the spotlight and seize the attention of all of New York. Human Curiosities were Barnum's greatest pride. He was forever boasting of our gifts. "My Curiosities are the royalty of the underworld," he would say. "Like everyone else, but more. So much more." In fact, when I first came to the Museum, Barnum cleared an entire room for my exhibit. He gathered every skeleton in the place—from a six-inch steppe lemming to the reassembled bones of a Romanian water buffalo—and placed them, smallest to largest, around the perimeter of the room. Full-sized portraits of yours truly in all my six-foot, sixty-seven-pound glory touted me as THE THINNEST MAN IN THE WORLD.

Barnum gave an equal introduction to Jonathan Alley, labeling the muscled newcomer The Giant Boy of Hungary and dressing him in bright red pantaloons and one of those tidy bow ties commonly worn by boys from the better families. Although Alley was nearly twenty-five years old at the time and bore the shadow of a rugged beard, Barnum worked the monster-child illusion perfectly. Alley came to the Museum with great flourish, caged atop a painted wagon drawn down the center of Broadway during the height of commerce. The "boy monster" rattled the bars of a cage full of bunting and big yellow balls. I laughed until my side stitched when I first saw the man. "I think it's a perfectly decent presentation," Matina had said, offended by my laughter. But then hadn't she started her career dressed as a cherub, wings and all?

When Barnum hired his giant, Emma Swan, The World's Tallest Woman, he flew flags off the balconies and made up twenty-foot posters of her seated with two midgets on her lap. He claimed that she stood eight feet high—what did it matter if she had to pile up her hair and teeter around on shoes with four-inch heels in order to measure up? Barnum even had Ricardo the Rubber Man stretched from one balcony to the next for an entire morning during the first week he came to us. Yes, all of us had been given a proper introduction to the public. So why would he sneak this newest act into the Museum in the dead of night?

I pulled the shutters closed and stuck my head into the bedroom. Matina was sprawled across two-thirds of the bed, her hair flaxen in the moonlight. Her generous breasts rose and fell like waves on the ocean beneath the blue silk of her dress. What if the woman I'd seen with Barnum was competition for Matina? She'd be furious. But no. The woman I'd seen outside did not look large. Had Barnum perhaps found a new Hottentot Venus? Again, no. The new woman was slim and elegant, with no protruding buttocks, at least as far as I could tell. Still, the real Hottentot Venus had been dead for years—I'd heard rumors that certain oversized parts of her had been pickled and now floated in a jar on display by special invitation only at Kahn's Anatomical Museum—and a new Venus would be a true coup.

Maybe I should wake Matina. Surely, she'd know who was coming up through the circuits. And oh, how she'd love the gossip of a mystery woman! But I decided it best not to disturb her. Instead, I settled into the small space beside her, pulled my mother's comforter over my ribs, and gave myself over to dreams of great and mysterious women.

chapter two

HE CLANGING BELLS OF ST. PAUL'S WOKE ME from a fitful sleep. Matina had slipped out sometime during the night without disturbing me, and, as I lay in bed, my thoughts moved again to the mysterious woman from the night before. If she was a new act, I hoped she'd be extraordinary. Too many of Barnum's recent discoveries had been less than stellar, and I'd begun to worry that he'd forgotten the difference between *new* and *unique*.

When curiosity finally bested comfort, I forced myself up out of bed and moved into the parlor, thrusting open the shutters onto a clear Sunday morn. Below me, early-rising sinners hustled up Broadway toward St. Paul's for the morning services. In less than an hour, our own in-house church service would begin, and though I'd planned to take a soothing bath before worship—and had reserved the bathtub days ago for this purpose—I'd now have to settle for a dose of tonic and a quick toilette in my room. The maid had already picked up my chamber pot from the hall and left fresh water by the door, along with the single boiled egg I sometimes ate for breakfast. Ignoring the egg, I hauled the pitcher to the bedroom. Water sloshed over the side onto the already stained marble of my dresser. I made a mental note to speak to the maid about not overfilling it.

Checking my image in the wall mirror, I shaved carefully, wishing Matina hadn't told me that her *Peterson's* claimed it was no longer fashionable to let one's facial hair grow. After applying a touch of pomade to my hair and slipping into my trousers, waistcoat, and

Sunday cravat, I decided I didn't look half bad. One good thing about being only bones: My clothing never bunched or pulled. Hurrying out into the resident hall, I took a moment to peer around and noted that none of the empty sleeping rooms had been disturbed the night before. Where on earth had the veiled woman slept? How curious. But I was already late for church, so I pushed through the door separating our living space from the fourth-floor exhibits and hurried along. An irritable kangaroo thumped her tail as I passed, her odor strong but not offensive. I tipped my hat to her and then cringed, as I walked by the glass cages where the boa and other unsavory snakes lay curled around the center stovepipe for warmth. Snakes bothered me, always had. And the last day I wished to see them was on the Sabbath.

Because the Museum was closed on Sunday mornings and there'd be no visitors to disturb me, I bypassed the service stairs and cut directly through the public part of the third floor, hustling past the exhibits in the curio salons. These rooms were filled from floor to ceiling with the treasures Barnum brought back from his expeditions. Cases of butterflies and insects, Chinese balls, and whistles made of pigs' tails were displayed in neat lines beneath glass. For good luck, I tapped the display case where the pear-shaped diamond called the Idol's Eye was nestled, then hurried by bows and arrows and stone heads, the poisoned shafts from the lost tribe of Kahil El Zabar, the Samoan Sea Worm that could gut a cat in seconds, and a giant hairball that had been rescued from the stomach of a black-bellied sow.

I scanned the second floor for any hint of the new act but found nothing: no packs of undistributed flyers, no announcements, and no word of her on the big Notice Board in the backstage Green Room. Not even an advance broadside on the marquee near the Moral Lecture Room, the Museum's famous theater. Though I was already late for services, I made one final dash to the first floor, sure I'd stumble across a pamphlet or poster announcing Barnum's latest discovery. But I discovered nothing new at all.

Strands of the opening hymn, "Holy, holy, holy! Though the darkness hide thee," wafted downstairs, and I ran up the Grand Staircase to the temporary "chapel." Every Sunday, Barnum had the chapel set up in the same minor theater in which I did my daily shows. There were three of these minor theaters flanking the Moral Lecture Room. This particular room boasted a small elevated stage, a plank floor, three portal windows peering out on an airshaft of floating dust, and ten or so rows of straight-backed chairs. The only truly elegant touch—and all three minor rooms had variations of the same—was the doorframe. Each room boasted a carved figurehead taken from an old warship, ram heads around one entrance, ancient Roman saints on horseback framing another. Today's "chapel" door showed two full-length carvings of the Greek goddess Athena in her half-naked glory.

I patted my hair into place and entered, scanning the dark room for the new act, but saw only Matina, the giant Emma Swan, three housemaids, and a handful of actors currently playing in *Ring of Fate*. Reverend Smalley glowered down at me from his pulpit as I dutifully slid into place next to Matina. I settled onto one of the same chairs our audiences sat in to watch me perform, wishing I had a cushion to protect my thin frame from the hard wooden seat. The stale stink of yesterday's crowd still filled the room. But Matina looked charming in a white bonnet and day dress of lavender silk with large puffing flounces running around the hemline.

"Why did you leave without waking me?" I whispered, leaning toward her.

"Shush now. You're late and the Reverend is staring at you."

"You'll never guess what I saw last night."

The little congregation starting singing "Fairest Lord Jesus," and Matina raised an eyebrow at me.

"I'll tell you, but you must keep what I say to yourself."

"Of course, Barthy, of course."

"Barnum is back."

Matina let her hymnbook slide to her lap. "He is? Why so early, for goodness' sake?"

I let her wait a moment, to build the suspense. "I think he's brought a new act with him."

"What do you mean, a new act?" Matina whispered. "Who in the world is it?"

"Not sure. Barely saw her, I'm afraid."

The good Reverend lifted a cautionary finger at us, and Matina lifted her book to her face again, studying it intently. Then she leaned over to me, her lips pursed. "*Her*, you say?"

"And today, no sign of her at all."

Matina said nothing else. We sat through a lackluster sermon about how we received grace through our own free will—drivel, in my opinion, since no man is the master of his own destiny—but I could tell that Matina was dying to hear more; few things pleased her as much as news that no one else was privy to.

As soon as the service finished and we left the room, Matina demanded, "Tell me everything!" I filled in all the details, but she kept asking questions I couldn't answer: Where did she come from? Could you tell how old she was? How tall?

"You *must* pay better attention to what you see," Matina admonished me, as we made our way down the service stairs, her hand wrapped around mine like warm bread. I let her squeeze my fingers as I led her out the staff door and through the back courtyard near the kitchens. When we reached the dining room, she said, more to herself than to me, "How odd that I haven't heard a *thing*. I usually get wind of what Barnum is planning before anyone else."

I opened the dining room door for Matina and gestured her forward. Ricardo the Rubber Man, resplendent in green pantaloons, leaned rudely across the table, fingering the fine piece of table linen that had been scavenged from Barnum's rooftop café after someone had written *Give us a kiss* on it in India ink.

"Now ain't lunch looking appetizing?" He snaked one of his arms out and wrapped it all the way around Matina's ample waist, tugging up the back of her hoopskirt so that it showed the bottoms of her petticoats.

I rapped Ricardo on the hand with my walking stick, which made a sharp cracking noise as it smacked against his knuckles.

"Bastard!" Ricardo whipped away his hand, intentionally dislocating his fingers. Normally, I'd admire a Curiosity with skills as unique as Ricardo's, but I must admit that his long tongue, his sloppy words, and his aversion to baths revolted me.

"Look what you did, you broke my fingers!" he hollered at me, dangling his hand in front of my face.

"Leave them alone!" Alley bellowed from the far side of the table, and Ricardo backed away grudgingly, pulling his ears long like a hound's and barking.

Alley and Ricardo had been rivals for years. Ricardo liked to claim that his own gift was vastly superior to everyone else's and took great pleasure in offending the ladies of our company. But Alley kept him in line. For all his slovenly habits and his sad eyes, Alley surged with power. No torn and baggy clothes could hide his massive legs and shoulders. Potency and good health gushed through him, and Ricardo had little choice but to respect his greater strength.

I took Matina by the elbow and steered her along the back side of the table across from the windows. She settled onto one of the reinforced benches, and I pulled up my customary chair, on which I kept a pillow to ease the pain of sitting. I nodded across the table to Zippy the What-Is-It? Next to him sat Nurse, a frantic woman with an overbite and thinning hair who'd been hired a few years ago to protect him from an elf boy who'd tormented him endlessly by lobbing rocks at Zippy's tapering head.

The giant Emma Swan scowled down the table at all of us. "Might it be possible to have a quiet lunch today? The good Lord favors the gentle and the meek." Emma was the daughter of a Nova Scotia preacher and wasn't about to let us forget it. She had a face as long and square as a horse's, but with a rolling chin instead of a neck. Her dogma was backed by little piousness, as Matina pointed out.

"For all her talk of meekness, that woman is quick to speak her mind," Matina muttered. "But for once I think she might be right."

She nodded toward a flyer hanging on the inside of the dining room door. IN MEMORIAM ran across the top of the flyer, above an

American flag and a bust of President Lincoln. In the middle, a poem was flanked by two pillars, one that displayed Lincoln's birth date, the other the date of his death. "Tomorrow is Lincoln's funeral. None of us should fuss today."

Emma seemed about to make a snide remark but changed her mind and bowed her head instead. "What a world we live in. What a world."

We all held our tongues when Cook shoved through the dining room door, pushing a cart loaded with huge platters of mutton and pails of boiled potatoes. Feeding a giant, a muscleman, and Matina took some work. Cook, a hardy Italian woman with broad cheekbones and a penchant for spiced fish and brandy, so hated to hear us gossiping that she sometimes refused to serve our food while we were in what she called "your snotty little moods." So we stayed quiet as she hauled the meat and potatoes onto the sideboard with the rest of our usual Sunday fare. Behind her, Bridgett, a pretty Irish girl with black curls rolling about her face like tiny serpents, carried in two trays of pie. She wore the blue striped uniform Cook insisted on, but it didn't hide the dirt ring around her neck or disguise the worn, oversize shoes that flapped around her soiled feet. She blushed a high red when she spotted Alley, who kept his head ducked, staring down at his plate.

After Cook left, we all calmed down and took to our food with different levels of appreciation. As usual, I counted out a dozen green beans, no more, no less, and placed them horizontally on my plate, along with a bit of horseradish to add zing. After cutting each bean into thirds, I dipped a piece into the horseradish and popped it into my mouth, chewed twenty-five times before swallowing it, then started on the next piece.

It wasn't until Cook returned with the pudding that Matina looked down along the quiet table. "I've got some very interesting news," Matina announced, sitting back until everyone appeared to be listening.

"Matina," I admonished. "I think it best not to—"

She waved me away with one hand. "Barnum's back," she said, measuring her effect. "Barthy saw him from his window last night. And apparently he's brought a mysterious person with him. A new act!"

Ricardo rolled off the bench and lay on the floor at Matina's feet, bugging his eyes out at her. "We've already heard, my sweet pumpkin. And not only that—"

Alley cut him off. "I'm the one who seen her."

"You?" Matina frowned, realizing she'd lost her thunder.

"What's she like up close?" I asked.

Ricardo uncurled. "I saw her, too! She was covered up like a convict so she's either a real monster or a looker."

"You did *not* see her. A liar giveth ear to a naughty tongue," Emma admonished.

Ricardo rushed to explain. "Alley was in the hall when they came in. He saw Barnum slip her into his office. He closed the door and locked it, and the two of them stayed in the office for at least an hour, all alone."

Matina heaved her body from the table and made her way toward the sideboard, poking Alley in the side of the head as she passed. "If you know so much, tell me her name," Matina said.

Alley's broad shoulders slumped forward and his stringy brown hair rested on his shoulders like a boy's. "The first name, it's like two letters: I. L." he said. "Last name Adams. Iell Adams. That's all I know." As usual when talking to a woman, he did not look at Matina's face but gazed somewhere over her shoulder instead.

"Have you ever heard of such nonsense?" Matina made a haughty face, then spooned herself out two bowls of pudding. "I. L. What kind of name is that? And who told you this?"

Alley gave Matina one of his rare smiles. "The carriage driver who brung her. I know 'im. He came 'round this morning to complain about Barnum."

"But where did she sleep?" Matina demanded. "Barthy told me there's no one new in any of the resident rooms."

"My bet," Ricardo said, "is she's a chippy . . . a hussy . . . a whore."

Zippy sang out in a girlish voice:

A hussy ain't the only gal,
She's the only gal for me.

"Go ahead, Alley. Tell her the best part," Emma said, suddenly a co-conspirator.

"He's housing her outside."

I dropped my knife. It clattered loudly on the china before falling to the floor. Who in the world could this woman be? All the Curiosities lived together in the fourth-floor resident wing; we had done so for many years. Barnum only made special arrangements for his most lucrative acts, like Charles Stratton or Jenny Lind, the Swedish Nightingale. Boarding those performers at the St. Nicholas Hotel elevated their social standing, as did renaming them Princess This or General That. It wasn't as if I envied their privilege. I had always liked Charles Stratton, even after Barnum named him Tom Thumb. Charles and I had met for a drink or two over the years, and sometimes Alley and I would join him at the pony races to share his private box along with a few well-dressed ladies for hire. When Charles got married, he insisted Alley and I attend his wedding, but Barnum would not hear of it. "They don't need the likes of you two taking away from their time in the sun," he'd said.

This I resented, though I also felt a surge of pleasure that Barnum thought my presence would attract so much notice. And good Lord, what a fuss that wedding turned out to be. A GREAT LITTLE WEDDING—MARRIAGE OF GEN. TOM THUMB AND MISS LAVINIA WARREN, the *World* headlines read, THE SOCIAL EVENT OF THE YEAR. Over twelve thousand people attended the reception, and President Lincoln and his wife received the newlyweds at the White House later in the week.

"Whoever this Iell is, she must really be something, else why all the mystery? And we're out of butter, for goodness' sake." Matina rang the little bell next to the soup terrine, and Cook's new assistant, Bridgett, came scurrying into the room, giddy as a girl. Her dark hair was tugged back so tightly from her face that her eyes flattened unnaturally, giving her an almost oriental appearance. Cook had obviously taken a hand in making the poor girl presentable.

"Ma'am?" Bridgett curtsied, an action that brought smiles to more than one of us. We were used to kitchen help coming and going—God knows we weren't the easiest group to service—but rarely did one of them demonstrate such admiration. We'd see how the girl felt about us after a few months of slinging piles of food and cleaning dozens of platters and bowls.

"Butter." Matina pointed to the butter plate, and Bridgett went running, causing Matina to lift an eyebrow in amusement as she maneuvered to her seat, a plate in both hands. I shifted a bit to accommodate.

"If she ain't no chippy," Ricardo said, "this act must be something that will make Barnum rich. Why else would he bother?"

I set my cup upright and poured myself some tea. "Money isn't everything."

"Barnum's like a dog on the prowl when he smells something he wants," Emma said.

"Or on a leash," Matina added. "At least if his wife is around." They both snickered, their usual rivalry overshadowed by their mutual love of good gossip. "Remember those acrobats? And that poor chambermaid? What was she called, Barthy?"

"Abigail something or another," I said, remembering only the poor girl's first name.

Matina shrugged. "Mrs. Barnum had her declared insane, and they toted her off to the asylum uptown."

"As well she should have," Emma said. "I swear, the only one around here with any sense is Barnum's wife. Lord knows, Mr. Barnum isn't worth the land he stands on."

"You think it made sense to have that poor girl carted off when all she did was mention an indiscretion or two?" Matina slathered more butter on her roll.

"An indiscretion?" I asked, surprised by Matina's stance. "That 'poor girl' caused a horrible fuss. Blathering to the *Times* and the *Herald*. Barnum's reputation was at stake."

"And what do you care about Barnum's reputation?"

"His good name reflects on all of us," I said.

Matina blew out a cheekful of air. "We do not need Barnum *or* his reputation."

But she knew I was right. Under Barnum's care we were celebrated as Curiosities and given proper respect for our gifts, but without his showmanship the public would see us simply as freaks. Barnum's Museum was at the top of the heap. Nowhere else in the world were people like us treated so well. There were other museums, of course, plus the theaters and some private clubs, which could guarantee at least a living wage. But after that came the long slide down—to the circuses, the pit shows, the traveling menageries, and the Bowery dives. The anatomy museums were the lowest rung of the ladder.

Among our kind, there was a clear class system. Although all of us were considered Curiosities, the True Prodigies were the highest among us. These were individuals born with such rare God-given gifts that they could never be confused with ordinary mortals: men with flippers, armless girls, parasitic twins. Barnum shied away from True Prodigies. With the exception of the connected twins, Chang and Eng, whom he had showed with smashing success a few years ago, he never hired them. "I'd sooner take on my uncle's donkey than an act that might offend a gentlewoman or inspire a man to drink," Barnum once claimed.

The next level down were the regular Prodigies like Matina, Alley, Emma, and me. All of us were more or less the right shape and pleasant enough of feature, but with unusual proportions. Our special gifts emphasized different aspects of human beings—their hunger, their strength, their purity. We traditional Prodigies were the type Barnum favored most, though I'd always thought that showed a lack of vision on his part.

After the Prodigies came the Exotics, those whose odd bodies were helped along by a touch of show business. Like Ricardo, for example. He boasted at every opportunity that he was a True Prodigy because of how he could stretch and bend. None of us agreed. As far as we were concerned, he was a talented trickster but little else—as was our other Exotic, Zippy, whose fame owed as much to Darwin's *Origin of Species* as to any innate skill. It was sheer luck that his elongated head and simian propensities made it easy for Barnum to bill him as the missing link, the lone survivor of an Amazonian tribe discovered during an exploration of the River Gamba. The truth? He hailed from Liberty Corner, New Jersey, and was the son of former slaves.

Last came the Gaffs, self-made Curiosities who faked what came to the rest of us naturally. They had no inherent worth whatsoever. I felt a surge of pride looking around the table at my colleagues. We had not a Gaff among us.

Matina dabbed at her mouth with a corner of a napkin. "Well, I think one of us should warn this new person, I really do. Accepting favors from Barnum is a dangerous path."

"Oh, I'll warn her all right." Ricardo bounded from his chair and pulled a box of phosphorous matches from his pocket. He struck a match until it flared, then threw it in the middle of the table, yelling, "*Ding, ding, ding, ding, ding!*" in imitation of a fire truck.

Everyone jumped.

"Stop that this instant!" Matina admonished Ricardo as she slapped at the match flame with her napkin.

"We need something heavier to put out those flames." Ricardo stretched his arms across the table toward Matina's breasts, prompting an outbreak of laughter.

I glared at Ricardo.

He just laughed. "What? Would you slap my hands for going where yours go every day?"

I rose. "If you continue to insult Matina, you will have to answer to me!"

Ricardo cackled and rose to my challenge, but Alley held up one of his huge hands and waved him down.

"Give me those matches," Alley said. "You know better than that."

Reluctantly, Ricardo tossed the box of matches at Alley, who tucked them into his pocket.

As I settled back into my chair, Matina patted me gently on the knee. "Look at you, defending me," she whispered. "Such a sweet man."

I nodded, grateful for Alley's intervention, but all I could think about for the rest of the day was Barnum's new discovery. Who was she? I was dying to know.

chapter three

ONDAY WAS THE DAY OF PRESIDENT Lincoln's funeral procession. Out of respect, Barnum closed the Museum and draped the building in black bunting. Thick rolls of it were battened down onto the roof with ropes and allowed to spill over the façade, creating a play of dark shadows both inside the Museum and out.

A special notice hung in the Green Room, our collective dressing room. It had been printed on the printing press, like all our notices, despite the ease and rapidity of simply hand rending the thing. Mr. Fish insisted that we had paid good money for the press, however, and he used it at every opportunity. The notice read:

☞ SPECIAL NOTICE ☜

MONDAY, APRIL 24, 1865

MUSEUM CLOSURE!!

ATTENTION ALL PLAYERS, ACTS, & STAFF MEMBERS:

Due to the death of our beloved and much Admired President Abraham Lincoln, and due to the City's plan to have his body lay in state in City Hall during the afternoon of April 24, the Museum will be closed for **A Day of Mourning.**

WHERE TO VIEW THE PROCEEDINGS:

There will be chairs set on the roof and along both balconies. Please do not litter. For those of you who wish to do so, you may visit the casket showing beginning at two o'clock at City Hall.

☞ Special Note: *Remember! You represent the Museum on or off the Museum grounds. It is a fine idea to* **take flyers** *of this week's performances and pass them to bystanders. Do so respectfully, and do not fear being inappropriate. A joyous time has never been so needed by all.*

Matina found me in the back hall midmorning. I could see tears behind her thin black veil. She held a large basket in her arms.

"His body will be on display right across the square, Barthy. I *have* to go. Cook has packed me a few sandwiches to take along."

"Don't be ridiculous. It's entirely out of the question."

Matina scowled. "Out of what question?"

What could I say? The streets of New York were no place for the likes of Matina on a quiet day, let alone a day of national mourning. In fact, as long as I'd known her, Matina had never ventured into the streets in broad daylight. I myself rarely went out, except for the occasional outing to McNealy's, a tavern frequented by Curiosities, and then only under cover of night.

"You know better than to expose yourself to the masses." I reached for the basket, but Matina pulled it away from me. "Think of the crowds," I went on. "And the heat. And the defenseless position you will be in. Why not watch from the roof with the rest of us, my dear? It's safe, and you'll see much better at a little distance."

"But he was *murdered*," Matina whispered, her voice cracking. "A great man is gone, and he deserves our respect."

I never expected Matina to go, but not an hour later I watched from my window as she tromped along Broadway to City Hall, blond hair flying, skirts flapping like a tent in a hurricane. I flinched for her when a group of gentlewomen sank against the storefronts as she passed, and again when a cluster of men, in flagrant disregard for the gravity of the occasion, yelled out what was most likely a string of obscenities. But Matina trudged onward. I had to admire her gumption.

I watched my friend until she disappeared into the crowd in front of City Hall, and then I went up to join the rest of the troupe. The day was cool and breezy, and dozens of performers and staff members stood along the edge of the roof, gazing down on the double lines of mourners, which stretched as far as the eye could see—all the way up Broadway and all the way downtown. Lincoln's procession appeared sometime after one o'clock. Six men dressed in black bore the coffin high on their shoulders, showing no fatigue even though they had carried it from the docks; the Seventh Regiment followed in formation, bells tolling the entire time. The procession stopped at City Hall, beneath a long banner that read THE NATION MOURNS, and the flags flapped at half-mast on the roof of the building.

None of us said much as we watched. What could one say? We simply stood together as the soldiers fired a round of shots into the air as a signal for the bearers to move Mr. Lincoln up the marble steps and onto a velvet dais inside the rotunda. After that, the mourners began their slow file through the square, crushing the grass but entering and leaving the building with uncharacteristic solemnity. It was Emma who spotted Matina in the crowd. "Is that who I think it is?" She pointed and everyone strained over the rail for a better look. Who could miss Matina in the middle of one of the lines, broad as three or four of the people around her?

"I'd no idea she would go out alone," I said, preempting any negative comments. "I would have attended her, had I known."

Emma shook her head. "Well, don't worry, Fortuno, she brings her hardships on herself. All that carrying on."

Alley grunted, his eyes fixed on Matina as the line inched forward.

"Maybe it's not too late," I said. "Surely I could find her in the crowd."

"For goodness' sake, why put yourself through that?" Emma said. "You'll do her no good now. Leave it be, Fortuno. She'll be back soon enough."

I shook my head. I'd let Matina down and needed to make amends. "I'll see you later," I said, and took off down the stairs. The least I could do was to wait downstairs at the service-entrance door. When Matina got back, she'd be tired and hungry, and I could lend her a hand on the way to her rooms.

How rare to be in the Museum on a workday with no people crowding the halls. My footsteps, light as they were, echoed along passages usually full of chatter and laughter. I walked briskly through the

Waxworks Room, the East Wing portrait gallery, and the large exhibit room where we used to sit in tableau before Barnum moved such exhibits to the ground floor.

Everything seemed normal enough until I passed the Ballroom. What I saw there stopped me cold. Wrapped in cotton batting and resting against the top of the stairs, the tall, flat, rectangular object stood nearly six feet tall. A new poster? I paced in front of it. Beneath its covering, it still smelled of fresh paint, which meant it wasn't simply a photograph but something more expensive, handcrafted. My first response was anger. Barnum had been promising me my own likeness for three years, and nothing had ever come of it. In fact, two months ago, when I'd again asked for a poster, he gave me an unequivocal no, blaming it on the demands that the war placed on poor Mathew Brady, whose photographic images had served as the basis for all our posters since well before my time. "The maimed and the dead fascinate Brady more than you do now, son." Barnum waved his hands across his eyes as if to sweep away visions of specters. "And his prices have grown exorbitant. You should see what he's asking for even the smallest daguerreotype these days." But curiosity bested my anger.

Twine held the white batting in place around the poster, and someone had scrawled black letters across the front: *Do Not Open or Disturb in Any Way*. How thoughtless to leave the thing in the hall for anyone passing to wonder about. I glanced across the wide Atrium. The doors to the Ballroom and the Moral Lecture Room were closed, and I couldn't hear so much as a footstep. Everyone was on the roof or outside with the mourning crowd. What harm would a small peek do? Carefully, I undid the twine and tugged at the cotton at the bottom.

Running along the base were the words NEWEST WONDER OF THE WORLD. The new act! Making sure again that I was alone, I pulled the batting back as far as I dared to uncover a posh skirt, a background reminiscent of Thomas Cole's *View from Mount Holyoke*, a lap in which an exquisite hand rested, palm to heaven, and . . . nothing. The top of the poster was blank, unfinished. My efforts thwarted, I rewrapped the damned thing and made my way over to the service entrance. Wait until Matina heard about this. Newest Wonder of the World, indeed.

✷ ✷ ✷

WHEN MATINA finally returned, she was so distraught that I held my tongue about the poster and, instead, spent the good part of an hour trying to stop her tears. The poor dear had clearly been harassed by the crowd. Later, after she calmed down, I snuck back up to the second floor to see what had become of the poster, and discovered that it had disappeared. I'd have to wait to show it to Matina. Until then, I supposed it could be my little secret. No harm in that. No harm at all.

The next morning, I skipped breakfast and rushed over to the Green Room, sure that something about the new act would be posted on the Notice Board. Backstage was already throbbing with activity. Dancers flexed and actors do-re-mi'd as they wandered in and out, awaiting the call for places. The room stank of greasepaint, smoke, camphor, and sweat, and no one knew a thing about the mysterious woman.

"Out of the way. Out of the way." Mr. Fish swooshed past in a sea of tooth necklaces and turkey-feathered hair before I had a chance to ask about the new act. He was shepherding a group of Indians between the mirrors and the mildewed costume racks, his flyaway hair looking whiter than usual against his bulging forehead. When the Indians stopped for no apparent reason, he stared at them, his eyes magnified by the spectacles that balanced on his long pointy nose, then waved his arms above his head. "To the theater," he commanded, though none of the Indians seemed to understand. God help him if the Indians figured out they were here as moneymaking attractions and not as emissaries of peace. I wondered how the chiefs would react when they saw the Moral Lecture Room.

Years ago, Barnum had ripped out the old theater ceiling and expanded the room into a three-tiered cavern. Mauve draperies now flanked its proscenium stage, velvet covered the seats, and hanging in front of the stage between acts was a canvas drop painted to look like our Capitol Building. Private boxes—protected by open trelliswork—glowed in the light from Viennese sconces. And the stage itself had been made over to reflect the most advanced achievements of the modern theater, with a sprung maple floor to ease the pain of standing, and backdrops of such realism that even the actors had to touch them to make sure they weren't real.

Barnum had installed all the latest technology, from moving panoramas to calcium and gas effects for supernatural spectacles and battle scenes. I still couldn't get over the hydraulic machinery and the footlights, which used a new method of mixing oxygen and hydrogen right at the burners with a blow-through jet. Barnum renamed the theater the Moral Lecture Room when he decided to make what was shown there respectable enough for ladies to visit. Now, instead of housing Prodigies or good old-fashioned spectacles, the big theater was wasted on performances of *Uncle Tom's Cabin*, *The Vicar of Wakefield*, and *The Drunkard*. These shows drew crowds, it was true, but crowds made of pinch-faced women dragging in spineless men without a bone in their bodies.

By the sounds of the thumps and bangs at the end of the hall, one of the Indians had fled from the theater and had crashed into the crates from the newly delivered steam engines.

"Good Lord, can't you do something about all that noise, Barthy?" Matina scowled into her mirror and tried to disguise the red in her eyes by rubbing makeup around them. In spite of her efforts, it was obvious that she'd been crying again.

I placed my hands sympathetically on the curve of her rounded shoulders. "You're looking lovely today."

Matina pressed some *papier poudre* under her eyes and along the sides of her nose. "Kind of you to say, but it would take an awful lot of beauty to counteract so much sadness in this world."

I gave her shoulder a friendly squeeze, the bones of my fingers sinking into her flesh. "How lucky we are, then, to have you."

"Such nonsense," Matina said, but I could tell my words pleased her. "Go along now. We've all got work to do."

I left her, checking the daily notices on the way to my first show.

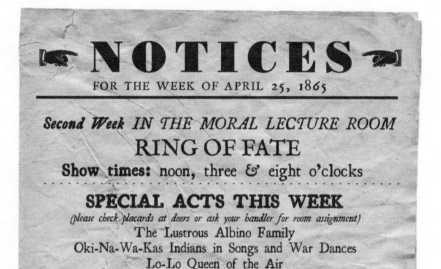

NOTICES

FOR THE WEEK OF APRIL 25, 1865

Second Week IN THE MORAL LECTURE ROOM

RING OF FATE

Show times: noon, three & eight o'clocks

SPECIAL ACTS THIS WEEK

(please check placards at doors or ask your handler for room assignment)

The Lustrous Albino Family
Oki-Na-Wa-Kas Indians in Songs and War Dances
Lo-Lo Queen of the Air

NEW EXHIBITS

Two Glass Steam Engines in full operation in Wax Figure Hall. New 2000 foot panorama of Gulliver's Travels in Lilliputian Land will be delivered and installed in minor room four where Mr. G. W. Herbert will give descriptive lectures.

MINOR ROOMS

The following will perform in the following order (in hour intervals) from nine until noon, and two until six o'clocks, with tableau schedule as usual:

Mr. William "Zippy" Johnson
Mr. John Alley
Mr. Bartholomew Fortuno
Mr. Ricardo Hortense

All others will appear in tableau only, as previously set on first or third floors

Note to all performers: *Tonight from 9:00 until 10:00 pm, you will report to the Ballroom and help cut the black bunting into six-foot squares to be delivered to New York widows who lost a loved one in the war.*

Aside from the extra task of cutting up the bunting, the only thing of interest was that the new act wasn't listed. I wondered if she would start in tableau, like the rest of us had, or if Barnum would put her right on the performance program. Either way, why was he waiting so long to introduce her?

When the warning chimes signaled time for places, I dashed a bit of pomade into my hair and hustled down the hall toward my little showroom. Backstage, Thaddeus Brown, lecturer and general master of ceremonies, grabbed my arm. He was a squat man, with short thick legs and a barrel chest that tipped him forward when he walked. Thaddeus's calloused, tobacco-stained fingers pinched my bicep and made me wince in spite of myself.

"Bone man. You're late."

I yanked my arm away from him. "I'm here, for God's sake." According to the usual schedule, my act followed Alley's and, as Alley was still onstage, I had plenty of time.

Pulling my performance suit off its peg, I tugged the trousers over my red tights and then paused to peek past the curtain into the house. Perhaps Barnum's mystery woman was out in the audience, observing our acts today. Why not? We were the best of the best, and she should be proud to be part of our company. I ran a hand down along the staircase of my ribs, past my nonexistent belly to the ridges of my hips. Yes, she'd be lucky to be one of us.

Thaddeus flicked the back of my head with a finger. "Places, bone man. Now!"

Frowning, I slipped into my jacket, the small rocks hidden in the bottom hem bouncing painfully against my thigh. Sewn in to keep the material in place, the rocks also kept down the white shirt and vest stitched to the inside seams, allowing the lot of it to be ripped away in a single piece. Quickly, I took my hat and brushed it clean of any dust, buttoned my jacket carefully, and slipped on my padded shoes. Two stagehands balancing a painted backdrop of a castle scene hustled past me, and I stepped back to let them pass.

Right on cue, Alley growled and took his final bow. When he

exited, he grinned bleakly, obviously glad to be done with his show, and tipped his crown to me in greeting. The stagehands carried my prop chair onto the stage.

"So what did you think of our muscleman?" Thaddeus crowed to the audience in his whiskey voice. "Wouldn't like to encounter *him* on a dark street, eh?"

I checked a loose thread, pulled myself tall, and breathed in to steady my nerves.

"But perhaps you'd like to see something even more shocking. Perhaps you'd like to see the human body pushed to the very edge of its endurance. Let me show you how much that quarter you paid for this show is *really* worth, my friends," Thaddeus crooned. "Let me show you the facts of your very own life."

Thaddeus moved out of my sight line, and I craned my neck to watch for my cue. When I'd first come to the Museum, my act was a bit more erudite. I still wore tights, but over them I'd layered a scholar's jacket and big fake spectacles. Most of my stage time was spent reading to my audience from Jules Cloquet's *Manuel d'anatomie descriptive du corps humain*. I quite enjoyed discussing the nature of the body. For a while, Barnum had even let me change my stage name to The Professor. But eventually he decided it was the sight of me that really carried my show, so out went the books and charts and in came a tight red body stocking. I remained philosophical. As long as I still got to share my gift, what did it matter how I showed it?

I straightened my coat as Thaddeus bent down close to the front row of the spectators, focusing on a young girl with lush chestnut hair. He squinted in mock concern.

"But first, answer one question, ladies and gents," Thaddeus said, directly to the girl. "What does it take to make a man? How much flesh? How much—dare I say—bone?" Even from the wings, I saw her blush a high red; Thaddeus could be such a scoundrel. "Decide for yourself what is real as you gaze upon Bartholomew Fortuno, the Thinnest Man in the World!"

Thaddeus stood back and waved his arm in a grand gesture as I marched onto the stage.

The audience gasped at the sight of me, some breaking into nervous laughter, others slipping into silent awe. Giving them time to adjust, I walked to my stool and dragged it downstage center, climbed onto its padded seat, and arranged the cuffs of my sleeves. The heat from the gas lamps warmed my chilly feet, and as I dusted lint from the front of my trousers, I peeked out from beneath the shadow of my gray fedora. From the stage, I could barely distinguish one person from the next. Short folks stretched into taller, darker versions of themselves, children grew into adults, then back into children again. I'd had this sensation for years. For lack of a better term, I called it Misting Over.

With concentration, I began to distinguish individuals. A handful of lads rumbled around in the rear, kicking the spittoons. A soldier silenced them. Directly in front of me, a handsome pair of nurses perched on their chairs, curled hair perky beneath their spring bonnets. They fanned themselves, inching forward to check on the emotional state of the dozen or so girls in their charge, all dressed identically in ivory-colored smocks. The girls looked me over with shock-filled eyes, the smallest of them sitting with her mouth open, pulling mindlessly at the strings of a whirligig carved into the shape of a queen that vaulted round and round, wooden head and crown *clap-clap-clap*ping against the stick that held it.

I waited for the audience to settle down, and a feeling of exhilaration washed over me. They already found me shocking, but they'd no idea how thin I really was. I couldn't wait to change their stares and snickers into gasps of fear and awe.

"Oh, he's thin, you say. Certainly he's that," Thaddeus called out behind me, "but do you have any idea how thin?"

One of the boys in the back shrieked, "No," and Thaddeus's broad, fox-colored mustache flickered up and down as he asked me the question we'd performed many, many times.

"So how thin are you, my skeleton friend?"

"Thin enough," I hollered out, bending over and rolling my pant legs just enough to expose the red tights that covered my legs, eliciting a few grunts from the watchers.

"Are those your *legs?*" Thaddeus mocked on cue. "I doubt you can even stand on those things."

I answered by hopping down from my stool, the rocks in the hem of my coat banging into my thighs. "I stand as surely as *any* man stands."

"But you show us only bones, sir. The fat of you must be above your knees, yes? Shall we see a bit more?" The spectators laughed and applauded, cheerful now in my presence, assuming they'd seen the worst. Gleefully I rolled my pants higher, securing them with the special hooks sewn in them so they would stay up. When I exposed my bony knees, the audience buzzed, but when I hitched the pants higher, revealing my long thighbones and suggesting the narrowness of my hips, their laughter stilled, and they whispered among themselves. If this kind of audience reaction didn't warrant a poster, I didn't know what did.

Right on cue, Thaddeus walked behind me and asked the final question. "And if your legs are that thin, what about the rest of you?" Staring directly into the crowd to engage them, he hooked the front of my breakaway jacket with the top of his cane.

"Shall we see?"

A few people clapped; a few yelled out, "No, no!"

"Shall we?" Thaddeus yelled louder, and more of the audience joined in, hollering, "No, no, please," while stamping their feet.

"You shouldn't be afraid, my friends. You deserve to get your money's worth. You deserve to see it all." Finally, one woman hungry to know screamed out, "*Yes!*" So, flourishing his cane and his smile, Thaddeus hooked the neck of my coat, the wood of the handle rough along my neck, and ripped away.

The audience swooned as I stood in front of them in my red tights and jersey, the bones of my torso and my ribs revealed. Sitting back on the stool, I smiled sweetly.

"It's good to be like me," I said, breaking the quiet of the room.

"What's that you say?" Thaddeus laughed. "Do you hear this, my

dear audience, my fellow seekers? He says it's good to be like him."
He scowled and turned to me. "Why would you say such a thing?"

"Because," I answered, preparing as always to use my gift to its
fullest, "nothing happens within me that cannot be witnessed from
without."

This gave folks back their voices, and chatter filled the room. That's
when I stood and pulled in my stomach muscles until every organ in
my body seemed to pop right out of my frame.

"Oh, good Lord, sweet Jesus," one woman sighed, and the entire
room went silent. The show was going well.

I propped one foot up on the stool to show myself at a different
angle, lovingly running my fingers down my rib cage. "Don't be afraid
of what you see. This," I said, "is what we're all made of. Me, you, every
single one of us. Do you see how my heart beats? And how my stomach waits for me to fill it? When you look at me, can't you understand
yourself a bit better?" I made fleeting eye contact with the silent faces
in front of me. "The only difference between us is that I do not hide my
inner self."

It took nearly a full minute for someone to snicker nervously, and
then a second joined in, and a third, until nearly everyone began to
laugh fully and slap one another on the backs or pinch each other's
body fat, eventually applauding when goaded on by Thaddeus.

But a few stayed silent. One or two sat with their heads hanging
down, the smoke-filled air encircling them as their feet shuffled against
the floor. These were the ones who mattered to me. The ones I taught.

chapter four

C HANCE, TOGETHER WITH A BIT OF LUCK, SOON
sent me along my inevitable way. It began with a
small fire in a corner of the Green Room. An acci-
dent. Someone dropped an ash, or an errant flame leaped from one of
the wall lamps; no one seemed to know for certain what had happened. Mr. Fish was frantic, insisting that the janitors check every
lamp in the room for leaks or faulty wicks. It would not have affected
me at all except that when the stagehands doused the flames with a
bucket of water, they pulled out the charred remains of my stage
tights.

"What in blazes?" I hollered out, poking at the soggy tights. Half
of one leg had burned completely away. It was impossible for them to
be salvaged. As a result, I had to dig out my old pair, the red faded at
the knees and the seams loose and frayed.

That Saturday, the last show of the night, my little theater overflowed with visitors. My spirits were high—I'd drawn in more people
than usual that month, proving my worth to Barnum—and even
having to wear old tights did not hamper my mood. The show went
as well as it always did, the audience reacting exactly as expected.
But then, near the end, just as I rose from my stool, I heard a horrible
tearing sound, and a wave of chilly air hit the inside of my thigh.

"Holy smoke, take a gander at that!" A farmer in the front row
nudged his neighbor, and they started a guffaw that spread through
the room like wildfire.

My tights had ripped along the inseam from my crotch all the way to my knee, the material cutting into my skin. I shot Thaddeus a look of desperation. His shrug said a million things: Be a soldier; act like a man; march on. So on I trooped, going through my paces as if nothing were amiss, dipping rather than standing tall, twisting where I normally stayed my ground. Of course I couldn't afford to suck in my stomach at the end for fear of more exposure, but I made do, altering my act as best I could. In the end, even though the audience clapped wildly, I failed to reach any of them at a deeper level.

Backstage, I flung myself down on an old salt box to examine the extent of the damage.

"What in God's name?" I cried, when Thaddeus came offstage. "You're supposed to help me, not let me dance about like a maiden protecting her virginity."

"It's not my fault you're a virgin, Fortuno. And, frankly, I did you a favor. They liked your racier act way better than your usual drivel."

"My *usual drivel*," I said, "is a revelation of the soul of man."

"Yeah, sure it is." Thaddeus pushed past me. I stomped along behind him, as he slipped off his stage jacket and brushed the back of it with his hand. "Anyway," he said as he put his coat back on and straightened the lapels, "it don't matter. You ain't got that much to show."

"It certainly *does* matter," I answered. "This is not about pride, it's about professionalism. You've no right to make me into a fool. And if you do such a thing again, I will have you dismissed!" I poked him once in his meaty ribs for emphasis.

Thaddeus grabbed my finger and pulled it, hard. An awful pain shot all the way up my arm.

"Maybe it's time for you to go back where you came from, Fortuno," he taunted me. A momentary shiver stopped me cold. *Back where I came from* meant the circus. Never! Just the idea made my head dizzy.

"I loved the circus," I lied to the back of Thaddeus as he

reentered the stage. "I was a star in the circus, and they treated me like a king."

The truth is, I was never a star in the circus; I was only a sideshow act, and I didn't belong on the fringes, I belonged as a main event. But even as a sideshow act, I knew, at the tender age of fourteen, as I sat shivering and bruised in the fancy Richmond office of Isaac Van Amburgh, my uncle Frederick beside me wringing his hands, that the circus was going to be an improvement on what came before. At last, I would be seen. *I'm getting out, I'm getting out*, I thought to myself as Van Amburgh eyed me from across his broad wooden desk. *My gift will soon be seen by all.*

"His parents are dead, you say?"

"The father, yes. The mother, mad as a hatter. Ward of the state."

"And you have full control of the boy?"

My uncle scrabbled about in his pocket, pulled out a wrinkled but official-looking document, slapped it down on the desk, and sat back nervously. "Like he was my very own."

Van Amburgh studied me. "He *is* magnificent, got to say that much. Let me see him up close." He waved a hand, and my uncle grabbed me by the scuff of the neck and hauled me to the front of the desk, pulling my coat open to show my bony chest. Van Amburgh stared at me with small black eyes.

"Can you speak?"

"Yes, sir."

"Do you eat anything at all?"

"Yes, sir."

My uncle piped up. "He might be an idiot. I hope that doesn't lower the price."

"Not as long as he can travel. You can travel, can't you?"

"I think so, sir."

"And you will live, eh?"

"Of course the little bastard will live," my uncle said. "He's strong as a horse."

It took Van Amburgh forever, but finally he slid the papers across the desk with a fingertip. "I want to tour him with my traveling show. People are getting tired of seeing only animals, and these human oddities make the menageries a little more exciting for our countryfolk. Might even put him with a tented show if he does well." He smiled and turned to me. I hated him already. "Better to work for me, boy, than some two-bit handler roaming about in the territories. You're a lucky little lad."

Within two days, his people had lashed my mattress to a flat rig, and I found myself traveling south. My education began then, and for a grueling two years I bounced from Maryland to the Carolinas, from New York to New England, first traveling with the animal shows, sitting in a little side tent reading to avoid talking to people as they passed. Later I joined an even lower-class sideshow. I was seen, yes, but only by pig farmers and vengeful little boys. No one who really understood my gift.

Compared to those years in the circus, life at the Museum was a pleasure. Like a good painting, I was best seen with a bit of distance and a proper frame. And I was my own master here—even if Thaddeus didn't care to acknowledge the fact.

I settled in the wings as Thaddeus leaned back on his heels, throwing his voice over the crowd. "And next on the roster, another lad who understands the meaning of transformation."

Ricardo went through his paces as I fumed. Eventually, the audience gave their final applause and the room emptied out, leaving me to wander into the house alone. What a mess. Discarded flyers littered the place as though a storm had recently passed; underneath the seats were abandoned apple cores, ends of meat sandwiches, crumbs, spittle, and smoldering Bull Durhams. So much of the disorder in the world was caused by men filling their bodies with food or drink! I took a seat in one of the chairs. My back prickled at the thought of Thaddeus's insults, but I realized how difficult it was going to be to revenge myself without putting my job in jeopardy.

Perhaps it was best to ignore his insults. I should concentrate my energy on obtaining new tights, since my current pair was torn beyond repair. And for that I'd have to go to Barnum. I sighed. Getting Barnum to pay for anything other than room and board wasn't easy. He claimed that costumes and props had been supplied at the beginning of our employment, and there was not a reason in the world to be replacing perfectly decent attire. If we needed something beyond what he originally supplied, he contended, we were to pay for it ourselves. I disagreed. None of us knew the extent of our employment, and though our salaries were generous, we had to save every single penny for the unknowable future. I, for one, had no intention of spending a dime beyond what was absolutely necessary.

Then there was the problem of finding a way to see the man. First, he had a rule that everyone must have an appointment, even though he was notorious for not being there at the appointed time. And second, he insisted that all complaints and requests be put in writing, though in the past I'd found that this action assured me of nothing. The truth was that Barnum was a capricious man. He acted on whim, and he traded in favors.

But I could hardly work without a decent costume. I had no choice but to go to Barnum's office after hours that night and insist that he see me. Maybe the sight of my torn tights would be dramatic enough to force some resolution. As insurance, I would abide by the rules and put my request in writing.

I found a piece of paper beneath one of the seats and, using the pen I always kept in the upper pocket of my performance coat, I wrote out:

Arguments for a
New Costume

Number 1: I've not had a new costume since my arrival five years ago and the holes in my tights prove my need.

Number 2: Due to circumstances beyond my control, I no longer have a back-up costume, a necessity in this business.

Number 3: The Museum is more than solvent and can most definitely afford the cost of the materials despite any war shortages and inflation.

Number 4: I am a most valuable member of the Human Curiosities and my past requests for a new costume (to say nothing of posters!) have gone unattended.

Not bad. Clear. Concise. With the illustrative hole in my tights and an argument list in my hand, my chances of getting a new costume looked very good indeed. I sat in the empty performance room until I heard the Museum's closing chimes. Soon after came the eleventh stroke of St. Paul's bells. I waited a few minutes more and then set out across the second-floor Atrium toward the Grand Staircase. Three of the housemaids came up behind me in the shadows of the hall.

"Evenin', sir. Nice legs, those."

"Off with you, girls," I snapped, and they scampered away, giggling like children, one smiling so broadly that her tin-capped teeth sparkled in the lamplight. Another, a pockmarked girl, covered her grin with a small grubby hand and cackled rudely. They'd seen me often enough not to be shocked by my appearance, but I remained a joke. They couldn't see far enough past their own noses to recognize my gift.

Downstairs, the front doors had been locked for the night, kept in place by velvet-covered chains looped securely through the brass handles, and the floor of the empty ticket vestibule sparkled from the reflected gaslights outside. As I walked past the shadows of the turnstiles and through the Cosmo-Panopticon Studio, my heart started to pound. Maybe Barnum wasn't in. Or, if he was, maybe he'd toss me out on my ear for bothering him after hours. I stopped to rest near the panorama of the Colosseum of Rome and pretended for a moment that I was a gladiator, fierce and fearless.

At the end of the hall loomed a door marked with the sign OFFICE OF P. T. BARNUM. ENTER BY APPOINTMENT ONLY. I forced myself forward and rapped lightly on Barnum's office door with the end of my cane. No one answered. I knocked once more, clutching the list I'd made in my free hand. The least I could do, I told myself, was leave the list on his desk so he could read it at his leisure and leave word for me as needed.

I pressed the door open an inch. Inside, I saw light and movement and then heard voices: Barnum's voice and a woman's as well. Generally, I would have left immediately—private conversations are private conversations, after all, and should be respected as such. But the woman's voice was unfamiliar. What strange lady could Barnum be entertaining in his office at this hour? It could only be the new act.

Peering around the door, I could just make out Barnum behind his desk, observable in glimpses as long as he didn't shift too much to the left or to the right. Uncharacteristically dapper, he wore a European jacket with ivory buttons and a satin lining; a watch chain dangling from his vest pocket caught the secondary light. He'd tamed his hair with ebony wax as he usually did, but his jowly face looked unnatural, smiling but strained, as if suddenly frozen in a daguerreotype. All I could see of the woman were the gloved hands resting on her lap and the tips of her walking boots peeking out from beneath her skirts.

"I see no reason for you to expect such treatment," Barnum said stiffly.

"Really?" the woman answered coyly. "I thought I'd given you more than sufficient reasons, sir."

His eyes pinched shut. "This was not our agreement. You promised me a decision by tonight."

"I did? How silly of me. Well, let's not create a stalemate over a little bit of time. I'm perfectly satisfied with the status quo for now, and I assure you I'll give you an answer soon enough."

Barnum banged the wall with a liver-spotted fist, the picture of Napoleon's march shaking askew. "Anyone else would jump at the opportunity!" he hollered at her.

"Anyone else? But I'm hardly like anyone else. Why are you so vexed?"

Barnum took in a deep breath and then slouched, adopting the posture of the meek and beaten. "Fine," he conceded. "I'll wait a little while longer. As for the other matter, I'll take care of it as I promised. But I'll not allow you to expose yourself. You've no business in such places. Is that understood?"

"For now, that is acceptable, yes."

Barnum stood behind his desk, and I heard and then saw the whip of the woman's skirts as she made her way out the door at the other end of his office, on her way, I assumed, to a private carriage waiting nearby. Barnum held his smile until the latch clicked closed, and then he collapsed into his chair, his face a storm of anger and disappointment. Ever so quietly, I pulled the hallway door shut.

I smiled. It was rare to see Barnum bested, especially by a woman. Even though I knew nothing of the details of their negotiation, it was clear that the beautiful stranger had taken the upper hand and Barnum wasn't pleased. Suddenly, I had a sinking feeling. Wonderful as it had been to watch him grovel, he'd be in no mood for favors now. Perhaps the wisest choice was to put off my request until morning, when I could either make a proper appointment or leave my list with a note.

Resolved, I folded the list and replaced it in my breast pocket. Then the office door flew open. Barnum stood glaring at me from the threshold, the backlight from his office making him look as huge and uncontrollable as a wild bear.

I took a step back.

"I knocked, sir. Twice. I waited and no one came so I assumed . . . I was making my way back upstairs."

"You do realize I only see people by appointment, do you not? Why are you skulking around like this?"

If it had been morning I could have said I'd been wandering past the carnivorous flowers or had decided to take a private clairvoyant reading, but at this time of night any excuse I made would ring false.

"You misunderstand," I sputtered instead. "My costume. Look here." I thrust my leg unceremoniously forward, hoping the light was strong enough to show the tear.

Barnum glowered at my tights as if he were about to rip them from my body, and my heart all but stopped. Then he turned on his heel and stamped into his office. "All right, then, Fortuno," he said, over his shoulder. "Come on in. I suppose I can have a word with you, as long as you're quick."

Holding my breath, I followed him in. The office smelled of embalming fluid and cigars, as always, but with a new layer on top of it, the lingering scent of roses. I stood at attention in front of Barnum's desk, and as he made his way to his chair, I surveyed the room. Despite its fancy decor—it had the same moldings and the same blood-red upholstery and gilded mirrors as did the Moral Lecture Room—I couldn't help but think of a morgue. Perhaps that had something to do with the floor-to-ceiling cases teetering with shrunken body parts, misshapen bats, rodents, calf fetuses, even a triple-winged canary, all floating in liquids of different colors and viscosity.

Barnum plunked down behind his desk and studied me silently. I swallowed hard, pulling my jacket closed to avoid feeling any more exposed than I already did. What on earth had I been thinking to come here for help? I tried to steady my nerves by staring at the heavy wood cabinet that stood behind Barnum's desk, but once I recalled the rumors that behind its closed doors were things so risqué Barnum would never exhibit them, all I could imagine was some future self of mine, dried, mounted, and stuffed inside it. So I concentrated instead on the sign carved in black teak hanging above his desk: NO INTOXI-CATING DRINKS ALLOWED. DRINK IS THE DEVIL'S LUBRICANT!

His voice made me jump. "How long has it been since I've had the pleasure, Mr. Fortuno?"

"A few months, sir."

"That long, is it? I hope everything is going well for you. Have your shows been doing all right? You've certainly held your own in the past."

Buoyed by the compliment, I dared to speak my mind.

"I need new tights, Mr. Barnum. I can't go onstage like this. It's a disgrace." I shoved my leg forward, the thighbone catching the lamp-light. "Half the women in New York nearly fainted this evening from fear of seeing my personal bits. Can you imagine one of your best per-formers being seen in such a sad manner?"

Barnum didn't even bother to look at my costume, just tapped his broad fingertips against the top of his desk. "I seem to remember you asking for shoes at the beginning of the year."

"Shoes?" I glanced down at the very shoes to which he referred, specially made with two inches of cotton batting inside to protect the bones of my feet. I'd forgotten about the shoes. "Yes, but I needed these. You can't ask someone like me to stand all day in normal shoes. I would die of pain."

Barnum seemed to be enjoying my discomfort. With me, he always had the upper hand.

"My costume is in tatters, and Thaddeus is worse than no help at all. He actually drew the audience's attention to my torn costume. I can't imagine you'd condone such disrespect, and I told him so!" My mouth went dry. What in the world was I doing? I'd not intended to bring up Thaddeus, though now that I had, I supposed that I should argue my case well. "He needs a formal reprimand."

Barnum half smiled at me and stretched back in his chair, the leather creaking with his movement. "And did you put this complaint against Thaddeus in writing?" he asked.

"No, of course not. It just happened tonight. But I did . . ." I fumbled in my pocket for my argument list.

"And no appointment either. I don't make exceptions, Fortuno. Surely you have learned that by now."

"Then why make an exception for the new act?" I couldn't believe I'd said that, and I gritted my teeth, ready for him to toss me out of his office.

Barnum seemed to swell up before my eyes, but before I could flee, he relaxed.

"Have a seat, Fortuno. You look uncomfortable." He nodded toward the stuffed chintz armchair behind me, and I exhaled in one short puff. The moment I sat, I smelled roses again. Perfume, perhaps?

"Why would you think there's a new act?" Barnum let loose with one of his famous smiles, the one that spread across his face like a rising sun, and now I knew I was in trouble.

"I caught a glimpse of her when she first arrived. And I believe she was here a moment ago, sitting in this very chair."

I shifted in my seat. Neither of us said a word as St. Paul's bells chimed once for half past eleven. Barnum stared down at me, a hawk eyeing a mouse in the middle of an open field.

"Refresh my memory. You started with Van Amburgh, didn't you?"

"I did, sir. Three years with one of his traveling menageries, then two more years with John Bindy." Where, I wondered, was he going with this line of questioning?

"Ah, yes, my friend Mr. Bindy. Seems to me I plucked you from his clutches, did I not? And in none too good a shape, if I recall. Bindy was such a quack. How was he to work for?"

"Absolutely horrid. He dressed me in spangles and stuck me in the lions' den as a taunt to the big cats."

Barnum threw back his head and laughed.

"I lived in utter fear, Mr. Barnum, I really did. And then Bindy coupled me with a young Hungarian named Josip, a famous funambulist." I was talking too much and knew it, but there was something about Barnum that loosened a man's tongue.

"What was his last name, this Josip? I remember Bindy lost a drunk from the wires a few years ago. Fell to his death. Made a terrible mess of the ring."

"Rigó, sir. Josip Rigó. We were a pair, early on, me in black tights painted with bones and Josip all in white dancing along a skinny wire, then coming down to earth to kneel at an altar in the center of the tent. As soon as Josip was deep in prayer, I'd sprint across the ring, sawdust flying, crowd yelling, and crawl up his back like a crab. He'd pretend not to feel my arms flung around his chest, while the audience yelled out, "Behind you, behind you!" and I'd lift a hand, shake a skull rattle, and glower. Then up the slanted rope we'd go. You should have seen me. Though I was much younger then. Couldn't do such a thing anymore, of course. And I was covered in bruises from the contact. Painful days, to be certain."

Barnum was still smiling. "Not a bad thing to have employees who understand how good they have it here with me. And if memory serves, you've been of service to me in the past, Fortuno."

I flushed in satisfaction. "You mean the sisters, sir?"

A few years back, Barnum had gotten himself into an awkward situation with a family of aerialists, three young sisters who barely spoke English but could tie themselves in knots or fly through the air like silver swallows.

It happened at night, in the middle of winter. Normally, I'd have been in my rooms at such a late hour, but I couldn't sleep, so I'd been sitting halfway down the Grand Staircase sketching. I heard someone clear his throat and when I looked up, Barnum stood above me.

"Fortuno, I need a favor."

I sprang to my feet. "Of course, sir. Whatever you say."

He gazed down the stairs to the ground floor at the last of departing crowd. "The acrobats," he said. "The little girls." His voice was low, and his half-closed eyes emitted a piercing intensity.

"What about them, sir?"

Barnum motioned for me to follow him, and we climbed the stairs together. At the top, he nodded across the Atrium toward the windows flanking the bank of doors leading into the Moral Lecture Room. The light of a full moon shone coldly through the glass, casting blue light across the white marble floors.

"That's the Wolf Moon shining in," he said, and shook his head as if he had shared some great and ponderous mystery. "The most beautiful moon of all."

Before I had a chance to comment, the sisters fluttered out of one of the Moral Lecture Room doors, together as usual, the eldest no more than fifteen, the twins maybe three years younger. Giggling and hopping about in tinsel-covered costumes, they looked like sprites.

Barnum locked his eyes on the girls. "Listen to me," he hissed, the words forced from the side of his mouth. "Go to the eldest and tell her I wish to see her one more time, but only once more. Do you understand? Send her to the Ballroom. I'll be waiting."

"Forgive my cheekiness, but why not tell her yourself, sir?"

"The walls have eyes, and I can no longer be seen speaking to them. I need you to deliver my message. And Fortuno, be discreet, if you can manage it."

This comment insulted me, but I nodded and walked across the floor, realigning my cravat. When I reached them, all three girls tensed but held their ground. "Guinevere." I acknowledged the eldest with a nod of my chin. She pulled herself away from the other two and sauntered toward me. Her heart-shaped face had a fey boyish quality, but her body, despite its youth, already looked well traveled. "I have a message from Mr. Barnum for you."

"What does he want?" Her heavily accented voice hinted of both laziness and anticipation. She wore a headdress of tin and cut glass, and it jingled when she moved.

After I delivered Barnum's short message, Guinevere smiled slyly. She glanced over her shoulder toward her sisters, who rested on each other like fairy vixens, shiny and wicked and so very small. Her headdress caught rays of the moonlight and bounced them along the marble floor as she nodded for her sisters to wait. And then, to my amazement, she placed her hands on the top of her tunic. Slowly and deliberately, she pulled the sleeve down, exposing her bare shoulder, then lower yet, until I could almost see the top of her white, budding breast. Turning, the girl walked toward the Ballroom with a roll of her girlish hips. When she got to the main doors, a booted foot from inside pushed the doors open, and in she went. The twins scurried away, leaving wisps of patchouli in their wake. That was it, the last any of us ever saw of them. The very next day, all three had left in a flurry.

Barnum tipped back in his chair, its springs squeaking for lack of oil, and lit a cigar. The office had grown quite warm, and I coughed as the end of his cigar puffed red and let out a smoke cloud that filled up my nose and throat.

"I must say," Barnum said, "you proved trustworthy in that case. Never said a word, least not that I ever heard. So maybe we have taken on a new act, maybe we haven't. But old Barnum has something he needs done again." For a moment, I couldn't see his face through the smoke. "Perhaps you could do him a good turn in exchange for that new pair of tights."

"What kind of favor would it be, if I may ask?"

Barnum laughed hardily. "Nothing much, Fortuno. I simply need you to pick something up for me on Thursday afternoon in Chinatown."

My breath caught in my chest, then broke into words. "Chinatown? That's not the neighborhood I'd choose for a stroll. And in the afternoon, you say?" I dabbed at my neck with the back of my coat sleeve, and then forced myself to stop. "I have a show to do, you know. Why not send Mr. Fish? It's his kind of errand, after all."

"Busy," Barnum mumbled. "Much too busy."

"Then someone from the household staff? Surely, any of them could fetch for you, sir. Because I rarely go out in public."

"This is a discreet assignment, Fortuno. Not just anyone will do. It will take an hour at most, and I'll see to it that your shows are covered for an afternoon. If you will do this for me, I'll see to those tights of yours." He winked at me in a gesture of camaraderie.

Doing favors for Barnum always had a slightly disagreeable air, but fetching a parcel sounded like a respectable task. It would be worth the trouble just to see the expression on Thaddeus's face when he saw my new tights. For a moment, I considered asking for a poster as extra compensation but decided I had better not press my advantage.

"Whatever happened in the end with those acrobats?" I asked him.

Barnum gifted me with the full force of his smile again, but rather than answer, he pulled a sack full of coins from his desk drawer. He scribbled an address and a rough map on a piece of paper and then painstakingly etched out three foreign figures at the bottom. He put the paper into the sack and made his way around the desk toward me.

I stood.

"The map will tell you where to go," he said, pressing the bag into my hand. "I will set up an appointment for Thursday. Try to be there at four o'clock sharp. The shopkeeper's name is Mr. Lee. Give him the paper and the money and bring what he gives you directly to me. You're a good lad, Fortuno. You won't regret helping out an old man like me."

"And Thaddeus?"

"Don't worry yourself about him. Barnum never forgets a good turn."

chapter five

HEN I TOLD MATINA ABOUT MY PRI-
vate conversation with Barnum, she
invited me to her rooms for tea.

"What exactly did he say?" She stopped at her door and rearranged
the things she carried: a large box of pastries, a parasol, and a fresh bag
of black tea. The afternoon sun shone through the windows and drew
long rectangles along the hallway walls.

"That I should go to see a Chinaman next week. Thursday, to be
exact."

"Not about the assignment, silly man, what did he say about *you*."
She balanced ever so lightly against me—a mountain on a tree—as I
opened her door.

"The first thing he did was ask about my days with Van Amburgh
and Bindy. He assured me that I'd done the right thing in coming to
work at the Museum."

"Well, now, that's an understatement. Everyone knows John Bindy
was a terrible man." Matina tossed her parasol on the floor and dropped
her packages on the round entrance table with legs carved like rococo
flowers and fruit. "What else did he say?"

"He called me trustworthy. Said the assignment required a special sort of man."

"A special sort of man?" She cocked an eyebrow. "I'm proud of you,
Barthy, Mr. Barnum singling you out like this."

"I could hardly have said no," I answered, but we both knew how
easily I might have refused. I liked my routine.

Matina popped wood in her small four-o'clock stove, lit it, and put a kettle full of water on top.

"Now," she said, plunking the pastries down between us and settling into the chair across from me. "Tell me more about this new act haggling with Barnum. What else can you remember? What color were her skirts? Her gloves? You can tell a lot by the style of gloves a woman wears."

"White gloves with pearl buttons. Blue skirts, perhaps. Or maybe brown."

"Brown skirts in the spring? Never." Matina fluffed up her own pink dress. "And to be unescorted in Barnum's office at such a late hour. A bit disreputable, don't you think?"

"Perhaps, but she bested Barnum every step of the way."

Matina smiled and piled three éclairs onto her dessert plate. "A little challenge might do our Mr. Barnum good, don't you think? What exactly did she say to him?"

I recounted what I could, including how Barnum was clearly waiting for some kind of answer from the new act, and that she had him by the short hairs. When the kettle began to whistle, Matina lifted the pot by wrapping a greasy cotton rag around its handle. A thin stream of perspiration rolled down her neck, disappearing into the abyss of her cleavage. Without comment, I bent forward and pushed the windows open, letting in the breeze. She gave me an appreciative look.

"It's strange," Matina said. "A week has gone by, and not a word about the woman. Not like Barnum to be hiding something this long. Think what he went through for those damnable white whales of his. He shipped them down from Canada in wagons and then ran ahead so he could stop at every Podunk town on the route to make sure the whole countryside knew they were coming."

"Or that idiotic Fejee Mermaid he touted twenty years ago," I answered, remembering the half-monkey, half-fish exhibit. What an atrocity! Barnum had planned everything, even hired an actor who claimed to be a famous British scientist who'd made the discovery. Restricted viewing ginned up interest for months, and in the end everyone and his brother came to see the dead shriveled thing, with its fins and its claws and its gaping, toothless mouth.

Matina poured tea into tiny porcelain cups, her hand shaking slightly. "Barnum must have something special planned for the new act. We'll find out soon enough, I suppose." She shoved a pot of honey my way. "You know, Barthy, it wouldn't hurt you to use a little showmanship yourself. Tonight at supper, brag a little. Tell the others that he's singled you out for this special task on Thursday."

I pulled my cup back. "Absolutely not."

"And why not? I'm sure Barnum's not asked any of *them* to do his bidding."

"I've no intention of boasting in front of everyone. And he's banking on my discretion."

Peeved, Matina popped an éclair into her mouth and tapped a sticky finger on the top of a stack of newspapers as she chewed.

"And you'll say nothing to them either," I added, knowing exactly what she was thinking.

Matina dabbed her napkin at the corner of her mouth. "Fine. But I think others would pay you a lot more respect if they knew Barnum had singled you out. People with remarkable gifts do not always end up rich or happy in this world, you know."

"I would never assume that they did," I answered, though in fact I *did* believe our gifts brought remarkable lives with remarkable insights. Otherwise, what would be the point? "And not many of us have been as lucky as you, my dear."

Matina had worked under Doc Spaulding, sailing the Mississippi aboard the *Floating Palace*, the fanciest boat afloat, so one couldn't take her complaints too seriously.

"They treated me like an animal on that boat!" Matina sipped at her tea, then reached for another pastry. "Threatened my honor day and night. You've no idea the drunken hooligans that hang around riverboats."

I laughed. "You've a perfect pedigree, and you know it. And it hardly sounds like Spaulding treated you poorly."

"Well, he never put me in the big show, did he? And that ghastly act I did for him!"

Matina had told me dozens of times how Doc Spaulding used two tugboats to haul his riverboat circus up the Mississippi. The first tug carried an African elephant and a steam-run calliope that squeaked out Stephen Foster songs to herald their arrival. The second carried Matina, along with an armless man named Theodore Bunt, a blackface troupe, a menagerie ring made up of monkeys riding Shetland ponies, and a few African cats in big cages. Folks had to walk through one of the tugs to get to the riverboat's big show, complete with a circus ring, stage curtains, horses, and clowns. Try as she might, Matina could never convince Spaulding to move her to the main theater. Instead, he made her serve as a warm-up act, playing the part of a British explorer—jungle gear, netted cap, oversized game rifle, the works—and had her tramp about the little tug shooting off firecrackers from a gun. After she bagged a fake bird or two, a pack of irate men in blackface came running out to "capture" her and drag her through an ingeniously constructed rain forest, all paper and paint, vines and stuffed parrots, with a twenty-foot paper snake let down from above. Then they stripped her to her bloomers and bustier and, with great effort, hoisted her up and plunked her into a huge black pot, displacing water over the sides. Lighting a fake fire beneath the pot, the natives threw carrots and cabbages in beside her and danced around her in a most frightful manner. Barnum encouraged Matina to perform her riverboat routine when she first came to the Museum, but he canceled her act at the beginning of the war, saying he did not want to engender any unnecessary fear among the white folks with so many Negroes becoming freed men.

"At least you were spared the wagon circuses," I reminded her.

Matina grunted. She reached across the table and grabbed a red berry pastry dripping with honey. "Putting a fat woman in a pot! Where's the artistry in that?"

Quietly, I sipped my tea. "You should consider yourself fortunate. The audiences here are much better than anywhere else in our world."

Matina frowned and sat back. "They're all the same, Barthy, you should know that by now. The circus, the riverboats, the private showings—they all pay us to show ourselves. What difference does it make who's watching?"

"It makes all the difference in the world."

"Oh, pshaw." She dunked her pastry into her tea. "Lowlifes to codfish aristocrats, they're all alike. People want to feel shock, envy, and delight. They just use us to fill them up. Which, by the way, is an impossible task."

Matina's callousness frustrated me. "That's not true. We teach the world. You know how I feel about this. Nothing in the world comes close to our artistry. To manifest ideals through the body! Your abundance. Alley's strength. My clarity. Why, it's as Godlike as one can become."

"We amuse and frighten, that's all." Matina invited me to quibble by placing her elbows on the table and making it jiggle slightly, her blue eyes challenging. "Haven't you seen that look in their eyes that shows how hungry they are? Just because some of us appear in books with the likes of Galileo and William Penn, dearest, doesn't mean we're any more than passing amusements. We are *not* respected." She smiled over the table at me, a sparkle in her eye. "Except for you, Bartholomew. Except for you."

Later, when I rose and left the table, I took Matina by the hand. "This Thursday, when I go on Barnum's errand, why not come with me? We could have an adventure."

"Go with you? Outside? Oh, Barthy, honestly, the funeral was difficult enough." Matina flipped open her fan and waved it zealously in front of her face. "I wouldn't even think of going out again."

"We could get a carriage, and you could ride—"

"Nonsense, Barthy. My last venture into the city nearly killed me. But it's kind of you to ask."

* * *

THE AFTERNOON passed pleasantly enough in Matina's rooms, but supper left something to be desired as Cook was in a most dreadful mood. She thrust her big-bosomed self into the dining room carrying a plate of sweetbreads, her helpmate Bridgett tagging behind.

"I want no complaints about the food tonight," Cook yelled. "And no third helpings. You people are working me half to death." Cook flung the plate of sweetbreads onto the serving table, and as soon as her back was turned, Ricardo jumped up and slid over to Bridgett. He held a burning candle in one hand.

"Ah, fresh little chicken. Have you ever seen my act?" Holding the candle an inch beneath his chin, he moved the flame back and forward, casting grotesque shadows across his face.

Bridgett's young cheeks drained of blood. "S'cuse me, sir, but I don't . . ." Her eyes darted to Cook's back, then down to the floor.

Cook whirled around and banged her fist against the serving table. "Stop that, you reptile! You'll scare the girl half to death. And put down that candle! You know better than to play with fire around here."

Feigning fear, Ricardo set the candle on the table and waited until Cook left the room, then reached down and grabbed his leg, snaking it into the air. He wrapped it around his neck, glaring over at Bridgett the whole time.

"For you, a special show." Ricardo's tongue stretched out and up, and he licked his own forehead, one hand already fussing with the buttons of his trousers.

Not knowing that Ricardo rarely made good on his obscene threats, the poor girl blinked wildly and began to wring her hands, until Alley pushed back in his seat. Ricardo grumbled a bit, but he dropped his leg and slunk back to his chair.

Just as things calmed down and I settled in for a nice cup of hot tea, Matina leaned close to me and said, "Barthy, would you be a sweetheart and go fetch my cape? I left it in the exhibit hall behind the riser."

Irritated at her forgetfulness, I scraped back my chair, fluffed up the pillow on my seat, and stomped out of the dining room, ignoring the snickers of my fellow Curiosities. I lingered for a minute in the back courtyard and lit a cheroot, complaining mildly to myself about Matina's assumption that I would do whatever she asked. The courtyard was a walled-in area that held the communal garden, benches and rickety tables for the help to use during nice weather, and some lovely trees. An ivy-buried storage shed sat at the far end of a weedy path. Ragged and unkempt though it was, the yard proved a godsend to those of us with aversions to the outside world. And it was an excellent place to waste a bit of time. I took a deep drag on my cheroot and blew smoke up into the leaves of a sycamore tree, thinking that while I didn't mind fetching for Matina, I didn't want her to take my help for granted.

My train of thought was broken when the service door leading onto Ann Street opened and two burly roughs skidded inside, lugging a six-foot wrapped canvas between them. One of them nearly dropped his end into a puddle of late spring mud, and the other cursed loudly, hefting his own side higher until his partner regained his balance. They navigated the canvas through the vegetable garden and down the flagstone walk toward the kitchens. I strained to read what was written across the covering. *Do Not Open or Disturb in Any Way*. It was the same poster I'd seen outside the Ballroom only the week before. It had to be.

Throwing my smoking cheroot to the ground, I took off after the roughs, trailing behind them to the far end of the kitchens, where the door to the south cellar stairway stood wide open. When they maneuvered the thing down the stairs into the bowels of the Museum, I followed, cringing when the poster banged against the stone steps and then scraped one corner of the east cellar wall. Mold and the scent of fish sent me scrounging for my handkerchief, and the chill of the cellar floor seeped through my shoes, despite the padding inside them, but I kept up. They stumbled on past discarded animal cages, wooden crates, piles of tomato jars, the hippopotamus tank and, finally, dragged the covered poster through another door at the far end of the cellar.

The two men shut the door after them, and I stopped. After a moment, out they came, holding nothing but the covering.

"Can I help you, mate?" Dressed in the dirty pantaloons and the ripped jerkin of a street thug, the shorter of the two seemed intent on blocking my way.

"I've got business inside." I stood tall, ignoring the thumping of my heart.

He stepped away from me as if I were a leper. "What sort of business?"

"What's it to you, my man? Tell me your name."

"He wants my name." The man turned to his ruddy-faced friend. His boss, I assumed.

"I will file a report saying you've hindered my task," I threatened, emboldened by my recent success with Barnum.

The boss eyed me up and down. Clearly I belonged here at the Museum.

"Let him in," he said.

"But—"

"Let him in."

"A wise decision," I said, pushing past them both.

When I first entered the room, nothing was visible but my own shadow across the dirty floor. The door slammed behind me, and I jumped, my satisfaction replaced by a sudden fear that they'd locked it behind me, burying me in the bowels of the Museum. But when my eyes adjusted, I chided myself for my silliness. I was simply in one of the storage rooms. A forest of paper trees obstructed my path, obliging me to duck and weave to make my way along; I started when I saw a life-sized portrait of the Cherokee chiefs gazing out from a broken gilded frame, but I knew the poster was in here somewhere. A dozen small oil paintings depicting the battles of Napoleon had been stacked along the wall, waiting to be rehung, and on a worktable to the left sat half-assembled chandeliers that, even unlit, reflected light from the wall lamps. I jammed my big toe on a disfigured carving of Marie Antoinette, sitting for some ungodly reason in the middle of the room, cursed loudly, and looked up.

And there it was! Her portrait.

Every ounce of me prickled with excitement as the image of Iell Adams stared down at me from atop a throne set in a background of olive trees and clouded skies, tinted a deep purple so rich it was almost black. She was stunning, simply stunning. Her face, her skin, her bright red hair: all beautiful. But most stunning of all? She sported the most astonishing beard I had ever set eyes upon. Fire-red and passionate, it erupted from her face like an uncaged animal, roaming over voluminous breasts and reaching out at the ends like the tentacles of some man-eating primordial beast. I'd seen bearded women before, of course, heavy-featured women cursed with thick arms and chins buried beneath an outbreak of unseemly hair—the effect more like a man in a dress. But this! Her sea-colored cape draped across one shoulder and the other was bare, its skin porcelain white. Her eyes were deep green, and they gazed imperiously down an aquiline nose as if in challenge to the entire world of men.

Instinctively, I reached my hand out toward the canvas.

"Even if I knew you, sir, I would have to object to your touching me like that." It was the same voice I'd heard in Barnum's office, coy and confident.

Stunned, I spun around and saw her: the new act. Iell Adams, in the flesh. She watched me from the doorway, and for those first few moments, the only thing I could do was manage to keep my mouth from falling open. I'd never seen such a magnificent woman in my life. She had the same flame-red hair, but in person it was fashionably parted in the center, swirling down into loops and braids. The dashing cape had been replaced by an elegant emerald Zouave jacket worn over a dress of dark blue silk. Black braiding and strings of lilac buttons decorated her skirts; and around her neck was draped a diaphanous white scarf, the very scarf she used as a veil when traveling in public.

But it was the beard that weakened my knees and took my breath away. It had none of the ferocity depicted in the artist's rendering. She had combed it smooth and decorated it festively with satin bows tied sporadically throughout, but nothing could hide how lush and full it flowed. Now I understood why Barnum's new act deserved such special treatment. She was one of a kind.

"Might I suggest that you move along, sir?" she said. "I am sure you haven't intentionally entered a place where you were not invited."

All I could do was take one step toward the door. I ordered my tongue to loosen and my ears to cease ringing. "You must be . . ." I croaked out, and she smiled, coolly.

"Iell Adams," she said. "Though if we're to be colleagues, you may call me Iell." She smelled of roses, and her perfume reminded me of my mother's, though the sweet floral odor was mixed with something deeper and more mysterious. When I said nothing, Iell looked at me dispassionately and cleared her throat. "But now, sir, if you wouldn't mind . . ."

I tried to leave but found myself paralyzed by her gaze.

Iell shook her head. "All right, I'll come back to see the poster later," she said, "but I hope you've found both your tongue and your manners the next time we meet." She shut the door behind her, leaving me insulted and already half in love.

By the time I fetched Matina's cape and slipped into the dining room, I could barely feel my body. Matina was talking, but all I could hear was Iell's voice. How horribly I'd bungled my own introduction. Somehow, I would have to find a way to see her again.

"Then that doctor came around again," Matina said to the table at large, and I tried my best to listen. "And this time he wanted to measure Alley's head."

"He wants to buy my body when I die. Offered good money for it, too."

"Don't sign a thing!" Emma glared over at Alley with true alarm. "Where is this so-called doctor from, the Medical College? Please don't say yes. Two years ago, they offered me three hundred dollars for my skeleton after I died and I almost agreed, but you should have seen the look in their eyes. I could just picture myself signing some paper and then meeting with a mysterious accident: a fall in the night, arsenic in my soup. Next thing you know, those butchers'd have my flayed self laid out on a slab in front of fifty doctors, and my parts sold to Dr. Kahn's within a week."

"Naw, it weren't no doctor," Alley answered Emma. "One of those scientific men. Kept measuring my biceps and writing in some book and talking about normal. Why are folks only interested in how big I am? Nothin' else." He shook his head and looked over at me as if I should have the answer.

"What?" I asked.

"Alley doesn't think anyone sees past those big strong arms of his," Matina said, causing Alley to choke out a red-faced guffaw.

My mind was spinning with images of auburn hair and fingers as light as smoke. Maybe I should tell them I'd met Iell Adams. But no. Better, I decided, to wait.

"You know people don't understand us," I said, forcing my attention on the conversation at hand, "and it's only getting worse. We used to be *Lusus naturae*, special beings, unclassifiable. Now the scientists just want to explain away our gifts."

Alley cut off a hunk of pork with a short hunter's knife. "I thought you liked all that measurin'."

In my mind, I wondered how a scientist would classify the new act. But aloud, I took a more certain stance.

"Indeed. I consider myself a man of science. But the whole point of Curiosities is to blur the line between reason and faith. Darwin and Linnaeus both have their place, but we represent something beyond evolution. Something mythical. Did you know that medieval naturalists used to believe in a sheep that was half plant?"

Emma smiled.

"Don't laugh. They imagined a sheep that grew from the ground, its belly attached by a fat stem. Supposedly, it lived by eating the grass that grew up around it. And these men believed so strongly that the thing existed, they classified it—named it a Scythian lamb—even though no one had ever laid eyes on such a creature."

"Whatever is your point?" Emma asked.

"We mustn't slaughter our Scythian lambs. Man needs a bit of mystery to remind him that the world still holds miraculous things. Unclassifiable wonders. And if scientists simply shove us somewhere in the grander scheme of things, the magic disappears." I wondered whether someone like Iell Adams might do for us what we did for the world. Open up our eyes. A Scythian lamb in the flesh. My heart soared.

Alley picked up his beer mug. "Here, here!" he said, hefting his glass to the ceiling and then taking a long, slow drink. Everyone else held up their glasses, and for a moment we were united.

Then Mr. Fish flung open the dining room door, letting in a breeze strong enough to blow the tablecloth over the breadbaskets and rustle the dried flowers on the wall.

"Children, children! I've got little time and much to say, so please pay attention." He pushed his way to the front of the table and stood stiff as a yardstick, white hair wild with electricity. He banged on the table once with his cane. Cook and Bridgett bustled out of the room and Matina settled into her seat, swallowing a half laugh aimed either at Fish or at me, I really wasn't sure.

"Mr. Barnum has returned, and he's not at all happy with your performance. He says you are all turning listless onstage, commonplace."

"He's never happy, is he?" Emma said, her legendary dislike of Barnum distorting her face. "And he's been out of town. How would he even know how we've been?"

Fish raised a disapproving eyebrow until Emma flushed and quieted. "We must attend to business, people. Your positions are always coveted by newer acts, and you should not for a moment forget that."

Ricardo snorted. "What other act could do this?" He bent forward and stuck his head between his legs, coming up the back high enough to kiss his own posterior.

Fish dismissed him with an impatient flap of his hand. "*Also,*" he said, "next week we will be joined by a new act, Mrs. Iell Adams. She has come to us from Boston and has never before been seen onstage."

Matina raised her eyebrows and mouthed the word *Mrs.?* My heart sank. She was married. Fish shushed us, and Matina rolled her eyes.

"She will be gracing us for an indeterminate length of time, and although I expect you to welcome her and treat her as a colleague, she'll not be staying here at the Museum, nor will she be paying any social calls. Please respect this; carry on." As quickly as he had come, Fish scurried out.

"*Nor will she be paying any social calls.*" Matina mimicked Fish's officious tone. "Now why in the world would that be?"

"She *must* be a Gaff!" Ricardo chimed in.

I almost spoke up in her defense, but I held my tongue, wanting to keep the unsullied image of Iell to myself for a little while longer.

"Barnum won't let us meet her up close 'cause she ain't real. Either that or, like I said before, she's his chippy." Ricardo waggled his tongue, swinging it back and forward, and winked at Matina. "What Barnum can't find, he makes. Though I'd like to see him make the likes of us, eh, my sweet?"

"Or me, or me." Tipping a chair over in his exuberance, Zippy bounced on tiptoe; Nurse grabbed him by the neck, wrestled him down into his chair, and said, "I seen the woman myself, going in the Arboretum. First a few nights ago, and then again last night." She peered down the table at us, the white of her scalp visible beneath thinning strands of hair. "Veiled head to foot, she was."

"But the Arboretum is being renovated," I said. "No one is supposed to go in there. And why at night? Perhaps she's staying there, secretly."

"Supposition takes us nowhere. Why don't we just wait until we see what her gift is?" Emma finished. "Much as I hate to defend the scoundrel, if Barnum's keeping her under wraps, he's probably got his reasons."

The conversation moved on to other things: our linen pickup day, ticket receipts, anticipation of the early summer corn. After lunch, I walked Matina to her tableau and took the service stairs up to my rooms. But on my way I stumbled upon Emma and Ricardo.

"Fortuno is such a ninny," Emma said, not knowing I was behind her. "I was dying to tell him that the new act is lodging at Mrs. Beeton's, just to see the look on his face."

"He thinks he knows everything," Ricardo responded, slipping his arm around Emma's waist in a most ungentlemanly manner. Although I felt my blood heat up—ninny, indeed!—I owed Emma a debt. Now that I knew where Iell was staying, perhaps I could arrange to cross paths with her again. But why would Barnum put her up in a board-inghouse halfway uptown? I could understand why she might not want to live with the rest of us. She was a star, after all. But why wouldn't she insist on the glamour and notoriety of the St. Nicholas Hotel, like others before her?

chapter six

THE MOMENT I OPENED THE SERVICE DOOR onto Ann Street Thursday afternoon, I realized what a fool I'd been. The smell that wafted in from the street turned my stomach, and I shut the door immediately. Why had I agreed to Barnum's request to go out?

I took a moment to compose myself, opened the door once more, and stepped onto the filthy walk.

Although the day was slightly past its peak, the sunlight crashed down over everything, and the sewage smells, mixed with the stench from the Brooklyn glue factories, brought tears to my eyes. Pulling my Panama hat lower, I lifted a hand in hopes of hailing a carriage. Ann Street was nearly empty. Only a few bankers loitered around the Oyster House across the street, and a wagon was pulling up to the dry goods annex of Hearn's. Not a cab was in sight, and my palms were already itching inside my gloves from the heat. I squinted toward the far end of Ann Street to where a river of folks surged past on Broadway at a most alarming pace. Good Lord, what a nightmare! Well, all I could do was swallow the dust in my throat and trudge forward. After all, how difficult could a little day trip be?

When I reached the corner of Ann and Broadway, I stopped, aghast. I'd spent many idle hours on the Museum balconies watching the wagons and carts battle for right-of-way along Broadway, kicking up dust or churning the street into a thoroughfare of mud in the rain. I'd laughed when the crossings logjammed, forcing the police to come and disentangle the mess, directing the drivers to reroute their goods to Vesey Street. It had been a long time since I'd been out in the daytime—two years at least—and then I had gone in the early morning, well before the crowds could swell. But now, face-to-face with the midday rush, I saw Broadway for what it was: a battlefield. Each man, each carriage, struggled to overcome the others, and my ears were bombarded with the screech of metal on metal, the drivers' shouts, the cowbells, and the wheels rolling by. I pitched myself into the throng and let it sweep me away. How in heaven's name had Barnum talked me into a trip in the middle of the day?

By some miracle, I maneuvered across Park Row without incident and moved toward City Hall, mumbling obscenities to myself. The sun reflecting off the municipal building nearly blinded me, but fortunately, the trees along Barclay Street provided a bit of shelter. After a block or so, however, the trees proved insufficient, so I hobbled over to a park bench to gather my wits. Careful to keep my hat down, I sat and slipped off my coat for a touch of air.

"Oh, mercy, look at that." An elderly woman had stopped on the walkway in front of me.

Her younger companion tried to pull her along, all the while hiding her face behind her fan so as not to stare directly at me. "Come away, Mirabel. He's probably sick."

"Sick?" the older woman said. "No. I think the poor thing is dead, I really do." She drew near me, cocking her head and fiddling with her spectacles to get a better look. "Probably killed by one of those Irish hooligans for the price of a beer."

The idiocy. I flipped off my hat and stood.

"It moves!" The older woman cried, bowing her head to genuflect. "In the name of the Father and the Son!"

"I am alive, woman!" I shouted at her. "Alive and well! Or at least I would be if it were slightly less hot outside today."

Startled, the woman stumbled backward and grabbed her companion's hand, and they scuttled off in the opposite direction, horror-struck that a dead man could have such appalling manners. This was precisely why I never mixed with people outside of the Museum. Normal people needed the context of my show to understand my place in the world. And I needed the distance from normal people. Idiots, every one.

I tugged my coat back on, buttoned it all the way up, and pulled out Barnum's map. According to the directions, I was to travel past City Hall to Chatham, then to Mott Street, then east to Pell. A half-hour walk at most, with the Elizabeth Street police station nearby in case I ran into trouble. At this point, my left ankle began to throb, and I noticed a pinch beginning to travel up my leg. Perhaps instead of walking I should flag down one of the horse trolleys and ride up Broadway to Walker. After that, it would be a short jaunt to Pell. Even relying on public transportation, I'd arrive back at the Museum a little late, but I was doing Barnum a favor. How could he mind?

When I waved down a trolley, it shrieked to a stop on six metal wheels, the horses shaking froth from their mouths and panting. I climbed the three stairs and slipped a nickel in the box. The driver eyed me suspiciously but said nothing, and I pushed my way down the aisle, taking a seat in the center near a redheaded woman with a child. I placed my hat respectably in my lap and pulled my coat sleeves down to cover my spindly wrists.

The woman and child got off the trolley at the corner of Leonard Street, a half block past the closed-for-repairs Steward's Department Store. Perhaps they were on their way to the Allen Dodworth's Dancing Academy, which I'd read about in the *Times* with, I admit, a small degree of longing. I hopped off a block or so later at Pell Street. Checking the instructions on my map, I found what I was looking for, a small storefront marked with a number nine and two sixes. The building, unpainted pine and shingle, had settled poorly on its foundation. It didn't look particularly old, but it had already begun to tilt southward toward the piers. In its window, several pink featherless ducks swung haphazardly on display.

Heat engulfed me when I pushed open the door. Behind a rickety counter, a shrunken Chinaman with hooded eyes and skeletal fingers smacked at vegetables with a cleaver; each dull *whack* thudded through my bones. A dirty mirror hung on the wall. Baskets of corn and beets, misshapen rutabagas, and a few unhealthy cabbages littered the floor. What a disgusting odor. Too ripe, but not quite rotten. I drew out my kerchief and covered my nose.

"Pardon me, sir." After removing my gloves, I pulled the leather bag full of Barnum's coins from my breast pocket and set it carefully down in front of him. "I've come to retrieve a package for my employer, Phineas Taylor Barnum."

The shopkeeper squinted at me, moving his face forward like a turtle's head. I pushed the note and the coin purse closer. The China-man sunk one hand into the purse and jingled its contents rather than dump it for a count. Then he took the note and ran his hand over the three Chinese figures at the bottom.

"Wait," he said at last. He took the bag of coins and held up a finger for me to stay where I was, then slid through a curtained door in the back, the top of his black silk cap bobbing as he moved. I glanced down and saw that my good brown pants had rings of dirt around the bot-toms of both legs. I'd have to wash them when I got back to the Museum. And what in the world was taking the Chinaman so long? After a few more minutes had passed, I'd all but made up my mind to leave empty-handed when he reappeared, holding a small parcel out in front of him.

When I reached out for the package, the Chinaman's other hand shot out and grabbed my wrist with his fingers, bone on bone.

"You have pulse?"

I pulled away, revolted by his touch.

Still holding Barnum's parcel in one hand and my wrist in the other, he let his eyes roll languidly along my torso, and when I grabbed again for the package, he moved it out of reach.

"You look like corpse."

"I most certainly do not! I am a performer and personal friend of Mr. Phineas T. Barnum, who will not be happy if you detain me any longer." As the Chinaman considered this, I sneaked a glance in the mirror on the wall. My cheeks were flushed from the heat. I looked nothing like a corpse. I snatched away my hand and stepped back from the counter, smoothing down my lapels and straightening my sleeves. Calmer now, I stood my ground. "Come, sir. Give me what I paid for so I may go."

The Chinaman held out Barnum's parcel in the middle of his palm, making me pluck it from his hand like a bird after food.

"Herbalist." The Chinaman glared at me, pointing at his own chest as I tucked Barnum's package into my coat pocket.

"Yes, yes, I am sure that you are, but no one here needs an herbalist." I pulled my gloves on and made my way to the door.

"I help!" he yelled after me.

But I was already gone.

The hustle down Pell Street brought me back to myself. What an odd and uncomfortable encounter. I stopped for a moment and sat on an empty stoop, realizing how distasteful the whole thing had been. At least I had gotten what I'd come for. I'd done Barnum's bidding and trusted that he'd compensate me for my trouble. Pulling the package out of my pocket, I held it up to the sky, squinting at it in the weakening light. What did it contain? And why had Barnum chosen me to fetch it? Out of nowhere, a hag of a woman rushed down the stoop behind me, flailing a broom and spitting out of the side of her mouth. "Monster! Ghoul! Whatever you are, go away! Get your festering body off my porch before I send you back to the hell you came from."

I scuttled away like a spider in the sun. It took me a block or so to calm down and slow my pace. By the time I got to Mulberry Street, I could feel a welt spreading down one side of my neck where the woman had hit me, and my tongue had grown thick as a stump from thirst. Nothing good had ever come from subjecting myself to the outside world. Just like the two women earlier that afternoon, this hag of a woman had seen only my thinness, overlooking my gift. But what did it matter if people on the street accepted me as one of their own? Hundreds of people paid good money to see me every day. How many of them had such a secure position in the world?

❋ ❋ ❋

I DIDN'T reach the Museum until the last of the evening sun streamed through my parlor windows, illuminating the charcoal drawings I'd hung on the walls over the years—portraits of Matina and Alley and Cook, our courtyard garden—and seeing them warmed my heart. My parlor smelled of books and blankets and Matina's perfume. "Nowhere like home," I said, and took in a deep breath of appreciation. Disposing of yesterday's *Herald*, I placed Barnum's package on my desk and took a good steady look. "Now let's see what all the fuss was about."

The package was three inches by four and weighed no more than a deck of playing cards. It had been wrapped in dirty brown butcher's cloth and sealed all along the top with red wax. Prying at the wax gently with my fingernail would cause evident marks of tampering. Shaking revealed nothing. I sniffed at the package and identified a slight dank smell but couldn't be certain if it came from the contents or the wrapping. Most likely, the parcel contained some new oddity the Chinaman had unearthed—a bright blue duck egg, perhaps, or a tuber grown into the image of a woman. But why go to all the trouble of having me fetch it? No, it had to be something more. All I could think to do was clean myself up and take the parcel to Barnum, hoping he'd open it in front of me. I was dying to find out what was in it.

After a quick wash, I rooted through my étagère, struggling over what to wear. I abandoned my usual striped scarf in favor of a bow tie, knotted with care. A visit to Barnum warranted wearing my father's stickpin, the one shaped like a stallion. I slipped it through the silk folds of my scarf as if I were going to a Richmond cotillion, and it gleamed like new even after all those years.

My father would have disapproved of my dressing to please a boss. And he would certainly have disapproved of Barnum. My father was a practical man. He did not believe in impresarios, circuses, or any other type of entertainment. A pity, actually, for he was a brilliant horseman and could have made quite a name for himself. For years, he trained French trotters at the Haras du Pin in Normandy before a Scotsman named Major Holmes lured him to Virginia to care for a stable full of Arabians and Plantation Walkers. My mother, a Bostonian girl, served as governess to the Major's daughter, and she lived and taught lessons in a small cottage on the grounds, the same cottage in which I would be born and my father would die.

"You should have seen your father when he first came to the farm," my mother told me. "The way he strolled out of the barn and into the kitchen to join the staff for dinner. So dashing. His accent. His broad back. Ah, and his smell. All saddle soap and sweat."

I remember him as a harsh man with rubbery skin and silky black hair. He spoke to me in French mixed with English, when he spoke at all, and spent most of his time in the stables or the corrals.

"There's no man in your father at all when he rides," my mother once said. "Just a saddle and a beast." And even that was an understatement. My father could sit, stand, turn, or throw himself sideways on a horse and pick up a nickel from the ground with his teeth. But he never used his talents to amuse. He hated trick riding almost as much as he hated little boys.

Somewhere I still had a flyer he once brought home. Where was it now? I rummaged through my bookcase, flipping through my history and botany books in search of it, remembering the night he'd come in after spending the day buying horses from the famous Pepin and Breschard circus. I'd found the flyer stuffed in the pocket of his coat. What young boy wouldn't have begged his mother to keep the thing, despite a father's mild disgust? Ah-ha! Here it was, tucked neatly into my volume of *Annuals of the Circus*. The faded handbill showed a huge horse, eighteen hands high, rearing up, a man straddling its bare sides with a whip in one hand, the horse's mane in the other.

According to my mother, Pepin tried to recruit my father in 1835. Wouldn't that have been something? I thought. Pretending to be on the back of a galloping horse, I lifted one arm in triumph, listening to imaginary crowds calling out for me, the son of a great rider, taking up the tradition, surpassing even his remarkable feats. I dropped my arm. Who knew the truth of it all, given my mother's propensity to imagine? And even if Pepin had approached him, my father would never have considered such a thing. Sighing, I replaced the flyer and shut the book.

I waited until I heard the closing bells, then tucked Barnum's parcel into the pocket of my vest and climbed down the service stairs. As I approached his office, my stomach churned. Calm down, I told myself. How easily one could slip out of an impresario's favor and back into a midway tent, dodging peanuts and bored to death. Better to do Barnum's bidding and be done with it.

Strands of cigar smoke spiraled out the open door of Barnum's office. Waving my hand through the smoke, I entered. The first thing Barnum did was glance down at his timepiece.

I held up the package. "I came as soon as I could, sir. The trip was much more difficult than I'd imagined. I had to change my clothes."

Barnum snatched the package from my hands and tucked it under his armpit, then led me to the stuffed chair. He poured me a snifter of brandy from a bottle on his desk and pulled up a slatted-back chair.

I nodded past him to the NO DRINKING sign on the front of his desk. "Does this mean that drink is no longer the devil's lubricant?" I asked, filled with a sudden spark of defiance.

Barnum scraped his chair to the right so that the sign on his desk was no longer visible. He examined the wax seal on the package, making certain I had not tampered with it.

"Perhaps it would be prudent to open it, sir. To be certain of its validity."

Barnum simply smiled. "No need for that, Fortuno. But I want you to realize how much I appreciate your help." Nodding toward the untouched brandy in my hand, he waited for me to take a drink before placing his own glass untouched on the desk. "And you'll be happy to know your new tights are nearly finished. Though a costume is hardly enough to thank you—especially since I might need your services again."

"Again?" Oh, how horrid! Who knew what ghastly thing he might ask me to do the next time? But I knew it was good for me to be in Barnum's good graces. To have him a bit indebted to me. It would make Matina proud. And perhaps it would even impress Iell . . . if I could find a way to cross paths with her again. I thought back on the discussion at lunch a few days past when Zippy's nurse told us how she had seen the new act lingering in the Arboretum after hours. Easier to access than some uptown boardinghouse.

"Assisting you is reward enough, sir; I deserve no more than that," I said, trying to warm him up. "But if you insist, there is one thing I'd like."

A flicker of pleasure jumped across Barnum's face. "Tell me, lad. Whatever you like."

"Actually, I was hoping to give you a gift of sorts." I loosened my collar, trying to appear nonchalant. "I'd like to feed the birds in the Arboretum."

Barnum seemed surprised. "Why in the world?"

"A wish to serve, sir, nothing more."

"Is that so?" Barnum stood, scraping the chair against the floor, and I could tell he didn't believe a word I'd said.

"You see, last week, I wandered into the Arboretum by mistake," I lied. "The poor little creatures. They need a personal touch, sir, they really do. I could make sure they're fed and that their cages are fresh. With the Arboretum closed, I expect you've been paying the charwomen extra to see to the birds. If I took over the job, it might save you money."

Skepticism narrowed Barnum's eyes and pulled his bushy eyebrows in toward each other. "Hardly seems like the kind of thing that would appeal to you." He let me stew while he resettled his body into the polished wooden chair and drummed his fingers against his desk. And then, just like that, he said, "But you know, the more I think about it, yes. Go ahead and feed the birds. Why not?"

Barnum removed a great ring of keys from the top drawer of his desk. Taking his time, he worked a small silver key off the ring, the rest of the keys jangling against one another as if saying goodbye to one of their own. He slid the loose key across the polished surface of the wide desk, and it stopped halfway over the edge nearest to me. "This opens the storeroom in the back hall," he said. "You'll find the birdseed in the corner. How about you start Wednesday? That gives me plenty of time to relieve the maids."

Pleased that Barnum had granted my request, I stood and clicked my heels together, grabbing the key before he changed his mind.

"One more thing, Mr. Fortuno," he added, as I backed out his door, the little key already seated in the watch pocket of my vest.

I frowned.

"I have given a certain new performer permission to sit in the Arboretum as she wishes."

"Sir?"

"And as long as you'll be in that room ..."

My breath quickened. Was Barnum asking me to do the very thing I most longed for? "I'm not sure I understand you, sir."

Barnum shuffled papers about and avoided my eyes. "It's not like I'm asking you to spy on her or anything."

"What then? Who?"

Barnum picked up a small obsidian paperweight rumored to be as old as time itself. Squeezing it as if trying to break it, he sighed, then tossed the rock back down and grabbed his glass of brandy.

"Just come see me next week. Share a cigar and a brandy, and tell me if you've run across anyone else lingering in the Arboretum or the hallway nearby. But Fortuno—say nothing of this to your companions, eh?"

"About which, the brandy or the bird feeding?"

Barnum laughed one more time before shooing me out the door with a great bearlike swipe of his hand.

chapter seven

"WHY DIDN'T YOU COME SEE ME LAST night?" Matina looked up at my reflection in her makeup mirror. "The second I'm finished, you're to tell me everything that happened on your"—she looked around the Green Room—"you know, your trip."

I was dying to tell all, but with Alley's huge body sprawled across the chair behind her, I held my tongue. What in the world was Alley hanging about for, anyway? Something must have happened. Otherwise, he'd be sitting alone as he always did. Instead, he loitered behind Matina, smoking a cigar and watching her swipe at her face with a cloth full of cream. Behind them, faded posters and clippings covered the wall, old pictures of Barnum, banners from *The Enchantress*, which ran for six months at Niblo's, and newspaper headlines such as CHILD DEVOURED BY PIGS and SHOCKING OCCURRENCE: FIVE MEN SMOTHERED IN GIN VAT.

Alley pulled on his cigar, his cheeks collapsing in on themselves like sinkholes. Then he puffed the smoke straight up, sending a cloud of it rolling past my face.

"I really wish you wouldn't do that," I said, waving my hand through the smoke. I pulled up the chair from the next dressing table and sat down on it.

"Don't pick on the poor man." Matina moved close to her oval mirror and squinted at the side of her nose, perfect from what I could see despite her eye for secret flaws. "Alley had a bad day yesterday, and we've been talking about what he might do, poor thing, to make some sense of it."

"My day wasn't easy, either," I interjected, but Matina seemed not to hear me or not to care. "All right then," I barked at Alley, "tell me what happened."

Alley looked the other way.

"The police picked him up," Matina answered for him.

"The police?"

"But I can't get him to tell me why. And now he says he wants to leave us, Barthy. Can you imagine?"

"I'm thinkin' o' maybe goin' west," Alley said at last. "Buy a farm somewheres. Maybe Indiana."

Matina threw up her hands. "Goodness, no! Have you any idea what a wilderness the territories are? Tell him, Barthy."

I'd nothing to say. It was utterly inconceivable to me that anyone would want to leave the Museum, let alone to go to the territories. Nowhere in the world would Alley be so well regarded as here. And God knows he could never manage to control himself outside the company of his peers. He knew that as well as I did.

Matina picked up an old photograph in a silver frame she always kept on her dressing table and waggled it in front of Alley's nose. Ah, yes, the husband's likeness. I knew it well.

"I myself am from Indiana," she told Alley. "Horrible place. Horrible people. My very own Paps, in fact, married me off to this Swede to pay his dry goods bill. It was barbaric. Look at this!" The photograph showed Matina, probably fifteen or so, standing in front of a much older man. Behind them was a pine building with an overhead sign that read SVENDAL DRY GOODS. Matina, already large by normal standards, was wearing the kind of dress that's only seen on young country girls, and her hair was braided. The man, her husband, Henrick, towered above her. He had legs like oak logs and shoulders as broad as she was wide. His pocked face bore the long nose and craggy cheekbones of his Nordic ancestry. "I swear that man was chiseled from a glacier." She sighed. "I had to wrap up in raccoon furs whenever he touched me. And here." She lifted the white sleeve of her gown and pointed with her chin to a scar on the inside of her left arm. "He cut me once with a kitchen knife for burning his bread."

Alley reached a huge finger out toward her scar.

"Don't fret." Matina pulled her arm away before Alley could touch it. "He left me for an Irish girl, a sheepshearer, and it was the best thing that could have happened. I didn't even petition for room and board, though with the way he treated me, Lord knows, I'd probably have gotten it. But no, sir. Just signed a paper of divorce, packed my bags, and got right out of there. I ended up in Indianapolis. Morty Howard— you remember him, Barthy?—well, Morty Howard saw my potential right away, and it took less than a year of eating pork fat and goose to become the girl I am today." Matina wagged at finger at Alley. "We make ourselves succeed," she said. "We don't run away."

"*You* ran away," Alley said, scratching his head.

Matina shrugged. "I hardly think it's the same." After turning to me for assistance and getting silence, she twisted around and reached beneath her chair. With a bit of effort, she pulled out a basket full of *cartes* and plunked it onto her lap. Flipping through the basket, she found what she was looking for and held it up in front of us.

"Here it is: Kaspar Hauser," Matina said, poking at the picture with her finger. "That boy lived in a tiny cellar until he was sixteen years old. He never saw the light of day, never spoke to anyone. His meals came each morning delivered by an unseen hand." Matina pulled out the battered picture and held it up: a short man with a large head, bowed legs, and hair pressed to his ears. "He's a wonderful example: the way he rose above his problems. I find it quite inspirational."

"His life sounds all right to me." Alley smirked.

"I'm serious. The poor boy lived in darkness for years until some kind soul found him and let him out. And he ended up quite famous despite his lack of language. The rumor—and I, for one, believe it— was that he was the son of the Grand Duke of Baden!"

Matina rummaged about in her basket, pulling out another picture, this one of a huge man dressed in a loincloth.

"Better yet, here's Charles Freeman, who could lift fifteen hundred pounds with one hand. This here says that even though he knew not a thing about boxing, he went into the ring with the Tipton Slasher."

At this point, I interrupted. "My dear, it might not be the best idea to compare Alley to Charles Freeman."

Matina knew how I felt about Alley. No matter how gentle his temperament, a man with a body like Alley's was subject to dangerous storms—storms that, should they break, could cause all manner of harm and destruction. Better to give him practical counsel than encourage him with stories of violence.

"I simply want to remind him that we succeed by being brave, not by letting our problems overwhelm us."

"I think you've made your point."

Alley reached over to take the *carte* from Matina, but his elbow hit the dressing table and knocked her hairbrush from the top. It clattered across the floor and slid under the adjoining makeup table. I let Alley jump to retrieve the brush even though it was probably as difficult for him to clamber beneath the table as it would have been for me. I didn't care. I wanted a moment to let Matina know I wasn't pleased about her fussing over Alley when I had so much news to tell her. As soon as Alley ducked his head, I gave her a searing look. She shook her head back at me, frowning.

When Alley stretched forward and reached his gigantic hand along the floor, his shirt rode up, revealing the beginning of three long, deep scars that disappeared beneath his broadcloth shirt. I flinched. Alley had once told me about those scars. His father had died in New York City's Great Fire of '35 and afterward, although he was no more than sixteen, Alley took to whiskey. Some days, he could drink all day and still be on his feet and lucid. Other days, a single shot could intoxicate him, and if someone provoked him while in that drunken state, Alley flew into an awful rage. One day, after drinking a few too many shots of whiskey, he nearly killed another boy over a game of cards at a dive in Five Points. The courts sent him upstate to a reformatory for two full years. Alley spent his time there quietly, causing no one else harm. But the moment he got out, he was at it again.

Barnum's scouts found Alley a few months later, brawling in a tavern on the West Side. The scouts watched him for two days, then sat him down, fed him, and gave him a free glass of whiskey. That was all it took to convince Alley to compete in the Fight of the Beasts, a notorious bear-wrestling contest Barnum put on for private clients with a taste for violence. Held on a pig farm near land the city had set aside for the new central parklands, the fights took place in an old barn that Barnum had refitted as a fighting ring, with rough-hewn oak benches lining the walls and, in the center, a metal cage on top of a huge pit of mud. Inside that cage, a black bear raged. Barnum would pit that bear against anyone crazy or desperate enough to fight it and made quite a sum, I've heard, on entrance fees and betting.

After Alley scrawled his name across the front of a one-page contract, he found himself propped up in a donkey cart on his way up the island, crooning love songs and drinking black ale under a cold winter sky. During the long ride, it started to snow. Alley didn't bother to shelter himself beneath his coat. He just stared wistfully out across the Croton Aqueduct and the open fields of Manhattan, dreaming, he told me later, about some girl named Eleanor. The snow floated down, and the cold kept him still. By the time he jumped off the cart and headed into the barn, his clothes, his hair, and most of his face lay buried under dirty snow and ice. He stumbled into the barn like a Himalayan Yeti, and he must have made quite an impression because the bear shook his bars as spectators flew to their feet, appreciatively. Alley yelled a ferocious greeting and jumped into the caged arena half blind from the ice. The bear reared up. They circled each other like warring brothers, equal in size and strength, and took turns swatting and showing their teeth. At one point, the bear knocked Alley sideways and the impact whipped him around on his heels, exposing his back. With one tidy swipe, the bear clawed down his skin like it was the bark of a tree. But rather than stop Alley, the swipe sent him into a fury. The powerful howl from this ice-encrusted wild man so stunned the animal it jerked back, and that hesitation gave Alley his chance. With a roar as loud as a crashing tree, he slammed his fist across the poor bear's nose, and with that single *thump* he knocked the animal to the ground, unconscious. Barnum did not waste a moment. He recruited Alley on the spot.

Now, as Alley pulled his shirt down to cover the scars—raised slashes like tiny mountain ranges that started at his lower back and twisted halfway up to his shoulders—I felt sorry for him. But pity didn't change a thing. A man built like Alley was destined for violence.

"Here it is!" Alley righted himself, handing the brush to Matina as if it were a precious gift.

"Perhaps what you need," I suggested to Alley, slightly repentant, "is a female companion. Someone to pass the time with. How about Bridgett, that black-haired girl from the kitchens? She's totally smitten with you."

But Alley wasn't listening to me. He stared mournfully at Matina, his long hair flopping over his face so that only the tip of his nose and his dark eyes were visible. When she took the brush out of his hands, he turned to go.

"You stay right where you are," Matina ordered, and Alley hesitated, then sat down. "Barthy, why don't you go check the schedule while I finish here. We can talk about your day later."

Irritated, I walked over to the Notice Board and waited until Fish came to hang up the new schedule. Over my shoulder, I watched Matina pat Alley on his arm. Why did she baby him like that? I turned back to the board and, to my surprise, found that a small crowd had already gathered.

I had to squeeze myself between two sweating acrobats to get a better look.

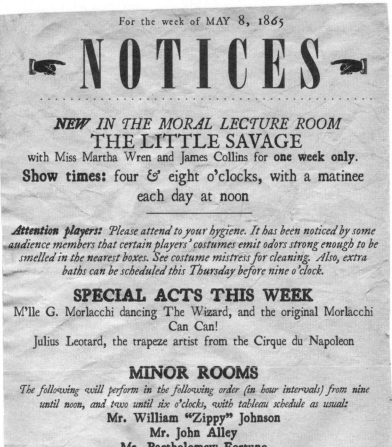

For the week of MAY 8, 1865

☛ NOTICES ☚

NEW IN THE MORAL LECTURE ROOM
THE LITTLE SAVAGE
with Miss Martha Wren and James Collins for **one week only**.
Show times: four & eight o'clocks, with a matinee each day at noon

Attention players: *Please attend to your hygiene. It has been noticed by some audience members that certain players' costumes emit odors strong enough to be smelled in the nearest boxes. See costume mistress for cleaning. Also, extra baths can be scheduled this Thursday before nine o'clock.*

SPECIAL ACTS THIS WEEK
M'lle G. Morlacchi dancing The Wizard, and the original Morlacchi Can Can!
Julius Leotard, the trapeze artist from the Cirque du Napoleon

MINOR ROOMS
The following will perform in the following order (in hour intervals) from nine until noon, and two until six o'clocks, with tableau schedule as usual:
Mr. William "Zippy" Johnson
Mr. John Alley
Mr. Bartholomew Fortuno
Mr. Ricardo Hortense
All others will appear in tableau only, as previously set on first or third floors

New Addition to House Acts:
Mrs. Iell Adams begins Wednesday for a special engagement. She will be presented in the Yellow Room for a separate admission fee. Due to her location and the expected number of visitors, space will be limited. We ask that no one other than paying customers attend these performances.

Aha! At last. Mrs. Iell Adams. Slated to start on Wednesday. But why would her shows be private, closed to all of us? And if Iell's theater assignment was any indication, she'd been struck a retaliatory blow. The Yellow Room was on the main floor between Barnum's offices and the exhibit hall where most of us sat in tableau between performances, and showing her there was a bit of an insult; all the real theaters were upstairs. The only good thing about the Yellow Room was that it was right next door to the Arboretum. Maybe I could use my newfound intimacy with Barnum to finagle a pass to get in.

"She's all yers." Alley grinned as he walked by me, nodding goodbye to Matina before ducking his head to clear the door into the busy hall.

"What in the world is wrong with you?" Matina asked me when I left the Notice Board and sauntered back to join her. She brushed at her hair with so much vigor, the vanity table jiggled in front of her. "The man needs your help as much as he needs mine."

I ignored this comment, sat myself down in the chair abandoned by Alley, and waited, knowing Matina's curiosity would eventually get the better of her. Not until she calmed down and asked me sweetly did I begin recounting my trip to Chinatown—"And you've no idea what was in the package? Couldn't you peek?"—as well as my interview with Barnum. I diplomatically omitted Barnum's suggestion that I monitor Iell's movements, telling Matina only that Iell's show was finally on the schedule.

"The woman has a separate showroom? Did Barnum say anything about her gift or what she'll be doing?"

"Not a word."

The bell rang for places. I waited as Matina poured water over her hands and into a bowl and examined herself in her mirror one last time. She patted her hair into place, pinched her cheeks, and held out her arm for me to help her to her feet.

"One other thing," she said, leaning on me a bit heavier than need be. "Did you really have to suggest that Alley find a companion? After all, he does have the two of us."

✳ ✳ ✳

I DON'T know how she did it, but Matina found out that Iell had a beard, and after that the news spread like wildfire. Then the rumors started. Iell had seduced a young Gypsy boy whose grandmother tricked her into drinking a potion that had caused her hair to grow.

She'd been improperly raised in Africa. She was really a man. Most of the gossip, told out the side of one's mouth or behind one's hand, was too wild to be anything but fabrication, but one interesting bit came from Cook, who told Matina that she'd heard two of the seamstresses complain about how fussy Iell was over the cut of her dresses and how they already hated her. They called her a prissy Boston Brahmin. That didn't surprise me in the least. Of course Iell would have come from a fine Bostonian family. She certainly gave off an air of gentility.

I learned nothing more about the new act until the next afternoon, when I went to join Matina in tableau.

Tableau was all Matina did for the present, spending most of her day in the first-floor exhibit room along with the other permanent exhibits, and I joined her there between my shows. Tableau wasn't hard work, but it wasn't my favorite. It required nothing other than placing oneself in a scene—backgrounds of mountain lakes, for example, or castle grounds, whatever Barnum deemed most interesting each month—and chatting with customers. We were encouraged by management to sell our visitors personal *cartes* with our pictures for a nickel and fake histories for a dime. I had always found it uncomfortably intimate to be stuffed into a corner with strangers standing so near that I could smell the horse manure on their shoes. It reminded me of the circuses. And it was hard to control a customer's response when dealing with them up close. Tableau subjected us to the full range of our viewers' reactions: fury, amazement, humor, and disgust. We were forced to put up with all manner of comment and slander.

This afternoon, I'd arrived late. Three boys in ruffian shirts and button-fly trousers already milled about Matina's platform and, worried that they might be harassing her, I hurried across the room, trying not to touch any of the customers as I passed. Her platform measured twelve feet by six. It sat flush against a wall and was elevated about a foot off the ground. Matina reclined on a plank bed made of oak slabs balanced across two stone pillars, pillows of blue patterned silk all around her.

"Finally," Matina said when she spotted me, smoothing her dress, its red and white skirts billowing like flags.

With effort I climbed up next to her, my day suit drab in contrast to her colorful veils, and scowled at the boys. They broke into whoops and giggles.

"Let me stand in front, my dear. So you're not unduly aggravated."

"Honestly, Barthy, if I haven't learned to manage a few boys by now, what have I been doing all these years?" Matina pulled out a red lace fan and waved it lazily across her face, causing her veils to move slightly in an artificial breeze. As Matina unhooked her veils, exposing her décolletage, one of the boys—a slick-haired youth with doe eyes and the beginnings of a beard—all but fainted, proof that what was shocking about Matina was the very thing that moved a certain type of man. When he reached forward to touch her ankle, Matina pulled her leg back only enough to make his quest impossible.

"Careful, young man. What would you do if you got hold of me?"

"I'd think of something, I'll tell you that." The boy flushed and spun to face his friends, slapping his thighs and sending up a puff of dust from his pants. But his friends had already abandoned him for other exhibits, one examining the comely portrait of the Prince of Wales's mistress, Mary Darcy Robinson, that hung along the wall, the other leafing through a copy of her novel, *Vancenza, the Dangers of Credulity*, a gothic romance full of references to the prince's sexual predilections. The boy walked off, but the look he threw her over his shoulder told me he would be thinking of Matina for a long time to come.

"I have a present for you." Matina pulled a folded clipping from her sleeve and handed it to me. From the width of her smile, I knew it held something of interest.

NEW YORK, FRIDAY, MAY 5, 1865

✳ ✳ ✳ ✳ ✳ ✳ ✳ ✳ ✳

BARNUM'S
AMERICAN MUSEUM

NEWEST
WONDER *of the* WORLD

In the form of a WOMAN OF GREAT BEAUTY with a MAN'S BEARD and of figure so beautiful and comely, she was previously MISTRESS to kings and arbiter of HIGH FASHION, the Newest Wonder of the World will be presented to society in a SPECIAL SHOW at this Museum.

You are invited to meet and view the most astonishing MRS. IELL ADAMS of BOSTON, the BEARDED ARISTOCRAT, the WIDOWED WONDER.

By special admission only, she will begin on Wednesday, 10th, and hold court daily at 10 A.M., 2 P.M. and 4 P.M. daily, with an evening show on Fridays and Saturdays.

"Not only is Barnum finally giving her press," Matina said, "but apparently, as the article says, she's not married after all."

"Do you think that's true?"

"Emma confirmed it. She went straight to Barnum and asked if she was an honest woman. He told her that the new act was a widow. And has been for some time, apparently." Matina shifted her attention to a group of ladies who had stopped to look us over. "Good day to you, ladies." Matina smiled, making one of the young girls giggle and turn her eyes away. "To tell you the truth," she said to me, "I have a bad feeling about this new bearded woman of ours."

"You're being ridiculous," I snapped.

Matina winced. "You don't think I know what I'm talking about?" She straightened her back regally, gazing over the heads of the customers, and ignored my apology. "Did I ever tell you the story about my pap's brother-in-law, Nathaniel?" she asked, considering the crowd. "He lived with my aunt on a pig farm in Indiana. A hard worker, that one, with muscles running up and down his arms like iron ropes. Well, you know how I can see people's colors?"

For as long as I'd known her, Matina had claimed she could see colors in people, much like pigs, they say, can see the color of the wind. I'd always thought it more of a joke than anything else, though she's been known to catch me on a bad day and tell me that my normal shade has gone too pale.

"One summer," she went on, "his whole color changed. Nathaniel left his wife with the farm and came down to help my paps with the planting." She paused for effect. "Nathaniel was a good man, Barthy, and he'd always read a good healthy orange. But he started to sneak off and spend his evenings with some harlot in town. The strain of the secret marked him with big purple spots." She tilted toward me, the weight of her forearms on the platform causing it to shift slightly. "It's the same thing with that harlot that Barnum has hired."

"You haven't even *seen* the woman yet," I said. "You're going on about nothing."

"It's not *her* color that makes me say this," she explained. "It's Barnum's. Have you noticed how yellow he's been looking? He's hiding something about her, and it won't be good for anyone. You mark my words."

"Let's just leave it be," I said, but my thoughts shifted back to Iell. She was a widow. And the mistress of kings, the flyer said. Just thinking of her made my heart thump as nervously as a boy's. I turned away from Matina and looked into the crowd, worried that she might read my excitement through my color.

I had to find a way to see Iell's show.

✳ ✳ ✳

THE DAY the new act debuted, I started my bird-feeding job, hoping to use the proximity of the Arboretum to help me sneak into the Yellow Room. First, I'd discharge my duty, then linger and wait for my chance. As the Museum hadn't opened yet, it was easy enough to drag a large bag of seed from the storeroom across the empty hall and past the Yellow Room door, where Iell's poster—the same one I'd seen in the cellars—sat propped up on a little platform next to a stack of advertisements.

I entered the Arboretum expecting to see what I'd always seen in the past: a few benches, potted plants, and rickety birdcages stuck along the back wall. To my surprise, I found the renovations quite remarkable. Lugging the seed bag down a twisted stone path, I marveled at the newly imported bamboo and palm trees, the big-leaf banana plants, and the flowers with heads like little hooded people. The farther in I ventured, the more junglelike the room became, and I went a bit giddy with the smell of tea roses, tree fungus, magnolias, and almond shrubs. When the path split around an oak tree dripping with Spanish moss, I stumbled to get to the rear of the exhibit, and there, to my surprise, I found a fog machine spewing overzealous clouds into the vines that covered the ceiling above.

I squinted into the artificial sunlight, hoping to catch a glimpse of Iell, but found I was alone in the room. I dragged the seed bag toward a large wire aviary recently built along the back wall. Inside, dozens of exotic birds—cockatoos, parrots, macaws, African grays, and snow-white canaries—cackled out to me from artificial roosts. They'd been singing, but they changed their tunes as I approached, uncertain if I were friend or foe. To give them time to adjust to me, I stopped near an exhibit. A stuffed ocelot hung from a tree, its bared fangs inches above a terrified brown bunny, which lay belly-up, recognizable only by its long, innocent ears. "I know how you feel, little fella," I said. A waterfall trickled down the wall behind the display. To the right was an artificial tortoise pond—dry, still, and full of pebbles. To the left was a café table with two ornate fan chairs, cobra-backed and shadowed by palm trees. Near it, a single raven had been shackled by one leg to a standing perch.

"Hello, in there." I dragged the bag of seed to the aviary doors and wiped my brow. "Aren't all of you something?" Propping open the door, I climbed into the big cage, pulling the bag behind me, and used a half shell I'd rescued from the tortoise pond to scoop seed from the bag into small cups hanging on wires. To my surprise, I quite enjoyed the experience. A rose-breasted cockatoo pecked at my hand and the sight of bird excretion was a bit hard to bear, but having said this I must admit that the bright plumage of the parrots lifted my heart, as did the lilting songs of the finches and the canaries. Even the raven pleased me. His ebony feathers gave him a most dignified appearance, and his claws—spindly and sharp—made my own hands look soft and fleshy by comparison. When I heard the bells alerting the staff that the Museum was about to open, I hurried through my remaining tasks with a bit of regret.

By the time I pushed out the door into the main hallway, a queue already stretched halfway down the corridor to the front of the Yellow Room, where Mr. Fish himself roosted atop the lecturer's platform. Drat. Slipping in was going to be harder than I'd thought.

"The rarest of gems in a setting of gold," Fish harked down the hallway. "A woman as nature never intended a woman to be."

At the front of the line, a young couple put their dimes into the basket at the door and slipped past the black velvet curtain into the room. The fellow's beard was almost the same color red as Iell's. I considered my tactics. All sorts of people were jumbled together in line: ladies in their spring corals attended by young girls aflutter over the prospect of spending the morning at the Museum. Half-grown boys pounding one another on the shoulders. A surprising number of tradesmen—

printers, gilders, clerks, and the like—some unhappily accompanied by their wives while others were alone and nattily dressed. Even a group of veterans waited to give over their dimes, their gruff guffaws unable to cover their haunted eyes.

I figured my best bet was to slip into line, keeping my eyes to the ground, and so I ducked in behind an old man who gave me a nod. As we moved forward, I lowered my chin and managed to advance a few feet, then a few more after that. No one said a word to me, though I could hear murmurs and snickering from behind me. As Fish continued his chant, I lingered for a moment in front of Iell's poster. God, she was beautiful! My mouth went dry at even the painted image of her.

"Move on," Fish ordered, not realizing it was me slowing up his line. By the time I shuffled forward and dropped my dime into the basket by the door, I felt invincible. I made it halfway through the curtain before I felt the yank of Fish's cane at the back of my neck, wrenching me out by my collar.

"What the hell are you doing, Fortuno? You know you're not allowed to take up space in here. Out with you."

"My dime, Mr. Fish. I've paid my dime."

But I'd already drawn too much attention to myself, and I knew I'd best retreat.

Later on, I went downstairs to try to determine the impact of Iell's show by canvassing people as they left the room. I approached a middle-aged man.

"Did you enjoy the exhibit?"

"Marvelous, marvelous."

"Well worth your money, then?"

"Would have paid a quarter more, but if you want to know the truth, the whole thing made me feel a bit squeamish."

Idiot, I thought, but I nodded my head politely and made my way back to my quarters. I'd have to find some other way into the show.

chapter eight

ITTLE DID I KNOW THAT FATE WOULD SOON intervene and give me my first real conversation with Iell. Two days later, Matina dropped into my rooms after the Museum closed for the night to borrow a book.

"Most of the botany books belonged to my mother," I explained, surprised to see Matina run her fingers over Kant, Plato, and Linnaeus, and then linger on *The Botanist's Repository*.

"Did they now?" Bypassing *The Botanist's Repository*, she pulled out another oversized tome and carried it to the table near my settee. It was one of my favorites: *A New Treatise on Flower Painting*, its spine loose from countless thumbing and knee balances. Inside was page after page of hand-colored engravings—bitter cress, nightshade, sundew, clover—along with lessons on how to render each image in watercolor or Conté crayon.

"Looky here, Barthy. The magnolia!" Matina glanced up from the open book with bright eyes. "My favorite flower. Isn't it gorgeous?"

I bent over her shoulder and looked at the sketch. "I learned to draw with that book, you know."

"Really?" Matina said, her head buried again in the pages. But I could tell she was listening. No matter how often Matina asked me about my childhood, I rarely talked about it. The past is the past, I always said. One should not waste his life looking back. But that night I was in the mood to talk.

"My mother," I said, rewarding Matina's restraint by offering a bit of information, "insisted I find exactly the right stroke of the brush." I demonstrated with a perfect flick of the wrist. "And if I got it wrong, or strayed outside the lines, she'd make me do it again and again."

"That sounds so unpleasant."

"Unpleasant?" Her response surprised me. "No, not at all. She just wanted me to fulfill my potential. She taught me everything I know."

My mother's voice materialized in my head. "Classification is everything, my boy." The morning sun dappled through our cottage windows. I sat atop a high stool watching my mother stab at a wall chart with a pointed stick. "Does it flower, or does it not? Is it a single or double seed leaf? Class, subclass, super order, tribe. Such an elegant system, don't you think? Most plants are happily classified by family, genus, and species. But there are a few special plants. Unique plants." She lifted my chin with one cool finger to make sure I was paying close attention. "Plants so special, Bartholomew, that they defy classification. *Those*"—my mother smiled broadly, her eyes cornflower blue—"are the exceptions that prove the rule!"

Matina and I talked briefly after that about other things—the schedule changes, how Alley had refused to speak to anyone about his beating, a bit more about the previous fire—until, around eleven o'clock, she scooped up the *New Treatise on Flower Painting* book and Aristotle's *Poetics* (the *Poetics* taken, I suspected, for my benefit) and returned to her room.

After Matina left, I got to thinking how lucky I was to have her as my friend. She never objected to my imperfections, never expected me to be anything other than what I was. How, I wondered, could I show my appreciation for her? She'd said that magnolias were her favorite flower, and I'd spotted a magnolia tree in the middle of the Arboretum a few days earlier. Should I pay a visit to the Arboretum and cut a handful of magnolia blossoms as a gift?

Despite the late hour, I trekked downstairs through empty halls, taking along a night lamp and a small penknife to cut the stems. When I pushed open the Arboretum door I was greeted by the squawks of the parrots and was pleased to find that someone had left the Arboretum lamps lit. I clucked a greeting to the birds, placed my lamp on the floor, and ventured in.

The tea roses at the front entrance caught my eye, so I clipped a few to use as a frame for the magnolias, then pushed deeper into the Arboretum until I reached the magnolia tree. Expertly wielding my penknife, I snipped off the best blossoms and laid them in the crook of my arm.

It was then I heard the voices. Female. Two of them, whispering and laughing together. Curious, I moved down the overgrown path, pushing away a stray vine or two until I came to the moss-covered oak where the path split. Straining to hear, I realized that the voices came from the café table near the aviary. I inched around the tree and stopped.

Iell and Emma Swan sat sipping tea together at the table like long-lost friends. I could not believe my eyes. What were they doing there at such a late hour, what with Iell being boarded uptown? Plus Emma had never said a word to any of us about having made the new act's acquaintance, and I'd have thought she'd be the first to brag about such an association. Whatever was she up to? In cahoots with Barnum, I suspected, despite her dislike of the man. Though why he would go to her and me as well, I hadn't a clue.

My wounded pride was relieved to see Iell looking slightly bored as Emma poured tea and chattered away. How utterly exquisite she appeared, in a silver dress that shimmered in the light. Nestled inside the palm-shaped wicker chair, she fluttered a fan beneath her chin, sending up loose strands of that beautiful beard. Perhaps Iell had decided to seek advice on navigating the dangerous waters of Barnum's business, something we all had experience with.

Taking my courage in hand, I shifted the flowers to my other arm, ran my finger along my eyebrows, and walked into the women's line of sight, stopping for a moment so as not to shock them with my unannounced appearance. The birds saw me first, and set up a racket, and both women looked over at the same time.

Emma frowned. I advanced and bowed crisply, my hands clammy and shaking.

"Pardon me, ladies. How are you faring this evening?"

Iell gave me a quick smile before dropping her eyes to her lap, and my heart leaped into my throat.

"This lady and I are having a private discussion, Fortuno." Emma's double chin folded into her neck, her lips crimson and tight. "You will kindly leave us to it."

"I have no wish to disturb you, Emma. I only want to say good evening and to give my regards to your new friend." A burst of steam blew out from the fog machine and covered a patch of lichen growing on the damp shale behind us. I was suddenly aware of how womanly I must appear, cradling a bouquet of flowers, with steam-induced tears running down my cheeks.

"Haven't we met?" Iell leaned forward to examine me more closely, and I cursed myself for not wearing a better jacket.

"The other evening," I said. "You came across me in the east cellars, looking at your lovely poster."

"Ah, yes. The gentleman who showed such a fascination with my image. I remember." She blessed me with an utterly charming smile. "Mr. . . ."

"Fortuno, Madame. Bartholomew Fortuno." I bowed, this time more deeply, blood rushing into my ears. Stand up tall, I admonished myself. Take up some space.

Emma pitched herself forward, half out of her chair, and set her hammy fists on the little café table. "Very nice, Fortuno. But now I'm sure you have plenty of other things to do." Emma's tone carried an edge, and had Iell not leaned over and gently touched Emma's arm, I might have been forced to leave right then.

"Perhaps," Iell intervened, in a voice as soft as a bird's wing, "we could take advantage of our uninvited guest for a minute or two." She waited for the scowling Emma to crunch herself back into her chair before addressing me directly. "My friend Emma and I have been talking about childhood," she said, "and I would love another opinion on the topic."

"Of course, Madam. What would you like to know?" I asked, heady in her presence.

Iell ran her fingers along the outside of her beard, and I looked away, a bit flustered. "We were discussing the Theory of Maternal Impression before you came in. What do you make of that premise, sir? Do you believe that we are all products of our mothers' traumas?"

"I do believe in fate," I said, choosing my words carefully. "But modern science has discredited the Theory of Maternal Impression."

"You see?" Iell smiled at Emma, rapping her fan in light emphasis against the metal top of the café table.

"'Thou didst weave me in my mother's womb, and I am fearfully and most wonderfully made,'" Emma said flatly.

Iell tilted forward in her chair, her eyes flickering with intelligence. I could see why Barnum was having a difficult time managing her— not that I wouldn't gladly trade places with him and argue with the woman until she tired of the game.

"And yet," Iell said to me, "even Aristotle and Hippocrates thought pressure to the tender parts of a woman's body altered a baby's development. Surely you can't disagree with minds such as theirs?"

I cleared my throat to give myself a moment to think, shifting Matina's flowers to my other arm. The Theory of Maternal Impression was well known. It posited that a shock of some kind—an unhealthy obsession, even thinking intently about something during the act of conception—might cause a mother to bear a child with a related problem. For example, a woman's unfortunate scare by a mongrel might produce a dog-faced boy, or a mother who dreamed of a wild beast might produce fierce progeny. But few people believed such poppycock anymore. Still, one did not speak of conception in mixed company, and I did not wish to offend my new acquaintance.

"I disagree only with the theory. Perhaps you recall the tale of Mary Tofts?"

"The woman who gave birth to the baby rabbits and blamed it on being lost in the woods?" Iell played her fingers across her lips, trying, I suspected, to hide a smile. "Pity she went to jail for it. I'd always found the story refreshing, though some think a woman should be punished for having ambition."

"I never said such a thing." Emma took a swift kick at the side of the aviary and set the cockatoos flapping.

"As far as I'm concerned," I continued, keeping a wary eye on Emma, "Mary Tofts was the worst sort of Gaff. To plant dead rabbits into her own womb, then pretend to give birth to them in front of ill-suspecting doctors? Of course she went to jail."

"So you object to artifice?" Iell stared at me with a directness quite rare in women. There was nothing flirtatious or coy about her today. Her charms were straightforward, strong and magnetic.

"More than anything in the world."

"And yet you yourself are the product of self-invention. You were not born thin, were you?"

"Pardon me?" My hands contracted into fists, squeezing the stems of the flowers until I forced my fingers to relax. I laid the flowers on the table.

"Your body. It has been this way from birth?"

"My change came a bit later than some, but, as you can see, I am all natural." I ran my shaking hand along my upper body to demonstrate that I was a Prodigy, not something constructed. How had she known about my history? Had she been asking questions about me? Or was it simply a lucky guess, an assumption based on the nature of my gift?

Iell's eyes sparkled, and when Emma snorted a half laugh, Iell waved her quiet. "How fascinating to think you might have elected this world, unlike so many of us who had no choice."

My temples pounded. "I assure you, Madam, I have never had a choice. I simply *can't* eat. My body won't allow it."

"Really, Mr. Fortuno? I'm certain that a man of your sophistication understands that sometimes choice is a complicated matter."

As discreetly as possible, I wiped my palms dry on the sides of my trouser legs and then cleared my throat, trying to regain mastery over the situation.

"There is but one thing certain," I said, changing the direction of talk. "No matter when we've received our gifts, we've all been blessed. Our uniqueness alone is enough to justify our special place in the world. But even more, our destiny insists we use our gifts to show others who they really are or show them what, in an ideal world, they could become. It may shock them at first, but, deep down, we open their eyes to greater possibilities."

Iell clapped her hands together as if my answer were a present. "So you believe that your act edifies your audience, Mr. Fortuno?"

"Not only mine, Madam. All of our acts."

Iell held up her index finger in a most charming way. "Now here I would disagree. I do not believe we educate our audiences. I believe we frighten them and, in doing so, make them feel better about the dullness of their own lives. We don't open their eyes, Mr. Fortuno, we give them permission to keep them shut." She glanced over at Emma. "Don't you think that's true, Emma? Are we not the nightmare? The gargoyles at the edge of their world?"

I didn't give Emma a chance to respond. "I think you underestimate us," I said.

Iell looked at me, clearly surprised.

"We're not gargoyles," I said, groping for something more significant to say. "We're gatekeepers."

Emma rolled her eyes. "If anyone's a gatekeeper around here, it's Barnum."

"Perhaps," I agreed. "But his protection permits us to reveal our true selves. We owe him our loyalty and appreciation."

"Appreciation?" Iell interjected.

"Absolutely. In fact, to show my personal appreciation, I recently fetched a parcel for him in Chinatown, and I did it in the full light of day." I was boasting, hoping to impress her with my bravery.

Iell's smile faded. She shifted in her chair, the crackle of the wicker setting the raven to sidestepping along its roost, its talons *click-clicking* against the wooden bar.

"I see. Well, then, it seems I owe you thanks as well."

I raised my palms heavenward in a gesture implying a lack of understanding.

"For helping Mr. Barnum," Iell said. "Chinatown."

"I don't understand."

"The package you picked up, Mr. Fortuno. It was for me."

It took me a moment, but then I saw the connection. Of course. Iell had pressed Barnum, and he'd made me do her bidding so he wouldn't lose face. My curiosity about the contents of the package was instantly renewed.

But Iell had chilled toward the conversation, and my heart sank. In an effort to renew her interest, I pushed the bouquet of flowers across the table toward her.

She shook her head and smiled.

"I think, Mr. Fortuno, that you had better take these flowers to the one for whom they were intended."

Iell made no further comment. As she stood, she gave me a half smile of dismissal, and I knew the only honorable action was to allow the women to depart, so I tipped my hat as they walked down the Arboretum path, the mist machine cloaking their backs in a heavy shroud of fog.

I would have been more disappointed had I not, at that moment, observed something on the floor behind the big wicker chair, something white and diaphanous. Iell's scarf. I whisked it up and held it to my nose; it smelled of roses. "Look how I've been favored," I said, to the silent birds asleep on their perches somewhere behind me. "Your new caretaker is blessed with a token of the lady." I squeezed the scarf into my coat pocket and rescued the flowers from where they lay. The raven let out a solitary squawk that brought a smile to my face.

✳ ✳ ✳

I RETURNED to my resident hall as the bells from St. Paul's chimed ten. Although I worried about having offended Iell by offering her Matina's magnolias, at least this time I'd held up my side of the conversation. I was so distracted I didn't even notice Matina sitting on a chair outside my door until I was almost upon her.

"Where have you been? I left my shawl in your room, and when I came to get it you were gone." Matina snapped her fan closed and rapped it lightly on my leg.

"Forgive me," I stammered, breathless. "I felt like a little walk."

"What are those?"

The flowers. I still had the flowers. The partially crushed magnolia blossoms released a heady scent, and when I thrust them forward, a few flattened petals drifted to the floor. "A present." I flushed. "For you. To let you know how much I value our friendship."

"Oh, you sweet man. Whatever did I do to deserve flowers?" Matina tucked her fan under the lace of her sleeve and held out her arms. I handed her the magnolias and considered telling her about my encounter with Iell and Emma. Emma now knew about my trip to Chinatown and might bring it up at any time. I knew I should confess, but I couldn't seem to make myself say the words.

"Would you like to go sit on the roof for a while?" Matina asked. "The weather is perfect."

I opened my door slightly but did not ask her in. "I'm rather peaked. Would you mind if we went some other time?"

"No, of course not," Matina answered, and as she put out her hand for me to help her to her feet, she smiled brightly. "I'll see you at breakfast, Barthy."

"Yes, of course. Tomorrow. Good night, my dear." I tilted forward to give her a brotherly peck on the cheek, but felt a slight tug and stopped.

"Barthy, whatever is this?" Matina stepped away from me. She had plucked Iell's scarf from my pocket and now held it in front of her, lifting it to the tip of her nose. Gingerly, she sniffed it. "My, my. How lovely it is."

Vainly, I tried to halt the river of heat surging up my neck and into my face. "Oh, that. I found it in the hallway. It must belong to someone. First thing in the morning, I plan to give it to Mr. Fish."

"Hmm." Matina frowned slightly. She returned the scarf to me, and I averted my eyes, knowing she was waiting for a better explanation.

I coughed but said nothing.

"Well. I'd best return to my rooms. You get a good night's sleep now, Barthy. I'll see you tomorrow."

I hadn't lied to Matina about anything important. Not really. But I found myself fighting the feeling that I'd done something dreadfully wrong. As I lay in bed, Iell's scarf on the pillow next to me, I wished I'd been more forthcoming.

chapter nine

T HALF PAST ELEVEN THE NEXT EVE-
ning, I knocked on Alley's door. His
openmouthed stare showed how surprised he was to see me.

"As long as you haven't moved to Indiana yet, I thought you might
go to McNealy's with me tonight." I'd already decided against telling
Alley about my serendipitous meeting with Iell, not wanting to take
the chance that he might mention it to Matina. What I really wanted
was his help. I'd not been able to take my mind off Iell since yesterday
and simply had to see her again. The only place I knew she would be
was performing in her show.

"You want to go out?" Alley asked. "It's been months since you been
out o' here, Fortuno."

"All the more reason for a change," I said, smiling.

I ran a finger around the inside of my collar, pretending nonchalance.
Alley knew I wanted something—I could tell by his heavy-lidded stare.
But I knew he'd be more likely to help me if properly distracted. And I
wasn't after much, really: just a little help getting into the Yellow Room. If
memory served, Fish owed Alley a favor. A few weeks ago the revolving
lamp on the Museum roof had come off its hinges and teetered on the edge
of the building. Alley had hauled it back in time to prevent it from crashing down into the street and crushing who knew how many passersby.

"I won't get in one of those fancy buggies," Alley said, thankfully
refraining from asking any further questions. "You know damned well
I won't."

"No reason we can't walk. And we can talk about your recent problems if you like," I added.

"I ain't got no problems, Fortuno."

"All right, then, we can always discuss mine."

Alley wrinkled up his forehead, closed his door, and then opened it moments later with his crushed hat in hand. Together, we headed down the service stairs and out through the Ann Street door.

"Good God, the air smells foul tonight." I dug into my pocket for my kerchief as we hit the street, sorry already I'd suggested that we step out. Parts of the city still relied on hundred-year-old hollow tree trunks buried in the ground to carry waste to the river, and clearly the system had overflowed again. Raw sewage covered half the walkway.

"Same as always," Alley answered, slowing his pace so I could keep up.

"How are you getting along with Mr. Fish?" I asked as I chicken-hopped along the filthy Ann Street boardwalk, bands of tension running through my shoulders and up my neck.

"Fine. Fine. Always fine."

"He's too strict with the rules, though, don't you think? Not as bad as Thaddeus, God knows, but still too officious for my liking."

"Rat!" Alley pounded his heel against the wooden walk, and a rat the size of my head bulleted across our feet toward the relative safety of the open street.

"Honestly, Alley, must you?" I waited for my heart to stop pounding before I went on. "As I was saying, you'd think Fish would be more receptive to us, wouldn't you? After all, it's not like he's talent."

"I hate rats."

"In my experience, the only way to get him to budge is to do him a favor."

Alley stopped under a streetlamp and looked over at me as if hearing me for the first time. "Get who to budge?"

"Fish."

"Budge what?"

"The rules."

"Ah." Alley shook his head yes—though who knew to what?—and off we went with nothing at all accomplished.

We hit Broadway in a matter of minutes, and I held my tongue so we could pass more quickly through the crowd of late-night strollers and streetwalkers slumped beneath the light of the streetlamps. I buttoned my coat against the night air. Both of us kept to the shadows. We made good progress, too, soon reaching the wrought-iron stairs of Loew's Bridge, the overpass that climbed up and over Broadway.

We picked our way up past discarded newspapers, handbills, and trade cards, a veritable forest of paper flattened out and filthy from hundreds of booted walkers. I was about to bring up Fish again, and how I might get into Iell's show, when we stumbled across the festering body of a dog lying belly-up halfway across the bridge. Alley slung a piece of broken cobblestone at the carcass, setting rats to scatter in three directions, and I hurried off the bridge so fast I beat Alley down the stairs to the other side.

At least the west side of Broadway was an improvement. There, the store windows sparkled; halfway down the block, the Western Union building towered above us. Higher than every other building in town, it was the city's timekeeper.

"I love that device," I said, pointing my chin toward the roof with its giant ball mounted on a cable. Every day, exactly at noon, the ball plunged downward. The entire city set their watches by it: bakers, grand ladies, the fire brigade, and the police; even the harbor ships used it to right their chronometers.

Alley grunted an acknowledgment of sorts, and we stood for a moment looking up. "So whaddaya want from me?" Alley asked.

No reason now to beat around the bush. "Does Fish owe you any favors?"

Alley waited.

"All right. I want to get into the new woman's show, but I haven't been able to manage it, so I thought, maybe, if he owed you, you could ask. And if not, maybe a little diversion in the hallway, just long enough to allow me to slip inside the room."

"I'm sure there's nothin' in there worth seein'."

"It's driving me mad. I *have* to see her."

Alley raised an eyebrow and took off walking again, but I knew he'd think about what I'd asked and would help me if he could.

The nearer we got to the river, the gentler the air, and by the time the tavern came into view, the smell of cherry blossoms from the Van de Clyff orchards inspired me to whistle "Saucy Kate." I'd done what I could for the moment, and I actually found myself enjoying the night air. When we reached our destination, the tension in my shoulders had completely disappeared.

The front of McNealy's tavern looked calm enough: a hound lying beneath the rangy oak branches that covered the shingled roof, and a man sleeping it off on the south side of the porch. The poor sot groaned as I clambered over his legs, and when he rolled to the side, I recognized the distended forehead and hollow cheeks of John Conklin in the flesh. Only yesterday I'd read a rumor in *The Clipper* that the New American Museum in Philly had dismissed him for getting into an argument over a girl. "Has our Modern Hercules shipwrecked once more against the cliffs of love?" the piece read. "How can the very man who caught balls fired from the mouth of a cannon be so weak as to be downed by the fairer sex?"

"If he keeps going like that"—Alley looked down toward John Conklin—"he'll end up on that wall." He tilted his chin toward rows of metal plates, the Plaques for the Dead, that McNealy had hung in honor of famous performers over the years. They covered the wall from the doorframe all the way to the far wall joint, most little more than tarnished tin strips with names etched in the center. James McFarland (*d. 1858*), the equilibrist who performed a free-wire ascension act outside Levi North's circus tent and died of a stab wound to the jugular in a fight over his wife. The great Hiram Franklin (*d. 1864*), the batule-board leaper who only this year was declared lost at sea somewhere off the Cape of Good Hope. I still had a clipping from the *Herald* that Matina had slipped across my desk one day. *In case you're thinking of sailing off,* her note had said. As if I'd ever. And in the far corner, a plaque for Josip Rigó, my old partner. AN ASCENT TO HEAVEN, the plaque read.

Glancing down again at poor John, akimbo on the ground, I suspected his trouble was whiskey and not women. Circus folk had it so much harder than we museum performers, and the poor man deserved to sleep off his misery in some comfort. Turning away from the plaques, I lifted his head and placed his hat underneath as a cushion. "Sleep in peace, old man," I said, and pushed through the door of McNealy's.

The familiar wave of heat and chatter inside the pub warmed my heart. I'd forgotten how thrilling the place could be, full of tattoos and third arms, feathers and spangles and golden crowns. The tavern used to be an old farmhouse. It had wooden plank floors and hand-hewn rafters, and, judging from the streaks on the walls, Mac still had its clapboard whitewashed with buttermilk and lime like most of the houses in the old days. But the family that lived here now was made up of show folk: handlers, bosses, specialty acts, and freaks. Here we were all welcomed. Despite the tang of stale beer and urine, and the fact that I had to brave the outside world to get here, I realized that I'd missed the place.

I stepped farther into the big open room. As always, the tavern was packed with performers: fire eaters, leapers, tumblers, slack-wire artists, contortionists, vaulters, trapeze swingers, pantomimists, even a well-known globe ascensionist (though why anyone would spend a lifetime rolling a globe up a wire and down again was beyond me). A dozen or so equestrians jigged in bowlegged abandonment to fiddle music coming from the rickety stage. In the far corner, a table of clowns wrestled over who was going to pay the bill.

When I removed my jacket, every agent in the room turned their eyes to look at my bony arms and chest. As Prodigies employed by the great Barnum, Alley and I were given a lot of respect at McNealy's, even though all performers had worth here. But my thinness was legendary, and it felt good to be admired by my own people.

"Alley!" McNealy lifted his arm above the crowd and motioned for us to join him. He stood six feet tall, his shaved skull covered in tattoos of vultures and flying peregrines. Although he wasn't a Prodigy in any way, Mac was a man who knew what it was like to be an outsider.

Alley pushed me ahead of him. I maneuvered through the crowd to a table laden with cards, lit cigars, and tankards of dark brew. Because of the spittoons on the floor, the sitters' knees knocked together beneath the tabletop in a twisted little bunch.

"Is that the great Bartholomew Fortuno with you? How long has it been, my man?" Mac scraped back a chair and beckoned me to sit. "The cards are falling well tonight. Glad you could come."

I saved the open seat for Alley—gone to answer a call of nature—and drew up an extra chair, tipping my hat in respect to Eli Bowen, who sat across the table. An Ohio boy with two feet of distinctly different sizes sprouting from his hip joints, Eli was one of the few True Prodigies in the business. He was famous for tumbling tricks and pole acrobatics, though what really made him a legend was his gorgeous sixteen-year-old wife.

The other person at the table was a tall swarthy man who was busy fondling the woman who sat on his lap. The woman looked a bit familiar, but for the life of me I could not place her.

"You remember Willie, don't you?" Mac asked. "Not the best poker player, maybe, but he sure keeps Niblo's hopping."

William Wheatley. An ex-actor, now manager of the prestigious Niblo's Garden. A bit of a nasty temperament, or so went the rumors, but exceedingly well placed in the theater. "A pleasure to see you, sir." I nodded, wondering what he was doing in our bar. Maybe expanding his repertoire?

"I've had the worst luck known to man," Willie said, poking at his cards while slipping a look at my arms and torso. "Not a decent hand all night."

Mac nodded to the woman still perched on Willie's lap. "And that there is his companion, Madame Zouve, a new face in town."

The woman smiled at me. "Evening, Mr. Fortuno."

She knew me. How could that be? I squinted my eyes. Maybe she was with one of Niblo's theater troupes that occasionally joined the

Museum. Or an acrobat or dancer. But she didn't look like any of those things. Her frizzy hair stood out wildly against a heart-shaped face punctuated with kohl-edged eyes and darkly rouged lips. It wasn't until she held up one arm as if carrying a tray that I recognized her.

"Bridgett?" Sure enough, it was Cook's helper, the mousy little Irish girl, all done up and wiggling about on the lap of some impresario in the middle of McNealy's. "What in the world do you think you're doing, girl? Cook will have a fit."

"I 'shure you," Bridgett said, nose in the air, "I don't know no Cook anymore. You have to call me Madame Zouve now. That's what Mr. Barnum says."

"What has that old coot gotten up to?" I asked, honestly surprised.

"He gave me a new position." Bridgett smiled again, a twinkle in her brazen Irish eyes. "I'm going to play a beauty, he says. Starting this week, and only in the mornings. I'm supposed to be from Circada—Cacasan—somewhere like that. I can't say the name yet."

I remembered then an ad Barnum had put in *The Clipper* a few months ago. He'd offered a reward to any agent who could bring back "one of the beautiful white women from the mountains by the Black Sea." The ad claimed that the sultans filled their harems with these girls from the slave markets of Constantinople. I examined Bridgett more carefully and noted her high forehead, deep-set brown eyes, and clear skin. Still, I couldn't believe that Barnum had stooped to using our kitchen maid.

"Circassian," I corrected her, tapping at the tabletop with my fingertips in order to avoid saying something rude.

"That's it!" she clapped. "Cacassenan."

"Surely you don't want to be a Gaff, do you, Bridgett? Look at that woman at the table over there." I pointed to a ragtaggle of a creature drinking shots of whiskey with a tattooed man. She slumped in the corner, her teeth filed down to razor-edged points and her hair shaved off to replicate the smooth head of a man-eating shark. "She used to be a perfectly respectable barmaid and now look at the poor thing. Works the Panny Palace, I think."

"Where?"

"A disgusting dive on the Bowery. A place for indiscreet practices. Men wearing dresses. That sort of thing." I gave her my best fatherly scowl. "That's where you'll end up if you don't watch yourself."

"Oh, no, sir. Mr. Barnum will take care of me just fine. And he don't ignore me, like some folks."

In truth, I suspected that Barnum had lied to the girl. Most likely, he dressed her up, telling her he would make her a star if she would be kind to him. He'd have his way with the girl and ship her off within a week.

Bridgett shrugged me off when Alley showed up at the table. As he slung into the empty seat between Mac and Willie, she stood and blushed wildly. When it was clear that Alley was not going to acknowledge her, Bridgett let Willie pull her back down on his lap, but she slapped away his hand, her eyes glued on Alley the entire time.

Alley stuck a cigar between his teeth, interested only in the game. He won the first hand, his mood high as he tossed in the greasy cards, and when he scooped up his winnings, Bridgett threw him a love-struck look.

"Look at that," Willie complained. "Didn't I tell you I was the unluckiest cad in this whole place?" But at the end of the fifth hand, Willie made a wild bet that Alley called, and when Willie tossed down his cards, calling out, "And there!" while sweeping in the huge pile of coins, Alley slumped into his chair.

"You said you didn't have nothin'." Alley lifted his arm in protest, and three women sitting behind him laughed nervously over the sheer bulk of his muscles.

"And you believed me, did you?" Willie gathered up his money, clearly debating whether to be afraid of the muscleman he'd just cheated. Once he was sure Alley wasn't going to harm him, he grabbed Bridgett by the hand. "If you want a bit of wisdom to take with you, my friend, there's a sucker born every minute. Try to make sure it ain't you."

"Well," I said to Alley as Willie walked away, "you have to admire the man's turn of phrase. We should pass that line about suckers on to Barnum. He'd appreciate it if anyone would." But Alley wasn't listening to me. He stared at Willie's back, his balled fists rapping steadily against his own thighs.

"If you like, we can set up a dart match in the back," Mac said, doing his best to comfort Alley. "Or how about some of our good boar stew? I'll get the girl to bring you a bowl." Although Alley had not been drinking—he and Mac had made an agreement years ago that as long as Alley stayed sober he was welcome in the bar—Mac moved the whiskey bottle out of reach.

But Alley's attention shifted again, this time to the front door. He stood stock-still and then hunkered down between Mac and me and whispered, "Find your own way home, Fortuno, I gotta go." Then, staying low, he slipped into the crowd.

I had to climb on top of my chair to see what had grabbed his attention.

There, at the front door, four policemen stood openmouthed, stunned for the moment by the sights and sounds before them. It took them a good minute to regain their senses, straighten their ragged uniforms, and lift their clubs, before they made their way cautiously into the room. By that time, Alley was nowhere to be seen.

chapter ten

*M*Y NEW TIGHTS HAD ARRIVED! My heart leaped at their vibrant red color and fine stitching, and they were almost enough to mitigate a stab of irritation at the changes in the schedule posted in the Green Room.

☞NOTICES☜

For the week of MAY 15, 1865

NEW IN THE MORAL LECTURE ROOM
JUNIUS BRUTUS BOOTH JR.
appearing with EJ Phillips in **OTHELLO**
Show times: noon, three & eight o'clocks

Attention players: Mr. Booth and Mrs. Phillips are on loan to us from
Philadelphia. Please treat them with the utmost respect and abstain from any
humorous jokes at their or Philadelphia's expense.

YELLOW ROOM
Iell Adams will continue as last week.
** *Note to Regular Performers:* Once again, players of any kind may NOT
view acts appearing in rooms of limited space. *Fines* will be levied.

MINOR ROOMS
Mr. William "Zippy" Johnson will be traveling for the next month.
Adjustments in the daily schedule have been made.
The following will perform in the following order (in hour intervals) from nine
until noon, and two until six o'clocks, with tableau schedule as usual:
Mr. Bartholomew Fortuno
Mr. John Alley
Miss Emma Swan
Mr. Ricardo Hortense

THE CIRCASSIAN BEAUTY will be showing in a **special daily tableau**
in the Exhibition Hall. She is an exotic escapee from a Turkish harem. Please
do not speak with her as she is easily frightened.

I couldn't believe my eyes. There it was in black and white: Bridgett slated to perform. Who would have believed such a thing could happen? She was a total Gaff, yet Barnum was going to have her stand next to Matina as if she were one of us.

And then there was Emma. Clearly she was on the schedule to replace Zippy, who'd been sent on the road. I could accept Barnum's political ambiguity—his support of Negro suffrage was fine and dandy, so long as no one mentioned that he displayed our one Negro performer as the missing link—but he had given Emma *my* slot, for God's sake, and scheduled *me* to go first! No one wants to be the lead-in act. I'd have complained immediately had it not occurred to me that changing my show times aligned me with Iell's schedule, giving me more of a chance to find her alone. Clever Barnum. Clever me. And maybe the altered time would allow me easier access to her show, lessening the need for Alley's help.

But opening the show set me completely off my stride. My new tights stunk of elderberry, and—though they fit like a glove—the material made me itch. Twice I missed a cue, and Thaddeus was so displeased that at one point he stopped his chatter. We might have come to words again, had I not seen Alley in the wings. Dark purple bruises covered the entire left side of his face, a cut festered across his lower lip, and one of his burly arms dangled in a sling.

"My God, what happened to you?" I demanded the second I got offstage. Standing next to him in the wings, I wiped down my neck with a towel and tried to avoid staring directly at his wounds, not that he'd done much to hide them. "Did the cops do that? What do they want with you?"

Alley shrugged. "Bar brawl is all," he muttered. "The other guy, that's who's really hurting."

Watching him slump by me, eyes darting everywhere but toward my inquiring gaze, I suspected he was lying. He tugged up the waist of his blue-and-gold short pants with his usual laziness and gave me an all-is-well nod that sent his tawdry crown off kilter. But his forearms, oiled and shiny, reeked of camphor ointment, and when I put a consoling hand on his shoulder he flinched.

"One of our finest specimens, ladies and gents. Once a Hungarian prince. Royalty from a wild country. With the strength of Atlas, the temperament of a wild tiger—"

"Don't go out there," I said. "I'll take you to Nurse." But Alley yanked the sling off, tossed it to the floor, and headed center stage.

I watched the act through the part where Alley picked up a boulder the size of a full-grown man and slammed his head into it once, twice, thrice, until it broke into a million pieces. As the audience squealed and broken rocks scattered across the stage, I hustled away to find Matina. We'd need to keep a closer eye on Alley.

✻ ✻ ✻

I WAS still thinking of Alley when I entered the exhibit room, but when I saw the unusually large crowd that had gathered a few feet down from Matina, curiosity took over. I scrambled onto the riser where Matina sat tableau and gave her an inquiring look. She shook her head in disgust and pinched her nose between two fingers in defense against a strong smell in the air. It took me a moment to recognize the odor: incense.

"Don't even *look* to your right," Matina said, rolling her eyes. "It's the kitchen girl, all made up and stinking like a whore."

I hoisted myself onto her plank bed, craning my neck to see. Sure enough, it was Bridgett who had drawn the crowd. She sat cross-legged on a pile of silver pillows, her eyes blackened with kohl, her hair dark and tempestuous as a storm. Standing near her, a musician dressed like a Turk strummed a long-necked instrument, the notes miserable and strange. My chest pinched at the sight.

"Whatever is Barnum thinking?" I shook my head, shading my eyes to better inspect the bystanders. "No one will believe such a thing."

Matina shrugged. "You wouldn't think so, but the crowds have been like this for nearly two hours."

She was right. Traffic had stopped in front of Bridgett's tableau. Lingering visitors blocked the way for those waiting behind them. Across the room, Emma nodded to me from the oversized chair where she rocked, knitting like a grandmama. It had crossed my mind at breakfast to corner her and demand to know how she'd become acquainted with Iell and how she seemed to know so much about her when the rest of us labored in the dark, then tell her I knew all about her being in cahoots with Barnum. But I worried that what I did might get back to Matina, so I said nothing. And now I feared we'd tied ourselves together in a mutual secret. Perhaps, later on, I would take Emma aside and speak to her privately.

Laughter. Bridgett had apparently said something amusing, because those nearest her seemed caught in the hilarity of the moment. I hopped down off the plank bed, my knees buckling slightly when I landed.

"Perhaps they are laughing *at* her, not *with*—"

"Please, Barthy. Let's not make it worse by pretending." Matina fanned around her face as if to ward off evil. "Though I must admit, Barnum has gussied her up nicely. She looks quite fetching."

"Don't be ridiculous," I scolded. "She's a Gaff, an insult to the rest of us. Barnum created her from nothing."

"Oh, honestly," Matina said, slipping on her veils, "how is she that much different from the rest of us?" She patted her belly. "You could say I created myself simply by eating."

"You did no such thing. You have a special capacity."

Matina ignored my look of dismay. "No. I believe that the prob-o-lem"—she articulated carefully—"is not that she's a Gaff but that she's done nothing to earn her spot. At least nothing we know of." She winked at me.

"I saw Bridgett in McNealy's last night with Willie Wheatley."

Matina's eyes lit up. "That little harlot. What did I tell you? Probably some arrangement between Willie and Barnum. Though you know, it really isn't right. Quite disturbing, in fact. I mean, if just *anyone* can get up here, how secure are we?"

The north door opened and Mr. Fish entered the exhibit room, clipboard in hand. Matina turned from me and focused her attention on the customers walking by, the professional thing to do, especially with Fish roaming around as he often did. But now my ire was up. All I could hear was Bridgett's silly laughter.

Matina was right. Bridgett was clearing platters and dirty knives one day and transformed into a Circassian beauty the next. Was it luck or guile or just trading sexual favors? When Barnum discovered me, I was risking my life for my craft. My face flushed at the memory of the night that Josip slipped off the wire and crashed to his death. A mere ten minutes more and he'd have come down safely, then climbed back up with me clinging to his neck. And then we *both* would have fallen. How many nights had I dreamed of the audience screaming in appreciation as we splattered onto the sawdust, bones cracking and blood and guts spreading everywhere?

"Sir, I'd like a card, but I can't stand here all morning."

An old woman stood below me, holding out a shaking nickel and scowling. She was dressed in expensive clothes and carried a parasol of Battenberg lace.

I fumbled through the basket we kept beneath the bench and dug out one of my *cartes*. She patted me on the wrist with a gloved hand, one of her bone buttons loose and dangling by a thread. Matina handed me one of my life-story pamphlets, arching an eyebrow to remind me of my obligation to try to sell it, but I didn't have the heart. The damned thing was such fakery. Exactly the kind of thing I'd been stewing about. I tossed the pamphlet into the basket and flipped over my *carte*, pen in hand.

"To Mrs. Harrington. Could you write that for me? And I'd like the pamphlet too, if you would be so kind."

Grudgingly, I wrote what she requested. She examined the *carte* and grimaced. It showed a likeness of me taken when I'd first come to the Museum. Still in my teens then, I smiled rakishly and displayed my thinness in a skin-tight harlequin costume of black and gold. The pamphlet contained an essay written by Barnum. It told a spurious tale of a dying woman who'd spawned me after successfully mating with a cadaver. It claimed that later I'd lived alone in a cave along the coast of the Aegean Sea eating nothing but sea crabs until pirates rescued me. Who could ever believe such drivel?

"My, my, sir. You *have* had a difficult time of it."

I caught a glimpse of compassion in the old woman's eyes and I decided to accept it. Aside from the obvious aches and pains, I'd lived a life of deprivation.

Softening to her, I said, "All trials have their gifts, Madam."

"Hers too, do you think?" The old woman held up a brand-new *carte* of a wild-haired, snake-charming Gypsy—that is to say, Bridgett—standing at the mouth of a cave in a poor man's Garden of Eden, big bold letters beneath her feet saying MADAME ZOUVE, THE CIRCASSIAN WOMAN. "Can you imagine living in the mountains with infidels? Makes me shiver all over."

I reached low and snapped my *carte* out of the old woman's hands. The woman flushed and grabbed her nickel back. "You are *not* a nice man," she said, and scurried away.

"That was brave, seeing as Fish is in the room," Matina said. She was reclining on top of her plank bed, watching the old woman push through the crowd toward Bridgett. "Don't let that floozy maid upset you, Barthy. The girl has no dignity, carrying on like that. She'll never last." A sudden streak of sunlight from a high window spread over Matina's face, and she tilted her head up to soak in the warmth. "By the way," she said, eyes closed, tender little smile, "I see that Fish has not posted anything about that scarf you found."

"No? I left it in his office this morning. With a note," I lied. "He must have already found the owner." I turned away so she wouldn't see me blush.

"Do you think so?" Matina mused, her eyes still closed.

My innocent omissions were building. After so much deception, how could I explain myself to Matina, even if I wanted to tell her the truth? She knew me as an honest man. I thought back on the previous day's conversation with Iell. How could I possibly discuss it with Matina when I'd never told her I met the new act? Pity, too, because I would have valued Matina's expert analysis. Iell hadn't said a word about her own experiences. Had her childhood been idyllic or wretched? If forced to guess, I would have said idyllic. Most likely her gift, like mine, didn't wholly reveal itself until puberty. I could easily picture her as a beautiful child playing in the sun.

A hard rap on the end of my shoe brought the Museum back into focus.

"Fortuno? Wake up, man."

Fish stood in front of the platform looking at me, knocking my foot again with the end of his cane. "Mr. Barnum wants to see you. Right now, if you please."

✳ ✳ ✳

When I got to Barnum's office, I found him slumped behind his desk, his head bent over something that required so much attention he didn't seem to have heard me enter. I waited—hands clasped behind my back for stability—and tried to still my racing heart. Eventually, Barnum lifted his head.

"Have a seat," he said, but rather than offer the cushy leather chair, he nodded me toward an old Brewster in the corner with a thatched seat and wooden back. "So tell me, Mr. Fortuno. Are you enjoying your new costume?"

The damned chair hurt. It was all but impossible to avoid pressing into the crossbars.

"Couldn't be better, Mr. Barnum. The tights are a thing of beauty. And I want to thank you for speaking to Thaddeus, because he's been most respectful to me all week."

Barnum unbuttoned his jacket and lifted his hands behind his head, then splayed back into his big chair, the springs squeaking with his weight. "And your new task. How might that be coming along?"

"The birds are fat with food," I said. Should I tell him that I'd seen Iell? What would Iell wish for me to disclose?

Barnum frowned. "Don't toy with me, Fortuno. Have you seen the woman or not?"

"Do you mean Mrs. Adams?"

"Of course that's who I mean." He slapped his hand hard against his desk, making me jerk upright.

"I had the opportunity to talk briefly with her yesterday in the Arboretum, sir. She was having tea with the giantess, Emma Swan."

"Yes, I know that." Barnum leaned forward, his forearms on the desk flattening the papers between us. "But what I'd really like to know is whether Mrs. Adams seemed to be getting along well with our Emma."

If he and Emma were working together, what was he after?

"They seemed to manage well enough," I answered, as calmly as I could, "though they are quite the unlikely duo, if you ask me. All the three of us did was exchange pleasantries, not much else. Mrs. Adams seemed quite interested in my opinion of current scientific thinking, though I'm sure she was only being polite. Then, on a more personal note, we discussed our childhoods—"

"Don't prattle on," Barnum chided. "Is that all you spoke of?"

"Not much else, I'm afraid. . . . Although we did speak for a moment about protectors."

"What about protectors?" The sudden fire in Barnum's eyes told me why he'd dragged me in here. What an idiot I was. I had told Iell about fetching the parcel in Chinatown, and Emma had reported this back to him. Barnum must be furious, and I didn't relish the tongue-lashing that was sure to come.

But Barnum said nothing. I looked at him. He was still waiting for me to answer. Maybe Emma hadn't spoken with him yet. But wouldn't he know soon enough? And wouldn't it be wiser to have it come from me?

Testing the water, I said, "I mentioned that we all owe an allegiance to you, sir. Thought a word on your behalf might help."

Barnum smiled. "Yes. I'm sure we could all benefit from a good word from you, Fortuno."

His sarcasm didn't sit all that well with me, but I preferred sarcasm to scolding.

A clock on the shelf behind Barnum chimed out the half hour. The clock was shaped like a woodland cottage, and at the sound of the chime, a small ceramic rabbit ran out the clock's door, a spring-wound hunter following in its wake. How fitting, I thought. Determined to ignore the growing tension in the room, I tapped my foot against the bottom rung of the chair. Perhaps it would be best to spit out the rest. Protect myself.

"I might have mentioned that I'd fetched a parcel from the China-man for you. Mrs. Adams seemed to think it was hers. It would have been helpful to know that fact in advance. It might have saved the lady and myself an awkward moment."

Barnum furrowed his brow; I could see that his interest in Iell ran deep. "She knows you went to the Chinaman's for me?"

"It was an innocent comment, Mr. Barnum. Nothing to be alarmed about."

"Alarmed? Don't be silly. I'm not alarmed." Barnum hesitated and picked up the obsidian rock that sat on the corner of his desk, point-ing it to his temple. "What was her reaction?"

"Quite calm. She expressed her gratitude. Nothing more."

"No anger? Histrionics?"

"No, sir."

Barnum tapped a finger against the desk. "She's just prone to fan-ciful notions, I'm afraid. And who knows what she's made of my ask-ing you to take care of something I'd promised to do myself." He searched my face for clues. "The truth is, Iell is quite valuable, and I am hoping to guide her career."

"Like Jenny Lind, the opera star?"

"Exactly. And for that she must trust me. But she must also know her limitations. So I will continue to need information about her com-ings and goings when I am not around."

"She *is* special, isn't she?" I said

"Yes, Fortuno, she certainly is that."

We sat together in silence for a moment, each aware that the other might have said too much.

"Perhaps if I had access to Mrs. Adams's show?" I said, pressing my advantage.

Barnum walked around the desk, placed his arm around me, and walked me forward. His armpits were damp through his jacket, his odor slightly feral. At the door, he hesitated.

"No," he said. "I don't think that will be necessary. But before you go, Fortuno, there is one more thing."

"Of course."

"Since this cat is already out of the proverbial bag, I'd like you to go again to the Chinaman's for me."

This was not the outcome I'd wanted, not in the least.

"Next week I might be able to manage," I said haltingly, hoping that by then I could find some way to avoid the task.

Barnum pulled out a sack of coins. "Actually, I was thinking of today. Tell you what, Fortuno. I'll arrange to have a carriage waiting on the other side of Ann Street after five. I'll have Fish tell the others you're excused from your shows this evening. So toddle along and bring the package to me as soon as you've collected it."

I'd managed the trip once. Perhaps the second time would be a bit easier. But I already felt the pinch of the tightrope I was walking. I suspected that it might not be so easy, in the end, to please both Barnum and Iell.

chapter eleven

T FIVE O'CLOCK EXACTLY, I SAT IN A private hack on my way to the Chinaman's store. This time, the traffic flowed smoothly. We slowed down only once along the way, at Chatham Street, where the latch at the rear of a hay wagon had come unhinged and bales of hay spewed across the avenue, an irresistible temptation to some of the less well-fed trolley horses. It took twenty minutes to navigate the mess, but soon we were on our way again.

The Chinaman's building looked quiet—too quiet—when we finally arrived, so I had the cabbie drive back and forth past the storefront until I caught sight of the proprietor's head bobbing past the window.

I banged my cane on the ceiling. "This should do."

As I got out, another Chinese man, humped over and wearing a skullcap and a dirty red jacket with a dragon on the back, came running. "No stop! No stop here!" When the driver didn't move, the man in the street started pounding on the side of the cab with a hickory stick.

"It's okay," I yelled to the driver. "Drive to the end of the block. I'll meet you there when I'm finished."

The stench of the trash piled in front of the rickety building gagged me, and I swatted away mosquitoes the size of horseflies that had gathered near the front door. My whole body shuddered. This really had to be the last time I did this. Ridiculous idea to involve me anyway. Surely someone sturdier could be sent to retrieve the package. I should be onstage now, in my element.

The front door stuck, and I had to give it a swift kick to open it. Inside, the stink of pickled onions assaulted my senses.

"No now," the Chinaman snapped, but when he saw who it was he wiped his hands on his apron and gave me a welcoming wave. He moved aside a jar full of pig snouts sitting on the counter and motioned me forward.

I held back, not wanting to move too near for fear of touching something unsavory. The first time I was here I'd not noticed how the ceiling above us sagged. Now I feared that at any moment the roof might tumble down.

The Chinaman wagged his head and smiled a toothless smile. Seemingly in need of more illumination, he tried to light the lamp on the counter but the wick sputtered, so he hauled up a hand lantern from the floor. I flinched. I'd hated hand lanterns ever since I was a boy, and seeing it flicker to life felt like a bad omen.

"I need the same thing as before. Do you remember? Last week I picked up a package for Mr. Barnum."

"Money?" He stared at me and waited.

I pulled Barnum's bag of coins from my vest pocket and tossed them onto the counter. The Chinaman stuck his hand in the bag, riffling through the coins, the late day sunlight streaming in from outside.

"You wait." He shuffled through a slit in the tattered curtain, leaving me alone in the stuffy room. I shoved open the window at the front of the store for a bit of air. Outside, in the growing dusk, a handful of Chinese boys in gray jackets and skullcaps loitered near the man who'd refused to let my carriage wait. One boy etched Chinese figures on the wall across the way with a burnt stick. Next to him, another drew a rough outline of a dragon with a limp bird in its mouth. They seemed to be preparing for some kind of ritual. Right at that moment, Emma was most likely performing in my stead. How disappointing for the audience. I sighed. I hadn't missed a performance in years.

I nearly jumped from my skin when the Chinaman grabbed the top of my shoulder with spindly fingers. In his free hand, he held a small package identical to the last one I'd picked up for Barnum.

"What you ask for." He handed Barnum's package to me.

I stuffed it into the side pocket of my trousers and turned to leave.

"Wait," the Chinaman said. "Another thing. A thing your heart want."

I did not understand until he held a dingy muslin bag in front of my eyes. A piece of tattered drawstring held the thing closed.

"A gift for you."

"What? No. No gift." I recoiled. "I want nothing else from you."

"You take." He dangled the disgusting thing in front of my nose, then grabbed my wrist and pressed the bag into the palm of my hand. "Eat and true self come alive."

I thrust the thing at him, wiping my hands against my pants.

"I don't want to eat that! Good God, man."

The Chinaman took me by the lapels and pulled my face close to his, his breath so foul I turned my nose to the ceiling to avoid it. With surprising speed, he snatched the pouch from my hand, shoved it into my coat pocket, and jostled me out the door.

It took me a moment to catch my breath. I could not believe that the Chinaman had manhandled me so! I looked around for a sympathetic soul, but the boys who'd been hanging about had mysteriously disappeared. In fact, the entire block looked deserted. Yet as I slogged to the carriage along a broken walk of bricks and soot, I could feel a thousand eyes watching me. What a relief to crawl into the covered carriage, safe again, and on my way home.

It wasn't until we turned onto Broadway that I felt secure enough to pull Barnum's package from my pocket. Whatever it was, it wasn't worth the bother. I held it up and shook it. Only the fear of what Barnum would do if he found me out stopped me from tearing off the wrapping and looking inside. As for the other thing—the mysterious gift—I left that package well enough alone. Whatever it was, I'd dispose of it the moment I returned.

Inside the Museum, I weaved through the dinner crowds—how wonderful to hear gasps as I passed—and made a beeline for Barnum's office. Thinking only to rid myself of his damned package, I rapped vigorously on Barnum's door. No one was there, so I slipped in and left Iell's package on the desk and then hurried upstairs.

I didn't even touch the sack that the Chinaman had forced on me until after I had washed up and changed my shoes. Then I dug the thing out of my pocket and pitched it into the trash bin.

A minute later, I fished it out. If I couldn't find out what was in Iell's package, at least I could satisfy my curiosity about this one. Fumbling with the greasy strings, I reached in and lifted out a tiny black root. It was slightly bulbous at its base and shaped like a deformed man. Disgusting. I held it to my nose and sniffed. It reeked of decaying mushrooms. The last thing I would ever do was eat the thing. True self be damned.

"Fortuno? You decent?" The sound of Alley's voice made me jump.

I stuffed the root into its bag, tossed it on my étagère, and opened the door. The hall light showed that the bruises on Alley's face had turned mottled and black. I retreated enough to give him room to duck beneath the doorframe, backing farther away when he passed.

"My God, that face of yours looks bad."

"Came by to see if yer okay," Alley mumbled. "Matina was worryin' 'cause yer missin' tonight's shows."

"Little stomach virus is all. Nothing of concern." I thrust my chin toward the oversized settee where Matina always rested. "Want to sit? You really should tell me what happened. Maybe I can help." I shoved open a window and tucked a pillow onto the sill, forming my usual perch. I crawled up, put my feet on the lintel, and sighed despite myself. My legs ached from trekking around the city like a servant. If Alley hadn't been there, I'd have fetched a pot of hot water and soaked my feet.

Slumping down on the settee, Alley dug behind his back and rescued the piece of lace Matina had been tatting. It was slightly misshapen, with jelly marks across one edge. He set it gingerly on the side table. Then he lifted both eyebrows, his way of asking for one of my good cigars.

"Be my guest."

He pulled a cigar from the side table's drawer, bit off the end, and lit it with a long match, the shooting sparks from the phosphorus making him grimace. It crossed my mind to tell Alley about my trips to Chinatown. I could really use someone to talk things over with, even if Alley rarely gave advice. But again, he'd feel obligated to share whatever I told him with Matina, and then she'd want to know why I hadn't said something to her myself.

"The Copperheads," Alley said, out of the blue. "The police says I helped them set off those fires in town. Ya know what I'm talkin' about?"

I knew all about the fires. And the Copperheads. They were a ragged bunch of Northern Democrats whose idea of preserving the Union was to prolong the war. A few months ago, a ringleader named Robert Cobb Kennedy masterminded a plot to burn down New York by torching a dozen hotels and other establishments while simultaneously lighting bales of hay floating in the harbor. The first fire started on the third floor of the Lafarge House, but the Fifteenth District put out the blaze. Then small fires shot up at the Winter Garden and the Fifth Avenue Hotel. Later, the police found evidence that someone had planned fires at the St. James, the Metropolitan, Tammany, the Belmont, the Hanford, and even the St. Nicholas and the Astor. Had the plan been pulled off, the fire brigades could have never stopped it, but most of the would-be arsonists ended up being tossed out of the hotels for the cut of their coat or their lack of a shave well before they'd time to light their kindling. Pity for them they didn't have Barnum's skill in putting on a show.

"And they beat you? The police?"

"Caught up with me three blocks from here." He flicked his cigar ash into the unlit fireplace and gave me a tilted smile. "Not easy for someone like me to hide, ya know."

"I don't understand why they're bothering you. They hung those fires on that poor Kennedy fellow last March, and the affair ended then. Why would the police suspect you now?"

"Someone left a new tip. Said they seen a freak that night pourin' phosphorus over a bed at the St. James and were afraid to come forward till now."

I slid off the windowsill. "Saw a freak? Only that? No physical description?"

"You know cops. They figured it had to be someone like me."

"You need to tell Barnum," I said, walking to my étagère and fingering the dirty sack with the root inside. "Don't tempt fate, my friend. The police haven't been the same since the Draft Riots."

"Nah," Alley said, getting up off the divan, "I can handle it." He walked to the window, and when he passed me, he glanced at the sack in my hand. Quickly, I opened up the top drawer and dumped the thing inside.

"As long as you were in the Museum that night, I suppose you've nothing to worry about."

Alley looked out the window down into the street. "I did do a job for them once." He half turned and gave me a sheepish look. "Guarded a meeting, but nothin' else."

"The cops will have to prove you were near the fires or they've got nothing."

Alley leaned out into the night sky. "Moon's up," he said. He shifted his weight back and forward, one foot to the other. He often fidgeted like this, the movement reflecting some flame inside him. Quite honestly, I suspected the worst. Not that Alley was an evil man, but God knows he had his rages. Perhaps arson helped him quiet the fires within.

"If you need an alibi—"

"Nah, don't worry, Fortuno." Alley flicked the ash of his cigar out the window and came back into the room. "By the way, Fish won't let you into that show. Sorry, friend. Tried my best. But I brung you a gift."

Alley rummaged in his pocket and pulled out a crinkled broadside that he set on the table and straightened out as best he could.

"These here are tacked up all the way down Broadway. Thought you might like to see one."

Might like to see one? I could barely contain myself as I snatched the broadside out of Alley's hands and held it an inch from my nose.

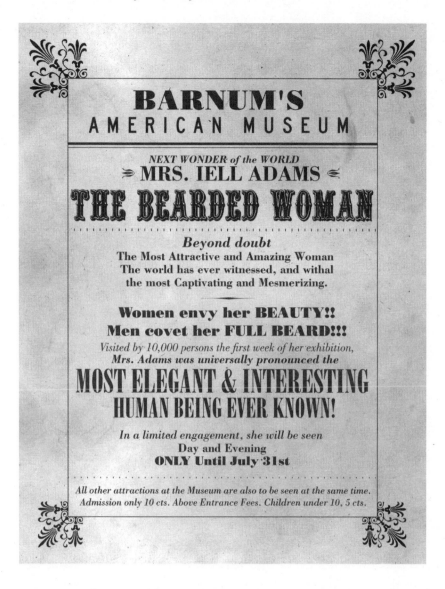

Quite a captivating broadside. But, oh! Iell would only be here through July 31!

"Did you see this?" I asked, stabbing a finger at the date. "This is only a few months away. I knew her engagement was limited, but this is no time at all!"

Alley shrugged. "What are you gettin' all riled up over? She's a woman with a beard, Fortuno. Nothin' more than that."

"Come, come, now. Help me think how to get into her show. Maybe you could start a little fire in the hall to draw Fish away from the door."

Alley grunted and looked at me in a way that made me uncomfortable. "What in hell is wrong with you?" he said, cigar ash tumbling down his rough shirt and onto my rug.

"Yes, all right. Maybe something less dramatic." I started pacing.

Alley stomped to the door and ducked into the hall. "You know what your problem is, Fortuno? You ain't learned what's important yet."

I admit, I'd already asked myself, Why the desperation to be near this woman? She was nothing to me, not really. But try as I might to maintain my normal balance, something inside of me yearned—no, demanded—to see her. From the first moment I watched her arrive in the middle of the night, to the remarkable moments we shared in the Arboretum, my need to know this woman had begun to grow beyond any logic or common sense. It was as if she held a secret part of me in the palm of her hand, and I needed only say or do the right thing and she would open her hand and I would fly free. And now, to learn she'd be here for such a short time? It all but took my breath away.

Normally I would have asked Alley to stay for a few hands of cribbage, but tonight I was glad to see him leave. Hadn't learned what was important, indeed!

I picked up my *Harper's*, flipped to the new installment of Dickens's book, and then shut it and pulled out that morning's *Times*. Alley was right. A man needed to decide what was important to him and then go after it, come hell or high water. I glanced at the clock. Seven–oh-five. The last show of the night was at eight. That gave me a little less than an hour to come up with a plan. What if I disguised myself and pretended to be one of the crowd? With the right disguise, Fish would have no idea it was me.

Fortunately, by the time I got down to the Green Room, most of the shows were already in progress, and those folks not working were in the courtyard waiting for the dinner bell. That left only a few extras from *Othello* and two of the cancan dancers downed by dancer's pains. They barely looked my way as I pulled my tights off the hook and moved down the hall to the costume room, an airless place full of racks and bins and baskets of everything from a king's crown to polar bear suits.

I lit one of the small wall lamps. It flickered, casting a glow across the cobwebbed corners. In the semidarkness, I took off my day suit and pulled on my tights, then rummaged through mildewed boxes until I found some sturdy cotton batting. It ripped apart quite easily, and I stuffed it into my tights in the hollow spaces beneath my arms, thighs, and belly.

An old cracked mirror rested on one of the walls, and I used it to inspect my reflection, twisting slightly to get the best view of myself. I looked a bit like a stuffed pepper. When I pulled my suit on over my tights, the jacket fit too snugly, and my pants would not fasten at all. So I pulled out the padding and shuffled through a nearby rack of costumes until I found another jacket two sizes too large for me. I slit open the lining, slipped the padding in, and used a needle and thread to quick-stitch it in place. Perfect. Then I found a drawer of mock mustaches in the wardrobe bin, drew out a handsome brown handlebar, and stuck it onto my lip with a bit of stage gum. A wig left behind by the last touring troupe, an abandoned cape, and a bowler hat rounded out my disguise. The wig looked a little suspect, the hair a sickly brown and curled out like a boy's, but yanking the bowler farther down on my head improved the effect. The mustache was a touch of brilliance.

I stripped off the costume and carried it upstairs, where I distracted myself by rearranging my books while the rest of the hour passed. Then I dressed and examined myself in my own mirror. I'd just gotten the mustache into place when I heard a light knock on my door.

"Barthy, are you in there?" Matina.

Heart pounding, I wrenched off the mustache and the wig, which sent my hat flying across the floor, and I barely made it to the front door before Matina twisted the knob and pushed partially into the room. My shoulder plowed into the door, and thankfully my strength proved enough to close the door nearly all of the way. I peered out through the slim opening. Matina's massiveness blocked all but a touch of my view.

"Goodness," she said, pulling back into the hallway, eyes wide, fingers fluttering to her hair. "Apparently, I've disturbed you."

"No, no. I apologize." I kept a firm hold on the door while trying to keep my voice even and unconcerned. "I'm afraid we can't visit tonight, my dear. I'm not well, you see. A stomach problem. Nothing serious."

Matina moved forward again, and rested a hand against the doorframe.

"Alley told me. I can't believe you were too sick to work. Poor thing. Look, I brought you a little food." She indeed had a basket with her, large and full of covered dishes. Patting the doorframe mindlessly, she pushed a hip forward. "Come now, Barthy, let me in. I only want to help."

"Thank you," I said, alarmed at her insistence, "but I will have to see you tomorrow."

Matina peered in at me quizzically, moving her head from side to side to see more of me through the crack.

"What's that you have on?" She scowled. I knew I hadn't the strength to keep her out if she insisted, but I also knew she wouldn't force the door. It wasn't her way.

"Forgive me," I muttered and pressed my shoulder firmly to the door. "Tomorrow, then." The door snapped closed.

Panting slightly, I placed my ear to the wood. Matina knocked softly one more time, undoubtedly confused by my behavior, but I did not answer. Eventually, she gave up. I could hear the rasp of her skirts as she retreated down the hall. Dastardly way to treat a friend, I told myself, but she would never have understood.

By the time I made it to the service door on the main floor, it was half past eight. Overheated, I pushed through the door and found myself flush in the midst of the evening crowd. Men rumbled about, smoking and talking beneath the gaslights, buying tickets and jostling past the turnstiles and up the stairs. Women moved through the halls in groups like colorful ducklings, listing to one side and then the other to look at exhibits.

I blended in completely. No one looked twice at me. I felt a surprising pleasure at passing. It wasn't that the idea of padding had never occurred to me. In fact, I sometimes padded myself slightly to go out. But I'd only modified my physique in self-protection—never with an aim toward becoming someone else. For what was I without my gift?

Now, buried within the costume's layers, I felt something stir within me. I took up more space in the world—and I liked it. But along with this feeling of pride came an undeniable guilt. Wasn't it dishonest to hide myself?

Pulling myself together, I walked to the rear of the line for the Yellow Room and took my place. People around me talked pleasantly of fruit pies, penny nails, and their children's problems in the new public school. The line moved slowly forward. Before I knew it, I stood in front of the door to Iell's showroom; I couldn't help but smile when I flipped my dime into the basket and Fish barely glanced my way.

Inside at last. The first thing I heard was music. Already impressed—the cost of a band was prohibitive, so most of us at the Museum performed in silence—I followed the man in front of me as we walked single file on a path kept narrow by velvet ropes. My steps felt lightened by the sweetness of a Rossini étude, one I'd often heard at intermissions of Moral Lecture Room ballets or wafting out of the Ballroom during an occasional soirée. Soft and slyly melancholic, its notes floated out of the corner of the room where a flutist, two violinists, and a cellist swayed on their chairs like young saplings. We shuffled forward beneath soft lights. I could smell the roses that had been scattered in clusters throughout the room.

In front of me, a light shone straight down from the ceiling, and I strained my neck to see ahead. There, in the center of an eight-foot platform delineated by head-high curtains, sat Iell, motionless atop a crimson throne. At her side was a table with an etched water pitcher and glass, a silver tea set, a porcelain vase of white peonies, and a mantel clock that ticked away the time. The light shone down from a hidden source and illuminated her while she sat serenely turning the pages of the current *Godey's Lady's Book*. She'd swept her hair into intricate curls, and she wore an astonishing dress that reminded me of an inverted sunflower, the skirts in layers of yellow crepe billowing out and flipping slightly, the bodice a sea-green satin. The entire tableau rotated in opposition to the moving crowd, powered by some unseen contraption. The whole thing was brilliant. She'd cast the scene in the style of a European masterpiece, a Vermeer or a La Tour, and women from the finest New York families could not have made a more elegant impression. Yet that beard marked her as a being like no other in the world. By highlighting the normal, she magnified her uniqueness. I could not help but contrast the subtlety of her show to my own, which struck me now as shabby and impossibly old-fashioned.

On I walked, gawking at Iell right along with the rest of her audience. Her profile was equally charming from either side. I struggled to maintain my composure like a peasant in the company of Queen Victoria herself, and I suspect it was the same with most everyone around me. The men seemed particularly affected, even those clearly discomforted by Iell's beard. A few loosened their collars in the face of her charms. The rise and fall of her fetching bosom sent an undeniable message of fecundity to even the most dimwitted male.

It's not easy for a normal man to find himself so taken by an aberration. In fact, I was surprised that no one lashed out. I looked about at the men nearest me. An elderly gentleman a few steps in front of me stared up openmouthed as Iell twirled by, the image of her in his eyes as bright as a candle in a dark window. And just behind him, a much younger man, a tradesman by the looks of him, stared up at her with a naked look of hunger, no matter how shameful he might feel at being so drawn to such a creature. There was no denying that Iell was a force of nature. Only her show of gentility kept the crowd under her control.

How proud I felt to be one of her kind. And to think she'd scoffed at the idea that we educated our audiences. Here she was, firing up men's instincts, then teaching them to control themselves. She deserved every bit of the special treatment Barnum gave her.

Time was up. I was supposed to make way forward for those behind me, but just before I reached the exit, I stepped out of line and pressed my padded self onto the rope.

"Your show is perfection," I whispered up at her.

As Iell rotated past, she glanced down at me, tilting her head like a bird on a wire. And then she bestowed on me a look of warm recognition.

"Mr. Fortuno? I hardly knew you! Apparently you *do* have a choice."

Her comment stopped me in my tracks. "What?" I asked. But her pedestal continued to rotate, and she turned to face the other way.

From somewhere behind, Fish hollered at the crowd to step along. I peeked one more time at Iell on my way out the door, but all I could see now was the back of her head—a grand lady, set above the rest.

chapter twelve

THE DINING ROOM LOOKED ESPECIALLY FES-
tive at supper on Sunday. Someone had cut handfuls of daffodils and stuck them into pitchers
along the middle of the table, and their color spilled over onto the tablecloth like sunlight. But the light mood in the room darkened when
Zippy walked in. He had returned early from the road with a sprained
wrist and a head gash that was still puffy and sewn with seven black
stitches. He dashed about wild-eyed, banging a knife against a china
plate, shouting:

"Stepped on my hand.
Walloped my head.
Strike up the band.
Black man ain't dead."

I picked up my fork and rapped it on top of the table in time to
Zippy's banging until Matina scowled at me to stop. So I dished out
my usual beans and watched Nurse manhandle Zippy into a chair,
calming him with a bowl of stew and a couple of pats on the thigh.
Unfortunate lad: so subject to the whims of the world. I reached across
the table and tried to muss the little patch of Zippy's hair, but he
moved away from me.

"The poor boy was at the Walnut Theater no more than five days
before them stupid Philly bohunks ruined everything," Nurse said. "I
guess they took offense at his being a free Negro, despite how sweet

the boy is. Threw all manner of things at him and scared him half to death. But then Barnum brought us home, didn't he?" She patted Zippy's shoulder. "And raised your pay, with a little more for me."

Emma yanked her nose out of her Bible to snap, "It isn't the whistle that pulls the train, you know." She gave Nurse a look that drained the blood from the woman's face. Emma was in a foul mood, her hatred of Barnum renewed. Now that Zippy was back, our usual lineup had been reinstated and she'd be demoted back to tableau.

"Why is that boy worth any money at all?" she groused. "What can Barnum be thinking?"

I hated to admit it, but it had occurred to me that Barnum might have masterminded the attack on Zippy in the first place. The old man always seemed to know which way the wind blew, and I wouldn't put it past him to use strife as a way of publicizing the lad.

When Emma eyed me with unexpected malice—Whatever for? It wasn't my fault Barnum treated her so cavalierly—I focused on my beans. Best to sit quietly and chat with Matina, who sat next to me piling new potatoes onto her plate.

It was almost a relief when Fish banged through the dining room door with Bridgett trailing behind. The crispness of new petticoats added to the swish of her fancy skirt. She smiled grandly at Cook, who harrumphed and stomped out.

Fish cleared his throat. "Although I suspect you've already seen this little lady in tableau, I am here officially to introduce to you your newest colleague, Madame Zouve." Sunlight ricocheted off Fish's stickpin, a gaudy green stone that looked like something Barnum had discarded. "She will be moving into Room Four upstairs and will sit tableau in the main exhibit room through the entire day. So far, she's shown extremely well, and we are proud to have her with us."

"Ha!" Matina plunked her glass down so hastily it hit a plate, clanging like a muffled bell.

Fish paid her no mind, just flourished one limp hand at Bridgett, waving her on into the room. "Although some of you may believe you have met this person at another time, let me clarify. She has just arrived from across the ocean. She barely speaks our language. You've never met a person even remotely similar to her in the past. Is this perfectly clear?"

Bridgett removed her bonnet and carefully hung it on one of our hooks by the door. When she slipped out of her day cape, the beads around her neck jingled like tin chimes.

"Wonderful. Now, quickly, on another note: Mr. Barnum may be sending someone around to assess the living spaces and the shows. Please cooperate, and do not act put upon if he should ask you questions."

"Why would Barnum do that?" I frowned at Fish, keeping half an eye on Bridgett as she advanced toward the table. The girl did have cheek.

"Cost cutting, Fortuno. This *is* a place of business, after all."

"Maybe if Alley didn't eat no forty pounds of meat every day." Ricardo turned his bug eyes to Alley. "He drinks it down with six gallons of milk every meal, sir. Six!"

"Or if kitchen maids didn't move upstairs," Matina added, fussing with her plate.

Fish shot them a pointed look and resituated his glasses. "This is not about food, and no one in this room is a kitchen maid. Mr. Barnum is simply considering expanding the fourth-floor exhibit space. Nothing to get in a snit about."

"Well, if Barnum *does* need more room," Matina offered, an innocent look on her face, "I'd be more than happy to move to a boarding-house like some others we've heard about." She snickered and looked about the room for corroboration.

Fish smiled. "Anyone unhappy with these changes"—he poked his chin at Matina—"might want to reconsider her attitude. That's all I have to say."

After Fish left, Bridgett made her way along the side wall, stopping at the seat to my left, directly across from Alley. I expected her to sit, but she continued to hover next to me until I realized that she was waiting for me to stand. I knew Matina would have a fit, but a man is bound by manners, so I stood and pulled out a chair for her.

"Why, thank you, Mr. Fortuno. I am so pleased to be in such good company." She enunciated her words carefully but with an odd foreign accent. She'd obviously been coached. And though she was ostensibly addressing me, she continued to face Alley. "Mighten I have a bit of that, then?" She gestured toward a platter of roasted sweet corn on the other side of the table. Alley glanced up, his face mostly hidden behind strands of hanging hair, and pushed the plate of corn toward Bridgett with a single hammy finger.

"I do so love hubris," Matina said to me, loud enough for everyone to hear.

I mouthed the word *shush*, and she returned to her pork and potatoes and said nothing more.

❋ ❋ ❋

THE NEXT day, the weather turned thick and wet in the late afternoon, making my hip joints stiff as a board and my back feel as if it had been welded into one unforgiving piece. After spending extra time in the Arboretum with the birds—I'd taken to naming a few of them: Twisty, Big Voice, Whisp, Esmeralda—I retired to my rooms, mixed two spoons of Mother Gray's Sweet Powders into a glass of milk, and added a double dose of my tonic. Settling in my reading chair, my legs covered with my comforter, I sipped the concoction as I made a charcoal rendering of my mother. It was a fine depiction: her hair pulled into a knot to show off her long neck, her stubbornly squared chin, and that expressive brow I had so loved.

My mother was a formidable woman. She could convey her desires by the slightest contraction or widening of an eye. But sometimes she could be tender beyond belief, cradling me in her lap and running the tip of her finger gently down my cheek. I felt a tightening in my throat. There was something of my mother in Iell, I realized, a similar mix of tenderness and toughness. Was this why Iell had such a hold over me?

A man and his mother were not easily separated. An uncomfortable thought enveloped me. What if Iell had been offended by my illicit visit to her show? Perhaps a note would clarify my previous intentions.

Inspired, I went to my desk and pulled out a pen and a blank card.

> My Dear Mrs. Adams,
>
> It was a true pleasure to witness your show yesterday evening. Quite remarkable! Highly refined!
>
> However, I would like to send my apologies for breaking your request that no fellow performers attend. Please note that I came to see you as any man would, paying full admission.
>
> Yours most respectfully,
> Bartholomew Fortuno

I sneaked downstairs to place the note on top of Iell's throne in the Yellow Room, but I still felt vaguely discontented. The rain had cleared, so I bought a copy of the *Times* from a vendor just outside the Ann Street door and found a free bench in the garden where I could sit and read.

The newspaper further upset my mood. I'd been following the trial of Lincoln's supposed assassins—God knows, I was all for executing the bastards—but I couldn't bring myself to believe that the authorities might hang Mary Surratt if she was convicted. They'd never hanged a woman before. I looked up at the sycamore tree across from the bench and imagined my mother dangling by the neck from one of the tree's branches. I pinched my eyes closed. Good God! Stop it!

I shuddered. The sun shot through the tree branches, making patterns in the garden grass. I believed strongly in fate, but would it really be Mary Surratt's fate to hang? Had it been Lincoln's fate to be shot in a theater? Or my mother's to pass away in a crumbling asylum? I had a sudden memory of my mother sitting by a window in our cottage, her beautiful cheeks already hollowed into caverns and her hands bone thin. On the windowsill behind her sat a glass bottle, green and slightly opaque. As my mother took it in her hands and lifted it into the sunlight, the light refracted through it beautifully. She turned and looked at me through the glass bottle.

"I believe you have a gift," she said.

"A gift?"

"You've been put in this world for something special. I have always known this, my baby. But if you want to fulfill your destiny and be who you are meant to be, you must learn to control your impulses. Control, Bartholomew, control."

I tossed the newspaper down on the ground and rose to my feet as a speckled starling flapped past me, snatching up a crumb at my feet. Control, my mother taught me. She was right. It was doing me no good to sit in the garden and stew. Better to take action, any action, and alter my mood. Up the stairs to the resident wing I went, determined to control a growing sense of discontent.

Kicking off my boots, I padded into the bedroom and studied my image in the mirror against the far wall. A trick in the glass made my reflection look taller. I moved sideways, to the right, and then to the front, my image changing and changing again. And then I remembered the root. I'd left it in my étagère. It took some digging, but I finally found it buried in the far corner of the top drawer, hidden like a hibernating animal. The bag felt smaller than I'd remembered, and when I unloosed the straps and drew out the root, I found it slightly sticky in my palm. It still smelled foul and earthy.

What foolish chatter had the Chinaman spouted? Eat the root to find my true self? Perhaps it *was* as the Chinaman had hinted. Inside each of us is another self, a truer self. And Iell. Hadn't she insinuated that I might have a choice about my appearance? Did she mean I could disguise myself, the way I had the other night, or something more?

I bit into the root, tearing off a gummy splinter, and let it sit on the top of my tongue. It tasted bitter, oily and dry at the same time. The stringy, barklike substance mixed with my saliva and let loose a tangy juice that settled hotly in the bottom of my mouth before slipping wickedly down the back of my throat. I spit the thing out and waited. At first I felt nothing, nothing at all. What in the world had I thought would happen? But then, something stirred inside me. A possibility; I'd no other name for it. And quick as that, it disappeared. I felt so alone.

Maybe it was time to talk to Matina. If I confessed all that had gone on since Iell came to the Museum, she could help me sort out my feelings, and together we would dispel my confusion. Despite its being late for a proper visit, I knew she would see me, so I pulled my boots back on and hustled down the hall toward Matina's rooms, only to run into Alley returning from his last show. His bruises retained a bit of color, but he seemed more or less himself again as he rested against the wall.

"Where you off to?" he asked, and I explained that I was hoping Matina was still awake.

He gave me a piercing look. "You need to talk so late at night, you can try me, ya know."

I looked up at him, his towering bulk overshadowing me. How could I explain this new sensation rising in me? As if suddenly I'd found a new door in a house I'd lived in all my life, but I wasn't able to open it.

"Have you ever felt like you were missing something but didn't know what it was?" I asked.

Alley flicked away a bit of dust from the front of his shirt. "I usually know what I want," he said. "I just don't know how to get it."

That wasn't at all what I meant. "So you've never felt like something was just out of your reach?" I tried again.

"Didn't say that, did I?"

I raised my eyebrows.

"Grabbing somethin' don't mean you can have it."

I searched Alley's unshaven face for a hint of irony, but he seemed quite serious. I changed the subject. "How goes it with the police?"

He shrugged.

"And those Copperheads. Any more trouble with them?"

Alley said nothing.

"You can tell me," I prompted. "It was the Copperheads that pushed you into starting those fires, right?"

Alley jimmied his fists into his pockets and kicked one foot back against the hallway wall. "No, Fortuno, I never started no fires."

"I understand what it's like to be forced to do another man's errands," I said.

"No, Fortuno," Alley repeated, straightening up. "I told you. It weren't me." The gruffness in his voice was enough to stop me from saying anything other than thank you and I would see him later.

After he stumbled off down the hall, I made my way to Matina's door, still thinking about Alley's crimes. He seemed so set on being seen as an upstanding citizen, but wasn't it natural, if one had no inherent control, to give in to one's baser instincts? I rapped lightly on Matina's door.

"Barthy? Is that you? Are you feeling all right? It's so late." Matina flung open her door, moving her yellow cloak—the newest spring fashion, she'd said—so I could sit on her settee. She put the heel of her hand to my forehead, checking for fever. I realized how glad I was to see her face. It was all I could do not to throw my arms around her ample waist.

"What have you eaten today? Your color has gone all ruddy." When Matina tilted forward, the neckline of her dress buckled, exposing the top of her ample bosom, and I found myself staring. "Everyone is asking after you. We can't believe how many shows you've missed recently. Not at all like you, Barthy. And did you hear that Mrs. Barnum arrived yesterday morning? The first thing she did was get rid of the Indians.

Said they smelled like holy hell and made Barnum ship them out to some circus in the Carolinas."

I stood and kissed her on the cheek. "Sometimes, you are my favorite person." Although the urge to confess remained strong, I thought it best to start slow, so I took her by the hand. "How about I read to you? Tell me what you'd like to hear."

"*Malaeska*," Matina said happily. She curled up on the settee, her tatting recovered and in her lap at the ready.

I dug out the dog-eared copy of *Malaeska, the Indian Wife of the White Hunter* by Mrs. Ann Sophia Stephens that she kept in a case by her front door, then read to Matina as she worked on her lace. But twice my eyes slipped off the page and wandered again to her neck and to the top of her breasts, all thoughts of confession washed away by the lushness of her. And then I felt a sharp stabbing feeling in my stomach. What in the world? I thought. It took a moment for me to realize the cause of the pain. That root! That horrible root the Chinaman gave me. Its juice must have reached my stomach! Could it be poisonous? Was it working its way through my bloodstream at that very moment, threatening my health? I forced myself to take a deep breath and waited. One more *ping* low in my belly, then nothing. I inhaled. Exhaled. Inhaled. Nothing more. For the moment, all seemed well.

Somehow, I managed to get all the way to chapter three without giving way to panic, but I breathed easier when Matina tossed aside her lace and stood. "I think I'll go downstairs and take a bite to eat," she said, "then come back and toddle off to bed. I'm so glad you're not horribly ill."

So was I. After walking her to the stairs, I returned to my own rooms and took stock of my body. The pain had ceased entirely, and I felt no nausea, just a slow feeling of potency spreading through my limbs, an invigorating sensation, as if I'd slept for hours and had just woken up, utterly refreshed. Is this what the Chinaman thought I'd experience, this feeling of strength? No. Ridiculous. The man had been toying with me, and having fallen for his silliness, I'd let my mind have its way. I was allowing my imagination to get the best of me.

I started to prepare for bed, but for some reason I couldn't shake the image of Matina from my mind. How luscious she had looked! Why had I left her without a word of confession? In fact I barely gave her a proper good night. How rude of me. Lately I hadn't been much of a friend, and I owed it to her to try harder. She might still be in the kitchens getting her snack. I should stroll downstairs and wish her a pleasant evening.

After throwing on my smoking jacket, I made my way to the kitchens, and sure enough, she stood in the larder loading a tray with dark rolls and sauce-covered mutton chops. The icebox stood open, its square oak door allowing the mist from the melting ice to escape and surround her in a soft fog. When Matina saw me in the doorway, she clutched her tray in surprise. "Barthy. You scared me half to death. Why are you staring at me like that?"

"I came down to say good night."

She studied me carefully. "Didn't you already do that?" She shoved the icebox door closed with one hip and moved toward a little table in the back.

"Let me help you."

Lifting the tray from Matina's hands, I slid it onto the table, then pulled a sprig of thyme from a bunch drying in a nearby jar and stuck it in her hair. Turning her hand over, I unbuttoned the top of her glove and kissed her wrist, the flesh yielding and pink. What are you doing? I asked myself. Stop it this instant. But try as I might, I couldn't seem to control my impulses.

"You look absolutely irresistible tonight," I said, and I meant it.

I leaned in and kissed her flush on the mouth—softly, at first, then a bit more aggressively.

Matina pulled away, her expression incredulous.

"I'm so sorry." I backed away, horrified by my behavior. "I don't know why in the world—"

"It's all right." Her voice was soft and full of surprise.

"No. You must think I'm an animal. It's only that your neck, your hair . . ."

Matina smiled. "How can a girl complain when a gentleman is overwhelmed by her charms?" She sat down to her snack, but the skin on her neck was still flushed with excitement.

"Well, good night then," I stuttered, and left before I could make any other mistakes. I hoped my rash actions hadn't changed anything between us.

chapter thirteen

EET IN THE DINING ROOM. TEN MIN-
utes." Fish's voice jarred me awake. The
clock at my bedside read five A.M.

"Wait, wait. One minute!" I pulled my dressing gown around my
shoulders and cracked open the door. Fish peered in at me. "It's the
middle of the night, for God's sake," I yelled through the crack. "Go the
hell away."

"Don't toy with me, Fortuno. Get yourself dressed, *in* costume,
and down to the dining room. We're off to Brady's."

Down the hall, Matina's door opened and closed after Fish pounded
on it loud enough to wake the dead. Normally, I'd have gone to check
on her, but after the kiss a few nights back, I was trying to keep my distance.

Neither Matina nor I had said a word about what had happened
in the kitchen, but it still worried me. I had chalked up my own action
to a moment of madness, and Matina had not pressed me for clarifica-
tion. But I wasn't entirely certain that she'd taken it in stride.

At least new photographs would please Matina. Mathew Brady
hadn't taken pictures of us for years. Before the war, we used to go to
his studio annually, always without notice and before dawn so that,
according to Barnum, "He can catch the purity of your faces in the
glow of the morning sun." Ha! We all knew why Brady liked to steal us
away in the wee hours of the night. In his own way, he was as much a
freak as we were. He liked to think of us as secrets that belonged to
him and him alone. I'd never expected to see him again after he ran off

to the battlefields, wild with the idea of documenting the war in photographs. The country was stunned by his audacity in displaying the battlefield dead. But now that the war was over and the country was eager to forget its horrors, he'd come back to us.

My toilette took me no time at all—just a dash of pomade on my hair and scuffing to clean my shoes. My tights had yet to soften and felt uncomfortable beneath my performance suit, but at least I'd look my best in the photographs. And maybe Iell would be at the studio. Lord, how I would love to have a portrait of her!

I hesitated. Where was that root? Digging about in the drawer, I found it hiding beneath my handkerchiefs, and carefully, I pulled it out and set it in my open palm. The first time I'd tasted it, it had given me a sense of confidence, and if Iell were at Brady's, I would need all the confidence that I could muster. Looking to heaven with a silent prayer to protect my health, I bit off a sliver and, to avoid the bitter taste, swallowed it whole.

By the time I entered the dining room, I felt marvelous. Matina swooshed up to me the moment she saw me.

Fish pointed a bony finger toward the clock and clucked his tongue at me. "You've kept us all waiting on you, Fortuno. What *have* you been doing?"

"Sorry, Mr. Fish." I made a mental note not to irritate him any more than necessary. Who knew if I might need him as an ally one of these days?

Fish looked again at the clock, fretting. "Dear me, I've got to leave. Miss Emma, here, will be in charge of getting you to Brady's safely. Please treat her with the same respect with which you would treat me."

Ricardo cleared his throat but dared not laugh. Emma stepped forward. She wore the fluffy white dress of a little girl, and she contrasted mightily with Alley, who had donned his animal skins and oiled his biceps. The two of them flanked the dining room table like pillars.

"Let's get on with it, dearies. He who waits, as the Good Book says."

Emma shepherded us briskly through the courtyard and out onto Ann Street. The city was doing repair work on the sewers, so our carriages were waiting a half block away. We moved in a cluster toward Broadway, lurching past closed doors and darkened windows. Zippy kept stopping to pick up bits of trash from the street, slowing our progress. It was still dark, but the air carried a hint of the dusky light that would soon wake the city to its frenetic state. Lingering behind the others for a moment, I stopped to listen to the starlings, remembering how, as a child, I'd sometimes crawl from bed at dawn to lie on the lawn between the barns, listening to the birds' morning song, happy to be out of earshot of my parents' arguing.

"Let's *go*, Fortuno," Emma called out. "We haven't got all night."

I quickened my step to rejoin the group. Just before we reached the carriages, Fish's voice came out of nowhere. He was talking to someone, but I couldn't see him. And then I glimpsed a smaller carriage beyond ours. In front of that carriage, Fish was chatting with a gray-haired woman in a dress the color of twigs. She rested against a cane, a small carpetbag with leather fittings and a lock in her other hand, and for one moment she looked at us over the top of wire eyeglasses.

Tension hopped from one member of my group to the next as we all recognized the woman at the same time: Barnum's wife, Charity.

"What in heaven's name?" I whispered to Matina, who looked as stricken as the rest of us.

"Watching out for her interests, I suppose," Matina said, keeping her voice low. "You know this can't be good."

Matina was right. Mrs. Barnum's proximity to us—as occasional as it was—usually bode ill. Ever since the scandal of the Jerome Clock Company five years ago, Mrs. Barnum owned more than half of her husband's assets.

You see, Barnum had gotten hoodwinked. He'd been trying to create a city—East Bridgeport; who else would undertake such a thing?—and his plan had been to buy parcels of land and sell them to companies who would then move to town. One such enterprise, the Jerome Clock Company, had accepted happily, providing Barnum would temporarily cover their debts. "They are gentlemen," Barnum said, "and the company is sound, just having a bad year. Why not extend a bit of trust and my good name?" He'd signed undated notes to cover incoming debts, and it ended up bankrupting him. He had to sell the title to the Museum, plus most of his holdings, and though the Museum soldiered on, it took two grueling tours of Europe with Tom Stratton and the rest of his diminutive company for Barnum to recover his holdings. The day he repurchased the Museum, Barnum addressed the staff and performers at a must-attend meeting after church services. Nearly sixty of us crammed along the benches in one of the minor rooms and listened to Barnum attentively.

He stood on the stage in the front of the room and rested an elbow against the lectern at his side. No one had fired up the footlights, so his strong eyebrows overshadowed his nose and eyes.

"I want to squelch any rumor of financial insolvency," he said. "As you well know, I have suffered greatly by ignoring my own business sense. I've been preached to, harassed, and made to dance to every jig our spectacle-loving fellows could impose on me." He lifted his face dramatically as if praying to a vengeful God. "I've tolerated everything and held my own, but"—here he held up a finger and wagged it at us—"what I could *not* tolerate was how my so-called friends turned into butterflies at the sight of me brought low."

He scowled across the room. We sat still as rocks, trying to hide from the light of Barnum's glare as he pounded his fist on the lectern, the fat of his belly and jowls shaking in response to the suddenness and strength of the gesture.

"Nothing is worse than false friends," Barnum hissed, and he scanned our faces as if to catch an unbeliever in the crowd. Then his expression changed; he beamed over us, a newly risen sun. "But you, my *true* friends, will help me return the Museum to its previous majesty. Together, we will reach an even greater height."

A cheer went up, and because I was still green and awestruck, I believed that Barnum had prevailed by being a man of character, a man of strength: a hero. In reality, he bought back his Museum with his wife's inheritance. It was she, not he, who saved the day. And ever since, Mrs. Barnum has had the upper hand—an unnatural and uncomfortable state of affairs.

I didn't relax until we climbed into the two carriages and took off, leaving Mrs. Barnum and Fish behind us, chatting in the street. Matina pulled out her tatting and worked at her lace as the carriages made their way through the empty streets. Bridgett and Alley sat across from us. Alley looked utterly miserable, his eyes glued to the floor. Bridgett glared into a small mirror, adjusting her hair, constantly checking to see if Alley was paying her any mind. When she started to hum some barroom tune, Matina rolled her eyes.

We halted in front of a gray building. Its roof was covered in creeping ivy, with two long skylights cut through the vines like eyes. Emma jumped out of the lead carriage and pounded heavily on the battered door as the rest of us gathered near an etched metal sign swinging from two iron poles: MATHEW BRADY: IMAGES AND DAGUERREOTYPES. One of Brady's assistants, a young man in a blackened apron carrying a lamp, let us in.

After staggering through the deserted reception room, we filed one by one through a narrow door at the assistant's behest and followed him down a long hall, our shadows skittering along bare walls, the sound of our footfalls echoing against the oaken floor.

Brady's used to be a grand old place, but apparently he'd moved his furniture and most of his portraits to a newer studio farther uptown. When the assistant pulled open the doors to the main room, however, I breathed out in relief. This, at least, remained intact. As before, a scarlet and indigo palace carpet, shopworn but handsome, covered the floor, and unframed daguerreotypes of Lincoln and Webster and the brave Clara Barton still lined the walls. I flushed with pleasure to see the famed portrait of Madame Jumel, wife of the fallen Aaron Burr, hanging along the northern wall as it always had.

Though the room lacked the brilliant light that would soon pour in from the skylights, the windows at least let in a limpid breeze. In the front of the studio, a handful of assistants draped a large raised dais in red velvet cloth. Six-foot ferns stood on either side of the dais like palace guards, and, in front, two cameras bordered a table covered with stacks of framed glass, pans of liquids, rags, and hanging racks.

"Beautiful creatures! How I've missed you!" Brady bounded in through a door in the back. Dust rose at his feet as he walked toward us. After wiping his hands on the sides of his trousers, he slipped on a pair of immaculate white gloves. He must have reopened his old studio just for us.

"Let me take a look at you. You bring an old man to tears." Collectively, we expanded our chests and stood a little taller, in love as always with his vision of us. Brady had been aged by the war, his hair thin and snowy now, his eyeglasses so thick and heavy that their metal frames cut into his nose. But he still radiated vitality and walked with the same businesslike intent he'd always had, circling us slowly and peering at each of us in turn. With Brady, we were all children. Ricardo stood up taller when Brady mussed his hair, and Matina giggled as he ran his gloved hand along her arm. When he pulled Bridgett forward and spun her around, her bangles clinked together, dust swirled around her like a squall, and she smiled from ear to ear. "A new girl! With such beautiful, beautiful eyes." He peered at her through his thick spectacles, then turned and blew a curdled kiss to Emma; I was happy to see how much it flustered her. Grabbing hold of Alley's leg, he used the palm of his hand to test the strength of Alley's thighs. Zippy surprised us all with a show of unexpected dignity, shaking hands with Brady like a peer.

As for me, I willingly allowed him to slip his hand inside my jacket and play the tips of his gloved fingers over my ribs, probing each bone, because I knew that he, like few others, truly understood my gift. And though he gave no indication that he sensed any difference in me—my vigor had increased considerably after my recent taste of that root—his glowing smile reminded me that he knew I was the real thing, no doubt about it.

But shortly thereafter, Mrs. Barnum entered the studio with Fish, and the mood shifted. Even Brady seemed a bit flustered when he saw her, gesturing for his assistant to bring out chairs and tea and dashing to join them up on the far side of the room as all of us stood at attention—afraid to appear too happy or sad or nervous or relaxed. It was never wise to draw undue attention to oneself when Mrs. Barnum was near. The same question was clearly on all of our minds: What is she doing here?

When Brady disappeared into the shadows, I prepared myself for the session. I felt a bit overexposed when I took off my jacket and pants, peeling down to my tights, but Brady needed to capture my true essence, so I didn't really mind. The problem was Mrs. Barnum, who stared down her spectacles at the lot of us, whispering God knew what in Fish's ear. When she finally glanced my way, I ran a finger across my eyebrows, hoping I looked at least presentable.

We waited, knotted together in the corner like schoolchildren, as Brady's assistants hauled in more glass and trays of foul-smelling liquids and ducked under the long black cloths attached to the viewfinders. Finally, Brady reappeared, dragging a potted fern behind him. His main assistant, a paunchy youth with skin the color of goat cheese, clicked his tongue and ran to help him bump the fern noisily up the steps and onto the platform's center. It was only when Brady stumbled and needed help down the stairs that I realized how much his eyesight had deteriorated.

"You!" Brady yelled out to Alley, who had slumped to his haunches to rest, and gestured to a collection of props in the far corner of the studio. "Could you kindly retrieve that chair at the top, my fine mountain of a man?"

Alley scaled the prop pile and plucked the gilded chair like a prize. He tumbled down, chair held high, and placed it carefully on the center of the dais.

I slid my eyes toward Mrs. Barnum, who seemed preoccupied with the tea that had just arrived. I glanced over at Matina and noticed how her gown made her skin look like alabaster. "Your dress is lovely," I whispered in her ear.

"Do you think so? Thank you so much." Matina sighed and tilted her body gently into mine, her upper arm pressing squarely against my side. Even with the extra vigor from the root, it made me nervous to support her great weight, but I didn't want to offend her by moving away. "You know, Barthy, I've been thinking. Perhaps we should plan an evening out," she whispered. "Just the two of us. This Sunday, perhaps."

I took a step backward. An evening out? Hadn't I offered to take her with me on my first trip to the Chinaman's and she unequivocally turned me down? And that was well before I found out how hard it was to navigate the streets. I could no longer imagine going out with Matina in tow.

Matina sensed my hesitation. "We needn't do anything fancy, Barthy."

"I'm so sorry, my dear. But I really don't think . . ."

Matina paled.

"Quiet now," Brady ordered. "I want the rest of you on the dais. We haven't much time, so up you go. We're going panoramic!"

We moved forward in a group; when I tried to help Matina by taking hold of her arm, she pulled it away.

Ricardo pushed his way to the front. "Christ almighty!" he cried out, and in spite of Mrs. Barnum's presence, or perhaps because of it, he pulled out a flask from his hip pocket and took a swig. Emma reached out to take the flask from him. Surprised, Ricardo lurched and lost his balance. When he tried to steady himself, he bumped against an assistant carrying a tray, and its black liquid spewed onto the floor behind us. The air stank of sulfur.

"My sweet peppers, you must take care! Come over here, you naughty lad. And watch the mess. Don't walk through that." Brady grabbed Ricardo's flask, slipped it into his own pocket, and led him around the oil spill and up the stairs. When Ricardo made a beeline toward the gilded chair, Brady tetched at him and pointed him to the far left.

Up we all went after that, and, like the characters in a minstrel show—the master of ceremonies, the banjo player, the fiddler, Mr. Tambo, and Mr. Bones—we arranged ourselves into a wide horseshoe. In the middle, the empty chair sat like a taunt. Brady rubbed his hands together and looked toward a closed door to his right, then up at the windows, where the sky perceptibly lightened as the sun rose higher. I tried to catch Matina's eye, but she avoided me. The air was musty and close.

The dour look on Mrs. Barnum's face as she sipped her tea caused Fish to hold up his watch and point. "Yes, of course." Brady answered Fish's gesture with a loud clap. "We'll fetch her now."

The assistant scurried out the side door, and when it reopened we all turned our heads. Matina snorted, Emma chuckled, and my belly went hollow with excitement as Iell walked into the room. Sunlight poured in from behind her, brightening her hair, which draped deep red against her bodice. Iell floated toward the dais and mounted the stairs, walking to the empty chair without hesitation and without so much as a glance in the direction of Mrs. Barnum, who was tracking her every movement.

"You'd like me to sit in this chair." It wasn't a question. Before she sat, she looked behind her at the lot of us, her gaze stopping briefly at me, her eyes running the length of my torso. She'd not seen me in costume before, and for a brief moment, I heard her words again: *Apparently, you do have a choice.* But she gave me a small smile, and my concern dissipated. What a charming woman. So like my mother but, thankfully, without my mother's unpredictability. My mother was strong, no doubt, but she was also superstitious and believed in odd omens. She could become hysterical if a cat stood crookedly on a windowsill, for example, or if a tree branch broke into some odd shape. In contrast, Iell seemed fully in control of her charms. She took her seat, and Brady dove beneath his black cloth.

"All right, now, I want you to look like a family." Head buried, he pulled one arm free to wave his hand like a flapping bird. None of us knew how to interpret such a request, so he popped out, his hair frazzled. "What is the problem, my beauties? Gather closer to the center. Come on now, it's not so hard."

Without thinking, I stepped forward and grabbed hold of the top rungs of Iell's chair, wisps of her red hair brushing against my fingertips. I heard Matina gasp behind me.

"And the rest," demanded Brady. "What are you waiting for?"

Slowly, the others followed suit until they had all shuffled closer to Iell. Matina was the last to move. When she slid behind me to my left, I stared straight ahead toward the camera, suspecting I'd made another error in judgment but unable to correct my path.

Two of Brady's minions stood at the table, dipping dark glass plates into an oily emulsion before sandwiching them in a metal drainer. The shorter of the two plucked out a plate and slid it into the back of the camera. Brady crawled beneath the cloth once more.

"Perfect. Hold still!"

We held our breath. *Flash!* A sudden explosion of light nearly blinded me. My fingers slid across the top of the chair a half-inch closer to Iell. *Flash!* Matina sniffled behind me. Were those tears? *Flash!* They couldn't be. *Flash! Flash!* Much too late to change position, much too late to move, I shut Matina from my mind and looked down my nose at Iell. If I dared, I could tangle my fingers through her hair and pull her to me. To my horror, I felt the stirring of my sex. For a moment I wasn't even sure what was happening. But yes, I could definitely feel movement below, like a serpent coming to life.

"I said not to move!" Brady yelled, but I had to inch to the left to hide behind the chair. Desperate, I glanced over toward Mrs. Barnum. Thank God she was busy putting sugar in her tea. I concentrated on the boards on the far wall after that, and counted ten more explosions of light before Brady dropped his waving arms, his hair plastered to his forehead with sweat. The sun had completely risen by then, and as it washed across the studio, its blinding light helped me regain enough control to move away from the chair. What in heaven's name had come over me? Never in my life had I had such a bestial response to a woman.

Brady waved us free. "All right, my lovelies, that's it! You can all go home now." Matina stood alone near the stairs and I stepped away with the intent of joining her, but Iell stopped me with a touch to my wrist, beckoning me nearer. She now seemed a bit unsteady, as if she could not feel the seat beneath her or had just awakened and was trying to orient herself to the living world.

"I got your charming note," she whispered, looking up at me with cloudy eyes. "I was thinking that perhaps you'd consider making another trip to the Chinaman for me. Mr. Barnum need not know."

Would I mind? Absolutely I would mind. Hadn't I already decided never to go again? But Iell was so fetching and so in need of my help, the words slipped out of me. "Nothing would make me happier than to make another trip for you. As often as you like."

"Ah, Mr. Fortuno, I cannot tell you how grateful I would be."

She held up a hand for me to help her to her feet, but before I could touch her, Brady's assistant swooped in.

"Not you, my dear. Barnum wants more pictures of you alone." The assistant helped Iell up from her chair, muscling me away, and led her toward a closed door in the back.

Immediately, I turned to Matina, but Alley had already helped her down the stairs. He shot me a wicked look, and I thought for one startling moment that he'd seen the change in my body. But that was not possible; all my colleagues had been standing behind me. No, Alley's ire was clearly in defense of Matina, and I supposed I didn't blame him. I'd upset her and needed to make amends quickly. But why should she be so upset over my eagerness to join Iell? Matina and I had never made such claims on each other before. Damn that kiss.

I let Matina and Alley go on without me. Alley would see her to the carriage, and it would be better if I waited and spoke to her later, after she'd calmed down a bit. Looking around, there was no sight of Iell. I was done here, and I would walk back to the Museum alone. Why not? It wasn't that far, and it was still early enough that the streets would be empty.

Fish called out to me after I'd finished dressing for the street.

"Over here, Fortuno. One moment more, if you please." He pointed to a wooden chair and motioned for me to occupy it. Mrs. Barnum sat expectantly next to it, her heavy black shoes rooted squarely on the floor, her cane propped against the nearby wall. Emma stood next to her, but she turned and left after Mrs. Barnum waved a dismissing hand. My throat constricted. Why in the world would Mrs. Barnum wish to speak to me?

I slipped on my gloves and forced myself forward, checking to see whether any of my colleagues were lingering nearby.

"Mr. Fortuno, how nice to see you again."

I bowed briskly to the woman and my heart pounded. Mrs. Barnum's iron-gray hair, pulled tightly against her scalp, emphasized her high cheekbones and a nose as sharp as a beak. Her black dress bespoke civility, but that external calm was clearly studied. One glance at her scorching eyes warned me against complacency. She smiled graciously, gesturing for me to sit, and I could think of no way out. The unpadded wood of the chair hurt the bones of my pelvis. Could she have planned that? Of course not. I was being ridiculous.

"I am told you and my husband have become close of late," Mrs. Barnum said, breaking the silence that had already grown between us.

"Kisses his arse," Ricardo yelled, from somewhere behind me. To her credit, Mrs. Barnum ignored him, and one of Brady's assistants hustled him out.

"He employs me," I said cautiously.

Mrs. Barnum lifted her well-groomed eyebrows. "As do I. People sometimes forget that."

"Of course, Madam, of course." I pulled my coat tightly over my jersey. The two of us were now alone in the studio.

Mrs. Barnum smiled again. "Do you enjoy your work at the Museum, Mr. Fortuno?" Her tone sent a shiver up my spine.

"Absolutely," I asserted, shifting on the chair. "How could I not? It's a big step up from the circuses."

Mrs. Barnum squinted as she considered me, and my palms began to sweat. "So you are an ambitious man?"

"No, not ambitious. Though I believe that a man can make what he wants of his life."

"Funny. I've always thought it was life that made what it wanted of a man." Mrs. Barnum played with a large garnet ring she wore on one finger, and even though my greater height forced me to look down on her, I felt like a child at his parent's feet. Mrs. Barnum regarded me skeptically. "Did you know my husband was a shop boy when he married me?" she said finally.

"Yes, I had heard that."

"Like you, he claims not to be moved by ambition, yet I have lived with him for many years, and if it isn't ambition that drives him, I don't know what else to call it. Perhaps it's something higher: a religious quest, a calling. Who am I to judge?" She sniffed dryly. "But he has peddled people like you for as long as I can remember. Don't misunderstand me; I don't entirely mind. His obsessions have kept him occupied, and until now they have been lucrative and relatively harmless. But this new fixation of his? That's another thing entirely."

"Fixation, Madam?"

"I think we both know who I mean."

I nodded in assent. Obviously, she was referring to Iell. The room grew much warmer, and I wondered where this conversation was heading. Brady laughed from some hidden room in the back, and I remembered that Iell was still with him. My stomach rolled over.

"What is it I can do for you?" I asked, the fear of what she might want of me stronger than my fear of offending her.

"It's my belief that you have been colluding, however mildly, with my husband. Helping this person obtain certain items. I would ask you to stop."

I flushed and looked away. "I've spoken to your husband only a handful of times, and I barely know this other person." How in the world did she know I'd traveled to the Chinaman's for Iell? Emma must have told her. Who else would have known? But if that were true, Emma was not in cahoots with Barnum, but rather with his wife. And what was I to do now? Not five minutes before, I'd promised Iell that I would go to the Chinaman's again.

Mrs. Barnum ran a dry thumb along the edge of her chair. "You have no doubt heard that we plan to assess the resident space."

"Excuse me?"

"Some of us might have to pull in our belts. Share our quarters with the transient performers. I trust that you and your colleagues will make do, if necessary, with such an arrangement, but you've been with us for such a long time. I'd hate to see your living accommodations compromised by practical needs."

I rose to my feet, avoiding the urge to shove my hands in my pockets so that she wouldn't see them shaking.

"I believe I should say good day to you now," I said.

"Relax, Mr. Fortuno." Mrs. Barnum smiled, revealing too many teeth. When she reached for my hand, I backed away, but she took it anyway and patted the top like a mother. "I'm simply asking you not to insert yourself where you're not needed."

Using my arm to steady herself, she stood, and at full height her head was no higher than the middle of my chest. Her sharp chin tilted up at me and her papery fingers continued to stroke my hand. "I can see from the look on your face that you're much too clever to risk what you have, so I think our talk has been fruitful." She released me. I had been warned and dismissed.

There was Fish, silently nodding toward the exit. He turned me out into the street with barely a word. I all but ran back to the Museum.

chapter fourteen

BRIGHT BLUE PARROT FLEW AT ME AS I unlatched the aviary door. I grabbed the broom and flourished it until it flapped back inside and perched on a branch of the acacia tree.

"It's going to take more than squawking to break free from me, little one." I held out my arm in front of the bird, and it hopped on. "I'm going to name you Arrow," I said, and fastening the door behind me, I set him onto one of the perches. He tilted his head and watched as I scooped seed into the food cups, but I lost control of the sack and seed poured out onto the floor. "And now look," I complained to the bird. "Do you see this mess?" He flapped his wings. "Proof that we can't always control our world."

God knows my last two days had illustrated *that* clearly enough. Matina had barely spoken to me since Brady's. She simply wasn't herself anymore. So emotional. So irrational. She was obviously jealous of Iell, but—one kiss aside—I had never promised Matina anything more than a friendship. With her acting like this, I could hardly ask for counsel, though I'd never needed it more. I felt the specter of Mrs. Barnum looming over me like a damned storm cloud. The memory of her patting the top of my hand made me shudder, and I grabbed the broom and swatted at the seed to get her out of my head. Perhaps I should tell Iell I'd changed my mind.

I dug into my pocket and pulled out the bag with the Chinaman's root. I'd taken to carrying it around with me lately, finding it reassuring to know I had it on hand in case I needed it. I'd begun to worry that, eventually, the root would be gone, though for now there was plenty left. I took a little bite and thought again about Iell. Never had a woman elicited such a response in me. There had been a girl once, Mary Louise Daley. She was dark-eyed and pale-skinned, and my pulse raced as she took my hand and tugged me into her kitchen pantry.

Stop thinking of such things, I told myself. *Focus on the task at hand.* But once I'd remembered Mary Louise's long dark hair, it was hard to put her out of my mind.

I was living with my uncle then in a little town in northern Pennsylvania. Mary Louise, fifteen or so—no more than a year older than I—lived with her mother in a small white house near the barbershop. I could still see her face in my mind: round, with an adorable dimple in her chin. She had a long neck, which disappeared into the top of her cotton dress, and shiny black hair.

We'd exchanged shy glances for weeks until one afternoon, with barely a word, Mary Louise pulled me behind the pantry door. Her mother, she said, was off selling yarn in Mason's dry goods store. My palms went sweaty as she put her hands on the small of my back and leaned into my neck. Her breath smelled like peaches. Our touches were hasty and blind, all knobs and knees and heavy panting. At the feel of her small breasts, I became so elated I could barely breathe. But then I realized how grave a sin I was committing. My mother had taught me that self-mastery was the most vital of virtues, and now that she'd been hospitalized it was more important than ever to stay in control and set my own course in life. I pulled away from Mary Louise. She clung to me for a moment, but when I persisted, her hands dropped to her sides, and she gave me a puzzled look.

It wasn't long after that encounter that my gift manifested itself. Ever since my father died, I'd had little appetite. For years, I'd treated food as a shameful necessity. But after touching Mary Louise, the very sight of food nauseated me. Sitting at my uncle's table, an image of Mary Louise's soft flesh arose when his housekeeper urged turnip pie on me; for a moment I was ravenous, but then it was all I could do not to vomit. "Come along now, hon, are you ill? Take a little bite or two." How could I explain the fact that my stomach now turned at the sight of a potato, a hunk of cheese, meat, bread, nearly anything at all? The mere idea of a soup or a stew threw me into convulsions. And if I tried to disregard my aversions and force even a morsel to my mouth, I could hear my mother's whisper in my ear, urging me to control my impulses, and the sound of her voice stopped me cold.

For months after that, the only food I kept down was green beans or berries. And yet, despite my lack of sustenance, I started to grow taller. Uncle Frederick said nothing when I sprouted up like a weed, but when it was clear that I was putting on no extra weight, he took me aside, shaking my arm roughly.

"What's wrong with you, boy?" Uncle Frederick scolded. "Whatever you're doing, I want you to stop."

But I couldn't stop. I had no choice in the matter. Children from neighboring houses began to taunt me, calling me Spindleshanks or Spider. Finally, when it became clear that my new tall body was not going to flesh out, my uncle dragged a mattress upstairs and arranged it in the corner of the slanted garret, suggesting I might enjoy the solitude. He was either embarrassed by me or thought I was touched. Either way, he separated me from the family. The housekeeper continued to bring me three meals a day, but except for a bite or two, I threw the food out the window for the dogs. Still, the situation was not all bad. My stomach sometimes cramped with hunger, and I often felt lightheaded, but each day the sun poured through the south-facing windows, burning off the chill of evening, and each night the dark delivered me into a deep, dreamless sleep.

And then one morning, I got up off my mattress, opened the door to pick up my food tray, and had a fleeting image of my mother walking toward me, a bowl of steaming soup in hand. I fainted straight away. Hours later, I opened my eyes. The sun had moved all the way across the room by then, and numbness covered me like a blanket. The song of the nuthatches, usually a delight, bored through my head like spikes, and when I forced myself to sit, my nose began to bleed. I hadn't even time to reach for a kerchief before a stabbing pain rammed through my belly, doubling me over. The only way to stifle my cries was to cover my mouth with a pillow rammed tight with my fist.

Again my mother's voice called to me, but this time as soft as an angel's. "If you control your urges, sweet boy, you will be rewarded." Suddenly I understood. As swiftly as the pain had come, it lifted. My heart beat normally, and my body felt as light as the late sun washing through the room. I stood and walked to the window. My new body made me special and pure. If I wished to fulfill my destiny, all I had to do was resist temptation. Beans were sufficient. And the Mary Louises in the world? What need had I for such blind and groping impulses? Outside, a brand-new world awakened: crisp, translucent.

I had always cherished this memory of the day my gift was delivered to me. But today, something about the memory didn't ring true. A feeling that I'd misremembered it threatened to unnerve me until I put it from my mind. I had work to do. I watched Arrow flap off the branch to join a young, white-breasted hatch I'd named Puff in one corner of the Atrium. His blue feathers looked like the sky to me, clear and sparkly, and I realized how enjoyable caring for these birds was becoming. It took me a few more minutes to finish sweeping the floor, and after clicking the aviary door shut and wishing each bird a good day, I sat at the café table to take a short rest. That's when I saw the envelope on the table, my name written across the front in a fine hand. My stomach leaped as I looked up and down the aisle, but the messenger had disappeared. I tore the letter open with shaky hands. The card inside smelled of rose water.

Dear Mr. Fortuno,

I have sent word to the Chinaman. If you pay him, I will reimburse you in full. Can you go soon? Tomorrow night would be ideal if that's possible. Leave me a note in the Yellow Room when you have accomplished the task.

And once again, my heartfelt thanks.

Iell

She'd signed it with a bold hand: *Iell.* I brought the card to my nose and inhaled. Had she been in the Arboretum and heard me chattering away to the birds like a simpleton?

My fingers trembled as I spread Iell's note flat in front of me on the table and read it over again. She wanted me to go to the Chinaman's tomorrow? Impossible. I would have to sneak out without Mrs. Barnum discovering it, and clearly she had a spy in the house. Someone had told her about my previous trip—I fully suspected Emma, though it could have been anyone. We all depended upon the Barnums' favor for our livelihood. Nothing less than invisibility would let me sneak out and back undetected. And Iell was boarding uptown. How would I find the time to deliver the Chinaman's package to her?

I brushed a hand over the pocket where the Chinaman's root lay hidden and felt a surge of strength. Why did I allow Mrs. Barnum to frighten me so? She herself had called me clever. Surely I was clever enough to help Iell without being discovered. And so what if Mrs. Barnum *did* find me out? If I was discovered, I could tell Mrs. Barnum that her husband put me up to the task. Lord knows I wouldn't be souring a good marriage. It was common knowledge that the Barnums already mistrusted each other. Pitting husband against wife would be an excellent diversion, should I need to create one. Iell had asked for my help. It simply wouldn't do to go back on my promise.

At the sound of the opening bells, I rallied and put away the broom, but before I made my way to the Green Room, a sudden urge to relieve my bladder drove me up the stairs and out onto a side balcony rarely used by guests. Streamers flapped limply from the railings, the morning's mugginess suppressing any hint of breeze. I headed for the public urinal built behind a protective four-foot wall, an innovation installed last year to prevent men from relieving themselves onto the unsuspecting walkers down below. I slipped inside and, holding my fingers to my nostrils against the stench, did my best to think of cool hillsides and mountain streams.

As I exited, I spotted Barnum standing at the far end of the balcony, overlooking Ann Street. I stopped in my tracks. It was never a good sign when Barnum showed up unannounced, but in all probability he had no idea I was there, and his appearance was nothing but happenstance.

Barnum turned and beckoned me forward. "Exactly the man I had hoped to see."

His face was pinched. Something was definitely awry. I crossed the balcony toward him and followed his gaze over the balcony wall. Down in the street, a couple argued violently. The woman yelled out an obscenity at the top of her lungs and the man hollered something equally as profane, his arms rising in frantic accompaniment.

"Look at them." Barnum stabbed his chin toward the couple. "Ever fight with a woman like that?"

"No, sir, of course not."

"You've been a bachelor a long time, haven't you, Fortuno?"

"Yes, sir." Though taller than Barnum by half a foot, I found myself hunching so as not to overshadow him. He still hadn't looked at me.

"Ever consider marriage, then?"

"No, sir." Rubbing my hands together did not stop them from shaking, so I interlaced my fingers and squeezed. Whatever was he driving at?

"Despite how it sometimes appears, marriage is a fine institution. Keeps a man strong. It's loneliness that makes a man weak, Fortuno. Makes him susceptible to temptation."

I looked slant-eyed at Barnum's profile. Had he seen Iell's note? I reached into my pocket and fingered the end of the card. No, no. Impossible. I'd just seen the note myself.

"I know my wife spoke with you at Brady's," he said, without turning.

"Your wife?" My breath caught in my throat.

"Come now. You don't think you're my only cohort, do you? She took you aside at the photography studio and spoke to you privately, and from my experience that means trouble." Barnum's shoulders sank unnaturally down into the bulk of his barrel chest. He looked exhausted.

"Your wife strongly encouraged me not to help you in any way," I blurted out, wondering who had told him of the meeting. "In fact, I'm happy you brought this up, sir, because your wife—she's quite formidable. She suggested that I would have to share my rooms if I helped you."

"Helped me do what?" Barnum moved away from the balcony's edge and stood along the weather-stained wall. The sun washed out his features, and for a moment he looked buried in dust.

"Mrs. Barnum knew you'd sent me to the Chinaman's and seemed quite determined that I not go again."

Barnum kicked the wall. Hard. Alarmed, I jumped away. Barnum pulled out a handkerchief and ran it over the side of his neck where a trickle of sweat had rolled. Don't say it, I begged him silently. But sure enough, he said exactly what I didn't want to hear.

"Perhaps the trips into the city weren't the best idea. Let's not repeat them, all right? How about you simply come to my office when I'm elsewhere. You could drop me a little note at the end of each week and let me know what Mrs. Adams is doing. You wouldn't mind doing that, would you?"

I stifled the urge to groan aloud. "Not at all, sir," I said.

Barnum's eyebrows lifted like foxtails. "And as far as my wife goes, you are not helping me in any way, are you?"

"No. Of course not."

Barnum took hold of my shoulder and stopped me when I tried to move away. "Let me speak frankly with you, Fortuno. You work for *me*, no one else. I found you and brought you here, so your only allegiance is to me. If you don't understand that, you might end up— well, let's just say in a place not as pleasant as our Museum. Is that clear?"

"Perfectly."

"Also, you are not to assist Mrs. Adams, not even contact her, unless I instruct you to do so. We need utmost discretion while my wife is here." Barnum rubbed his hands together decisively. "So then, what can I do for you to show my appreciation?"

"Do for me, sir?"

"Your help has been invaluable, and I'd like to show my thanks."

I swear I didn't mean to say what I said next. Maybe it was a reaction against the fact that now both Barnums had expressly forbidden me to go to the Chinaman's. Or maybe it was the root I'd swallowed that morning. But out came the words. "My mattress is so thin that I find my sleep quite painful at times."

Barnum smiled. "Is that so? Well, as long as you remember who your boss is, Fortuno, painful sleep will be a worry of the past."

✳ ✳ ✳

I HAD the devil of a time falling asleep that night. As if my request had angered the gods, my old mattress felt even harder than usual and I tossed about on it for hours, worrying. Now that aiding Iell would be an act of disloyalty to both Barnums, surely she would understand if I wrote her a note begging out. But I'd promised her, hadn't I? And a man is only as good as his word. But again, she wouldn't ask me to do something that would threaten my well-being.

Back and forward I went until finally, to help me sleep, I pictured the delicacy of bird feathers and recalled the sounds of their songs. But I'd no sooner slipped into oblivion than Fish's voice tore through my dreams.

"Up, up, up, up, up!"

I shot out of bed, wide awake. Fish was in the resident hall, yelling and banging a gong. The air smelled like smoke.

"Fire!" I cried. "Oh, my God, fire!" As I threw on a jacket and ran down the hall, my first thought was for Matina, but she was already on her way down the service stairs, Emma and Alley on either side, giving her a hand, Bridgett looking surprisingly calm. The rest of the floor residents, in various states of dress, staggered across the hall and down the stairs.

Ducking back into my rooms, I grabbed my mother's comforter, Iell's note, and the root and took off down the stairs after them. Cries from a few of the caged animals stopped me at the entrance to the third floor. How many of them could I free, I wondered, before I threatened my own well-being? And the birds. What about my birds?

Thankfully, there was very little smoke rolling up the stairs. The animals seemed riled more by the bells of the approaching Fourth Brigade than by any real danger. By the time I made it to the courtyard gardens and huddled with the rest of the shivering staff, the peril seemed to have passed.

A handful of ruffians from the Fourth Brigade soon burst through the Ann Street entrance—long hoses and axes flying every which way—and charged through the door leading to the first-floor exhibit rooms. Nothing happened for at least a quarter of an hour, and then out they tramped, carrying two blackened pails of charred rags, sodden now with water but still sending off smoke.

Even though the fire was small, Barnum went berserk. He kept us in the garden until well past sunrise, tramping up and down the stairs with the chief of the Fourth Brigade, hollering out questions a mile a minute as the fire chief stole wide-eyed looks at the lot of us. At one point, Alley fetched a chair for Matina, and the two of them stayed near the dining room door, talking quietly. In the old days, I'd have gone over to them, but now I hesitated. What if they were talking about that kiss of mine? Maybe Alley had spied on me? No, that was ridiculous. I'd told Matina about my first trip, but that was all she knew. And why ever would Alley care what errands I ran?

Around seven, two policemen showed up and joined Barnum, Fish, and the fire chief. They gathered near the pails, poking through them for any final clue they might provide. Then the police lined everyone up. In front were the Curiosities, behind us the theater talent, then the staff, the stagehands, the chambermaids, and even Cook—all forced to stand in line like common criminals. Barnum waited along the side, fiddling endlessly with his watch fob as the police questioned first one and then another of us. "Where were you in the last hours? Do you have any complaints against the Museum? Have you ever been to jail?"

When they got to Alley, they lingered. Alley answered their questions with his usual truculence, and when asked to show his hands, opened his palms upward as passively as everyone else, but the younger of the two cops, broad across the shoulders and bowlegged, didn't seem to like his answers.

"What's that black stuff under your nails? And who says you was asleep?" The bowlegged cop poked his nightstick in the middle of

Alley's chest. "How are we supposed to believe a chap as nasty-lookin' as you?"

Alley shrugged. The cop thwacked him so hard on the side of his leg with his nightstick that he staggered back and grimaced. Matina cried out, "Hey!" and even Emma stepped forward to complain.

"That will be enough of that!" Barnum bounded over to the two cops. "What do you think you're doing? These are my employees. You're not to harm any of them."

"We've dealt with this one before, sir," the pockmarked cop explained patiently. "We know what we're doin'."

"That will be quite sufficient, thank you."

The officers grumbled but complied; after taking a number of notes they conferred one last time with the fire chief, and Fish led them out.

After all of the outsiders had gone, Barnum addressed us.

"I am not a happy man," he said sternly. "Fire is our biggest threat, you all know that." He ran a shaky hand through his hair. "How many theaters have been lost to fire in this town? The National, Sans Souci, Tripler's Hall. I still weep over what got destroyed at the Crystal Palace; that venerable establishment only took half an hour to go up in smoke. Think about that."

The expression on the stricken faces around me said we *were* thinking about that. Every one of us knew how quickly flames could grow out of control. And anything could set them off: gunpowder, gas lamps, pipes, foot lamps catching curtains on fire, wooden stairs like tinder. I looked over at Alley. Little was as frightening as a match in the hand of an arsonist with a bone to pick.

"Clearly, the fire last night was no accident." Barnum indicated the pails with his chin. "I have my enemies. Any manner of skullduggery is possible."

Fish came scuttling in and whispered something in Barnum's ear. They glanced briefly over at Alley, and Barnum shook his head no before again addressing the group.

"I will consider what is to be done in terms of protection, and

Mr. Fish will report back to you shortly. For what it's worth, I think the arsonist is someone from outside, not one of you. But—and I cannot emphasize this strongly enough—if one of you *is* responsible, Lord help you if I find out."

A quick look at Alley revealed nothing. I certainly hoped Barnum was right about the threat being external, because clearly he was in no mood for mercy.

chapter fifteen

T HE NEXT EVENING, THE MOON WAS ON THE rise, a good omen for my third trip to the Chinaman's. Also, talk of the fire had worked in my favor. Everyone was preoccupied with the previous night's events, making it easier for me to slip away undetected. Still, I took great care with my preparations. I'd decided to make the trip after the Museum closed, which would allow me to claim I was on my way to McNealy's, should anybody ask. I'd wear the padded disguise I'd made to get into Iell's show. It would help me navigate the city streets without drawing too much attention.

In order to discourage evening visitors, I'd pinned a note on the door to my room: *Do not disturb—I've taken a sleeping potion and will see you on the morrow.* And just before leaving, I swallowed not one sliver of root but two. Almost immediately, a surge of well-being helped vanquish any fear I had had of discovery.

Timing my exit to the closing bells, I slipped out into the hallway in my disguise, skittered down the public stairs and through the crowds, and left by the front doors. A gypsy carriage stopped in front of the Museum without my even having to flag it. Excellent.

In I hopped. It felt marvelous to be free and outside. The evening lamps flew by, and whatever foreboding I'd had slipped away like a dream. By the time I reached Broadway and Spring Street, my blood ran so hot, I rapped on the roof for the driver to stop. I was burning up inside and simply had to get out into the open air. After scribbling down the Chinaman's address, I handed it to him along with a silver dollar—a ransom for a man like that.

"I'm going to walk the rest of the way. If you wait for me at this address, I'm good for another dollar."

The cabbie tipped his hat and took off, leaving me alone in the street.

The first thing I did was look about for anyone I knew. No fleeting shadows, no mysterious persons ducking into alleys. As long as I kept my padded coat closed and bowed my head when people passed, I made my way along quite nicely. My distaste for leaving the Museum was fading with every trip. In fact, it felt so good to be in the bigger world, I actually whistled as I passed Wood's Minstrel Hall, where Brooker and Clayton's Georgia Minstrels had performed the previous year. Maybe after I picked up Iell's package and delivered it to her, I'd invite her to go to the theater with me. Perhaps I could wear my padded suit. And if I took Iell with me, she could wear her veil. We both had a choice, didn't we? This thought sat well with me, and I made a mental note to say as much to her when next we met.

A small group of gentlemen came up behind me, smoking cigars and chatting idly. I straightened my mustache and pretended to be part of their group as they crossed Broadway. On the other side of the street, the St. Nicholas Hotel loomed up, dwarfing the nearby Haughwout Building and the Prescott House. Saloon pianos and jig bands threw music out of the rows of brothels over on Greene Street. This side of Broadway thrummed with life.

A man in front of the St. Nicholas stopped us. He wore a uniform, a faux military jacket and trousers sporting a gold stripe along the outside of the leg. "You gentlemen all right then?" the doorman asked, his eyes sliding past me to the middle-aged man to my right.

"Looking for a bit of company is all." The man winked, pulled out a watch from his vest pocket, and snapped it open. "Or is it too early for such pastimes?"

The hotel man waggled his finger. "Sorry, sir, but you ain't gonna locate such company anywheres near the St. Nicholas." He was probably one of those "cleaners" hired by the finer establishments to keep their immediate vicinity clear of ladies of the night. He grinned, revealing a missing tooth, and snapped a card from his pocket. "Although, if you want to go to an establishment and walk out with your wallet still on your person, this here is good for a free drink at Harry Hill's up on Houston." I reached out to take the card, but the doorman passed me by and handed it to the gentleman next to me. That was fine with me. I'd almost been accepted as one of them, and I admit to enjoying it for as long as it had lasted.

As I left the group behind and neared the Chinaman's shop, I pulled out the root and considered swallowing one more sliver but changed my mind, realizing I'd become increasingly dependent on the rush of energy I felt when I sampled it. The Chinaman's gift had undeniably improved my well-being. But the root was getting smaller; I would have to ask the Chinaman for more.

Pell Street set me back a step. In front of the Chinaman's shop milled a crowd of Orientals. All were dressed in gold or black and the street was filled with pinwheels and roaring gongs. It looked like some kind of festival. What a mess to push through. Thank God I saw my carriage at the far end of the block, the driver sitting patiently in his seat. At least I wouldn't have to worry about making my way home when I was done.

I pushed through the door of the shop without knocking. A little bell above my head, newly installed, announced my arrival. No one was in sight. As I waited, I peeled off the fake mustache and wig, placing them on the counter next to a bouquet of gold and silver flowers. Next to it sat a sand bowl full of burning joss sticks.

The hiss of the water kettle on a stove in the corner brought the Chinaman hustling through the curtain. He wore a yellow gown with stripes of black along the sides, and he waved at me to wait as he poured water into a teapot tucked into a basket for insulation. I could hear the scurrying of feet behind the curtain, and the sound of clicking doors, and for the first time I wondered whether the building might also function as a boardinghouse. I'd heard such places often held more than thirty beds in each small room, built in tiers like a ship.

"Is late," the Chinaman admonished me. "Have party."

"I do apologize. But time is of the essence." I pulled out my wallet and slipped a number of bills into his hand, not at all sure what the price might be.

"Late," the Chinaman said again, tapping two spatula-shaped fingers on the counter.

I added another bill. Seemingly satisfied, he disappeared, tossing a package onto the counter when he returned.

"One other thing," I said, reddening. "That root you gave me. Do you think I could possibly get another? I'd be glad to pay, of course, as long as the price isn't too dear."

The Chinaman slanted forward and flung my jacket open, glaring at my chest.

"No different?" he asked, obviously disappointed.

"Much improved," I said. "No aches. No pains."

"No different." The Chinaman crunched up his forehead. It took a moment, but then he smiled, his hollow cheeks caving in where teeth should have been. "Ah. Before you swallow. Must chew. Chew many, many times." He demonstrated, his jaw moving up and down, his Adam's apple dropping as he swallowed. Then he came round the counter and pressed his hand to my ribs, pushing me toward the door. "Makes different. Different thing."

I made a grab for my disguise on the counter as he shoved me into the street. In a blink, I found myself outside in a sea of revelers. The screeching of their instruments overwhelmed me as I plunged forward, and it took nearly ten minutes to work my way to the carriage. The driver was holding the door open, a stricken look on his face.

During the ride home, I felt a stab of anxiety that the Chinaman hadn't given me more root. But he had aroused my curiosity. Chew the root, he'd said. Chew it many times. Why not? I pulled the root out and bit off the smallest sliver, grinding it between my back teeth. The revolting taste all but numbed my tongue, and I could only chew a few times before I swallowed. Almost immediately, I felt that familiar surge of potency, but nothing else happened.

I left the carriage up on Broadway and stuffed my wig and mustache into my hat as I made my way down Ann Street. If anyone saw me now, I would say I'd been out for an evening constitutional. I ducked quickly through the Ann Street entrance. Who knew who might be watching from a darkened window or half-opened door? Even with the strength of the root in me, my heart thumped low and hard.

Fortunately, no one seemed to be about. Once I made it to the kitchens, I breathed a bit easier. The bitterness of the root still filled my mouth, so I went in search of something salty to take away the tang. I could not remember the last time I'd eaten anything outside of an obligatory meal, but I picked up a piece of dried beef and chewed until my mouth felt fresh again, thinking that tomorrow I would leave Iell a note letting her know I'd accomplished my task and suggesting she find another carrier for the next trip.

When I pushed open the door to my rooms, Matina sputtered awake on my divan.

"What in the world are you doing here?" I asked, quickly hiding the hat with the wig in it behind my back.

Matina forced herself up, her shawl draping provocatively off one shoulder.

I had to blink. She looked wonderful. Good enough to eat.

"I let myself in to drop off some tea, but when I saw you weren't here I decided to wait. I hope that's all right."

"It's the middle of the night, you know."

Matina gave me a quizzical look. "Is it? My goodness. I must have fallen asleep." She frowned. "Help me up, would you? My back is bothering me."

I peeled off my jacket before she could notice its extra padding, and dropped my hat onto the table behind me. Making certain that there were no other signs of my disguise, I went to her.

Matina's warm fingers felt marvelous against my arm. She balanced herself against me without applying much weight. "You can lean a bit more on me if you need to," I said. "I'm not as frail as you think."

"No one ever said you were frail, Barthy. Of course you aren't."

Matina let go of my arm as soon as she stood. "But you scare me, lately, you really do." As she crossed her arms over her ample chest and gave me an irritated pout, I saw a touch of her old sweetness underneath her expression. Her face glowed. Soft. Appealing.

"I fully expected to find you here, asleep, and then I find you gone again. I used to know you so well, but you've become quite capricious of late."

I couldn't take my eyes off her.

"Why are you staring at me like that?"

"Have you done something to yourself? You look so beautiful tonight, you really do."

"Maybe worry is good for a girl's looks," she said.

"I'm sorry you worried. I really am. I couldn't sleep so I took a quick walk."

"A walk? At this hour?"

It was a pitiful lie, and Matina knew it. But rather than press me for the truth, she glanced over at my parlor windows, which were opened to the night sky. "Would you mind terribly if I took a bit of air?"

As Matina walked to the windows, I watched her skirts move across her uncorseted hips. Her weight had not changed. Nor her hair. But something about her attitude was different.

My suspicion was confirmed a moment later when she reached the open window. For as long as I'd known her, Matina had wanted to lean out of my window to look at the view, but despite hundreds of assurances that the frame would hold, she'd never done it. But out went her head, then her shoulders, and the next thing I knew, she'd thrown her full weight against the mantel, her entire upper body outside beneath the stars. Whatever had gotten into her?

"It's lovely out here," Matina called. "And you were right, Barthy, I *can* see the harbor if I try. Though I am a bit chilly. Would you be a dear and bring me my cape?"

I gathered up her cape and took it to her, draping it across her shoulders. Something had definitely shifted between us. The old Matina would have given me a piece of her mind and been gone by now.

"The fire last night," she said, coming back in long enough for me to place the cape oh-so carefully across her shoulders. "What do you make of it? The police were just terrible to poor Alley, don't you think!"

"That's what comes of being built like Alley," I said. "Why don't you come sit on the sofa, my dear? You're making me nervous leaning out the window like that."

"You've been telling me for years not to worry! I think I'll stay here awhile and enjoy the evening skyline."

I rearranged her cape, my hands lingering on her shoulders. Her skin was warm and smelled of lavender soap.

"I've been thinking about my mother a lot lately," I whispered, offering Matina the kind of intimacy I knew she craved. "About how she used to smile at me when I got a lesson right. Or at my father, if he did something unexpectedly kind."

Matina retreated from me slightly, tilting out the window once again. "Your father was not a kind man?"

"No, but he had his moments. I remember watching him make saddle wax behind one of the barns," I whispered in her ear. When she didn't object, I tilted into the back of her, ever so slightly. "He plunked me on top of a hay bale and went about tossing horses' hooves and shin bones into a caldron of liquid, stirring it with a stick, scaring me silly when the fire spit up and over the pot sides." I ran my hands down the outside of Matina's arms.

"And?"

"When he was finished, he scooped a few cups of the oil into a tin pan and added handfuls of rose petals, stirring the potion until he could work it with his fingers into a cream. He spooned the cream into a little yellow jar, and later, when my mother rubbed the cream into her elbows and hands, she gave my father that same smile that you just gave me."

"They loved each other, your parents?"

"Love? No, I'm not sure I could say that. But when he wanted to, he could please her, and that should count for something."

"Well, I should think so. Yes."

My arms encircled Matina's back, and I rested my chin on her shoulder. Together, we looked out across the New York sky. I pulled Matina close. She stiffened and pushed off my embrace, then turned around to face me.

"What are you doing, Barthy?"

"I can't seem to help touching you tonight," I told her, and it was true. Her skin, her hair, the tilt of her chin, everything about her was so seductive. Rather than tell me what a fool I was, Matina left the window and moved into the parlor. I fully expected some show of anger, even tears, but again she surprised me, turning and walking into the bedroom.

"Matina?" I followed her into the other room. When I reached her, she held a finger to my lips to keep me silent, studying me carefully, as if searching for an open door or a way around a problem. She unfastened her cape, letting it fall to the floor. My heart thumped madly, and when Matina's fingers pried open the top button of her dress, then the next, my body ached with desire.

I hung back, a motionless idiot, as Matina's dress slipped around her feet in a puddle of silk. Her gauzy undergown barely hid her body, a continent covered in fog. When she let down her hair, it spread wildly behind her. She showed no flirtatiousness—no embarrassment or shame. She simply stepped out of her undergown and stood in front of me in her white chemise. I had no idea what to do until she took my hand and led me to the bed, where she stretched out, passively, and waited for me to act.

"It's all right, Barthy. Just this once. It's what we both want."

Was this what I really wanted? I wasn't certain, but I knew for sure that whatever happened next, it would change us more than that single kiss ever had. Most likely, it would be the end of our friendship, but I simply could not resist. I moved my hands gently along her body, kissing her behind her ears, stroking her soft arms. With shaking fingers, I undid the buttons at the bottom of her chemise. Matina stopped me.

"Wait," she said. "That mirror."

I moved my hands away from her, not understanding.

"Cover up the mirror."

By the time I'd thrown my comforter over the mirror and returned to the bed, Matina had closed her eyes and spread her limbs in acceptance. I was utterly beside myself at the sight of her, so flushed, so bountiful. The room filled with the scent of lavender mixed strangely with something else, a mushroom smell. As Matina breathed, her breasts lifted and fell as if the earth had come alive.

Matina proved hungry for the feel of my hands on her skin. She groaned softly as I peeled down her stockings and ran my finger along the insides of her ankles, lingering on the soft under part of her knees. When I brushed aside the edge of her chemise and pressed into her, she accepted my passion openly. Halfway through the act, she sat up, pulling me into the mass of her fulsome bosom.

"Let's stay here for a while," she said later, when I started to get up. She rolled onto her back so as not to crush me, and I drifted to sleep on top of her. I found myself dreaming of great oak trees and woodland paths where I kicked dried leaves and covered my eyes against an autumnal sun. But soon the dream twisted. Clouds gathered and blacked out the light. Knowing something terrible was coming, I started to run.

"Barthy?" Martina's voice called to me.

I flew awake, heart thundering, and the first thing I thought was that she'd discovered Iell's package in the pocket of my coat.

Ringlets of her blond hair were plastered across her cheek like little question marks. "You were dreaming. It's all right, now. Hush." She covered us both with a bedsheet, and I clung to her for a moment.

"I'm sorry," I said, embarrassed by my weakness.

"Don't be silly."

Matina stroked my cheek to silence me and rolled over to sleep, leaving me to toss and turn on a sliver of mattress. I stared at a water mark on my ceiling, the heat from Matina's body a guilty respite from the cold night air. I could not believe what had happened. Had I initiated such an act? Had she somehow seduced me? It took me until nearly dawn to make the connection to the root I'd chewed earlier. What else could have driven me to such a wild, thoughtless act? When the Chinaman said it would awaken my *true* self, he must have meant this: my animal self.

I got up and padded into the parlor, looking for my coat. Listening for the sound of Matina's even breathing, I reached in the pocket and pulled out the root. I walked to the opened window and swung back my arm with the intention of throwing the root out into the street. Only when I saw that a crow had roosted on my window for the night did I allow my arm to drop back to my side. Grumbling, I tossed the root into the drawer with Iell's package, hid my costume beneath the sofa, and went back to bed.

In the morning, I woke teetering on the edge of the mattress, full of shame and remorse. Matina lay on her side, still asleep. Careful not to disturb her, I pulled open my bed jacket to survey my ribs in the morning light. My body was unscathed, but for a few fingerprints and a darkening patch on one shoulder where she had unwittingly thumped me. I didn't hold Matina responsible. Even a normal woman might have damaged me, given a moderate amount of exuberance and an urge to please. Anyway, I deserved a beating. I'd compromised a woman for whom I felt not love but the greatest admiration. And rather than take responsibility for my actions, I'd blamed them on a piece of root. I was a fool. What would become of our friendship? How could we carry on from here?

The parlor was awash with sunlight and didn't even resemble the same room from the night before. I dragged the chamber pot to the front door and pushed it into the hall with my foot, then brought in the water pitcher left by the morning maids. I had a sudden frightening thought. Would Matina want me to marry her? But no, she'd said we would join together only the one time.

"Good morning." Matina stood in my bedroom door buttoning her undergown. "How are you feeling?" she asked.

All I could do was stare.

"Cat got your tongue?" Matina gave me a sweet smile, which sent a wave of shame flushing through me. "Well, come along then." She nodded, and I followed her dutifully into the bedroom, where I stood mute as she pulled her petticoats up off the floor. "It's late and I have to hurry." She struggled into her dress, and I fumbled as I closed her buttons. Without looking at me, she stepped away and bundled up her corset and stockings.

"No need to go so soon," I said, forcing myself to speak. She'd opened the bedroom shutters halfway, and the early sun at her back haloed her great body in gold.

"If I don't get to my own rooms before the maids do, who knows what they'll say," she said lightly. "Can you imagine the gossip Emma would spread if she found I hadn't slept in my bed?" Matina uncovered the mirror and stood in front of it, twisting herself this way and that. Clucking her tongue, she patted down an errant ruffle and pulled her stomach in tight. "You look absolutely peaked this morning, Barthy. I don't want you to fret over this. Last night was a wonderful gift for both of us, and not something I will easily forget."

"Lovely," I stammered.

"But sometimes," she went on, trying to hide her disappointment at my response, "gifts turn bad. I don't want that to happen with us, so let's leave everything be. Don't you agree that would be best?"

Even though I so much wanted to say something kind, something true, I couldn't bring myself to tell her I loved her.

Matina waited until it was obvious that I was not going to respond.

"Well, then. I guess that's agreement enough. We shall continue as we always have. You will, I hope, take me to church service on Sunday as usual?"

"Of course, my dear, of course."

I bent to kiss Matina's hand and caught a quick flash of myself in the mirror. Who in heaven's name was that person staring back at me?

✳ ✳ ✳

THE MOMENT the door closed behind Matina, I let out a huge breath, ran to my étagère, and yanked open the drawer. Where had I hidden that root last night? Groping, I shoved aside Iell's package and reached for the bag with the root in it. I had to rid myself of the damned thing and do it now. Throw it into the chamber pot, that's what I'd do. Like to see someone save it from that. But at the last moment, I hesitated. Who knew what would become of it if I tossed it aside. What if someone fished the thing out and reported what they'd found to Barnum? Better, I decided, to keep the thing with me until I could dispose of it properly. In the meantime, it would serve as a reminder of my shameful loss of control.

The bag with the root in it stayed in my pocket the entire day. In the evening, after feeding the birds, I set it on the café table in the Arboretum and relived my night with Matina one more time. Gritting my teeth, I took the root to the rock garden and used my bare hands to dig a hole at the base of the jojoba tree. I buried it, bag and all, piling dirt over the thing, and then covering it for good measure with a brick, a handful of gravel and a large speckled rock. Never, never would I lose control like that again!

chapter sixteen

NTIMACY CHANGES EVERYTHING. EVEN A MAN with as little experience as I have knows this. Friendship takes forever to build and can collapse in a moment. My heart sank when Matina walked into the Green Room later that morning wearing a red dress and a frozen smile. Although she joined me at the Notice Board as Fish posted the weekly notices, she faced into the room, away from me. There was a wedge between us now. We were a thousand miles apart.

Fish pounded his cane on the Green Room floor to get the attention of the performers, most still in partial makeup or half dressed for the stage. I tried desperately to focus, but all I could think was, What kind of fool have I been to believe Matina's assurances that everything will be all right?

"Mr. Barnum has asked me to speak to you about the recent fire," Fish said. "As you know, this blaze was set in the public hallway outside the kitchens, and management is quite concerned."

Matina coughed, and I moved closer to her.

Fish cleared his throat. "Precautions must be taken. First, no one will smoke in the public rooms." A groan went up, and Fish held up his hand. "This restriction applies to nighttime only. If you wish to smoke during the day, that's fine, but please dispose of smoking materials with extra caution.

"Second, pails of water have been placed under every staircase and empty corner in this Museum. Heaven forbid the need should arise again, but if you discover a fire, douse away as you call for help.

"Finally, we plan to install a fire gong in the service stairway. If you see anything suspicious or smell smoke, bang the hell out of it."

Alley walked in during questions and, surprisingly, sat down next to Bridgett. Matina scowled.

"Will you excuse me, Barthy?" Matina patted my arm.

"Are you all right?" I asked, though what I really wanted to know was whether we—together—were all right.

"There's something I must discuss with Alley." As Matina pushed across the room, I wrapped my arms across my chest and tried to squeeze myself back together.

"Now, on quite another note," Fish continued, pointing to the weekly schedule. "This Wednesday, Mr. Barnum has planned a Day of Remembrance for those fallen in the war."

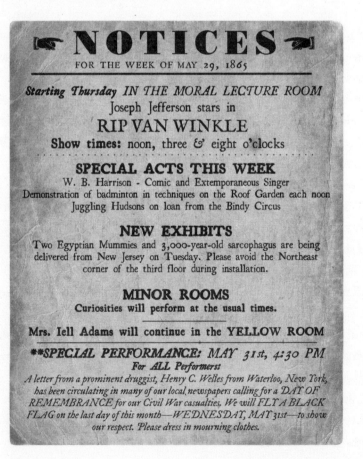

≈ NOTICES ≈

FOR THE WEEK OF MAY 29, 1865

Starting Thursday IN THE MORAL LECTURE ROOM
Joseph Jefferson stars in
RIP VAN WINKLE
Show times: noon, three & eight o'clocks

SPECIAL ACTS THIS WEEK
W. B. Harrison - Comic and Extemporaneous Singer
Demonstration of badminton in techniques on the Roof Garden each noon
Juggling Hudsons on loan from the Bindy Circus

NEW EXHIBITS
Two Egyptian Mummies and 3,000-year-old sarcophagus are being
delivered from New Jersey on Tuesday. Please avoid the Northeast
corner of the third floor during installation.

MINOR ROOMS
Curiosities will perform at the usual times.

Mrs. Iell Adams will continue in the YELLOW ROOM

**SPECIAL PERFORMANCE: MAY 31st, 4:30 PM
For ALL Performers:
*A letter from a prominent druggist, Henry C. Welles from Waterloo, New York,
has been circulating in many of our local newspapers calling for a DAY OF
REMEMBRANCE for our Civil War casualties. We will FLY A BLACK
FLAG on the last day of this month—WEDNESDAY, MAY 31st—to show
our respect. Please dress in mourning clothes.*

"On Wednesday, at four o'clock," Fish instructed, stuffing a newly penned script into each person's hand, "you will find special costumes in the Green Room. Since the set for the Van Winkle play is going up in the Lecture Room, you're to dress and report directly to the first-floor exhibit hall at fifteen minutes past. Is that understood? We're using a temporary stage and will be doing a Civil War reenactment, Mr. Barnum's gift to the veterans of this fine land of ours."

Everyone leafed through the script, and hands shot up with questions and complaints, but I was too distracted to pay the answers much mind. For the first time, my colleagues seemed like potential enemies. Emma and Ricardo stared at me from the other side of the room. They probably knew about my recent visit to the Chinaman and were plotting about how to use the information. Matina was whispering to Alley about God only knew what, and I prayed it had nothing to do with our night together. Did anyone suspect what had happened last night? I blushed with shame to see that even Zippy's nurse looked over at me disapprovingly. Undoubtedly, everyone already suspected I'd had a liaison with Matina. One look at her expression and their suspicions would be confirmed. I thought of Iell's package in the bottom drawer of my étagère. How was I ever going to slip away with everyone watching me?

The moment Fish had his back turned I yanked my costume off its hook. I had to get out of there, even if it meant passing Matina and Alley to get out the door. I decided to buck up. Why not take Matina at her word that everything would go on as it always had? I tipped my hat jauntily to the two of them and kept my scowl hidden until I reached the anonymity of the hall.

✳ ✳ ✳

FOR THE next two days, I put aside my worries as best I could. No one called me to account for my whereabouts, and no itinerant actor showed up at my door with suitcase in hand. Iell's package lay tucked away in my rooms. I'd heard nothing from her about delivery, so I put that worry out of my mind for the moment.

The problem was Matina. She continued acting strangely, clearly straining for normalcy every time she saw me. We sat in our shared tableau and chatted about nothing, but for three days in a row she came to her meals a half hour late. I made a concerted effort to stay out of her way, eating early and leaving before she arrived, and I waited in my performance room for my shows to begin instead of in the Green Room. But on the afternoon of Barnum's Memorial show, we found ourselves thrown together again. The Curiosities were all jammed uncomfortably behind a strung-up curtain at the north end of the exhibit hall, a makeshift stage designated by magenta cords. Everyone wore renditions of war outfits. Mine was a ragged Yankee uniform reeking of someone else's sweat. Only Matina, whose flag-inspired gown was already the bill of the day, got to wear her normal costume.

Because Matina was standing, I dragged over a chair and offered her a seat with a gallant wave of the hand, which she accepted with a chilly nod. "No special costume for you then?" I said.

"Fish seems to like my costume fine the way it is. Thank you for the chair." I could see her struggle to find something more to say.

"Would you like to join me for tea this evening?" I asked.

Matina shook her head no, but despite her lukewarm response, something in the slope of her shoulders gave me hope that she would soon forgive me. Knowing better than to press further, I kept my peace and moved toward Fish, who was busy inspecting the performers, tucking in a gray shirttail here, a bit of red pantaloon there. After getting the nod for my costume, I moved to the wall to wait for my entrance and nearly tripped over Ricardo, who was crouching in the shadows.

"Good God, man, you nearly knocked me down."

Ricardo, dressed only in his long johns, popped up and eyed me suspiciously, his expression uncharacteristically contented. Cupped in his hand was a scrawny calico kitten.

"Look what I just found!" Ricardo pinched the animal gently on the scruff of its neck and gave it a loving shake. "A cat. A little baby cat."

From out front, I could hear the applause. "You better get dressed before Fish sees you," I said.

"I was comin' through the garden, and there it was, all by itself. Ain't it the cutest?"

"Ricardo!" Fish yelled from a few feet away. "Where is your costume? Get moving, lad. We haven't got all day." As Fish bore down on us, Ricardo threw him a salute with one hand and reached around me with the other, slipping the kitten into the pocket of my uniform. If I hadn't seen that fleeting look on his face—what a shock to discover the boy in Ricardo, and a sweet lad at that—I would not have allowed it, but I slid my hand into my pocket and stilled the tiny mews until sounds of the growing audience made Fish move on.

Ricardo snatched the kitten from my pocket and started looking about for another hiding place. "I'm going to call it Poke," he said over his shoulder.

I motioned toward a small discarded costume basket. When Ricardo smiled at me as if we were now friends, I put him right.

"Don't think I won't tell Fish you have a cat if he asks. We have house rules for a reason, you know."

But Ricardo kept the smile on his face, placing the kitten ever so gently in the basket. "There's something changed about you lately, Fortuno. Maybe you ain't so bad."

The "enactment" turned out to be such a cheap event that even Thaddeus Brown seemed embarrassed by the drivel he had to recite. The crowd was rowdy, and many had brought their own food. We opened with the Juggling Hudsons in spangled tunics, hurling dozens of flags, Confederate and Union, up into the air while a band of pipers toodled out songs in accompaniment. Then Thaddeus dribbled out a tale of the "splitting" of the North and the South, while Ricardo, performing in body tights painted like a Confederate uniform on one side and a Yankee uniform on the other, stretched himself across the stage. Then we moved on to a sad little scene with Emma that Thaddeus called Saving the Innocent. I stood in the wings watching Emma lumber out dressed like a Southern damsel, her horsy voice booming out over Alley's head, "Ah'm really a Yankee. Don't hurt little ol' me. Save me!" as Alley pretended to try to untie the ropes that bound her.

In the middle of this travesty, Ricardo, who stood in the wings opposite me, began gesticulating wildly toward Emma. When Emma looked his way, he held up a pocket watch, pointing at it with an elastic finger, but Emma clearly did not understand. She shrugged her shoulders, causing the rope that tied her to fall down around her hips, much to the delight of the audience and the chagrin of poor Alley.

Ricardo called out across the stage, abandoning all discretion, "You was busy, so she came to me and changed the time. Told me to tell you." He passed his hands down his front, miming a very long beard. "In the Lecture Room. Half an hour."

Soon enough it was my turn to perform. All I had to do was walk across the makeshift stage two or three times, Bridgett dressed as a nurse trailing behind me, as Thaddeus nattered on about how the war had depleted us all. Missing the strength that the root might have given me, I foisted my sword up at great cost to the muscles in my arms and made some feeble stabs in the air, all the time keeping an eye on Emma, who had waded into the crowd. An irritated Fish grabbed her by the arm before she got very far and marched her back behind the curtain with the rest of the performers.

Once finished, I waited patiently for my own chance to escape. It came when Barnum entered from the other end of the exhibit room dressed as Lincoln. All eyes turned toward him as he made a great show of himself. Despite my costume and the sweat that covered my forehead, no one seemed to notice anything untoward as I walked the other way, determined to reach the Moral Lecture Room before Emma did. It occurred to me that I might even have time to run upstairs and get Iell's package, saving me the dangerous trip outside, but I needed to be sure I spoke with her first.

A breeze hit me as I pushed through the bank of doors into the Lecture Room. No sign of Iell or anyone else. At least I hadn't missed her, I told myself, as I hurried down the aisle toward the pastoral set of *Rip Van Winkle*, with its oversized crags and bluffs and stunted paper trees, a woodsman's "cottage" and a wooden bell tower off to the side. The orchestra pit in front of the stage was already full of instruments awaiting the play's musicians.

When I climbed the side stairs and mounted the stage—one of the few times I'd ever been on the stage of such a grand theater—the cavernous space opened up in front of me. I sat down on a bench in front of the cottage and rested my elbows on my knees, gazing out across the empty seats and the balconies. What would it be like to perform in a real theater such as this? Did I have the presence to command such a stage? Would my voice carry? Would my message?

The house doors opened. Iell! I popped to my feet as she walked down the aisle, but she threw up one hand and frantically waved me away. I didn't understand until the theater door at the rear of the house opened again, and I caught a glimpse of Emma's bonnet. Quickly, I slipped behind the wooden tower, managing to make it to the wings before Emma entered. The last thing I wanted was anyone else to see me talking with Iell. Especially Emma, who would surely report back to Mrs. Barnum.

The heavy wing curtain was ripe and discolored from years of stage smoke, and I gagged as I folded myself behind it, finding relief only when I stuck out my head far enough to see Iell make a beeline for the stairs.

"No, dearie, stay where you are," Emma hollered. Still dressed as a Southern belle, she lumbered up the stairs onto the stage and greeted Iell with a kiss on the cheek. Their footsteps echoed through the empty house as Emma led Iell past the cottage and the fake trees and stopped right in front of where I was hiding, as if hitting a mark onstage.

"Come," Iell said, looking as put out as I'd ever seen her. "Let's go down into the house. We can sit in the front row and chat."

Was she trying to move the conversation out of my hearing range or trying to protect me? Quiet as a cat, I shifted the wing curtain until I could see their profiles.

"Right here is fine." Emma reached out and gently touched Iell's beard. "All I want to say is that you don't need him. You know you don't. The Lord giveth, my dearest, and there are other ways to get what you want."

Him who, Barnum? She couldn't possibly mean me. I had to step slightly forward if I had any hope of hearing Iell's response, and the stage floor creaked. Emma glanced back. Had she seen me? I held my breath, and Emma turned back toward Iell, who was now facing away from the slumping giantess.

"I think it's the best way, I really do," Iell said, looking out into the empty house.

Emma grabbed hold of the back of Iell's dress between two fingers the size of billy clubs and gave it a tug. Surprisingly compliant, Iell turned around and faced her. My chest expanded with secondary pleasure. Oh, to be that near to Iell! To touch her dress!

"But you know I can help you, my sweet. Why not let me?" Emma pulled Iell closer, a heartsick girl clinging to the waist of her beloved, and I swelled with pride at the thought of the Chinaman's package waiting in my rooms. It was I who was helping Iell, not Emma.

"I find it hard to believe that you want to help me without any expectation." Iell looked up at the giantess. "Do you?"

"I only want to be with you. Hold your hand, maybe a kiss or two. That wouldn't be so bad, would it? And I know you, dearie. I really know you. You've no secrets from me. I love every single part of you, however strange. That should count for something, don't you think?"

I felt a touch of pity for the woman. I knew what it was like to long for Iell's company. But why did Emma think Iell would be interested in her? I'd heard of women who preferred their own gender; it was not outside my experience. But Emma should have known that anyone who wielded as much power over men as Iell did could not possibly be interested in another woman.

"I'm sorry," Iell said.

Emma took a step backward, her expression inscrutable. "All right then," she said, "but you'd be better off with me as ally than as enemy. You should know you can't rely on Barnum's good favor."

With perfect show-business timing, Ricardo flung open one of the house doors and barged in.

"A Barnum is coming down the hall!" he shouted down the long aisle. "You'd best be off." In his arms, he held the basket. I could imagine a faint mewing from within it.

Emma took in a lungful of air, moved down the stage stairs, and all but ran for the back doors. When she reached Ricardo, she took a swipe at the basket, but he stretched it out away from her and took off at a run. The theater doors swung open and shut, and they were both gone.

"Mr. Fortuno?" Iell called. "Are you still back there? You'd best leave as quickly as you can!"

I clambered out from behind the curtains with as much dignity as I could muster, nearly stepping into a bucket of water in the wings— part of Fish's new fire prevention protocol. My rib cage knocked about as if it held a flapping bird inside, and I willed my nerves steady. I knew I should leave, but there was no sign of Barnum yet. I rearranged my sword and patted down my hair.

"What can I do to ensure that Emma won't bother you again?"

"It's fine, Mr. Fortuno. Really. A dispute between friends, nothing more." Iell glanced toward the theater doors, then took hold of my arm. "Really, you should go." God, she was lovely!

"I wanted to tell you that I have your package. I didn't dare leave a note," I stammered as her fingers slid away. "But I shan't be able to go and fetch for you again."

Iell tilted her chin. "That's all right. Would it be a terrible imposition for you to bring the package to my boardinghouse some day next week? I am staying at Mrs. Beeton's uptown."

Exactly what I didn't want to hear, but who could refuse such a woman? "No imposition at all, though I'd prefer to go out after the Museum has closed, if that is all right."

"Ten o'clock, then. Let us say Wednesday. Someone will be there to let you in." An unidentifiable bang made us both jump. "Now go," Iell said, and rewrapped her scarf around her head, tucking in a stray strand of hair with the end of one finger.

"My hat," I said. "I forgot my hat!" I dashed into the wings to retrieve it, and thank goodness, because I never would have made it out of the theater without being seen. The door swooshed open just as I reached the wings, and I dove back behind the curtain, knowing what a disaster it would be if Barnum found Iell and me together. What a shock to hear *Mrs.* Barnum's voice wafting down the aisle.

"Mrs. Adams. We meet again."

My heart hammered into my throat. No matter how bad the consequences of Barnum's discovering me there, if his wife found me she'd dismiss me on the spot. I took no chances and did not so much as poke my head out from behind that curtain, despite the fact that I couldn't hear a bit of what the two women discussed. I waited until their muffled voices faded completely before venturing out. My hands shook like a crone's.

When I was absolutely certain that the theater was empty, I tore down the aisle, fretting that I might not make it to the doors before someone returned and discovered me. I didn't relax until I slipped into the evening crowd, welcoming their stares as proof that I was still a Curiosity and still worthy of my billing.

Before returning to the Green Room, I slipped into Barnum's office and hastily penned him a note to cover myself.

To report, I wrote with a shaky hand, *I briefly witnessed Mrs. Adams speaking with Emma Swan in the Lecture Room after the Memorial show, but I did not approach or speak to either lady. No other sightings to date.* I set the note on his chair and scurried out of there.

chapter seventeen

EDNESDAY TOOK FOREVER TO ARRIVE, and once it did, I found myself in a terrible state. I kept my mood in check, but after dinner I sat on my haunches in the gravel garden of the Arboretum café and considered digging up the root. My impending visit with Iell coupled with the ever-present fear of discovery sent shakes through my entire body. I simply had to pull myself together. The root would give me energy and courage, but how could I dare use it if I could not control its effects?

"What should I do, my friends?" I asked the sleeping birds. I'd come to rely on the birds more and more. Not that I expected real counsel, but they were a gentle presence, and when I needed to express myself out loud, they'd become my substitute friends. Of course, there was not so much as a squeak in answer to my question.

Moving aside the speckled rock I'd used to mark where I buried the root, I brushed away the gravel underneath until I saw the top of the bag. Think how strong you'd feel if you swallowed even one little sliver, I thought. The bag came out effortlessly. Dirt and gravel covered the outside; I shook it clean and then held it by its strings and let it dangle in front of me. My mouth watered. Oh, but I couldn't. Not after what happened with Matina. The trip to Iell's boardinghouse might be easier with a bit of root in me, but what would happen when Iell and I stood face-to-face, the two of us alone in her room? If I couldn't control myself with Matina, I'd no chance with a woman like Iell. No, it wasn't a good idea at all.

I dropped the bag back into the hole, brushing the dirt from my knees. One sideswipe from my foot set the loose gravel tumbling into the hole, filling it in seconds. It took only a few well-placed steps to pack down the gravel with the sole of my shoe and replace the rock. Done.

In no time at all, I'd be dressed and making my way uptown. I refused to let unfounded fear break my resolve. My reward would be seeing Iell.

✱ ✱ ✱

Hours later, in full disguise, I slipped into the public rooms just before the Museum's closing bell rang. It was easy enough to blend in during the rush at the end of the day, though I ran the danger of bumbling into one of my colleagues, who would no doubt recognize me despite the wig and mustache. If Alley had been with me, I could claim that we were on our way to McNealy's, but I hadn't trusted him enough to bring him into my confidence. For the first time, I began to see how isolated my predicament was making me.

I managed to work my way out the front door and onto Broadway without incident. When it was clear that no one had followed me, I hopped a trolley and headed uptown toward Iell's boardinghouse. I'd stuck her package in my coat pocket along with the white scarf. I felt quite passable in my padded jacket until a woman on the trolley dropped a quarter into my lap, saying, "Get something good to eat, sir," and it wasn't until I jumped off the trolley and started walking toward Mrs. Beeton's that my uneasiness began to pass. Nevertheless, I all but ran the last few blocks.

By the time I reached the boardinghouse, I was out of breath. This part of town was rather shabby—it had long ago lost its old stylishness and most of the houses were now residences for single gentlemen or show-business types—but Mrs. Beeton's still retained an understated elegance. The house was set a few yards back from the street, delineated by a perfect white fence, and even in the dark I could see its handsome redbrick façade. Its gardens were abloom with lilies and azaleas, and the walks on both sides of the house were lined with small saplings. In front, a discreet metal sign read: MRS. BEETON'S BOARDING HOUSE FOR WOMEN AND YOUNG GIRLS.

I peeled off my mustache and wig, stuffing them in my hat, and ran a hand though my hair. I didn't belong in such a fancy place. Now I wished I hadn't come, but I forced myself to open the gate. A woman whom I could only assume was the matron of the house stood in the front door, light from inside leaking out onto the darkened walk. She beckoned me in and left me standing there.

I examined the entryway with its inlaid tiles, windows draped in scarlet, and walls a swirl of hand-painted grapevines with purple leaves. Potted palms blocked off a small sitting room, and I heard the distant murmurings of women. It took an eternity for the matron to return and wave me forward, and I followed her silently, up a stairway, curving my fingers over the carved wood handrail.

The matron opened the door to the second floor and nodded toward the end of the hall. How I wanted to run away! This was even more nerve-racking than facing Mrs. Barnum. Beneath my feet, the rug was so thick that my heels sank an inch into the pile, and by the time I got to the end of the hall, my neck had gone sweaty with the effort of walking.

But there it was: a carved white door, a silver handle, the number seven in gold-plated metal in front of me. I adjusted my gloves and tapped lightly on the wood with the end of my cane.

Iell flung open the door and greeted me as if I'd just arrived for tea.

"Ah. Mr. Fortuno. How nice to see you again." She smiled deliciously and gestured me into a sitting parlor.

My head went empty of everything but light and air. Had my nose begun to bleed? I dabbed at it with my kerchief: nothing, just nerves. In I went. Trailing behind her, I breathed in the rose perfume that wafted back to me. When Iell stopped, I stopped, and because I didn't want to stare directly at her, I glanced about the room in front of me: a sitting parlor with a sea-green velvet divan, a visitor's chair, an ebony chest embellished with carved crests and medallions, and, on the far wall, a large English cupboard, sturdy as a giant. The room had three closed doors and a single window, outside of which silver willow trees sparkled in the moonlight. Matina would have gone green with envy.

Iell took my gloves and walking stick and placed them on a table in the hall, but I set my hat on the table myself so as not to expose the hairpieces inside it. I debated whether or not to remove my padded coat.

"It was so kind of you to make this trip for me," Iell said, as she led me across the bloodred rug into the parlor. Silently, I squeezed between the divan and the tea table in front of it. Iell cut a dramatic figure as she stood against the brocade drapery, her beard curled slightly at the ends, her dress some kind of oriental sarong. No hoopskirts for her, at least, not in private.

"Brandy, Mr. Fortuno?" Iell turned to a sideboard carved with gargoyles and demons.

"Thank you, but don't feel obliged. I'm happy enough to deliver your package and bid you good night."

It took every ounce of my strength not to stare at Iell as she poured brandy into a pair of small Prussian glasses and moved toward me, the two glasses chinking together on a copper tray. What was it about the woman that intrigued me so? It wasn't just the beard, it was so much else. She made me feel as if I were empty and full at the same time. Hungry and satiated. When she bent forward to place the drink in front of me, I could just make out the curve of her breasts beneath her silk bodice. The only other time I had been this close to her was the morning in Brady's studio. Thank God I hadn't eaten some of the root this time. I couldn't risk a strong response in such close proximity.

Flustered, I fumbled in my pocket and pulled out the package from the Chinaman, placing it on the table in front of us. I crossed my arms over my chest and waited. Iell said nothing. She simply gazed at me, amused, her eyes slightly hooded, then took a seat.

"You must think me improper for entertaining at this hour," she said.

"Not at all," I said, wishing she would acknowledge the package.

"Then let's enjoy our drinks. I don't see why we can't mix our business with a little bit of pleasure, do you?"

She coiled one ankle around the other, balancing her weight on the tip of one toe on the floor, and we chatted. We spoke of the weather, and of the problems with the New York streets. She confessed to reading the *New York Enquirer* twice a week, and when I told her about how I'd spent years under the tutelage of my mother conjugating Latin verbs or reading Wordsworth and Coleridge, her face lit up.

"Ah, a literary man! I remember that about you."

"May I tell you a secret?"

Iell interlaced her fingers and leaned forward. "Mr. Fortuno, I adore secrets."

"I never told my mother this, but my personal taste in novels ran more toward Hugo's *Hunchback of Notre Dame* and Mary Shelley's *Frankenstein*. She would have disinherited me had she known."

Iell laughed at this, and I started to relax a bit.

"Tell me, where were you raised?" she asked me. "Who were your people?"

The brandy had warmed my stomach. I sank back against the divan. "My father was French," I said. "He trained horses for a certain Major Holmes, who ran a stable in Virginia, one of the best in the state. My mother was employed as a governess there. The three of us lived in a cottage on the grounds and got on quite well."

"You spent your days with your mother?"

"My mother and I were very close."

"And did your father share your taste for literature?" With every question, Iell moved forward a bit in her seat, like a slowly advancing soldier. "Did he approve of you?" she challenged.

I ran a finger beneath the edge of my collar and shifted on the divan, glad to still be wearing the padded suit. What good could come from admitting to her that I'd been a terrible disappointment to my father? That he wished I'd been someone or something else. One of my first memories of him was when I was three, maybe four years old, and my mother had left me in his care—a rare event. I was giddy with excitement as she straightened the brass buttons on my black velvet jacket and tugged at the waist of my short pants. She walked me to the barn and shoved my small hand into his calloused palm. "You watch this child," she said, and he nodded and hoisted me up, the wool of his shirt rough and dank with sweat and horsehair. He cradled me in his arms, and my heart absolutely sang as my mother waved to us and walked off. But the moment she was out of sight, he grunted and tossed me onto a hay bale at the far end of the barn. Leaving me there, he sauntered away to join his roughshod friends for a game of poker, the four of them paying no attention to my screams as they rolled their fat cigarettes.

Once, years later, he'd insisted I help him drag hay into the horses' stalls. Some groom had made a derogatory comment about my delicacy, and he decided to make sure I ended up a proper man.

"Just watch me, *mon fils*. This is all you have to do. It is nothing!" He hoisted up a hay bale and gave it a good toss into the first stall. "Just do it once. Prove to me you can do something practical in this world. Then you can go and play beneath your mother's skirts if you want." Filled with the drive of a young boy wanting to please his father, I watched him intently as he hefted a bale into the back of the next stall, setting the horse to rear up and claw the air. Then, gritting my teeth in determination, I grabbed hold of a bale and strained mightily against its weight, the rope cutting into my fingers and the ends of the hay digging into my palms. I dragged that bale a quarter of the way to the cracked and manure-stained stall before my arms started shaking, but no matter how I tried, I could move it no farther. A wave of anger tore through me. I ripped into the bale, grabbing up handfuls of hay and throwing them wildly about. I can still hear my father laughing.

"Must we talk about such dull things?" I asked Iell. "You haven't examined the package I brought. Don't you want to make sure it's the right thing? Or we could talk about Emma if you like."

Iell stood abruptly, so I rose to my feet. The comment about Emma must have struck a nerve. But my hostess motioned me to sit back down and then stood behind her chair, resting her elbows on the backrest, tilting forward like a man.

"Answer my question, Mr. Fortuno. Did your father approve of you?"

Iell was nothing if not direct. Should I refuse to say more? Lord knows, she hadn't answered *my* questions. I found myself speaking in spite of myself.

"My father was a man of action. I think he would have preferred a son with a stronger constitution."

Iell nodded, then moved off to the window, brushing aside the curtain with the tips of her fingers. Stars filled the sky.

"Thankfully, my change didn't come until after my father died," I said, wanting to keep her attention. "Who can say what he might have made of the man I am now."

Iell let the curtain fall in place and faced me. "What do you *think* he would have thought?"

I sighed. "I think he would have hated me."

Iell struck the palms of her hands together in punctuation. "And your mother? Did she understand you when you changed?"

"She was no longer quite herself by then."

Iell moved again to the back of her chair, and from that safe position she looked me over more carefully, searching my face for information.

"What do you mean?"

"My mother spent her last years in the Eastern State Hospital."

Iell's turquoise eyes sharpened. "An asylum?"

"Public Hospital for Persons of Insane and Disordered Minds." I couldn't understand why I'd told Iell this, but once I'd said it, it was as if that long-closed door inside of me opened up a crack.

"What had she done?"

I pointed a finger to my temple. "She got lost." From somewhere in the street, a crash resounded, the collision of a cart or a wagon perhaps. We sat in silence for a moment. "Afterward," I went on, "the State sent me to live with my Uncle Frederick. Everyone seemed to think, because he was blood, he would be the best caretaker for me, but after a few years, he sold me to a circus."

"The State," Iell scoffed, walking around the chair and sitting once more, "is not known for its wisdom."

She did not press me to continue. Instead, she stretched her legs out in front of her, lost in some memory of her own. Good, I thought. Her attention is on something else. I touched a stem of bluebells in the vase, the peppery smell of the brandy mixing with the flowers' scent, and tried to rid myself of unpleasant thoughts. I concentrated on the laces of Iell's black shoes. Her feet were quite small. When she reached over and lifted the brandy canister to ask if I wanted more, I shook my head no.

Pouring herself a snifter full, Iell set the canister down, ran her fingers lightly across the Chinaman's package, and stared at me again with that same directness.

"Could I ask you one more personal question? Then I promise to stop prying." She dipped her little finger into the brandy, then put it in her mouth.

"Of course."

"Please do not take this the wrong way, but what does it feel like to be as thin as you are? Do you feel substantial?"

I recoiled. "Of course I feel substantial." Even as I said this, all I could see were my skinny thighs against the brocade of the divan. I did not appreciate Iell encouraging me to reveal myself, and then insinuating . . . Well, I wasn't certain what she was insinuating, but I did not like it.

"Ah, I've embarrassed you. I apologize. I've been told I can be too frank at times." Iell reached across the tea table and laid her hand across my wrist, the same way she had that afternoon on the stage. "It's only that so much about you fascinates me, Mr. Fortuno. For example, your choice of companion. What is your lady friend's name?"

"Do you mean Matina?"

Iell squeezed my wrist ever so slightly. "You have a relationship with her, yes? Perhaps you crave her company because she makes you feel whole."

"That's between Matina and me."

"There's also the fact that you came to see my show disguised as a regular man."

Red-faced, I pulled away my wrist. "An entirely different matter, I assure you."

"And even now you sit in front of me padded and hidden."

"Please, madam. Enough!" In an effort to stop her questions, I reached into my pocket and yanked out her scarf, holding it in the air. "Surely you can't think your veil is any less of a subterfuge than my padding?"

Iell reached out and took the scarf from me, letting it trail across the little table and over the still unacknowledged package. "Where in the world did you find this?" She laid the scarf around her shoulders like a shawl and did not seem the least bit disturbed over my sudden show of temper.

"I found it in the Arboretum a while ago," I said, already sorry for my outburst.

At this point I was all turned around. Iell had exposed me, flattered me, embarrassed me, and somehow insinuated a failing of character on my part. In my confused state, I barely heard the tapping. First muffled, then louder. Someone was at her door. Iell remained calm, but she grabbed my hand and pulled me around the table into the center of the room.

"This night is full of surprises. Forgive me, Mr. Fortuno, but if you don't mind, I need you to come with me." Dragging me by the hand, she led me to the large English cupboard at the far end of the parlor. I understood that she meant me to climb in and hide.

"Why?" I asked.

"Because this visitor won't be as pleased as I was to see you," she said, a cheerless smile on her face.

I squeezed myself into the cupboard as she flew across the room to grab my hat, gloves, and walking stick. Returning to the cupboard, she tossed me my things. She did not even look at me as she clicked the doors closed.

Humiliated, I sat girdled between long silvery gowns and wraps made from beaver and mink, their odors mixed with oak bark and hemlock. This visit was not going at all as I'd expected. I listened to muffled words through the door's slats and could not imagine who would be at her door, uninvited, at such an hour. By hunching down and twisting slightly, I could see the back of Iell's head. She stood in the entrance, one hand on the doorknob, the other dangling behind her like a small sleeping animal.

Her voice seemed to come from a great distance. "Good evening."

"Ah, you look enchanting." Barnum! Blood rushed into my head.

Though I could only see Iell's skirts at that point, I distinctly heard her say, "I'm not feeling well tonight, so forgive me if I'm unable to ask you in."

"Surely you can spare a moment for me."

My fists clenched at the sound of rustling cloth. The scoundrel had forced himself past Iell and stood now inside. I wiped a line of perspiration from my upper lip. Get out of this damned closet and stand up for the woman! But Barnum would have my hide. And if Iell had wanted me to protect her, she would not have stuffed me away. If only I'd dug up the root and brought it with me. . . . But I *had* brought the Chinaman's package for Iell with me. Where was it?

I jockeyed my position until I could just make out the tea table. The package sat right in the middle, next to the bluebells and our two purple glasses. Damn it. What should I do? Iell was still at her front door, but Barnum was stepping past her, his hair flying wildly about his head, his mouth frozen in an angry grin.

"You don't look the least bit sickly," Barnum said, staring openly at Iell's figure beneath her dress. I lifted my fist to pound out my frustration against the cupboard door. No good would come of my bursting out unnecessarily, but I readied myself to do so, just in case.

Iell shut the door behind him. "How ill-mannered of you to insist on coming in after I have told you I am feeling poorly." Barnum walked toward the parlor. Iell followed. Any moment now, he'd see the package. Barnum stopped abruptly.

"You've had a guest?"

The time had come. I took a breath, readying myself. But Iell had somehow gotten around Barnum and now shimmied onto the divan where I had been sitting. She pulled the scarf I'd returned to her off her shoulders and smiled brightly. What was she doing? Barnum hovered over the tea table, staring at her intently. Then I understood. She was controlling where Barnum was looking, and, with a flick of the wrist, she knocked the package off the table and onto the floor without his noticing.

"I demand to know who visited you," Barnum barked.

"I'm sure that's no business of yours, sir." One graceful readjustment of her skirt, and Iell covered the box.

"You should answer my question," he said.

"And you should control your curiosity." Iell wagged her finger at him like an exasperated mother. This seemed to please him mightily. I'd seen Barnum in a lecherous mood before, but Iell was a serious woman, not some acrobat bent on improving her condition by succumbing to her boss's baser requests. Clearly, she needed no protection at the moment, but I was horrified by his lack of decency.

"Are you at least going to offer me a drink?"

Iell stood, pushing the box beneath the divan with one foot as she said, "It's obvious that you've already had a drink or two this evening. This is why it was a mistake to let you in."

"Don't be like that, my dear. I came here for your charming company." Barnum's flattery clearly meant nothing to her. She was dismissing him. Barnum trailed behind her as she walked to the front door.

"Are you sure you want me to go? Because if I leave, I can't give you the little present I brought you."

Just before Iell reached the front door, she threw her white scarf around her neck, covering much of her beard. "You can give it to me or not, as you wish."

"Pity." Barnum burrowed into his pocket and pulled out a small brown box, most likely the same one I myself had fetched for him not so long ago. "Not only is your reliance upon this precious stuff growing, but no one but me can fetch it for you now. I've told Fortuno to stop going, and I'm quite certain he'll obey. Scared to death of me, that lad."

I blushed furiously. I wasn't afraid of him. I wasn't.

Iell stepped out of sight to open her apartment door, and I had to change positions to keep her in sight. "I don't know why you had him go in the first place," she said.

"Killed two birds with one stone. Saved me the trouble, and gave him a little punishment for his cheekiness."

Even alone in the dark closet, my mouth flew open. What an idiot I was. Of course, he'd been toying with me.

"You're a perverse man," Iell said. "You know that, don't you?"

Barnum towered over her. "You call me perverse?"

A silence. Then, "If you don't mind, it's late."

Barnum pressed the brown box into the palm of Iell's hand. "You really should reconsider, you know," he said heavily, his voice full of desire. "You've only two months left on that contract of yours, but if you do as I ask you can stay as long as you wish. Sit up on your high throne the way you like it. No one will ever know. And I could make you a very wealthy woman."

He was propositioning her. What a scoundrel. Had he no respect for any of us?

They disappeared through her door and out into the hallway, and I felt the closeness of the cupboard fold down on me again. My heart pounded in my chest as if resting from a chase, and my bones hurt. How dare Barnum call me a coward in front of Iell? Then, the click of the door closing, and the tap of Iell's heels on the floor.

Iell smiled as she opened the cupboard to me. Such an ambiguous smile. "So," Iell said. "You see."

I peeled myself out of the cupboard and grabbed my things, avoiding Iell's gaze. "It's not true, you know. I knew exactly what he was up to when he asked me to go to the Chinaman."

Iell took me by the shoulders. "He likes to exert himself. Nothing to be concerned about, I promise you. Are you all right?" She brushed dust from my shoulders and the front of my coat.

"He treats you shamefully. I trust that you have fended him off?"

"Fended him off?" That splendid mouth smiled, but I could take no meaning from it. Iell went to the divan and snaked her arm beneath it to reclaim the package I'd fetched for her. Her white scarf floated to the floor.

"It is not like that," she said. "The bond between myself and Mr. Barnum is—how can I say this?—sometimes uncomfortable, but it is not unsavory in the way you are suggesting."

"Let me help you. Surely there is nothing that a good friend can't make better."

"I'm sorry, but some things need to stay private. That's simply how it is."

What in the world could be so private she couldn't tell me? Feeling rebuffed, I stood and moved toward the front door, assuming she was merely trying to keep me at a distance.

"Wait! You needn't go." Iell waved me back to the divan on which she now sat in a grand manner, spine held straight, hands in lap. In front of her on the table were two identical packages.

"Come, let's finish our nice evening, Bartholomew. May I call you that?"

I inched down into the chair, unsure but charmed by the sound of my given name coming from her lips.

Iell retrieved the scarf, laying it across her lap. "I hope you won't take Barnum's comments about you to heart."

"Let me be clear, madam. I am *not* afraid of Barnum." My palms went sweaty. I couldn't even think of telling Iell that it was *Mrs.* Barnum who really put the fear of God in me.

"Of course you're not afraid. And he'd never have to know if you decided to go to the Chinaman for me again."

I shook my head. "It's not that I don't want to help you." Another trip would be insanity, though part of me thought there was no better way to avenge myself against Barnum than to aid the lovely Iell.

"I could go myself, of course," Iell said, paying no mind to my resistance, "but it's not the safest neighborhood. It wouldn't do for me to show myself in full daylight. And there's no one else I'd rather confide in." She lay back on the divan, lifting her arms up in a languid stretch. "You're the only one I trust."

I teetered on the very edge of my chair. "Trust should flow two ways, don't you think?"

"Absolutely." Iell's gaze held no challenge, but no intimacy either.

"At the very least, I'd like to know what I've been fetching."

Iell looked at me pensively, then smoothed down her skirts. "All right, Bartholomew. I owe you that much."

She rose and walked into another room, returning with a scarlet pouch in her hand. Resettling herself on the divan, she untied the drawstrings on the pouch and pulled out a long bone pipe, its bowl blackened from use, its mouthpiece marred by little nicks and indentations. Teeth marks. Setting the pipe on her lap, she opened one of the boxes on the table and removed a wad of some gummy black substance. She rolled it about in the palm of one hand, forming it into a small ball. After positioning the substance in the bowl of the pipe, she lit it with a match pulled from the tall silver holder sitting on the floor next to her, drawing the smoke deep into her lungs, holding it for an exquisite second, and then gently exhaling. The tension in her thin shoulders melted away.

"I have heard that smoking too much opium is not good for a person," I said.

"You've tried it?"

"No. Of course not."

Iell held the burning pipe in the palm of her hand. The smoke curled upward like tentacles.

I'd never smoked opium, but I knew all about it. We'd had a knife thrower years ago who'd used it to the point of total dissipation. Barnum eventually had to remove him from the Museum; he found employment for a while as a rat killer, then disappeared in Five Points. Iell's eyes took on the same quality as the knife thrower's, and I remembered that morning in Brady's—how Iell hadn't seemed to know where she was, how she'd appeared drained and transported. I chided myself for not recognizing her habit then.

"You should not judge me." Iell closed her eyes and sank onto the divan again, her lovely face partially obscured by the smoke. "My life has not been easy."

For a moment, I thought she'd fallen asleep. Then she spoke again.

"I was fifteen when my beard began to grow," she said softly, her eyes closed. "My mother was a woman of decent breeding, but she was burdened with an overblown opinion of her social position. Appearances meant everything to her, and she found my condition very upsetting. So, despite evidence to the contrary, she insisted my hair growth was nothing but a passing confusion of adolescence that would disappear once I made the transition into womanhood. She stole a straight razor from my father and taught me how to scrape the whiskers carefully from my face. This worked for a while. I even fell in love and was married for a short time."

"Of course," I said. I was beginning to understand her previous obsession with whether I'd had a choice in who I was. Perhaps it had been *she* who had made the choice to show herself rather than blend.

Iell shifted her position and slowly opened eyes as blue as a robin's egg. The pipe burned slowly on the table next to her, but she did not reach for it. Her hands lay in her lap. "He was an amazing boy, Bartholomew. Not unlike you, in fact. Handsome, long-legged, kind. We married in the heat of love. He understood and accepted me, every bit of me, but he died, unfortunately. Fell from a wagon and broke his neck. Only twenty years old."

"I am so sorry." Handsome like me, she'd said. I felt for her loss, of course I did, but it was a struggle not to smile at the generosity of the comparison.

"After that, I decided it was futile to hide my real self, though I do not always reveal everything. A girl should have her secrets." She winked at me mischievously and pulled herself out of her chair. "Wait. I have something I'd like to show you. I'll be right back."

It was impossible to take my eyes off her as she walked away, but once she left, I realized I'd been holding my breath. I could hear her rummage about in another room, and it only took the sight of her unhurried gait as she returned to set my nerves off once again. She carried a paper yellowed from age.

"You might find this interesting." Iell settled onto the divan and spread a small watercolor on the table between us. It was unframed, the paper rolling and a bit discolored from age. She had to struggle to get it to lie flat. Once she did, she looked over at me in satisfaction. It was a drawing of a three-domed building set on a hill surrounded by well-tended grounds, and I could tell that the building had once been quite elegant. But a restraining fence at the bottom of the painting gave the viewer the sense that the place would soon be swallowed up.

"It's the old McLean asylum," she explained, childlike and proud. "I painted it when I was young, and I've always been proud of it. Look there." She pointed to the lower left-hand corner. "They had recently built a train line nearby. It ruins the tranquillity of the countryside but also adds a sense of mystery and escape, don't you think? I thought I rendered the smoke quite admirably."

"You stayed in an asylum?" I asked, surprised.

"Like your own mother," she said, "I also became lost for a while. But that is a story for another time."

Iell took up the pipe again, and I stayed silent, watching her smoke. Now I saw how much she needed my protection and how villainous Barnum was to take advantage of such vulnerability. Their supposed bond surely had to do with Iell's weakness for opium.

"Barnum," I said. "Tell me exactly what he wants of you."

When Iell spoke again, her voice was heavy with the effects of the opium. "He knew I had an attachment to the drug and offered to supply me with what I needed as long as I promised to keep to my rooms and not let it interfere with my shows. But then he began asking for things in return."

"Does he wish to compromise you?"

Iell's eyes had taken on a remote quality, and when she looked at me she barely focused on my face.

"No, not at all. He just"—she hesitated in the most charming manner—"he knows things about me. It has more to do with sharing my secrets."

"Is that all?" I asked. "I don't see how that could be so damaging."

Iell turned her eyes from me—though from artifice or true embarrassment, I wasn't certain.

"What are we but our secrets, Bartholomew? You of all people should understand that."

I thought about the root. "And you are asking me to help you. Why?"

"Because I believe you will accept me for who I am and not try to use me."

Carefully, Iell stood, and I rose with her, understanding that our time together was over.

"I know that I have pressed you, Bartholomew. I would understand perfectly well if you'd rather not be involved. But please, do not answer me yet. Simply consider my request."

On my way out, she quoted Robert Browning: "Truth lies within ourselves: it takes no rise from outward things, whatever you may believe." And then, to my astonishment, she rose on her toes and kissed my cheek, her lips the softest things I'd ever felt, and slipped the scarf around my neck. "A remembrance," she whispered, her voice encircling me like the flutter of angels' wings.

✳ ✳ ✳

MY FEET must have taken me down the stairs and out into the streets, but I've no memory of making my way home. All I can recall is the sparkle of the New York night. It was the perfect reflection of how I felt. I did not regain my senses until I slid off the trolley at Broadway and Ann. I should have gotten off earlier to be safe, but even so, I almost missed my stop.

I ran into Emma as I cut through the kitchens toward the service stairs. She was sprawled over a small wooden chair, a candle and a cup of tea on the table in front of her, and before she could see what I wore, I slipped off my padded coat and folded it over my arm, hiding the hat that I'd carried home. Did she know I'd witnessed her humiliation on the big stage with Iell? Was she sitting in wait to even the score?

"What in heaven's name?" Emma stood when she saw me, and her expression slipped quickly into suspicion. "Not like you to be out and about, Fortuno, especially without Alley to watch over your skinny behind." The half-light of the kitchen lamps turned Emma's face into a parody of itself. Her forehead thrust out like an overhanging cliff, and her large feet spread on the stone floor like islands. My whole body went cold. She could not possibly know I'd been with Iell. I just had to act normal. Breathe easy. She'd be a poor enough spy if I gave her nothing to report.

"Felt like an evening out. There's nothing wrong with a beer at McNealy's alone, is there?"

Emma took a step toward me and stared straight into my eyes. "Lying lips are an abomination to the Lord," she said, and plucked Iell's scarf from my neck. I'd forgotten I wore it.

I snatched back the scarf. "I ask you to keep this to yourself, much as I will keep your little talk with Iell after the Memorial service to myself."

She raised an eyebrow. "How do you know about that?"

We stared at each other in silence until I muttered, "Forgive me, but it's late," and forced my way past her.

Emma nodded her great head and held two fingers to her lips, pretending to turn a lock. "You're lucky it was only me who found you out," Emma said. "Best be more careful. The Lord hates a liar, dearie. And a snitch."

I left Emma in the shadows and all but ran up the service stairs. When I made it to my rooms, I sprawled out across my bed, panting. I had seen Iell, and Emma knew it. If my meager attempt at blackmail did not work and she chose to tell Mrs. Barnum—or Matina—my career was over.

chapter eighteen

ITTING WITH ALLEY THE FOLLOWING WEEK AT the bar in McNealy's, I tried my best not to rush him. Utterly out of character, he'd approached me the previous afternoon, telling me he had to talk to me and could I meet him at McNealy's? Though there had been no repercussions from my visit with Iell, I worried that he might have learned something bad—Emma telling him that I had Iell's scarf, for example, or, on a different note, Matina confessing why my relationship with her had become so tense. I could barely sit still. But I waited patiently, as he sat on his stool and nursed an ale.

The havoc in the room filled up the mirror that hung behind the bar, and I watched the reflection of a man tattooed from head to foot as he took the seat next to me. He flung a small cage onto the bar. Inside was a hen with no beak. A black-and-white sign hanging by thin chains from the cage's rusty bars read: HEN WITH A HUMAN FACE (10¢). I grabbed hold of the bar rail—a long piece of oak carved to look like a serpent—and tilted toward Alley.

"Come on, man. Out with it already!" I shouted, over a chorus of "Old Bob Ridley" being sung in drunken harmony by a group of minstrel players from one of the Bowery shows. Scowling, Alley lifted one giant finger to tell me to wait and then another two fingers toward the barkeep, a wild-looking girl named Esmeralda. Then he wrangled a piece of paper from his dingy trousers and spread it out across the bar in front of us. An application: THE HOMESTEAD ACT, MAY 1862.

Underneath it, a clipping from the *Chillicothe Scioto Gazette* showed a large tract of land cut in half by a wide river.

Now that he'd presented the papers, Alley was a bit more talkative.

"Hundred and sixty acres, right next to the river, for two hundred dollars. Just have to fill this in and plant my shovel, and I can own it in five years."

"Where *is* this?"

"Ohio."

"Good Lord, man. Are you out of your mind?"

We sat in silence and looked over the paper. Esmeralda—whose eyebrows formed a solid ridge above her eyes—slung two more ales down in front of us. Alley downed his in one gulp, then held up one of the bar candles to shed more light on the announcement.

"What does Matina say?" I asked, looking over his shoulder at the clipping. "She'd be horribly upset if you left us."

"Don't know, Fortuno. She ain't been herself lately. In her room all the time. Is she sick or somethin'?"

A pang of guilt shot through my belly, then fear. What if I'd impregnated her? No, I needn't worry about that. I'd used great caution at the end. I glanced at Alley's reflection in the bar mirror, glad he didn't know about our tryst. And I wasn't quite ready to confess it to him.

"Frankly, I don't see why you'd want to do something as ridiculous as farming, and in Ohio no less," I told him, shifting the subject away from Matina. "The bugs alone will kill you."

"It's time for a change, is all."

I shoved my ale forward for him to drink. "Nowhere in the world beats the place we have with Barnum."

Alley took up my beer and downed it in one gulp. "What's so great about the Museum? I feel like a caged animal."

"Good evening, gentlemen," Bridgett said, stealing up behind us. Her eyes were still kohled dark as a Gypsy's. Even in the short time since she'd been performing, her girlish face had begun to change into something harder, more knowing, and her rouged lips were red as a wound.

Accompanying Bridgett was a most unsavory fellow dressed in tall leather boots, red flannel shirt, and a tasteless stovepipe hat. I couldn't believe Bridgett had had the effrontery to bring such riffraff into McNealy's. Most likely, he was one of the thugs hired by City Hall to keep the peace.

"Mr. Alley, my friend Alfred here says he'd like to speak to you." Bridgett spoke to the back of Alley's head and, though he flinched at the sound of her voice, Alley did not turn around and did not respond. Undaunted, Bridgett winked at me and went on. "Wants to hire you to do a little door-watching for him, like you did before. What do you think? Pays real good." She moved closer to Alley, her bracelets jingling like some voodoo instrument.

"Bridgett," I intervened, "this is neither the time nor place—"

Alley scraped back his bar stool and stood without a word. I was flabbergasted.

"Surely, you're not considering . . ." I said, but Alley nodded to her companion and, after gathering his papers and shoving them into his shirt, led the man to a nearby table.

Bridgett sighed and fluffed her hair as she slipped onto the stool Alley had left empty. "And I was so hoping he would ask me to join them." She squinted at her image in the mirror behind the bar and rearranged a hair clip that looked like a silver bird.

"Why would you do that, girl?"

"Rumor is, Alley needs money, so I'm trying to help him out." Her eyes followed Alley's movements as he shrugged his shoulders at something the thug had said. He nodded his head no, and then yes. "Maybe help myself out a little while I'm at it."

"Well, Alley shouldn't be encouraged to keep bad company. The police are already watching him."

Bridgett sighed and plunked an elbow against the bar, resting her chin in her hand. "He's so . . . big, isn't he? Tell me something personal about him," she said. "What does he like? Where does he spend his free time?"

"I think he's engaged to some gal in Indiana." A lie, but I hated to see the girl hook her heart to something she couldn't possibly have. And I meant it when I said Alley shouldn't keep bad company. The last thing he needed was more involvement with the Copperheads.

"Engaged." Bridgett sighed again, stretched her arm farther out on the bar, and rested her head along it. "Don't it figure."

Bridgett seemed genuinely stricken and, for a moment, when she looked up at me with the unsure face of the servant I used to know, I softened to the girl. Perhaps there were worse things than her striking up a romance with Alley. At the very least, it might keep him in New York.

"Maybe he isn't engaged," I offered. "In fact, honestly, I'm not at all certain that he is."

Bridgett's eyes shone as she sat up on the bar stool, the jangle of her bracelets setting off the chicken still in the cage on the bar.

"Now, ain't *that* good news. But I wanted to ask you a question. Would you consider giving me a bit of help with my show? Maybe you can watch me sometime. Tell me if I miss any marks. How I can stir folks up more." She moved closer and whispered in my ear. "Our kind has to stick together."

Our kind? Oh, the audacity! Was she really unable to grasp our differences? My momentary kinship with her disappeared. I swiveled to face the room, an empty glass of ale still in my hands.

"I'm sorry, my dear, but you will have to figure out your show the way all of us did."

A storm crossed Bridgett's face. Once she got it under control, she called for Esmeralda to bring her a glass of whiskey and then said, "Guess I see why Barnum's old lady is having your shows watched special."

I swiveled to face her. She was probably making things up, a petty attempt at revenge for my not helping her.

"Barnum's wife hired some man to come around to all the shows. Didn't you hear?"

The assessor Fish had mentioned. This was nothing new.

Esmeralda plunked down her whiskey. Bridgett made no move to pay for it. It wasn't until I put cash on the bar, and Esmeralda swooped it up, that Bridgett continued. "Mrs. Barnum told the man, when he sees your show, to write down everything you done wrong."

"When did you hear this?"

"A few days ago, not that it matters. If you ask me, you people really shouldn't take yourselves so seriously." She hopped off the stool with a flip of her skirt and made her way into the crowd. That's what I got for trusting a Gaff.

I never did get Alley's ear again. He didn't notice me waiting at the bar to go on with our conversation. Instead, he sat sprawled across two chairs, a great thigh on each. He'd gotten hold of *Leaves of Grass* by the bohemian Walt Whitman, and he held it to his nose, reading out loud from "A Song of Joys" to anyone who might listen:

> "To rise at peep of day and pass forth nimbly to work,
> To plough land in the fall for winter-sown crops,
> To plough land in the spring for maize,
> To train orchards, to graft the trees, to gather apples in the
>   fall."

I didn't know he could read like that.

✳ ✳ ✳

THE NEXT few days were uncharacteristically quiet. I heard nothing from Iell. No assessor showed up, and neither did the Barnums. Every night, Alley disappeared to do who knew what for the Copperheads, and Matina continued to vacillate between truculence and an awkward coquettishness. She was sweet enough during the morning tableau, happy to chat about idle events—concern over the fire; how surprisingly tender Ricardo was with that cat, which he now carried with him everywhere; and how, any day now, our photographs from Brady should be completed—but she avoided spending any real time with me. She no longer visited my rooms as she used to, and she refused an invitation to walk with me along the rooftop. She never once mentioned the night we had spent together. I hoped that if I continued to behave as usual, she would return to her old cheerful self.

And me? As the days passed, I'd started craving the root and thought constantly of how it lay buried under the rock in the Arboretum. The birds were a consolation—spending time with them had become a daily ritual of real joy—but, sadly, my mind wandered constantly to the root. Some ridiculous part of me had begun to believe that it held the key to my salvation. Not having it was becoming worse than the consequences it caused.

Then, during my last show on Sunday, Mrs. Barnum showed up with the assessor in tow. The man jotted down notes in a small book as he stood with Mrs. Barnum at the rear of my little showing room. The sight of them sent me into an absolute panic. I stumbled over several of my lines and nearly missed a cue, to the disgust of Thaddeus. But then I reminded myself that, unless Emma told her, Mrs. Barnum knew nothing of my recent activities, and I stood a little straighter, drawing in my stomach and enunciating every syllable. I even made a point of displaying the inside of both legs to show off my new tights. I was so confident I'd given a good showing that it came as quite a shock to find out the following morning that Fish had taken me off the performance schedule.

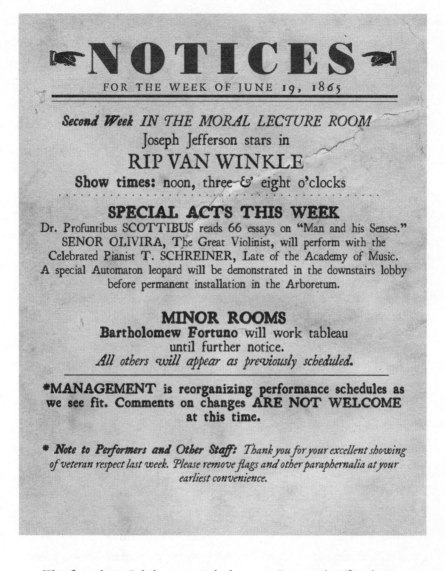

☞**NOTICES**☜

FOR THE WEEK OF JUNE 19, 1865

Second Week *IN THE MORAL LECTURE ROOM*
Joseph Jefferson stars in
RIP VAN WINKLE
Show times: noon, three & eight o'clocks

SPECIAL ACTS THIS WEEK
Dr. Profuntibus SCOTTIBUS reads 66 essays on "Man and his Senses."
SENOR OLIVIRA, The Great Violinist, will perform with the
Celebrated Pianist T. SCHREINER, Late of the Academy of Music.
A special Automaton leopard will be demonstrated in the downstairs lobby
before permanent installation in the Arboretum.

MINOR ROOMS
Bartholomew Fortuno will work tableau
until further notice.
All others will appear as previously scheduled.

***MANAGEMENT is reorganizing performance schedules as
we see fit. Comments on changes ARE NOT WELCOME
at this time.**

* *Note to Performers and Other Staff: Thank you for your excellent showing
of veteran respect last week. Please remove flags and other paraphernalia at your
earliest convenience.*

The first thing I did was march down to Barnum's office, but a sign
posted on his door said he was out for the day, which sent me sweating
into Fish's office a few doors down.

"I can't understand why management would *do* such a thing."

"Only following orders, Fortuno." Fish was on his feet and moving
a mile a minute, rearranging account books, gathering papers, and
making last-minute changes to lists posted on the walls.

"Whose orders? Why?"

Fish shot me a look over his shoulder. "You're still showing in tableau. Just bide your time and keep your nose clean, and all should be well."

No one said a thing to me at breakfast, though they'd surely seen the schedule change. Matina raised an inquiring eyebrow, but when I sat and silently sipped my tea, she let the matter be. Calmly, I accompanied her to the Exhibit Hall as instructed, and I was quite pleasant to the crowds.

I finished around eleven, and with little else to do, I hung about outside the Lecture Room, relishing the crowd's reactions to me. At least I still had the power to make them look. This raised my spirits for a while. But then I made the mistake of walking by my performance room. Thaddeus was nattering away inside, and I could hear the audience laughing at familiar cues. I knew Alley was breaking the rock on his head at that very instant, and Ricardo was limbering up in the wings. No one seemed to miss me at all.

I slipped off my coat to invite more attention from the crowd in the hall, but even the swoon of a young woman dressed in orange taffeta failed to bring me any lasting satisfaction. What had Alley said to me about desire? That he knew what he wanted but couldn't always get it? That same longing threatened to suffocate me now.

"Hey, freak! How much do you weigh?" A yokel came up the hallway behind me and poked me between the shoulder blades with his finger. "What do you eat, little chicken feet? And where did you get that fine hat?"

I sighed. Perhaps I should go fetch the root after all. I'd just passed the Yellow Room, heart thumping as it always did in Iell's vicinity, when I stopped in my tracks; Mathew Brady and Barnum were making their way up the main hall toward me. Barnum had draped one arm over Brady's shoulder, and he was gesticulating toward the exhibits as if Brady were a cherished Museum patron come for the first time to witness the splendor of the place. They cut a swath through the crowd as if they were parting the Red Sea. And under one of Brady's arms was a cloth portfolio. The photographs!

Pressing myself into the corner behind a mock thrashing machine, I watched them go into Barnum's office. After they closed the door, I crept forward and pressed my ear against it. Barnum's voice boomed from inside; there was no mistaking that laugh.

"Oh, these are excellent! They always are. But where . . ." I couldn't hear the rest of what he said, but I did hear parts of Brady's garbled answer: *wonderful, matter of time,* and *many interested parties.*

When Fish started his patter in front of the Yellow Room, I reluctantly moved away from the door. I knew the photographs were in Barnum's office, and I was dying to see them, but I'd clearly have to bide my time.

After what felt like an eternity, Brady and Barnum stepped into the hallway. They passed within inches of me, and only Brady acknowledged me, greeting me with a tip of his hat. I waited a good five minutes more before I ducked into Barnum's office, closing the door tight behind me.

The black portfolio sat on top of Barnum's desk. After I stuck my head into the hall one final time to make sure Barnum wasn't on his way, I moved a chair to the side of the desk and pulled the portfolio near. Heart pounding, I took hold of the cover. Then I had a sudden and paralyzing thought. What if Brady's camera had caught my physical indiscretion that morning? I'd be the laughingstock of the Museum.

I flipped open the portfolio cover. Inside, dozens of photographs were piled, one on top of the next. I thumbed through them as quickly as I could, praying that nothing in the images showed my compromised condition, and thank God, there was not a hint of it. In every single photograph, I stood enough behind Iell to hide my lower body. Thoroughly relieved, I laughed aloud.

Then I went back through the photographs again, more slowly this time, and with a considerable amount of pleasure. In the middle of each photograph sat the lovely Iell. Her regal face beamed out like a candle in a dark cave. Even on paper, her heavy-lidded eyes bewitched me. And her beard, exceptionally dark in the photographs, lay proud against the whiteness of her skin. Matina appeared quite content behind me, her sweet face smiling and serene. Hadn't she been upset?

I'd heard her cry, I knew I had. And afterward, there'd been no mistaking her distress. She must have masked her pain. I hadn't thought her capable of such deception.

I took a closer look at my own image in the photographs, surprised by how—I hated to use the word—insubstantial I appeared. My cheekbones looked almost ghoulish, and my body, carved by shadows, was little more than angles and planes. Even my hand on the rung of Iell's chair looked like a collection of brittle twigs serendipitously arranged to resemble a hand. Is this why Iell had asked me if I felt substantial? Could this be how others saw me? I thought back to the stunned faces during my show. Was it possible that their shock came not from the philosophical truths I laid bare but from something simpler and less noble?

I slammed the portfolio shut and loosened my tie. I had always been proud of my gift. I'd been chosen to show people the truth. So why did I suddenly doubt myself?

Then something else hit me. Brady had asked Iell to stay for solo photographs. Where were they? Flipping though the portfolio again, I couldn't find a single one of them.

"Are you looking for these, perhaps?"

My heart rammed into my throat. Matina stood in the doorway. In her hand, she held a second portfolio.

I struggled to keep my voice steady. "What are you doing here?"

Matina sank down on a chair by the door, its wood creaking from the burden of her weight. She let her fingers play blindly along the leather straps of the portfolio, teasing them until they dangled free, and then she quite purposely let the book slide from her grasp. It fell to the floor and burst open. Dozens of photographs flew across the green-and-red rug. My breath caught in my chest. They were the portraits of Iell.

"Oops. What a clumsy girl I am."

Without thinking, I fell to my knees and gathered the fallen images into a neat pile. In the first photograph, Iell posed regally on a daybed, her expression playful. My breath quickened.

"Where did you get these?"

"I am wicked to have them, I suppose." Matina tucked a loose strand of her hair behind her ears and looked above my head. "Our Mr. Brady left them inside one of the ticket booths unattended, can you imagine? But no harm done. I was just coming to return them."

Obviously, Matina had stolen the portfolio. I was flabbergasted, but I couldn't resist what lay before me. I remained on my knees and worked through the photographs slowly. Matina sat silent above me, her breathing low and heavy. At first I felt shame, crouching at the feet of my friend, knowing she was watching me, but I forgot her completely when I saw the next photograph—a likeness of Iell lying across a daybed, her eyes focusing on a strand of light passing above her head. Her face glowed, but she also looked undeniably available. I blushed to see it. In the next, she sat—no, slouched—in a manner so unbefitting a proper lady that I had to loosen my collar. She smiled with illicit intimacy; you could see the tip of her tongue protruding from between her perfect teeth. In another, more provocative still, she posed with her hands inches from her own breasts. At this point I'd gone well past blushing and was, frankly, in shock. But the one that most upset me was at the bottom of the pile, and I held my breath when I saw it. She had untied the laces of her dress so that the upper parts of her sleeves slipped halfway down her arms, revealing bare shoulders and amazing décolletage. She straddled the daybed like a man and had thrown back her head in utter abandon. Her hands were underneath her beard, lifting it up like an offering.

I forced myself to look up at Matina. "Has everyone seen these?"

"Some of us took a peek." Matina shrugged her shoulders, her flesh wavering, her look a mixture of supremacy and remorse. "Correct me if I am wrong, but I thought you might want to see them, too. In fact, Barthy, I think you *needed* to see them. You've already been pulled from the schedule, Lord knows why. Don't you think having as much knowledge as possible is a good plan? You have to protect yourself."

When Matina touched me, I pulled away. What did Matina know? And how could Iell have allowed someone to take such pictures of her? Surely, she'd been forced. I remembered her telling me that Barnum was after her secrets, and now I understood. In all likelihood, she'd been under the influence of opium. Barnum was a scoundrel.

"What will Barnum do with these?"

Matina stood then and loomed above me, blocking out the light. "Whatever he wants, I suspect."

I must have made some weak gesture, because her voice softened and she drew toward me. "I'm sorry, Barthy, but you simply had to know."

✱ ✱ ✱

THAT NIGHT, I sat at the café table in the Arboretum, desperate to dig up the root. Head in hands, I asked the birds why the root existed if not to make me strong enough to carry on without my performances? Their silence was expected. I thought of Iell and her opium and once again decided to leave the root buried. It was bad enough that one of us required a foreign substance to survive.

chapter nineteen

LTHOUGH I WENT ABOUT MY BUSI-
ness as usual the rest of the week, sitting
tableau and caring for the birds, thoughts
of Iell and those photographs plagued me. By Friday morning I'd
had enough, and, hidden in my padded suit, I took the trolley all the
way to Iell's boardinghouse with the intention of telling her what I'd
seen. In the end I lacked the courage to present myself. What could
I have said, that my heart was broken? That my poor addled brain
now burst with images of my True Prodigy half undressed, painfully
compromised, and not living up to the standards her gift required?
But no matter how I struggled to reconcile my previous impressions
of Iell with what I'd seen in print, one thing seemed certain: Barnum
had made Iell sit for those photographs. And given that fact, I could
not abandon her. She obviously could not protect herself in our world.

After lunch, I lingered in the Green Room as the company got
ready for their afternoon shows. The room was unusually dark—after
the fire, most performers had stopped lighting the candles on their
dressing tables—and I had to squint to see. Matina surprised me by
moving a stack of clothes from the chair next to her dressing table to
make room for me. She seemed willing to have me near her. Perhaps
she felt she'd evened the score by showing me the photographs.

When Fish poked his head into the dressing room, Matina
reached over and gave my arm a little pinch.

"Now what does *he* want?" she said, for a moment her old self.

"Attention, children," Fish hollered, into the chatter of the room.

He pulled a piece of paper out from under his arm and waved it in the air like a flag. "I'll talk to you tomorrow at lunch, take your questions and all, but for now—hep, hep." He tacked the note onto the Notice Board with a piece of spirit gum, waggled a bony finger at us, and left as quickly as he'd come.

Ricardo reached the note first. He stretched one arm unnaturally long and snatched it before anyone else had a chance to get to it. We all knew Ricardo couldn't read, but he pretended to be utterly engrossed, laughing and scowling until he tired of the game and passed the note on to Emma. Towering above us, she read aloud, one finger following each word as she reached it:

"'On 4 July 1865, the great Phineas Taylor Barnum will celebrate the eve of the day of his auspicious birth by hosting a soirée beyond all others!'" Emma looked up. "That's only a week and a half away."

Zippy clapped his hands and spun around in his seat. The rest of us waited to hear more. However late in announcing it to us, Barnum always threw himself a birthday party. One year, he'd had the servers painted gold. Another, he'd packed the menagerie onto wagons and sent them up and down Broadway like a circus train, all the animals sporting party hats. And for his fiftieth, he'd roasted fifty giant pigs, each one branded with a number carved into its flesh, and served them on fifty silver platters pounded out in-house by an imported silver-smith from Sheffield. That was a most astounding party. Many of the big impresarios of the day came. Aaron Turner, who, despite his legendary cheapness (he ran one of the first real circuses in America, reported to cost him less to show for a week than many circuses spent in a day), made an appearance, giving Barnum a full-grown ostrich. George Bailey, son-in-law and eventual heir to Aaron's great show, brought him a hippopotamus. Even Seth Howes showed up with a dozen donkeys dressed in girls' clothing—though Barnum didn't seem to appreciate the joke. The war toned Barnum down a bit, and he'd canceled last year's party entirely, claiming it was out of respect to our soldiers, though I suspected it had more to do with a paucity of finances.

The mere fact that Barnum was throwing a party wasn't surprising. What was different was what came next. Emma held up a finger for attention, then continued to read out in her gravelly voice:

"'As honored members of the Museum's talented ensemble, your presence is requested at the behest of the generous Mr. Barnum. Come dance and drink away the separations that keep brother from brother, mother from son, and man from his blessed counterpart, woman.'"

He'd invited us to attend! Instead of working the whole night, amusing the bigwigs and their indistinguishable wives before slouching off to our rooms, we were to go as guests. It was unprecedented.

"Whatever will I wear?" Matina fretted, and even Alley showed a bit of enthusiasm, standing up and walking over to read the notice for himself. But I couldn't imagine Barnum publicly treating us as peers, and I certainly couldn't see his sacrificing the amusement of his guests to make us happy. I said nothing to my colleagues. Let them dream while they could.

"We'll have to get the old buzzard a gift, you know." Emma looked across the room. "Volunteers?" The room went stone quiet. "Then it's straws."

Nurse nodded her head, hustled off, and returned in a moment with straw from a kitchen broom. Together she and Emma measured and cut, and when they couldn't find something to put the straws in, Emma asked Ricardo for his hat. He pulled his kitten out, turned the hat over, and we all drew straws. Matina came up short. She immediately turned to me, but I was out the door in a flash.

Just before I made it to the kitchen, Ricardo caught up to me.

"Fortuno, Mrs. Barnum wants to talk to you in fifteen minutes."

The blood drained from my face. Here it finally was, then: dismissal. "Did she say why?"

"Christ! How should I know?" Ricardo's head began to wobble about like a nodding doll.

Just then, Matina came out the dining room door, her lacy shawl draped over one arm, her feet sausaged into a pair of cheap leather dancing shoes. When she stopped, she smiled at Ricardo, not me.

"Barthy? Why did you run out like that? I wanted to talk to you."

"How lovely you look, Miss Matina," Ricardo said, twisting backward and then bending over to gaze at her through his legs. He plucked at her skirt hem.

Matina acknowledged this liberty with a shameless tilt of her chin.

"Ricardo was just leaving." I scowled down at him and he righted himself, bumping into me as he passed.

"Emma's rooms. Don't be late."

"Ta-ta," Matina sung after him. She turned to me, smiling. "He's so sweet since he found that cat."

"Why would you let that rubber creature near you? I don't understand you at all." Had Matina also succumbed to the will of the Barnums? That might explain her barely speaking to me for a week and now being so chatty and flirtatious. And all this with Mrs. Barnum waiting for me upstairs.

Matina stepped around and blocked the sunlight; her shadow swallowed me.

"I want you to come with me to buy a present for Barnum. Alley told me about this little curio shop in the Bowery." Rays of light splintered past her as she shifted position. "I'll take up a collection this week." She gazed wistfully into the sky, one finger playing with a strand of yellow hair, and drew in a long breath. How could I say no? Most likely, I'd be fired before then anyway, and I wouldn't have to worry about carrying it through.

"As long as it doesn't take forever."

"Really? You'll go with me?" Matina gave me an overblown smile, not entirely real.

"Seven o'clock, Sunday evening," I told her, watching Cook run down the hallway, a dead goose in her hand. "I'll order a cab and we can leave together."

✳ ✳ ✳

WHEN I knocked on Emma's door that night, Ricardo threw it open with a flourish.

"The scarecrow is here, madam," he yelled over his shoulder. "The magnificent, the wondrous—blah, blah, blah. May I take your coat, sir? May I take your hat?" He made great show of pulling my hat from my head, dusting it off, and overstretching his arm to place it on top of an armoire near the door. "Wait here," he ordered.

To steady my nerves, I tried to study Emma's sitting room. The small space was stuffed full of large furniture—a ten-foot sofa, a bureau almost as wide, and a massive chair. I'd expected her decor to be Gothic or religious but, instead, red streamers hung from the ceiling and bowls of cut daisies overflowed every available surface.

Ricardo beckoned me into the room, and though I feared my legs would not move, I somehow advanced. Mrs. Barnum sat on the bench of an upright piano along the back wall, Emma the spy perched right next to her.

"So." Mrs. Barnum waved me forward. "Again we meet."

It felt as if someone had stolen all the air from the room. As I stumbled toward her, Mrs. Barnum dangled her legs off the bench, her practical shoes knocking into each other. She did not ask me to sit.

Mrs. Barnum turned to Emma. "Why don't you go and make some tea, my dear? Mr. Fortuno and I have some difficult things to discuss."

This wasn't good. I threw a desperate glance at Emma, but she grunted and moved away at Mrs. Barnum's order. It took no more than the flick of a hand for Mrs. Barnum to send Ricardo scurrying from the room as well. When she turned her attention to me, every muscle in me went rigid.

What if I ran? No, no, that wouldn't do. If she was going to harm me in some physical way I might as well get it over with. I suspected that my work hiatus had been on her order, though sharing my bedroom with a foul-smelling tumbler would have been far worse. Had she somehow found out about my last trip to the Chinaman's? Oh, what I wouldn't have given for a bit of the root right then. But the root still lay buried, and Iell still needed a protector. I would simply have to find a way to appease Mrs. Barnum.

"Good afternoon, madam. Let me tell you right off that, since we last spoke, I've done exactly as you asked."

"Have you now?"

I glanced furtively toward the door, calculating how long it would take me to grab my things and make a dash for it, until she said, "I'm here to discuss a different matter today, Fortuno."

"Madam?"

"I've actually come to ask for your help."

My heart slowed, but my hands went damp.

"A little birdie told me that you've continued your friendship with that new abomination of my husband's," she said.

I interrupted. "Abomination? Madam, *please*. You shouldn't use such a word to describe Iell. She's a perfectly decent sort, I assure you."

"On a first-name basis now, are we?"

Mrs. Barnum's gaze was unwavering. My heart began racing again, and from some unseen place, Ricardo's cat mewed. I swallowed and waited as Mrs. Barnum resituated herself on the bench, stretching her legs down until the tips of her toes touched the floor.

"Now, if this were true," she continued, "it would distress me greatly."

I had to force myself not to look away. She needed to see that I could protect myself and, if necessary, Iell as well. I pulled my jacket open as if in a casual gesture, hoping to remind Mrs. Barnum of my many gifts.

"I will be frank with you," she said, ignoring my efforts. "My husband seems to have special plans concerning this person, and though it's not at all unusual for him to take to an act with special enthusiasm, I find this particular affair unacceptable. In fact, it's an embarrassment to me. So I am preparing new arrangements for Mrs. Adams, and when I present them to her, I hope she will see the wisdom of change."

"Why worry yourself so? She's only here until summer's end."

Mrs. Barnum laughed. "Mrs. Adams has no intention of leaving. My husband has made her a private offer, which I believe she will accept."

I could have kicked up my heels and done a jig, inspired by the knowledge that the beautiful Iell wasn't about to disappear from my life.

"Mr. Fortuno? I suggest you take this conversation a bit more seriously."

Had I shown too much delight? I fixed my expression on the piano behind Mrs. Barnum, using my reflection in the polished wood as a steadying device.

"I assure you—"

"The favor I would ask of you," she interrupted, "is a simple one. Do not get in my way. That woman will leave on schedule. Once I tell her what I have in mind, she'll see the wisdom of my plan. But I believe she will leave much more readily if she has no internal allies. Therefore, you're not to befriend her further or help her in any way. Is that clear?"

"I've no intention—" I began, but Mrs. Barnum interrupted me again.

"Are you enjoying your recent freedom? Much nicer than sharing your rooms, as we spoke of before. You still have your privacy, and now you've extra time as well. And of course, this vacation can always be extended."

So the schedule change had indeed been her idea: and now this new threat. She was suggesting dismissal, and Barnum could not be counted on to protect me. He'd already admitted to Iell that he'd used me, and hadn't he himself threatened me with expulsion? But I still had my popularity to bank on. My gift. Barnum was a businessman, first and foremost, and I was a valuable asset.

"Your husband would never allow me to be permanently removed."

Mrs. Barnum all but laughed aloud. "Oh, goodness, he has bigger battles to fight than protecting you, sir. And as for Mrs. Adams, I've no desire to harm the woman. I simply wish to see her moved elsewhere before my husband does something we might all regret. She's quite desirable to other establishments, you know. They will pay highly for her. And should a new position displease her in any way, I'd see to her future comfort. I have done so before."

Before? Was she was referring to the acrobats who had disappeared years ago?

"Do not befriend this person any more than you already have, Mr. Fortuno. The result would be disastrous for you, simply disastrous."

The sound of Emma lurching back into the room halted our conversation. I gathered my wits as Emma staggered past with cookies and minuscule teacups teetering on a tray no bigger than the palm of her hand. She balanced the tray on the end of the bench next to Mrs. Barnum.

"I think a single cup will be sufficient, my dear. Mr. Fortuno, unfortunately, cannot stay for tea."

Under the diversion of the rattling of china, I followed Emma to the front door.

"I'm assuming the *little birdie* Mrs. Barnum referred to was no other than you," I said. "You told her about Iell's scarf after all, didn't you? In fact, you've been in her service for quite some time."

"You've no idea how much I've been privy to, Fortuno, not that it matters. But Mrs. Barnum needed another set of eyes as much as her husband did, and in exchange I got some very privileged information."

"What kind of information?"

"Never you mind. If the good Lord wants you to know more, more will be revealed." And she all but shoved me out her door.

I beat a hasty retreat down the hallway, understanding that Iell needed me more than ever. I left a note in the Yellow Room that night, folded and wax-sealed, telling Iell I had to see her as soon as possible, and my news was not good.

chapter twenty

UNDAY EVENING I MARCHED UP THE HALL promptly at seven and knocked on Matina's door. She answered in a flourish of excitement.

"Give me one minute," she said, so I stood in the hallway, overly warm in my padded coat. I'd be responsible for Matina in public, and I didn't want to draw any more attention to us than was necessary. I wondered why I was the one she'd asked to accompany her. Most likely, this was her way of reestablishing our old relationship. With a bit of patience, I might have her once more as a confidante, and that would be worth the trip to the Bowery. Perhaps she could tell me how to manage Mrs. Barnum's demands. I simply couldn't let Iell leave, not until we'd spent more time together. Not until she knew me.

Matina swooshed out her door, bringing my mind back to the task at hand. "Well, look at you." She raised an eyebrow and fingered my padded sides, and I forced myself not to blush.

"Traveling can be difficult," I started to explain, wishing I hadn't put the damned coat on, realizing at the same time how much I'd used the thing since concocting it. Matina seemed nonplussed and passed me her cape to lay over her shoulders.

"We are to be at the shop no later than seven forty-five and ask for a Mr. Giovanni," she said. "Hopefully, we can find something irresistible in formaldehyde."

There are summer evenings in New York marked by soft, calming breezes and gentle sunsets that can turn the clamor of the city streets into a lullaby. It was that kind of evening, and for a moment it felt as if the last few months had never happened. All was as it used to be, and all was well.

"Look at that woman, Mama. She's fat!" Some young brat hanging on to the arm of his mother was pointing at Matina. I instinctively stepped between her and the boy, but Matina merely loomed over him and grimaced. The child took off with a squeal.

The carriage I had called waited on the corner of Ann and Nassau, but it was smaller than the one I had requested. The driver leaned on his horses, smoking a foul black cigar.

I frowned at him once we got close. "This contraption you call a carriage is not what I ordered."

The driver didn't answer at first. He was mesmerized by Matina. "Do you hear me, lad?"

"The other rig broke down, sir. I had to bring this one. Though I don't know if it will accommodate the lady, no offense to her."

Matina pushed me aside. "Open the damned door, you fool. We're late." The driver stared helplessly toward me, but when I slipped a silver dollar into his hand, he shrugged and flicked his smoke into the gutter. It took the efforts of both of us to pop her through the doors, and the carriage tipped slightly under her weight, but the wheels held. Matina gave a hearty laugh, and I climbed in beside her.

The trip uptown was bumpy. The gas lamps on Nassau Street were still unlit, and the few private houses remained hidden beneath the full foliage of the surrounding trees. Once we skirted up along Park Row, the walkways grew more active. Matina fanned herself and hummed as we trotted along; she was in high spirits. For a moment I considered talking to her about Iell, but I wasn't sure we were ready for that yet. The last thing I wanted to do was raise the subject too soon and have her clam up again or, even worse, give her the chance to talk about our own intimate past. So instead I sat quietly.

We turned east on Canal Street. Who lived in these tidy houses, with their picket fences and well-tended gardens? What would it be like to live such a life? I felt a twinge of excitement until we drove past

Mott Street and the dark secrets of the Chinaman and his herbs. My heart pounded, but I said nothing aloud.

"I wanted you to come," Matina said, her voice startling me, "because I thought you should see the Bowery."

"Why ever would I want—?"

She put a finger to my lips. "I have thought a lot about it, and I've decided that much of your recent behavior has come about because you are bored, Barthy. Our lives are so similar, day after day. Sometimes we take actions simply to wake ourselves up. I understand that now. So I thought a little trip to the other side might be a good idea. A reminder of how lucky we are to be at the Museum despite your diminished performances."

I flinched.

The driver hit a large hole in the road and the carriage bounced into the air. I nearly hit my head on the roof, and when we landed Matina's weight caused the carriage wheels to creak dangerously. Was Matina warning me away from Iell? Or was she simply worried about my position and trying to bring me back into the fold?

We turned onto the Bowery. Even on a Sunday, sailors jostled past girls in beads and secondhand dresses peddling their wares. Hungarians, Russians, Italians, and Irishmen hung from rickety second-floor windows and awnings that lined both sides of the street, selling everything from petticoats to potatoes. In this part of town you could buy whatever your heart desired—glassware, bed linens, strawberries, porcelain, china dolls, whitewashed chairs—all of it shabby and gray and much cheaper than in other parts of the city. In the shadows you could find other things to smoke or smell or touch or eat. A thousand ways to feed your hunger, and all the prices were negotiable.

As we passed the Worth Museum and the Pig & Whistle Tavern and then turned up Delancey Street, Matina shot me a meaningful glance. "Barthy, I need some advice from you."

Instinctively, I tensed.

"Barnum wants me to play Mazeppa at his party like Adah Menken in San Francisco does. I don't know what to do."

Utterly astonished, I swiveled in my seat. "*Mazeppa* is obscene! How could Barnum even suggest such a thing?"

The play was about a Tartar page named Mazeppa, who makes love to a nobleman's wife. In the last act, the townsfolk punish him by stripping off his clothes and binding him to the back of a wild horse. In civilized renditions, a dummy is strapped onto a stuffed horse that dashes against papier-mâché cliffs before disappearing into cotton clouds. But the actress Adah Menken took San Francisco by storm by riding a real horse on stage while dressed in flesh-colored tights. The scandal hit every newspaper, and it was rumored that audience members fainted or ran from the theater. A woman playing a man onstage? And barely clothed? Bad enough for a common actress to do such a thing, but Matina? I flushed at the idea.

Matina shrugged and twisted toward the window, fanning herself vigorously. "At least it would give me a chance to be onstage again."

"It's totally outside the boundaries of good taste. You can't do such a thing. You would be nearly naked!"

"I could negotiate with Barnum. Do this for him in exchange for a real act later on. Something that would show off more than just my body."

"Wasn't it you who told me, moments ago, to be content with my lot in life?"

"Content?" Matina snapped her fan closed, eyes darkening. "Settle for being a fat woman and nothing more?"

"Trust me, Matina. Barnum understands that doing this will make you look foolish, and I don't want that to happen."

"Foolish?"

"Yes. Absolutely."

"Not as foolish as some, I assure you!"

We rode the rest of the way in silence until, at the corner of the Bowery and East Second Street, Matina rapped her parasol on top of the carriage. We'd finally reached our destination. With effort, Matina struggled out of the cab without my help, and we stood uncomfortably in front of "Madame Theresa's Hall of Wonders." The street smoldered with cheap marquees advertising minstrel shows and sensational plays such as *The Scaffold* and *Ten Nights in a Barroom*, and everywhere we looked were seedy displays of iron-skulled men, tattooed women, and human pincushions, not one of whom Barnum would employ.

Strangers jostled past us on the street, some staring, a few stopping nearby to point and laugh.

I clutched Matina's elbow and steered her roughly into the little shop, desperate to leave the throngs behind. She pulled away as soon as she could and left me standing at the door as she disappeared down an aisle full of horses' hooves and tails strung on dirty rope.

"Hullo?" she hollered. "Anyone at home?"

The Hall of Wonders was disgusting, full of filthy-looking items with hand-scrawled labels. There were wood remnants marked as coming from the True Cross—enough crosses to crucify an army—and bits of bloodied sheet claiming to be the one Mr. Lincoln lay on while dying. On the walls hung mildewed charts giving obscene instructions for ensuring a happy marriage, with illustrative casts of body parts propped up nearby in case you didn't understand the charts. Bloodied uniforms and muskets filled the left wall, and one could almost see sewage seeping up from underneath the floorboards in the rear of the store.

I wandered the shop, horrified. Matina stood in the rear, chatting with the proprietor, a pock-faced man with a round belly and trousers covered with unidentifiable stains. I'd seen his type. At one point an emporium master, he'd fallen to hawking cheap replicas to unwary buyers, and he was always on the lookout for goods that could pass for real.

"Madame Theresa, I presume?" I tried to get their attention, but they ignored me in favor of a discussion I could not hear. I watched as Matina's expression went from sweet to animated to sweet again, and eventually the proprietor disappeared into the bowels of the store.

"I think I've found the perfect gift! It took a bit of convincing, but

Mr. Giovanni has promised to bring out the best he has." Matina's face glowed as the proprietor returned with several fingers pickled in bottles of formaldehyde. One finger sported a great black ring, indecipherable markings etched into its face.

"Those are disgusting." I pulled out my handkerchief and pressed it to my nose.

"That one!" She pointed to the ringed finger.

"What superb taste, miss. This finger comes from the hand of the great pirate Blackbeard."

"Oh, Barthy!" She turned to me. "Barnum will love it!"

She was probably right. "It's a sham," I said, "and probably too expensive."

The shopkeeper passed the jar to Matina. "This finger comes right off the ropes of the *Queen Anne's Revenge*. The old pirate hung on to the very end."

I rolled my eyes at the stupidity of his assertion.

"He was a nasty one. They say he'd dip candlewicks in gunpowder, tie them all over this big beard of his, and then light them for battle, so his whole face was spitting fire."

"Barthy, why don't you conclude our business with this gentleman while I look around the shop."

Irritated at Matina for leaving the hard part to me, I snapped, "Simply tell us how much."

The proprietor eyed me warily. "You know," he said, making certain Matina was out of hearing range, "I also got something you might like. I can give you a better price on the finger if you want to buy both." He reached across the counter behind him and opened a cabinet; then, using his body as a shield, he held out another bottle. Instead of a finger, this one held a severed penis, shriveled and gray.

"That, sir, is absolutely revolting! You should be put in jail."

"What is it, Barthy?" Matina came scurrying down the aisle, not wanting to miss anything.

The shopkeeper realized he'd misjudged me and slid the second jar into his coat.

"The price," I stammered. "He quoted me a ridiculous price."

"How much?" Matina asked him directly.

"For you? Fifteen dollars."

"You can't be serious! Surely you can do better than that." Matina leaned into the counter, her bosom all but touching the man.

"Perhaps the lady would consider a trade? I have customers who would love a bit of time alone with someone like you."

To my horror, Matina put her hand on his arm and squeezed. "Between us, all we have is six dollars fifty."

"Har-har-har." His laugh made me flush with irritation. "How's about eleven dollars? You wouldn't wanna steal from me, would you?"

The man's eager expression turned my stomach, and I detested the syrupy expression Matina had adapted. But I wanted to break back into Matina's good graces.

"You'd be bringing pleasure to a good woman's heart," I reasoned.

"This heart?" he said, reaching his slimy hands toward Matina's chest, looking at her as if he were about to gobble her up.

"Why not?" Matina barely stepped back.

"Sold," he said, just like that.

I forced myself to look away, glancing out into the street while trying not to listen to Matina counting out the dollars. The transaction complete, we returned silently to the cab. I refused to even look at Matina, and when I rapped my walking stick repeatedly against the floor to hurry the cab forward, I used unnecessary force. The driver sped through the streets, dark now except for the light from the streetlamps.

Eventually Matina spoke. "I don't see why you're so upset, Bartholomew. A girl must use what wiles she has."

"I am hardly upset." I turned toward the window, stonewalling her, figuring silence would be the best punishment, but it was me who suffered as a leaden quiet filled the carriage. Halfway home, I couldn't take it anymore and reached over and tried to touch her hand.

Matina yanked her arm away. "I have tried to be patient with you, Barthy, but I must tell you, I am close to the end of my tether."

I was shocked. Why was she annoyed with me when it was *she* who had acted so badly with the shopkeeper?

"You are being quite unreasonable," I said, and she turned on me, her face red, her eyes livid.

"And you are acting quite the fool! If I had known a shopkeeper could elicit this kind of reaction from you, I should have brought one with me the day after our little soirée, because, Lord knows, you've barely looked at me since that night."

"I have simply tried to respect you."

"And how might you treat me should some decent man court me? Would you never speak to me again? Try to marry me?"

Mention of another man took a little breath from me. "Are you being courted? By whom?"

"Oh, believe me, I've no one so intriguing in my life as you do in yours."

The carriage hit a pothole, and her bonnet bounced sideways. We rode in uncomfortable silence.

"I would at least like to know what you see in her," she said at last.

My palms dampened. "What I see in whom?"

"I know all about you and Iell Adams, Barthy. Everyone does. Though no one can understand the attraction. I thought the photographs might show you the truth, but clearly she's bewitched you."

I ached to lean across the seat and rest my head on Matina's bosom. Tell her it was all a lie. But she wanted answers. It was the least that I could give her.

"You and I, we have cared about each other for a long time," I said carefully.

Matina looked over at me, her shoulders tightening. "But you prefer her. Is it because she's so thin?"

"Goodness sakes, no! *Nothing* like that." I slid across the carriage seat toward her. "She's just . . . amazing: intelligent, witty, not like anyone I've ever met. When I'm with her, Matina, no one else exists."

"How nice for you."

"Please. Don't take it the wrong way."

"It's fine, Barthy. Really."

The carriage slowed to a halt. Matina turned from me and didn't move for what seemed like forever. Then she straightened her bonnet and gathered her things. She allowed me to help her from the carriage, but she refused to walk with me once we entered the Ann Street door.

"I think I'll take myself up to bed now," she said. "I'm sure you'd be happier down here in the garden for a while."

Dutifully, I sat on a garden bench for ten minutes or so—long enough for Matina to make the climb upstairs alone—as, above me, gray clouds tumbled in, covering the stars one by one. I'd hurt her, I knew that. I hadn't meant to be cruel. But even the mention of Iell's name sent me into an enraptured state. I tried to dismiss a feeling of discomfort as I walked up the stairs to my room, but I didn't worry long. When I pushed open the door to my rooms, a note lay on the floor. Sometime while we'd been gone, Iell had sent a message asking if we could meet at her boardinghouse the next morning. She also wrote that, if the bad news I warned about had anything to do with her, I wasn't to worry.

Wasn't to worry, indeed.

chapter twenty one

HE NEXT MORNING, I WAS SO NERVOUS ABOUT the impending visit to Iell I barely cared that my name still did not appear in the weekly notices. Even Bridgett's noisy entrance into the Green Room—she wore bells that she'd sewn into the hem of her skirt—barely struck a nerve. She looked particularly pleased with herself as she chimed her way through a group of workers and headed to where Alley sat, changing his shirt for the first set of shows. When she cozied up next to him and fussed maternally with the ends of his collar, he looked toward me for help. I shrugged my shoulders. What could I do? Even though we'd a bit more than a week before the party, Fish had insisted that we consolidate our dressing room space for the acts that would join us. He'd put Alley and Bridgett together on one mirror. Alley would have to make do.

Temporary name plaques listing the incoming dignitaries already hung above each mirror. No one wanted to sit next to Signor Fuego the Fire Fiend—rumor had it that a stagehand with two buckets of water would follow him everywhere he went—so some of the regulars tripled up next to John Mulligan, the six-foot Ethiopian minstrel, and the clog dancer Joe Child. Others drew straws to sit next to Dan Rice, the clown whose picture already hung at the top of my old mirror. According to the plaques, I was to sit with Ricardo. That had to be Mrs. Barnum's doing. What better way to keep an eye on me than to pair me with one of her henchmen. Well, I would see about that.

Claiming that I could barely see my reflection—true enough, too, since Ricardo had nearly buried the mirror with his own *cartes*, yellowed articles from the trade papers about his act, and old broadsides where he'd circled his name with red ink—I took my costume and flung it on a hook in the corner. I could do perfectly well without a makeup table. I did only tableau now, after all, and as long as my ribs showed, it barely mattered how the rest of me looked.

Both Alley and I turned when Matina walked in. She wore a new dress of pink crepe de chine, and she did not so much as look at me when she passed. Our last conversation still hung between us, but I would find a way to repair the damage.

"What do you have there, Zippy?" Matina flapped her hand at him as she plopped down in front of her makeup station, squinting at her image in the mirror.

The boy was busy tacking a curling broadside to the Notice Board that read *The Negro is a FREEDMAN.*

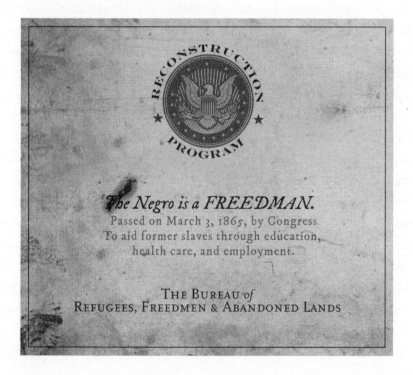

"Free!" Zippy said to Matina, chin over shoulder. "See here?" He poked at the poster. "Free." The black letters F-R-E-E-D-M-A-N jumped out against the background of coffee-colored paper.

"*None* of us here is free," Alley scoffed, as he struggled to secure his crown to his ragged hair, his eyes on Matina.

Like a schoolmarm, Matina shushed him. "Quiet now. No need to rile the child."

Alley blushed bright red. He steadied himself by putting a great hand on Matina's dressing table as she rolled a pair of stockings into a small bundle. His fingers, like mallets, drummed out some tune of frustration on top of the battered wood. "Gotta talk to you." Had the poor bugger become so trapped by Bridgett and the Copperheads that he needed Matina's counsel? Hadn't I'd already told him involvement was a mistake?

Matina wrinkled her brow and struggled to her feet. She nodded for Alley to follow, and together they made their way out to the hallway. Bridgett, alone at her mirror, watched the two of them, a look of hatred in her eyes.

Heads pressed together, Matina and Alley whispered who-knew-what. I could see them talking but couldn't hear a word they were saying. Alley stood entirely too close, swiping his stringy hair from his eyes while Matina talked, and at one point he cranked himself down to her like an old oak tree trying to bend in a gale. Matina grabbed his forearm with her fingers. She shook her head no, and neither of them moved. They just stared at each other, faces an inch apart. For a heart-stopping moment, I could have sworn she leaned forward and kissed him right on his rough lips. I shifted my gaze, and no more than thirty seconds later, Alley straightened up and stumbled off down the hall looking stricken.

I kept seeing the lunkhead bending down and Matina leaning toward him, over and over again, but I was certain she hadn't kissed him. No. Matina was only being kind. By my reckoning, Alley had run into some kind of trouble, and Matina was counseling him. Simple as

that. Even if it wasn't so simple, what did it matter? I would be with
Iell within the hour.

I waited for Alley at the end of his early show, hoping to inquire
about his talk with Matina. I would ask him discreetly if everything
was all right. Would he prefer a man's counsel to Matina's? But he only
grunted as he walked by. I didn't dally any longer for fear of running
into Barnum or his wife.

✳ ✳ ✳

Nothing to fear, I told myself, as I watched Iell's boardinghouse
from behind a tree across the street. The building glowed with
respectability, and climbing ivy softened the crisp exterior. Slipping
out of the Museum had been quite easy—everyone I knew had been
onstage or in tableau, and Cook and Fish both had midmorning
duties—but it still took all my nerve to step out from my hiding place
and into the sun. Patting the tree for good luck, I crossed the street
fast and hustled up the boardinghouse walk. This time I had not worn
my padded suit. *Disguise be damned,* I'd told myself, *I am who I am!*
When I knocked at the front door the matron nodded me in without
a word. For a moment, I was relieved, but then I got to thinking. What
if the matron was reporting my comings and goings to one of the
Barnums? Mr. Barnum was already paying for Iell's lodgings. Why
wouldn't he also slip the mistress of the house a few pennies to keep an
eye on her? Who else had witnessed my visits? Stop it, I told myself.
Iell is waiting upstairs. Buck up. Be a man. With fake bravado, I
straightened my jacket and climbed the stairs.

The moment her apartment door opened, Iell pulled me in and
kissed me lightly on both cheeks. All my fears evaporated, and it was
all I could do to feel my feet on the floor. We had difficult things to
discuss, but I grinned like an idiot, wanting only to tell her how lovely
she looked. As usual in her presence, the words stuck in my throat.

"Before we sit," she said lightly, "I've something I'm dying to show
you."

Taking my hand, she walked me through the parlor. The bluebells, still on the little table, hung limply over the edge of their vase now, and a touch of opium hung in the air, but in the high light of day it looked like another room entirely. Clean. Illuminated. Iell led me on through a half-opened door into a second chamber with an embossed fainting couch and two opposing wing chairs flanking an unlit fireplace. On the far side hung a huge portrait of Barnum as a much younger man. Other than that, the room held nothing personal. No pictures of friends or family, no books or clothing, nothing intimate that I could see.

"Just look at my newest toy." Iell made a sweeping gesture toward a pianoforte, delicately carved with miniature heads of wolves, hawks, and lions. Leaving me, she walked to it and placed a long white finger on one of its keys.

Plink. The sound danced through the room.

I moved to join her, overwhelmed to be in her presence. "I didn't know you played." For the first time, I noticed a small freckle on her neck, the loveliest little flaw.

"Oh, I don't. It is a recent gift. It's lovely, don't you think?"

Smiling, she slipped an arm through mine, sending a shiver through me. I had to fight not to reach over and tuck in a strand of red hair that arched down around her ear. But then that loose strand reminded me of one of Brady's photographs: Iell straddling a daybed, her hair free and wild, a single lock falling over one eye. How comfortable she'd looked. As if she'd been caught unawares in her natural state. Although she hadn't been in a natural state. She had posed, hadn't she? What was I thinking? She wasn't comfortable. She was an actress. A performer. That look had been faked. Of course it had. Pushing my doubts away, I followed her to the high-backed chairs, and we sat.

Although I considered broaching the subject of Mrs. Barnum, it felt too soon. "I played a bit of piano in my youth," I said instead.

"You played?" Iell asked. "How wonderful. I suspect it was that mother of yours who taught you."

"My mother taught me many things."

Iell dropped her gaze slightly, giving me a chance to examine her aristocratic nose and the swoop of a cheekbone. She seemed almost like a different person in the daytime. Much more relaxed. More forthcoming. And with her beard rolled up as it was, I couldn't help but observe the roundness of her breasts beneath the silk of her dark green dress. Her charms pulled at me even without the root in my belly.

"What do you think your mother would say if she saw how you are looking at me right now?" Iell said. "Surely she didn't teach you that?"

I was mortified. "Please forgive me! You must find me unspeakably rude." I rose, fighting to regain control. "I am not normally so forward, I assure you. I would never presume to gaze at you as I've seen Barnum do."

Iell laughed. "Now *that* is certainly true enough. Sit down. Don't worry yourself so."

Her slender hands on her lap, she gave me a moment and then said, "I see you have come to me this morning au naturel, Bartholomew. No padding? No disguise? I've been thinking quite a bit about you lately, and I must say I envy you. I really do."

She'd been thinking of me? How marvelous. "I can't imagine why you'd envy me."

Iell stretched her legs out straight in front of her, as a man might. "Adaptability is quite a gift."

"My gift is being observable, Iell, not adaptable," I reminded her. It occurred to me that I'd never before used her Christian name in her presence.

She smiled. Her heels dug deep into the plush of the rug. "Let me ask you quite a different question, Bartholomew. Have you ever dreamed of changing your life?"

"Yes, of course. Haven't we all, at some time or another?"

"No. I don't mean daydreams. I mean, planning to make it happen?"

I thought back to the time before my change. "Yes, on occasion, I suppose," I said. "But more often than not, change has come to me. For the most part, I am quite content."

"Are you? Perhaps that's because you have more possibilities than some others do."

"Forgive my forwardness," I countered, charmed and irritated in equal doses, "but perhaps it is *you* who is intrigued by the notion of choice. If you feel you need to change, why not simply hire a trustworthy barber?"

Iell lifted an eyebrow.

A shaft of sunlight cut across her lap. She smiled at me with real amusement, and I shifted uncomfortably in my chair.

"I'm quite serious," I said. "I think a woman like you could choose to do just about anything you wanted."

"And if that were so, what would you have me choose?"

I would have you stay here with me, I thought, but I held my tongue and said instead, "Perhaps a life free of opium."

"Ah, but that opium makes my destiny much easier to bear."

"Are you saying that my life is defined by choice," I challenged, "while yours is defined by destiny? That doesn't seem quite right to me."

"And what does seem right?"

An image of the root flickered in my brain and disappeared. Flustered, I said, "Perhaps we should get to the matter at hand. I've come to tell you that I was summonsed—"

"No. Not quite yet."

Iell picked up something from the side table next to her, a lacy white fan with tiny tassels hanging off the bottom. The tiniest flick of her wrist snapped it open, and she moved it side to side beneath her chin as she considered me.

"I want to know a little more about your father first. Last time you were here, you mentioned that he died when you were a boy. He must have been a young man, still."

I'm not sure why I confided in Iell. Maybe it was the softness of her smile or the clear sunshine that flowed through the windows and warmed my face, promising me safety. I stretched my legs out in front of me, my fingers playing across the chair's lush material.

"I don't remember much," I told her, closing my eyes, "but I know it was very early in the morning, in springtime. I'd come in from the garden, where I'd been building a little house from rocks and twigs, and saw my father spread out on his back on our cottage floor. My mother saw me and put a finger to her lips, as if he were sleeping. She sat on the floor next to him, and I don't know why but I think she held a lantern." A wave of uneasiness forced my eyes open. Something about what I was saying wasn't quite right, but I couldn't put my finger on it.

"Go on," Iell said. "Shut your eyes again."

Obeying her, I let my eyes close, and pictures from long ago crept into my head. "When I got close enough," I went on, "my mother forced me into her lap, grabbing hold of my hand and squeezing it so hard she cut off the feeling in my fingers. And a doctor came eventually. Someone put me to bed, even though it must have been late morning by then. Down below, the adults scurried about, and I could hear my mother sobbing, saying, 'No, no, the poor child was out playing in the garden at the time. Didn't see a thing.' Two days later, we buried my father in the Episcopal Church cemetery—her church, not the Catholic one of my father's kin. My mother had her head bowed, tears dripping off her chin. And when she tried to hold me in her arms, I must have felt it a strike to my manhood, because I pushed away."

I opened my eyes, startled at a new memory. "And then she laughed," I told Iell.

"What do you mean, she laughed?"

"As they lowered his body into the ground, my mother laughed aloud."

Why ever would she do that? I tried to think, to remember more, but all that flitted through my mind was the image of my mother holding up that glass bottle she had kept by the window and peering through it at me.

Iell rose. After touching me sympathetically on my shoulder, she left me sitting in the chair alone. I felt a tug in my belly as she slipped through a door into what must have been her bedroom. Why *had* my mother laughed? I stared out the window into a sun-filled sky, running my thumb across my own ribs, one by one.

Flustered, I called to Iell through the empty sitting room. "We still have a delicate matter to discuss."

I heard the slight rasping of Iell's dress as she reentered and stopped at my side. I knew she was staring down at me, and I was glad to turn the conversation back to practical matters.

"As I was saying, someone summoned me to tell me I wasn't to see you again," I said, looking up at her, "or to help you in any way."

"Who?"

I hesitated. "Mrs. Barnum."

"Phineas's wife?" Iell's voice took on a tension that I'd in no way expected, and the next moment she was in tears.

I sprang upright, my jacket flying. "Oh, my dear. My goodness." Like a manservant, I took her by the elbow and, as she continued to cry, I helped her into her chair. "Whatever is the matter? I'd no idea my words would upset you so."

"How I hate my weaknesses." Struggling to regain composure, Iell dabbed at her nose with my hanky. "Would you mind fetching me something to drink?"

I went to the outer parlor and found a pitcher of water and glasses on the sideboard. When I returned, Iell stood near the pianoforte, facing away from me.

"What do you think this woman wants?" she asked.

I handed her a glass of water. "I must ask you a delicate question first, and of course, you needn't answer."

"Please."

"I've seen the photographs." My chest tightened. "Is that what Barnum wants from you? Is that his price for you to stay? I know it is not my concern, but please, what is the truth about your relationship with that man?"

I'd expected some physical reaction from Iell, some contraction between the shoulder blades, perhaps, or a heaviness of stance. Instead, she took a slow sip of the water, then put the glass on the table in front of her.

"As I've told you, he is a mentor and nothing more." Her voice was flat.

"Even if evidence indicates otherwise?"

"Yes." Iell faced me now, her eyes sharp and dark. "Even if evidence indicates otherwise."

"All right," I said, trusting her. "Well, Mrs. Barnum must think it's more, much more, because she is quite insistent that you leave the Museum. She has plans to place you elsewhere."

"My contract at the Museum is so limited. Why should she concern herself with my placement?"

"She says she knows her husband has offered you some kind of private arrangement."

"I see."

"And she says you cannot accept it. Also, she explicitly warned me to keep out of it."

"Did she?" Iell's face changed, the lines of distress smoothing over so completely, I couldn't believe she'd been so recently upset. I fought the urge to go to her, but the rigidity of her posture told me to keep my distance.

"I've upset you again," I said.

"No, of course not. But I've suddenly come down with a most terrible headache."

"How on earth have you made so many enemies? First Emma, and now Barnum's wife."

"Emma?"

"You know that I overheard you dismiss her in the theater. And it was she who hosted Mrs. Barnum in her room for our recent talk."

"You might be surprised by who my friends are and who they are not." Iell was a different person now, hard and self-contained, any touch of intimacy between us gone. "Don't look so tragic, Bartholomew," she said, her voice strong and controlled. "I shan't let that old woman deter me."

Iell took me by the elbow and led me through her parlor and out into the hallway. Wordlessly, I followed her down the stairs. The matron joined us on the first floor, and stood behind Iell, who opened the front door and gestured me out. Obviously no longer in need of my compassion, she dismissed me. "Thank you again for your assistance. As always, you've been most kind."

The door closed behind me, and, when the sunlight swallowed me up, my head began to pound. There I was, risking everything for her, and Iell had put me out without a touch of warmth. I shouldn't have been so surprised. She was an opium addict, wasn't she? And those photographs. Perhaps that was the real Iell after all. Coy. Obscene. Matina was right. I kicked at a loose flagstone as I left the boardinghouse behind me and walked up the street. Maybe Matina would sit with me at lunch, I thought, but even as such an idea rose in my mind, the memory of Iell's smile overcame me.

Without even checking to see if anyone followed me, I walked all the way to Broadway, late-morning strollers gawking at me as I passed. By the time I crossed the avenue, I'd convinced myself that Iell had acted out of shock from the news and nothing else. My dismissal hadn't been personal, and only a fool would have taken it as such. I shoved away a nagging voice and, flagging down a public trolley, headed homeward.

But sitting on the trolley, all I could think of was Iell tipping her chin up, her eyes her own but her mouth clearly my mother's, laughing aloud and whispering, "Have you ever thought of changing your life?"

And a memory came to me—my mother and I stumbling to our cottage after my father's funeral service was over. With a bang, she kicked open the door and sat me on a window seat, where she made me face her. She took my head in her hands and pushed her palms against my temples so hard I felt my head would burst like a melon. Nose to nose, her breath smelled slightly sour, like bad milk. "Always obey me, Bartholomew." She stared at me and I did not cry, even though she kept me locked between her hands for an excruciating time.

That very same day she went missing, and it took me hours of searching the barns and the outbuildings before I found her in the overgrown glen, on her knees, half nude in the creek. Her camisole was covered in muck; in her lap was a bouquet of weeds and sticks. I dragged my mother home, where, meek as a lamb, she let me peel off her outer clothes and lead her to the bath. The water that I poured through her muddy hair flowed in brown rivulets down the base of her neck and ran in thin streams across her half-naked shoulders, dripping onto her chemise. When I moved closer, hoping for her to look at me, to know me, she said nothing, and at that moment I realized that she did not love me.

And then another memory. Deeper. I stared out the trolley window and tried to think of something else, but all I could see was my mother traipsing across the lawn behind the Major's kitchen. It had been days since the funeral, and I'd been sitting in our cottage window watching her pick her way across the footpath, still dressed in mourning clothes. She balanced a wooden tray above her head, and she shoved open the cottage door with one foot, plunking down the tray with so much fervor that food flew off the top. My stomach rolled.

"You have to eat," she said watching me separate the meat and the fruit. She slapped my hand when I lifted the greens off the plate with a long pronged fork, plunking them into the trash. Why had I discarded the food? I couldn't for the life of me remember.

chapter twenty two

DURING MY SECOND WEEK OF NO PERFORM-ances, I began to enjoy my limited schedule. True, I felt out of sorts not being seen on stage, but I had time to catch up on my reading and was able to spend more time in the Arboretum with the birds. I even went out for a walk on Thursday afternoon, though on returning I had quite a shock. A handful of police officers tumbled out of the Ann Street exit just as I was coming in.

The first thing I thought of was that I'd been discovered missing. I threw myself into the shadows and tried to decide what to do next. But would Barnum send officers to fetch me? No. Something else was going on. I hunched down and scurried into the courtyard, hidden by the flurry of activity. I barely managed to sit on one of the benches and get my breathing under control before Cook marched up the flagstone walk toward me.

"What are you doing out here?" Cook wiped her hands on her apron and scowled at me. "You'd best hurry along, Fortuno. Everyone else is already in the dining room, waiting for Fish."

"What happened?"

"We had a fire on the roof an hour ago. One of the cleaners saw smoke and beat a floor gong until the house crew dragged water buckets up and put out the blaze. Thank God none of the customers knew what was happening."

Cook veered off toward the kitchen as Zippy ran past in a helmet that he must have snatched from the new Debtor's Prison exhibit. He clutched a long sword—most likely also filched—that clacked and bounced along the flagstones, and he almost tripped me as I followed him into the dining room. Matina raised her hand in weak greeting when she saw me. Alley sat next to her. They hadn't saved me a seat. Disgruntled, I rested my spine painfully against the wall and crossed my arms over my chest.

When Fish came into the dining room, a new wisp of a beard blending into his speckled sideburns, he was beside himself.

"As I'm sure you all know, we've had another fire today." Fish wrung his hands but was clearly trying to exhibit control. "It was small and of no real threat—only a pail full of rags set alight once again— but because the roof is off limits to everyone but staff, Mr. Barnum now fears that the menace is internal."

"The firebug's one of us!" Ricardo yelled out.

Alley's ears went bright red.

"Maybe it's *you*, Rubber Man, if you had the nerve." Bridgett hollered this out from the far end of the table, and we all looked over at her, surprised at her outburst.

"Oh, I have the nerve, fancy girl, *and* the strength." Ricardo stood and wiggled his hips obscenely.

Fish waved Ricardo back to his seat. "This is arson, sir, and not a joke. Mr. Barnum is mightily concerned. Setting fires, however small, is a deranged act, and we need all of you to help us catch the culprit. From now on, you are to watch one another. If you see anything suspicious—anything whatsoever—you are to report it to us immediately."

All I could think about was how much harder it was going to be for me to travel undetected—though it might no longer matter after the way Iell had dismissed me.

Fish continued, "That said, we do not want you to be unduly alarmed."

"Too late for that," Matina chimed in.

"My dear, I assure you, all will be fine." Fish mindlessly pinched his nose between two fingers. "Mr. Barnum has decided to employ a dozen firewatchers, two on each floor, including the cellars and the roof. They will be with us day and night. I promise you, we will not be seeing another fire around here anytime soon."

No one said a word.

"Now. As long as we're all here, the fourth of July is less than a week away. A great day in this great country, and a great day for Mr. Barnum's party."

Fish paused for effect. Ricardo applauded, while the rest of us waited mutely for him to continue.

"I will be posting a special schedule for the next few days. You must attend to the notices, and I expect each of you to adjust as needed. As for now, Barnum has sent you this message."

Fish reached into his side pocket and pulled out a handkerchief, mopping the sides of his neck. Then he took out a crisply folded paper, cleared his throat, and read:

"*Please convey to the staff this vision for the week leading to the party: We will close or change every exhibit in order to restructure the Museum for the party. Visitors will still be welcome, but only in the great rooms. As far as the Curiosities go*"—he took a moment to emphasize the importance of the next part by peering down at us—"*I want the very sight of them to sweep the crowds into the unexpected. Shows will continue in a limited fashion, but for most of the day, they will perform in tableau in as many places as possible.*"

Matina groaned audibly and snapped shut her fan. "I certainly hope Barnum doesn't expect me to be switching floors for this new plan of his." Her breath came in short gasps, and I worried for her health. "The fires," she went on, "were far better news."

Fish held up a hand to quiet her. "*Suggestions will be posted on a daily basis, and new ideas are welcome. In conclusion, in anticipation of the party, our collective goal is to have visitors see us now not as a Museum but as an awakening!*

"And so you have it." Fish folded the paper in crisp quarters. "Now, beyond assuring certain persons that they will not be unduly pressed, do you have other questions?"

Bridgett spoke up again, this time all ladylike. "Excuse me, Mr. Fish, but what does Barnum mean by an *awakening?*"

"An awakening," he said, clearly happier to be addressing a question in place of a complaint, "is what happens to a person who comes across something so novel, so unspeakably new, it rattles the doors of their mind. Mr. Barnum believes that the surprise of you roaming about with the normal guests will accomplish something similar. I suppose we shall see. And Mr. Barnum also wanted me to warn those of you with—uh—greater appetites, that special food will be available for you here in the dining room. He'd prefer you not take your dinner from the buffet lines or there'll be nothing left for our guests."

With much scraping of chairs, everyone rose and milled about, chattering and complaining among themselves. No one asked me for my opinion, so I slipped out of the dining room and into the courtyard and up the walk. The service door on Ann Street stood wide open, and a cartful of workers blocked an open-bed wagon carrying bolts of cloth, and large barrels of ornamental trims, tassels, and decorative fringe. I stopped for a moment to watch.

The fires concerned me, of course they did, and I was irked about having to perform at the party, but my overwhelming thoughts still lingered on Iell's recent dismissal of me. I couldn't help but think that she no longer needed me. And my growing distance from my colleagues was painfully evident. How had that happened? Surely, Matina and I should have made amends by now. And Alley. I'd not had a decent talk with him since he hauled out that paper and told me he planned to move to a farm in—where was it?—Ohio.

"Enjoying your time off?" Barnum's voice came from directly behind me, and I jumped at the sound of it. He stood at the end of the garden, looking a bit seedy in an outdated black cutaway he must have pulled from the bottom of his closet, and judging by the expression on his face he wasn't a happy man.

"My God, sir, here you are again, out of nowhere."

"Step this way, Fortuno," Barnum commanded, grabbing me by

the elbow. He dragged me sideways along the courtyard walk, jarring my bones. We didn't stop until we reached the gardener's shed on the far side, a wood hut with a tin roof and square windows partially obstructed by duck-foot ivy growing along its whitewashed walls. Both my legs felt as if he'd yanked them from my hip sockets, and I feared he'd strained my left wrist.

"What in God's name have you been doing to get my wife all stirred up? Do you have any idea what trouble I went through to save your position here?"

The look on Barnum's face sent blood racing through my veins. "What are you talking about, sir?"

Barnum loomed over me. I rubbed my throbbing wrist, looking desperately toward the Museum in hopes that one of my colleagues had witnessed his cruelty. The stink of boiled cabbage rolled through the air, and Matina's laughter floated out from the half-opened dining room door. Perhaps if I inched to the left a bit, she might see us.

"Don't fiddle with me, Fortuno." Barnum grabbed hold of me and backed me up against the wall of the shed; his head bobbed like a dog considering the trustworthiness of a stranger. "I'm no fool."

I counted the markers rising from the even lines of peas and soybean plants in the garden to calm myself. "We had a private discussion, your wife and I."

"Why?"

What did he know? I had better speak truthfully. "She'd found out somehow that I'd visited Mrs. Adams, sir, and warned me to keep away."

Barnum slammed his hand into the side of the shed, displacing a shower of dust from behind the ivy. "So it *was* you in Iell's room that night! I knew it." Red-faced, he shoved open the shed door with one big boot and goose-stepped me inside. I struggled to remember Iell's response when I'd asked her point-blank about her relationship with Barnum. Had she ever given me a clear answer? Yes. She'd said he was a mentor and nothing more. Yet here he was, acting like a thwarted lover. Barnum shoved me toward a mud-crusted workbench.

"I think Mrs. Adams has a secret." I threw out the words in desperation.

Barnum jerked as if I'd hit him, and I saw that I'd hit a nerve. "What are you talking about, Fortuno? Out with it this instant!"

"Opium, sir."

"Opium?" Barnum's eyes softened, and he smiled. I wasn't sure if this was a good sign or a bad one.

"That is what I fetched for her at the Chinaman's, wasn't it?"

Barnum crossed the shed and laid his heavy hand on the bones of my shoulder. One of the rakes fell, clattering onto the shed's dirt floor. "Did you tell this to my wife, by any chance?"

"No, of course not."

Barnum stared at me with such unyielding directness that I barely felt the pain as he gripped my shoulder tighter still.

"Perhaps, Fortuno," he said after a considerable pause, "we've reached the end of our collaboration."

"The end?"

"My wife is a persistent woman, and it is not wise to rile her. You've spoken to her; surely you know what I mean. Best, I think, to conclude our private arrangements here and now. You need no longer concern yourself with anything regarding the affairs of myself, my wife, or the good Mrs. Adams. Is that clear?"

"Yes, sir. Perfectly."

Barnum let one of his famous smiles pour over his face and set me free. My shoulder pulsated as the blood returned to it.

"So thank you for all of your help, Fortuno. I am sure I can trust you to be discreet about what has gone on. Why don't I send you something nice? A token of gratitude, let's call it. Then we can consider ourselves even."

"Fine, sir, fine."

There it was, then. Iell was wedged between the two Barnums, one wanting her to stay, the other insisting that she leave, and both were telling me to break off all contact with her. What was I to do, ignore their threats and put my livelihood at stake? Even with Iell's recent coldness to me, how could I do such a thing? How could I not?

I spent the rest of the afternoon in tableau and skipped dinner entirely, opting instead to spend extra time in the Arboretum with my birds. Lately, to calm myself, I'd taken to trying to understand their songs. Sometimes I could almost hear words as they sang, a private language slipping back and forward between them. A different world. When, I wonder, would the Arboretum reopen? I'd have to fight to keep my bird-feeding tasks, because I doubted Barnum would want me to continue. I realized what a loss it would be for me not to be their caretaker.

After the Arboretum, rather than sit in my rooms while everyone else performed, I went up to the roof to check for signs of the fire. Other than a bit of dirty water near the big searchlight, nothing appeared out of the ordinary. The setting sun had turned the sky a beautiful mandarin color, with big streaks of pink slashing across the horizon, and not wanting to waste the sight I pulled an old wine carton up to the roof's edge and took a seat.

What could I do to make Iell safe? Perhaps Iell and I could renegotiate our contract as partners. Maybe do a joint show. That might alleviate Mrs. Barnum's concerns over her husband's growing attachment. On the other hand, if Iell wished to leave, maybe Peale's in Philadelphia would take us. Of course they would. Why not? Or perhaps we would even leave the business entirely.

I got to my feet and walked to the edge of the roof. From up high, the trolleys and coaches chugging back and forth looked like children's toys. Get out of the business entirely? I couldn't believe I'd even *thought* of such a thing. Without the business, I would have no reason to exist.

The sun finally disappeared, and when the sky turned black, I left the roof and made my way downstairs. As I lit the lamps in my rooms, a large object in the middle of my bedroom caught my eye. A bed. A brand-new bed. Barnum must have had my old one hauled out sometime that afternoon, and now, in its place, stood a fine, full, goose-feather mattress on a doubly reinforced frame, with new pillows and my mother's comforter folded neatly at the foot. I sat down on the bed and sank deep into the soft mattress. No doubt it was a bribe to keep my silence. I'd have to return it, but oh—it was so welcoming. Perhaps I could take a bit of rest first. Only a moment or two.

I curled up in the bed and pulled the comforter over my head. My mind raced with a jumble of images: Barnum yelling down at me, telling me our relationship was over. Matina slapping her fan closed in anger. Alley kissing her.

❋ ❋ ❋

HOURS LATER, muffled voices and the scuffle of many feet dragged me back to wakefulness. I checked the clock. It was a little past midnight. What was all the commotion about? Had there been another fire? I threw on my bed jacket and popped my head into the hall. Down at the other end, several of my colleagues huddled together in the light of the dimmed-down wall lamps. Their attention was riveted on a flickering light coming from inside Alley's room. What in the world had happened? Had he been struck sick? Keeping close to the wall, I inched my way through the shadows and slid silently into place next to Matina.

"Oh, Barthy, here you are. Isn't it horrible?" Matina grabbed hold of my arm when I joined her, our estrangement temporarily suspended. "Fish came upstairs an hour ago and searched Alley's rooms, and now they're in his parlor, shouting. He's saying Alley can't live here anymore and can only work with us until after the party, and even then only if he agrees to have a chaperone with him all the time. It's ridiculous, Barthy, and so upsetting."

"I don't understand."

"They found kerosene in his room. And rags. He swore that none of it was his, but no one paid him any mind."

"I don't think you need be so distraught," I said to her. "Fish most likely doesn't mean a word and is just venting his anger."

I thought for a moment that she was going to cry. "Thank goodness Alley was already thinking of leaving us," she went on. "Otherwise, the poor dear would be devastated."

Just then, Alley and Fish burst out of the door. Armed with a look of determination, Fish marched Alley toward the back stairs. Alley hung his head and did not look at any of us.

"Go back to bed, everyone!" Fish yelled over his shoulder. "Nothing here to concern any of you."

"They're removing him in the middle of the night? Just like that?" I asked Matina, both of us shocked by such brutality.

Matina watched them go, turning from me to wipe her eyes with her hanky. Then, to my surprise, she left me standing alone. A moment later, she was leaning against Emma and letting out great sobs. Surely we were all upset. Alley was our friend. And the idea that Fish could haul him out of the Museum so unceremoniously in the middle of the night was horrible. I could understand some tears. But why was Matina weeping with such distress, and on Emma's shoulder, not mine? For a horrible moment, it came to me that Matina was crying because there really was some deeper connection between her and Alley. My stomach flipped over. It was true that she and I were no longer easy companions. Much had passed between us, and I doubted we would ever be as close again. But Matina and Alley? Impossible. I knew them both like the back of my hand. Matina was simply emotional over how expendable Alley was.

Then a thought made my stomach turn again. Were *all* of us equally expendable? With a wave of cold realization, I realized that Alley's removal proved that the Barnums would not hesitate to fire a popular act. None of our positions at the Museum were safe. Even though I had just toyed with the idea of leaving the Museum, it was quite a different matter to be dismissed, and if I wanted to guard against that, I needed to make provisions to stand on my own.

chapter twenty three

HE RAVEN SQUAWKED TWICE WHEN I entered the Arboretum the next night, and the parrot I'd named Arrow flew up from his perch like a rising star. All day I'd been lost in thoughts of my troubles— Alley being removed, the loss of Matina, the Barnums and Iell—and the next thing I knew, I was kneeling in the rock garden where I'd buried the root. My hands moved by some unseen force. They plucked out the stone I'd used to mark the spot and then brushed away the gravel until I saw the tip of the bag.

One good yank and out it came, dust and gravel flying, and when I lifted the root to my nose, I smelled that familiar odor, fungal and dry. My mouth watered as my tongue touched the end of the root. The raven squawked.

With nary a thought, I ripped into the root. The bitterness clung to my tongue and spread along the inside of my mouth.

I chewed and chewed until none of the bitter taste remained. I swallowed the pulp and waited, then shuddered at a vision of Iell sitting near a stream, her skirts splayed out in the water. She held her beard with one hand and snipped at it with a tiny pair of scissors, the clippings falling into the stream, carried away toward some distant sea. My blood grew hotter. I could feel it bubble beneath the surface of my joints, down my thighs and through the back of my knees. My stomach burned as if it were full of fire.

I had to see Iell. Not later but now. What did it matter how late the hour? I needed to share my intentions—to let her know I was willing to take her away or keep her here, whatever she wished. Despite her cold dismissal of me when last I saw her, she must know I loved her. My headache blurred with excitement. Yes. I loved her. I loved Iell!

Ignoring any fear of discovery, I put the root into my pocket and ran out of the Arboretum, whipping through the Museum's front door and into the street with nary a thought. Let them see me. Let them throw me out on my ear like Alley. What did I care? Although it was after midnight, dozens of carriages still trolled the street looking for passengers. I hailed the first one I saw and shimmied onto the seat, shaking like a leaf. The fire in my belly spread through my limbs, and by the time the driver dropped me off at Mrs. Beeton's, I was a man possessed.

I pushed quietly through the wooden gate, the boardinghouse completely dark. Best not to disturb the matron, I decided, and moved stealthily along a path that led to the far side of the house. Through a window, I saw a darkened kitchen on the first floor, with a cast-iron stove, a brick oven, and an empty table covered by a lace cloth. To my left was a curved wooden stairway that snaked up the side of the house toward a sleeping porch. At the far end of the second floor, I spotted Iell's window.

From the shadows, I studied the black rectangle. She'd already gone to sleep. Of course she had. Yet I couldn't bear the idea of leaving without at least a glimpse of her. I paced the dark walk, up and back and up again. I knew I shouldn't be standing outside her window in the middle of the night, but I had to tell her that I loved her and would make her safe. Quite unexpectedly, her light went on. I took it as a sign.

I hopped onto the landing and swung myself up to the sleeping porch, inching past an unmade bed. It was easy enough to slip into the house through a curtain-covered arch and creep down the second-floor hallway toward Iell's door. I tapped lightly so as not to disturb anyone else. She did not respond. I knocked one more, this time with more force, and waited. Nothing. Not able to help myself, I hit the frame with my fist, fighting disappointment, but just as I turned to leave, Iell opened the door.

"Bartholomew, is that you? However did you get in here?" Iell was wearing a long mauve walking cape that covered a hoopskirt and swept all the way to the carpet. Her beard hung loose. Every few inches she'd tied tiny white feathers into it, like she was transforming into a dove. But her eyes had a hawklike sharpness I'd never seen before, and she smelled of smoke and incense. "Is something wrong?"

"Forgive me," I said, relieved just to be in her presence. "I felt terrible about leaving you the other morning with such bad news, and I simply had to see you."

"Come in then. Sit. Just give me a moment to get my bearings." Iell took hold of my arm and steered me into the half-lit parlor. A parasol rested against the wall inside the door, and I realized that she herself had just returned home. She walked me past the English cupboard where I'd hidden not long ago, and then into her private sitting room. Taking me by the shoulders, she guided me down into a chair and then drifted around, lighting wall sconces and lamps.

Sitting back, I watched her in awe. She *was* the medievalist's Scythian lamb, the *Lusus naturae*, the rarest creature in my mother's classification system. Although some might consider Iell's androgynous beauty unseemly, for a man like me—a connoisseur of remarkable bodies and gifts—she was perfection.

When she disappeared into her bedroom and returned in a lounging dress of pale gray—no hoop beneath the skirt now, so it hung free and close to her hips—my loins stirred. This time I did not fight the sensation. I simply allowed it to happen.

Iell dropped onto the chaise longue, her red hair floating down around her like feathers before settling onto her shoulders.

"Despite the late hour, I'm delighted to see you," she said. "I've not had an easy night, and I could use a little companionship."

"Iell," I began, heart thumping. "I have something to tell you."

She sighed. "You must give me one moment more, I'm afraid. As I said, I've not had an easy night."

I crossed my arms over my chest and waited while Iell repeated her ritual, pulling the pipe from a drawer in the table near her, along with an ivory box out of which she plucked a wad of opium. She rolled it into a ball, tucked it snugly into the pipe, and lit it with a long taper. The sticky smell of the opium turned my stomach a bit, but the smoke lulled me into a sort of stupor, quieting my urges. I sank deeper into my chair, woozy, as if I were smoking as well.

After a while, Iell seemed to fall asleep, and although I was still dying to confess my feelings, I was now content simply to watch over her. The muffled ringing of unfamiliar church bells pealed from parts of the city I had never seen. A night owl screeched from some nearby perch. Iell opened her eyes.

"Did you hear that?" She looked at me. "Soon some poor city mouse is about to be snatched up for dinner." She plucked at the top of her skirt, playing the silk between her thumb and finger. "Unless of course the mouse can find a way to escape his fate."

I wanted to proclaim my love but said, instead, "Have you recovered from my news about Mrs. Barnum?"

"Honestly, Bartholomew, you mustn't worry so. I'm an adult and am used to finding my own way in the world."

"Mightn't it be easier with a little assistance?" I said, inching toward the truth. "Some people in the world care very much for you, you know."

One of Iell's eyebrows, thin as the line made by a fine quill pen, arched slightly. "People?"

Now was the time to confess my love. I froze. What if she denied me? Or, worse, laughed?

Iell let my silence pass. "Are you still close with that woman friend of yours?"

I hesitated. "You mean Matina? Well, we've been friends for years." A vision of Matina's pretty face crossed my mind. "But we've had many differences lately."

"I see." The opium smoke flitted across Iell's eyes and mouth. "And did those differences get in the way of your pleasure?"

"Our pleasure?" It took me a moment to understand what Iell meant. "Just the opposite, in fact." I remembered Matina's warm, rolling flesh, and how lying on top of her was as soothing as a warm bath. I crossed my legs at the knee and leaned forward in my chair. "Her differences were quite delightful."

"Ahhhh." Iell closed her eyes once more, giving me another opportunity to study her face, the planes of her cheekbones rising smoothly out of her beard. How easy to imagine what she would look like as a normal woman.

"What gets in the way of *your* pleasure?" I asked boldly, attempting to take control of the conversation.

Iell stirred and ran one hand down the length of her arm. "What gets in *my* way is too complicated to explain right now," she answered. "But perhaps soon, together, we can explore such a question in more depth."

Together. We would be together soon. Once I confessed my love to her, I could tell Iell that I was willing to take care of her. If only I could find the right words.

Iell's skirt rustled as she stood and walked over to my chair. She slid in next to me, the backrest supporting us both, the armrests pushing us up against each other. When she kissed me, her beard tickled my chin to the point of ecstasy. I pulled her closer and slid a hand up the length of her fine back, rolling my fingers along her spine. I reached down and slipped off one of her satin pumps, wrapping my fingers around her ankle.

"I have something to tell you," I whispered.

"A secret?" Iell asked, pulling away her foot. "Would you like to know one of my secrets first?" Her voice was raspy and deep.

"I think I've already guessed it."

"Have you now?" She let her shoe dangle, then drop. It fell to the floor but made no sound.

"You want a protector," I whispered into her ear. "Someone to care for you and take you away from all of this."

She did not pull away. "Is that what you think?"

"That's why you speak of choice. Of change." I ran a hand across her hair, inhaling her rose perfume. "You thought Barnum would protect you, but now, with his wife in the way, you want me to help you be free of them both."

Iell stiffened in my arms, then withdrew. She stood, her beard spilling across her chest. One of the white feathers she'd woven into it came untied and floated toward the window. "If all I wanted was to go away," she said, "I would have accepted Mrs. Barnum's fine offer without reservation."

I looked up, surprised. "You've spoken to her?"

"No, of course not. Not directly. One of her agents brought me her terms, and I thought about the proposition longer than you might suspect."

Many feelings overwhelmed me—astonishment, awe, guilt, the urge to hold Iell and never let her leave me.

"You'd be a fool to trust her," I said.

Iell nodded.

"Once you'd left, who knows how long she would keep her word." I reached up and took hold of one of Iell's hands, tugging her back into the chair with me. She let me hold her. "What is it you really want?" I asked, her perfume making me dizzy. "Tell me what you want," I repeated, knowing I was at risk of being told what I might not want to hear. "We can stay here in the Museum if we band together. Or we could go to Peale's in Philadelphia. They'd take us, I'm certain of it. I could write a letter to them today." I swallowed my fear. "If you'll just tell me what you want, I will do anything to help you get it."

"Quite honestly, Bartholomew," she answered, again taking up the opium pipe, "I'm not really sure."

The lamp near our chair flickered and went out. The two of us sat together in the darkness, Iell curled against me, nodding in and out of sleep. After a time, I carefully lifted the pipe from her limp fingers and placed it on the table. She sighed when I got up. She may not have known what she wanted, but it was clear she needed me more than ever. And even though I'd never actually confessed my love, saying that I would do anything in my power to help her was almost the same.

I kissed Iell gently on the forehead and let myself out. As I walked through her door, I took a last look at my own image in the gilded mirror near her door.

✳ ✳ ✳

SATURDAY MORNING brought with it the sense that I'd skirted some terrible disaster the night before. Why did my stomach ache so? I looked over to my bedside table, where I'd put the root. Thank God it hadn't driven me mad last night the way it had with Matina.

As soon as I rose from my new bed—it had felt like sleeping in the clouds—I took a thin slice of the root, chewed it, and swallowed the desiccated pulp. I had been eating it with increasing frequency, and I tried to ignore how small it was growing. I needed to go to the Chinaman soon and ask for more.

Dressing in haste, I hurried to the Green Room and was unusually pleased to find many of my colleagues chattering in the dressing room. My effusive greetings and backslapping raised an eyebrow or two, but it felt good to be back where I belonged. And when Fish came in at his usual time, and posted a special notice, I was thrilled to discover that I was listed to perform in the first of the morning shows.

Who cared that he'd only put me down for one appearance? I couldn't wait to perform again. And my morning show went better than it had for years. Not since I'd first joined the Museum did I display myself with such pleasure. A woman sitting in the front row fainted mid-show, and I could not have been happier. For some reason, though, the Misting Over I so often experienced in performance was completely gone. Rather than people's faces blurring as I gazed out over them, every face was now distinct, with its own story to tell. I wondered if this was another side effect of the root.

Minutes after my show ended, Alley showed up backstage with a house escort and my mood plummeted. He told me that Barnum had put me on the morning schedule only because Alley couldn't make it in time. But what did it matter?

"Are you all right?" I asked Alley, and he gave me a brave nod as his escorts shoved him onto our little stage. He only had a few more days before he'd leave the Museum forever. But he looked almost joyous. I knew he wanted to move to Ohio, but I would have expected a bit more sadness on his part, given what he was losing.

On Sunday, guest performers started to arrive. Cook set up a picnic outside in the courtyard. Everyone sat scattered on the benches and across the patches of green grass, balancing plates of food on their knees. Zippy and Nurse sprawled across an old horsehair blanket that they'd spread out on the eternally hardened ground, playing a game of dice, and behind them loitered two midgets on loan from the Boston Museum, one a youngish man with a slightly oversized head, the other a perfectly formed woman only three feet tall and dressed like Martha Washington. Beside them, Bridgett sat laughing on the lap of the owner of the Boston Museum, who'd come to watch over his midgets.

On a flat stone bench at the far end of the courtyard, Matina sat fanning herself, and next to her, Emma argued with two visiting giants whom I recognized as the sharpshooter Captain Bogardus and his brother Ethan. The two giants gesticulated and poked long fingers into each other's chest. I raised my hand to catch Matina's eye, but she turned away. I looked around and not a single other soul returned my gaze. Fine. It was a beautiful day. No reason I couldn't enjoy it all alone.

Besides, the food table called to me. Why had I never noticed how comely a roasted chicken could be, or how plump a loaf of bread? And the smells—so rich, so mouthwatering. I piled my usual green beans onto a plate, adding a few extra, and then spooned out a dollop of mustard. I found a seat on an empty bench and laid my napkin across my lap. As always, I sliced each bean into equal parts before methodically dipping each piece into the mustard. I thought about the China-man's root and ignored the quick flip in my stomach. Then, surprising myself, I walked back to the food table, picked up a piece of bread from the communal basket, and gingerly lifted it to my nose. The wheat, ripe and vaguely nutty, dredged up some deep craving within me. I turned away from the group and took a huge bite of it. The bread sat heavily in my mouth. I dared not move. Saliva poured into the bottom of my mouth. Instinctively, I chewed. Then, unable to resist any longer, I swallowed.

Almost immediately, a memory rose up. I was a boy again, a boy who hadn't eaten in days. A boy who, late one night, crept out into the dark orchards and ate three fallen apples. The next night I stole radishes and squash from the garden, eating them raw, and the next day I hid in the kitchen, waiting for the household to finish their supper. The kitchen maid had piled trays of leftovers on the big oak table, and when no one was looking, I snatched up the cornbread ends, ham bones, half-eaten potatoes, and chicken legs that were meant for the pigs. Stealing food. Why would I do such a thing?

I ordered myself to step away from the food table, but instead, I wrapped the half-eaten piece of bread in my napkin and, after making sure there were no witnesses to my indiscretion, stuck it in my pocket. Across the garden, Matina was frowning at something one of the giants had said, her arms crossed defensively across her chest. I desperately wanted to join them, but they were in another world.

Feigning a calmness I did not feel, I set my plate down and poured myself a cup of tea. Ignoring the tantalizing smell of a pork loin roasted with garlic, I forced myself to return to the empty bench and sipped the tea slowly, washing away the taste of the bread I'd eaten. By the time the one o'clock bell rang from St. Paul's, I'd calmed myself. Eventually, my colleagues moved on to their afternoon work, and when Cook's new assistant came hustling outside to pick up the empty platters and clear away the condiments, I pushed up from the bench feeling back in control of my world.

That's when the first real wave of hunger hit me. At first, I failed to recognize it for what it was; I felt only that same ache at the bottom of my belly that I'd felt before. But then a desire rose up in me, a craving for something, anything, to take away the ache, and, by the time that urge changed into a brutish growl, it was much too late. My feet marched me out of the courtyard and into the kitchens, and into my pocket went a pork chop, a pink apple, and a huge hunk of yellow cheese.

Desperate for the courtyard to empty out, I paced behind the kitchen door until the last of the troupe had gone and then dashed up the cobblestone walk to the gardener's shed. Crouching down in the weeds, I pulled the pork chop from my pocket and tore into it. The taste of the meat shocked me: fleshy, firm, peppered to the point of burning. I chewed until my jaw hurt, the smell making me woozy, juices rolling down my throat like a river. After that, the apple tasted so sweet and crisp it brought tears to my eyes. I used my back teeth to rip off chunks to the core, and I even ate the seeds, the crunch of them between my teeth remarkably satisfying. When my belly started to swell, I told myself to stop, but, looking furtively through the weeds, I pulled out the cheese. I polished it off within a few glorious seconds. How wonderful the texture was, giving but insistent. Rich and heavy on the tongue.

I managed to go back to work after that, sitting in tableau and then lingering in the Cosmo-Panopticon Studio, chatting with customers and selling my *cartes* as if it were a normal day. The first spasm in my belly passed within moments, and I covered up the pain by smiling broadly and feigning interest in the story a lad was telling me about a neighbor's dog who died of malnutrition. The next spasm was more insistent, and within minutes I was pushing blindly through the crowd. As if in a nightmare, I could barely move forward. The food in my stomach had turned into a two-ton rock, dragging me to the ground. What I needed was fresh air. I forced my way through the public spaces, past the kitchens, and back out to the courtyard, stumbling through the vegetable garden. There I fell to my hands and knees, gagging. And finally, heaving with violence but great relief, my body rejected all the food I'd eaten.

chapter twenty four

THE NEXT DAY, I WOKE UP RAVENOUS. THE Museum was closed for the day in preparation for Barnum's party, and despite the battery of cleaners engaged to assist him Fish had pinned up a list of job postings on the dining room wall.

☛ **SPECIAL NOTICE** ☚
JULY 3, 1865

All regular performers have extra tasks as here outlined. **Please!** *No comments or complaints to management concerning these assignments.*

Report TODAY, 11:00 a.m. at assigned locations.

Bartholomew Fortuno - Oversee transfer of birds from Arboretum to Moral Lecture Room.
Matina Johansson - Napkin folding, Staff kitchens.
Bridgett O'Flannery - Glass polishing, Staff kitchens.
"Zippy" Johnson - Rolling of crepe, Ballroom.
Ricardo Hortense and Emma Swan - Rolling out carpets, first-floor service area.

Thank God for the diversion. All I wanted was to keep busy and pretend the previous day hadn't happened. It had been a fluke, I told myself. Nothing but nerves. But no matter how hard I tried to convince myself that all was well, I couldn't push away a growing dread.

What else could I do but take my normal tea at breakfast and then go back to my room? There, I snuck a tiny bite of the root. After chewing it thoroughly, I pitched myself into the day, hoping a bit of physical activity would bring me back to myself.

Staff members had spread across the Museum like locusts, polishing marble floors, dusting staircases, and setting up potted trees and seats along the walls near the Ballroom. Without being asked, I pitched in, dusting and straightening with forced heartiness. Come midmorning, three wagons pulled up to the back entrance and unloaded dozens of animals that had been stuffed by a zealous taxidermist and dressed hideously in party clothes and hats. In came a lioness in a pink dress; two bulls in neckties; a coyote, a handful of raccoons, and a fox all costumed as waiters; plus a huge black bear in formal evening clothes. I helped place them in the niches along the Ballroom walls. When workers hauled in twenty-foot renditions of Brady's photographs—including a solitary but discreet one of Iell—it was I who gave them a hand tilting the huge portraits out onto the lower balconies, securing them to the railings so they faced down to the street for all to see.

By the time I reported to the Arboretum at eleven for my scheduled assignment, I had all but exhausted myself. Just outside the door, dozens of slatted crates full of new songbirds had been stacked. The crates were stamped RICHE BROTHERS—the same company that had shipped three thousand canaries to the California gold mines and sold them for a fortune. I tromped down the pathway and ran smack into five burly men who had already transferred my Arboretum birds into pens and were carting them out. One uncoordinated buffoon banged the end of the pen he was carrying against the wall, sending the birds into a panic.

"Here, here! Barnum appointed me supervisor of these birds. You'd best take care with them or I will have your job."

"Sorry, sir, sorry," one of them mumbled, and they moved more carefully after that, toting crates of birds slowly up the main staircase to the Moral Lecture Room. The birds squawked as if it were the end of days until the men pushed the pens through the bank of doors lead-ing into the theater. Then they fell silent. We all did.

Barnum had completely transformed the cavernous theater for his party, and the effect was breathtaking. Across the gigantic stage, hun-dreds of prisms hung from strings. At some crucial point during the party, one of Barnum's handymen would fire up the Gothic torches hung high on the walls to bring these prisms alive. To the right, against the side wall, long tables were covered with Belgian linens, stacks of gold dishes, rows of goblets and decanters, candles, and a gigantic three-tiered crystal punch bowl. But most impressive were the fifty-foot runners of silk hanging from the ceiling of the cavernous room. Multi-colored and festooned with pounded-tin ornaments in the shape of Barnum's profile, they listed from one side to the other, and when I pulled the door closed behind me, the breeze set all the runners in motion.

It took us the rest of the morning to transfer the songbirds from their pens into the gilded cages piled in the rear of the theater. After that, I helped place my Arboretum birds. We put the parrots on cov-ered perches at the front doors, Arrow looking proud and handsome. The cockatoos were displayed in oval cages lit from behind by candles, and the macaws and African grays went into an oblong box hung high above the Lecture Room doors. The raven roosted alone on a perch in a black iron cage by the exit.

By noon I'd finished my tasks and went searching for Matina. Surely she'd know how Alley was faring. When I stuck my head into the kitchens to find her, I saw only the fruits of her labor—a mountain of folded napkins—and discarded empty plates everywhere. I hung about outside the dining room then, expecting Matina to come to lunch, but she never appeared. Anxious and tired of waiting, I walked into the room to ask after her, but from the moment I set foot in the dining room, all I could see was the food table: roast duck, pureed potatoes, tomato soup, baskets of fruit, all smelling heavenly and call-ing out to me. I didn't know what to make of this strange new impulse, but I wanted that food more than I'd ever wanted anything else.

Straight to the table I went and, pretending to serve myself my usual beans, I surreptitiously slipped a piece of duck into a napkin and then my pocket, followed shortly by a corn fritter and an orange. I caught Zippy staring at me from across the table. He tapped his spoon against his glass and sang out:

> "Eat the sacred.
> Whatcha got?
> Stomach naked.
> Lost the lot."

The floppy fur hat and deerskin boots he wore no matter what the weather infuriated me.

"Why don't you speak up," I hollered at him. "Say what you mean to say, boy. Stop speaking in riddles."

Zippy stopped in mid-tap, an unexpected gleam of intelligence in his eyes. "Maybe you should attend to your own riddles."

Everyone in the dining room looked over at me. Standing mute in front of the others, a big chunk of bread in my hand, I was horrified. The Chinaman had told me that chewing the root would reveal my true self, but this couldn't be right. If I lost control of my appetites, I would lose what made me special. My God, what was I doing? I looked around the table, everyone's eyes on me. Without my gift, I'd be like everyone else, and the world was already full of normal people. It was *us* the world needed, we Curiosities. I yanked out the food from my pocket and threw it onto the serving table. A piece of duck slid over the side and landed on the ground below.

"That's a clean floor!" Cook hollered after me, but I was already running out the door.

Up the Grand Staircase I skittered. I didn't stop until I reached the Moral Lecture Room and ducked inside to regain my bearings. Breathe deep. Breathe deep. My heart calmed as I looked at all those birds in cages. A bird or two had begun to sing, and it warmed me. Maybe we were all Gaffs in the end, all of us hungry to be different from what we were. Before Barnum threw him out, Alley had already decided to leave. Was he any less of a man for choosing a different path? Who really cared about this gift of mine? If I ate, I would be normal, and as a full-bodied man, I could be of much more help to Iell. What would it matter if Barnum dismissed me then? I could work in the world like any other man. I could take care of us both.

The birdsong grew, and I noticed that all the birds were singing—all of them but one. She was a white-breasted nuthatch with under-developed wings. I stuck my finger through the wicker bars, and the nuthatch looked up at me silently. I knew what had to be done: I slipped the bird and her tiny cage beneath my jacket and maneuvered into the hallway and up the stairs.

As soon as I got to my rooms, I set her cage on the sill of my window, and the nuthatch began to sing just as she was born to do. I sat down next to her and started to draw. It was a self-portrait. I worked fast, but when I was done, I thought the lines looked too thin, so I took up a thicker quill and drew hastily until the lines thickened, each outline building on the layer beneath it, making the figure more substantial by burying the first lines I had drawn. I stared at the picture, aching for the old times, when things were plainly this or that and I understood my world.

An hour later, I sneaked down to the kitchen and stole a leg of lamb.

✳ ✳ ✳

I DIDN'T mean to go looking for Alley that night. Some part of me simply had to get out of the Museum, and I thought McNealy's might remind me of what was important. The hope that Alley might be hanging about playing cards was an added attraction. Climbing the porch stairs and tipping my hat to the Plaques for the Dead, I felt almost like my old self, and when the chaos of McNealy's swept over me, I felt certain that going there had been the right thing.

Bridgett sat on the far side of the room, swilling ale with some of the theater players. Ducking to avoid her, I moved toward where Mac usually played cards, and sure enough, there was Alley. A Polish midget sitting across from him sparkled with gold jewelry, including several watch chains and wrist bangles and an oversized belt buckle in the shape of New York. Next to him sat the good Reverend Smalley from our Sunday services.

I pushed my way over to their table, tipping my hat to the three-antlered moose head hanging above them on the wall.

Mac kicked an empty chair toward me. "Three times in one month, Fortuno? You're almost becoming a regular."

"So God lets his servants have a night off, does he, Reverend?"

The Reverend smiled. "Even God likes to live it up now and then." His pile of chips was quite impressive.

Alley looked up at me and shoved a loose mop of hair out of his eye. He seemed quite cheerful, even though the skin on his knuckles was broken and bruised. I pulled my chair closer to his and took a look at the cards he was holding. Three queens and a two. An excellent hand.

"How are you, my friend? Where are you staying?"

"Over on Vesey Street with the house musicians. Ain't all that bad, really." Alley shrugged, rearranging his cards. "And it won't be for long. I'm leavin' in just a few days."

"I thought you needed to make a bit more money first," I said, pulling my chair closer to the table.

"I made a little extra, and I'm doin' great tonight." Alley tossed five chips into the pot, then, on impulse, two more. "Sure hope it ain't true what they says about a man who's lucky at cards bein' unlucky in love." He laid his queens on the table, dropping cigar ash onto the front of his shirt in the process. Mac snorted and tossed in his cards facedown. The midget pushed away from the table and left without a word, and Reverend Smalley sighed. Alley pulled the pot to him, stacking his chips a dozen high.

"What's the matter, Bridgett doesn't want you to leave her? She's just over yonder, you know. I'd be happy to fetch her for you if you like." I rose to make good on my threat.

"Bridgett?" Alley looked at me, clearly surprised. "I thought you knew, Fortuno. I've asked Matina to come to Ohio with me."

The raucousness around me disappeared. I sat down with a decided thump. "You did what?"

"Yesterday. Don't know if she'll go yet. She turned me down, but you know how she is, sayin' one thing one day and doin' something else the next."

"Why in the world would you ask Matina to do such a thing?" My voice came out louder than I'd meant it to, but surely he knew that Matina didn't belong anywhere else but in the Museum. "Don't you know how hard she's worked to get where she is? Barnum even asked her to do a show for his birthday. A real break for her."

"She told me you said not to do it."

"That's not the point." I felt betrayed. Matina and I used to keep our conversations to ourselves. "For God's sake," I said harshly. "Why would she throw everything away to go live on some farm in the middle of nowhere?"

The lines in Alley's forehead deepened. "What's the matter with you, Fortuno? You're all red in the face. You two are only friends. But Matina and me—"

"You don't know anything about Matina," I yelled. And then before I could stop myself, I continued in a harsh whisper. "We're more than friends. We've been . . . intimate."

"Intimate?" Alley scratched his head and sat up straighter in his chair. His muscled arms went rigid, his hands rolling into fists.

I wished to God I'd kept my mouth shut, but didn't Alley have a right to know the truth about the woman he was trying to steal away?

"It wasn't anything serious, Alley, not really. But I don't want to see you disappointed. Take someone else if you think you need a helper. Bridgett would go with you in a heartbeat."

Alley didn't move for the longest time, and then he grabbed Mac's glass full of whiskey and tossed it back. He reached for the bottle and poured himself another drink. Then a third. By that time, he had turned alarmingly cheerful. Glass in hand, he yelled out into the tavern,

"Let's drink to my friend here. Come on, you sluggards. Glasses up to becoming a man!" Then he settled his huge arm down around me like a fallen oak, and I winced. I met eyes with Mac, who gave me a what-can-I-do shrug.

As soon as I could slip out of his grip, I left Alley at the table and pushed through the crowd. Truth was, aside from being afraid of Alley when he was drinking, I also felt guilty as hell. I'd broken my promise to Matina. But then again, no one was guarding *my* feelings. I rubbed my belly, which was aching again for food.

I settled onto a bar stool next to a man with a bone in his lip who was arguing vehemently with Esmeralda over the price of a scotch. Esmeralda gave me a wink when she saw me. Pulling out my handkerchief, I wiped the sweat from my brow, determined to lose my worries in a glass of something strong.

"Whiskey," I said, when Esmeralda got to me. "And a plate of your lamb stew if you've got any this evening."

"Lamb stew?" She poured my drink and looked around to see if anyone else had heard me ask for food.

I sipped at the whiskey. My reflection leered back at me from the crackled mirror behind the bar, and I had a vision of my cheeks filling out, my neck growing thick and strong.

"Fortuno!" Alley's voice boomed from behind me.

I swiveled on my stool and stared into the face of a miserable man. His eyelids drooped, his nostrils flared, and tears ran down his deeply creased cheeks.

"It's *your* fault she said no!" he cried.

"I'm sorry I upset you, my friend. Sorry I said anything at all. But what would Matina want with a farmer's life?"

"She mighta said yes if it hadn't been for you. She never woulda been like a"—he shut his eyes in misery—"like a wife to you, if she didn't love you."

"She doesn't love me!"

"And now you're gonna marry her, and I'll never—"

"Marry Matina? Goodness, no. In fact, I'm in love with someone else. Someone so remarkable—"

Although I saw it coming, I barely had time to duck. Alley's fist whooshed past the side of my head, and I threw myself sideways, all but flying off my stool. I landed on the hardwood floor, and by the time my ears cleared a crowd had gathered, laughing and jeering.

"Come on, Skinny, let him have it!"

"Two bucks the skeleton won't survive a hit."

"Four says the strong guy's too drunk to find him."

I lay there, my left eye swelling shut. From the corner of my other eye, I saw Bridgett standing on a bar stool, craning her neck to get a better look.

An inch from my face, Alley stomped his mud-crusted boots against the filthy floor. I rolled over onto my back.

"Get up, Fortuno." He gazed down on me, swaying from side to side and almost sobbing. "I can't let you treat a lady like that."

And I understood how stupid I'd been. How long had Alley loved Matina? I thought back to how he always looked at her like she was a precious thing, how he defended her name. He had been courting her for some time, hadn't he, and some part of me had known it but could not accept such a thing.

My thoughts disappeared when, glowering like a mad bull, Alley bent down and grabbed me by the collar, lifting me with one hand. I peered into his drunken eyes and watched helplessly as his other arm lifted over my head to strike me a fatal blow. The crowd watched open-mouthed as he slashed his arm down like a guillotine, but he stopped two inches from my neck.

"Fuck all!" he cried, and dropped me painfully onto the stool. "I'm all fired up over nothing, just another whore without a heart."

I could have left it at that. It wasn't Matina I wanted, was it? Alley was clearly the better man for her, and I should have told him to take her away, to care for her in the manner she deserved. We could have parted as friends. But my pride was hurt and adrenaline surged through my veins. It was as if I were a lion kept too long in captivity and some gigantic hand had loosened the door of my cage. Who was Alley to ask Matina to leave her life at the Museum just to be with him? Who was he to attack me for telling him the truth? I hopped on top of the stool and faced him, sternum to sternum.

"You're an arsonist," I hollered into his rheumy eyes. "You can't control your impulses, and a hundred acres of farmland isn't going to change that. We are what we are, and that's that."

Alley swung at me again, but this time, I ducked and let his arm sail past me, the weight of it turning him around. While he was distracted, I jumped on his back and held on for dear life. Alley went spinning, and within seconds he tumbled over a bar stool and careened, forehead first, into the wall.

I got McNealy and three others to carry him to the carriage and send him back to Vesey Street. Then I pushed back into McNealy's, the crowd parting as I passed. Placing the bar stool back on its feet, I hopped up and slammed my hand onto the bar.

"Esmeralda," I yelled out. "Where is that bowl of stew I ordered? I want it. Now!"

chapter twenty five

S SOON AS I GOT HOME FROM THE BAR, Matina rounded the corner of the resident hallway like a runaway wagon.

"Bartholomew. Tell me exactly what happened!"

I braced myself when I saw her coming, gripping the doorknob, my hands still filthy from the fight in the bar. A dusty breeze blew in from the open transom of one of the hallway windows.

"Bridgett told me you had a run-in with Alley at McNealy's. Have you totally lost your senses? Barnum will have a fit if he finds out you've been fighting."

"I was rude. He was drunk."

Matina reached over and touched my eye. "He might have *killed* you, Barthy." I held my breath to hide any telltale odors from the lamb stew I'd just eaten. "What do you mean you were rude?" she asked.

"Must we discuss that now? As you can see . . ." I gestured at my filthy clothes and pushed open the door to my rooms, nodding her inside. Light pooled around us when I lit the lamp on the entrance table. Thankfully, the stolen nuthatch on my windowsill stayed asleep beneath the cover on her cage.

I helped Matina off with her cape and guided her toward the parlor couch. She sat down in her usual place and untied the strings of her bonnet, mussing her hair in the process. Although she ignored the old piece of tatting abandoned on the back of my settee, she made a point of turning over the embroidered pillow she'd made me so that its message—*He who stands with the Devil does himself harm*—lay faceup.

"If you would give me a moment," I said, "I need to change my jacket."

When I opened the door to my bedroom, Matina sucked in her breath. "What in the world is that?"

"What?" Surprised, I followed her gaze. "Oh. The bed. It's nothing. A gift from Barnum."

Matina snapped open her fan and waved it rapidly back and forward in front of her face. "Why would Barnum give you such a thing?"

My face flushed. "I did some extra work for him. You remember that trip to Chinatown."

"Yes, but a bed? That's quite a reward for one trip into the city, don't you think?"

"It's nothing, I assure you. Now, if you could give me a moment," I said again. "Pour yourself a brandy if you like. I shan't be long." I shut the bedroom door behind me and pressed my shoulder against it to hold it closed. How could I explain the bed? And how much of what had really happened with Alley should I share?

"Just look at you," Matina said, when I finally rejoined her, concerns about the bed apparently put to rest. "All black and blue. I warned you that people change colors when life gets away from them." She chuckled at her own joke, then patted the sofa seat next to her, urging me to sit down. "Do you have something to put on that eye? Otherwise, it's going to swell shut."

"Why didn't you tell me Alley asked you to go to Ohio with him?"

Matina snapped her fan shut and sat up a bit straighter. "My goodness. Is that what the two of you were fighting about?"

I said nothing.

"Barthy?"

I walked to the window and pushed it open for a bit of air. I looked up into the cloudless sky. "I cannot believe he asked you to move to Ohio."

"Why ever not? I'm not getting any younger, you know. You should know I am considering it."

I said nothing to this. What could I say?

"You *are* coming to the party tomorrow night, aren't you?" Matina asked.

"Yes," I said, still looking out the window.

"If you wanted to, I would allow you to escort me."

My heart slowed to a deep thump. I turned to face Matina. "I'm sorry. I have other plans."

Matina winced but maintained her cool bearing. "All right," she said, nodding quietly. She smoothed her skirts into place. The little songbird scrabbled in her cage, awakened by the sound of our voices. I returned to the couch and sat next to Matina and tried to put my hand on top of hers, but she took hold of her bonnet and pulled it onto her lap.

"I could change, you know," she said, her fingers playing with her bonnet's satin ties. "I could lose a bit of weight. Find another profession."

I felt as if I were standing on a cliff, the bottom so far away I couldn't even see it.

"No, my dearest, you shouldn't change. No one in the world is like you, and transforming yourself would require too much discipline and denial."

"But this other person. Iell. You think she's capable of changing herself?"

"She's so much more than the rest of us, Matina. Really she is. I believe she's even capable of living in the real world, if she should wish it. As can I. One can't depend on Barnum all one's life, you know. Eventually, the child must become a man."

"And how is it she could live in the real world?"

"She'd only need to shave."

We looked at each other for what felt to be an eternity, and then Matina began to laugh. She threw her head back and laughed so loudly her jowls shook and her eyes teared up.

I flew to my feet, desperate. "Stop! Please. What are you laughing at?"

"Oh, Barthy, so many things!"

Tears streaked down Matina's cheeks and she struggled to pull herself together. She wiped at her cheeks with the back of her hand and pushed a strand of hair from her forehead.

"I'm sorry, Barthy. Truly I am. But what about your fancy philosophy? All your talk of gifts and how Curiosities are so much better than everyone else? What about all that?" The lamplight illuminated Matina's face now, and I could see that she was perfectly serious.

"There's no reason why some of us can't live in both worlds. With padding, I could pass. I could perform in the daytime, then live in the city. Or quit the profession entirely and run a little shop somewhere. Haberdashery, maybe. Or sell equestrian gear. That wouldn't change my true self. A Prodigy born is a Prodigy for life."

Matina gave me a quizzical look. "Is this why you were eating bread at lunch?"

I stepped away. "I wasn't."

"Don't be an idiot, Barthy. Everyone *saw* you. Stuffing food into your pockets like a common thief. You did that because you want to live out in the world?"

"Of course not."

"Well, you'd better be sure this Iell wants the same things you do, that's all I can say."

When I offered to help Matina up from the couch, she refused—not with malice, but with determination—and I understood that not touching me was her way of letting me go. She tied her bonnet under her chin and moved toward the door.

"Matina." I stopped her. "There's one more thing I think you need to know."

She stood waiting for whatever I had left to say.

"About tonight. At McNealy's. We fought because I told Alley about us."

She jerked her chin as if I'd hit her. "What are you saying? What did you tell him?"

"I told him about our being together. That night."

"You did *what*? How *could* you?"

"That's why he attacked me, Matina. I shouldn't have said anything,

I know that, and I'm terribly sorry. But at least everything is out in the open now. I think it's better this way."

A gust of wind blasted one of my windows open, sending the charcoal etchings flying off the walls. Hurrying to the window, I pulled it closed and did my best to gather up the drawings. Then I looked up to see Matina's skirts billowing out like storm clouds.

"Better what way?" she said, in a voice that froze me to the spot.

"Matina. You have to understand. It was in the heat of the moment."

She headed for the bedroom, her heavy steps shaking the floorboards and setting the glass in the wall sconces tinkling. Hesitantly, I followed.

"Oh, I know all about the heat of the moment. Yes, indeed." She seemed to grow even bigger as she stood over my new bed. "You inspire me, Barthy, you really do. New friends. New beds as gifts. Maybe I could use a little change as well."

"It was only Alley," I muttered, praying she would calm down.

"Perhaps I should change the color of my hair or do it up a different way?" Matina's hands yanked at her chignon. The restraining pins tinkled to the floor like metal rain, hunks of hair tumbling across her face in feral waves.

"Alley will understand, once you give him some time."

Matina took a step closer to me and gripped the material at the top of her bodice, her breathing shallow.

"Or this plain old dress of mine, eh? Maybe I should change it?"

She drew in one deep, unnatural breath and pulled. There was a great ripping sound, and then the top of her chemise was exposed, the tatters of her blue bodice fluttering down her front in a horrifying parody of a party dress.

I inched away from her slowly.

"Then I could starve myself and grow a little fuzzy goatee."

"I want you to calm down, Matina."

Matina's eyes tapered and got very, very dark. She gave off an animal smell that made my tongue tighten against the roof of my mouth.

"Then again, maybe I'm not the one who needs to change. Maybe I should be helping you along instead." Her voice grew louder. "How about a little help, my love?"

She moved toward the bed, eyes narrowed, perspiration dripping from her forehead. In one frightening gesture, she yanked off the comforter and threw it toward the window. I dove after it, catching the edge just before it went out and over the building's side.

Matina snatched a pillow from the bed. "Do you have any idea how horribly you've treated me?" She grabbed the pillow between her hands and yanked so violently that it exploded, filling the room with an avalanche of pale feathers. "And now, on top of everything else, you've shamed me in front of Alley." She grabbed another pillow and held it aloft.

Fish started to bang on the other side of my door, yelling, "What's going on in there?" I could hear the nuthatch in its cage by the window chirping in alarm.

Matina raised her voice even louder. "And this bed of yours, eh? This brand-new, who-knows-how-you-got-it-or-who-the-hell's-been-in-it bed." Matina ripped the second pillow apart and then threw a wild kick at the bed frame. Her hair flew around her head like a cyclone.

"You stop it now!" I yelled, but this seemed to enrage her all the more.

"You want me to stop?" she screamed. "Do you? Oh, I'll stop, you pathetic little man. This is the end!"

The pounding on the door got louder.

Matina turned and stormed to the far end of the room. Then she hiked up her skirts, dropped her chin low into her neck, and came at me. My whole body went cold as she started running. She thundered forward, full of ferocity and grace. She bellowed once, then somehow pushed away from the floor and flew into the air, yelling out, "I am nobody's whore!"

When she landed on her belly in the middle of the bed, the entire left side crashed down, reverberating through the floor and nearly knocking me off my feet.

That's when Fish smashed through the lock. I remember the crack of the door and his yelling at us to cease, but by that time, I had lost all fear and had leaped toward Matina and grabbed hold of one of her ankles. From somewhere deep in my belly came a banshee yell of such intensity that the wall lamps shook and I was lost in the roiling sea of her flesh.

"Break it up, you two!"

Fish grabbed me by the legs, and for one moment the three of us stretched out in a screaming human chain. I hung on as long as I could, but my fingers gave way, and when I let go, I flew backward into Fish. The two of us tumbled to the floor, sweating and panting for air. Matina loomed over us, her face a raging tempest.

"You!" she screamed at Fish. "How dare you people make poor Alley leave? He is an innocent man! And you!" She glared at me, and when she spoke again her voice was so rough the hair on my neck rose. "You deserve exactly what you'll get!"

She stormed out of the room, the tatters of her dress whipping behind her like flags in a gale, and feathers flew once more up into the air.

Fish turned to me. "One more outbreak like this and you are dismissed, Fortuno! Do you understand?"

"Barnum would never allow—"

"You've been hanging on by a string for quite a while. This is the last time any of us will warn you."

Fish took off after Matina, leaving me buried in a mountain of plumage.

✳ ✳ ✳

A SMALL table kicked aside in the scuffle had a gash along the top of the wood. I righted it, and then examined my mother's comforter for damage before placing it carefully on the broken bed. Feathers had traveled like a snow squall, spreading from my bedroom into the parlor, dotting the checkered floor and sticking to the window lintels and walls. I swept what I could into the bedroom and began to stuff the feathers back into their casings.

My new bed was ruined. It tilted to the left, one leg of the frame splintered nearly in half. The best I could do was to haul in a pile of books from the parlor and prop them underneath to make it even, but it still looked like a battered ship washed up on some isolated shore.

Everything but Iell was lost to me now: Matina, Alley, and my self-control. Perhaps my very livelihood, since Fish would surely report my fight with Matina to one Barnum or the other. It was one thing to go out in the world by design, and quite another to be forced into doing it. The bells of St. Paul's rang twice. It was two in the morning. Barnum's party was only a few hours away. I heaved myself on top of the broken bed and lit a cheroot. Alley must have loved Matina for a very long time. My ankles throbbed. I dug into my pocket for the Chinaman's root, ripped off a piece with my teeth, and chewed until it turned to mush.

chapter twenty~six

THE SONG OF THE NUTHATCH DRAGGED ME back from some dreamless place. Slivers of light pierced through the ill-fitting slats of my shutters, forcing me to lift a hand in front of my face. I tried focusing my gaze, but my left eye was swollen shut. It was the fourth of July. I was ravenous. And I'd have to face both Barnums at the party tonight. Where was Matina now? Where was Iell?

The broken bed settled an inch or two as I shifted my weight and shoved open the window slats with my foot. What an absolutely exquisite day. The sun glistened, and the winds from across the river blew as gently as the valley breezes of my youth. I forced myself up out of bed and pulled back the cover from my little bird's cage. "Despite the ruckus last night, you sing like an angel," I told her, which made her sing all the harder. A quick peek in the mirror told me that my eye looked terrible, so I slathered on paste makeup to cover the mottled skin. What could I do if I stank of zinc and oatmeal? I took a small bite of the root and put the rest back into my pocket, a momentary panic striking me that if I didn't go to the Chinaman's soon I'd have nothing left. I'd simply have to deal with that later. For now, more important things awaited.

My heart pounded as I sneaked downstairs and took a trolley to Iell's boardinghouse. The house matron welcomed me warmly, in spite of my strange appearance, but I still ended up sitting in the downstairs parlor for nearly an hour before Iell would receive me. It gave me plenty of time to organize my thoughts. *This is the end!* Matina had screamed the night before. Yes. She was right. Time to stop being afraid. Time to decide my future. Either Iell wanted me or she didn't, and I needed to know one way or the other.

When Iell finally summoned me upstairs, my relief was short-lived. She greeted me through a half-opened door.

"I can't really speak with you right now, Bartholomew," she said, as she fussed with her gloves. "I have an important appointment." But when she saw my eye, she grabbed my arm and pulled me into her room.

"Whatever have you done?"

She plunked me down in the little parlor and disappeared into another room, returning in moments carrying a piece of heavy brown cloth that reeked of something foul.

"Rest your head and breathe quietly."

I let my head fall against the arm of the couch and stretched out my legs. Iell placed the poultice on my eye, pressing it down lightly, and I relaxed a bit, despite the fishy, astringent smell.

"How do you know how to do this?" I asked, gesturing toward the poultice.

"Growing up like I did, a girl learns to fight." Her smile was worth every bit of pain I felt.

I lay on the couch and watched Iell bustle about, gathering her hat, her parasol, and a scarf to cover her face. Yes. We'd manage quite well out in the real world, she and I.

"Now," she said, after setting her things by the door and coming back to me. "Do you want to tell me what happened?"

What could I say? That I'd lost all my friends? I squinted at the portrait of Barnum with my one good eye, then turned my head just enough to take it out of my line of vision.

"A misunderstanding," I said.

"There are so many misunderstandings in this world," Iell said softly.

I took her hand and brought it to my lips. "Let me take care of you." My words poured out. "Let me—"

Iell put a finger over my mouth. "Don't. I can't talk about the future right now, but I will know more soon. Then we can talk, I promise."

"Know more about what?" I took hold of her wrist, wanting to pull her close.

But Iell stood, dragging me up with her. She pressed my hand to the poultice to keep it in place and all but pushed me out the door. Before I knew what had happened, the matron was escorting me out of the house.

A few minutes later, as I stood mute in the middle of the walk in front of the boardinghouse, Iell came out. She'd covered her face with a scarf. "Tonight," she said. "We can talk then, but you must come late."

"Why?" I asked. "Where will you be before that?"

She said nothing as she disappeared into a waiting carriage.

❋ ❋ ❋

By the time I returned to the Museum, everything was in chaos. A line of young boys snaked out of the Museum's front doors wearing cowbells, tin clackers, and sandwich boards announcing the evening fireworks. For the nickel that Barnum would pay them, they'd be out the rest of the day wearing down their shoe leather as they trolled the streets and handed out flyers.

Inside, I had to all but beat my way through an army of workers—bow-backed delivery boys who looked like moving gardens, weighted down as they were with bundles of iris, plumeria, hibiscus, and lace-cap hydrangea. The florists clucked and fussed as they pulled the flowers from the boys' backs and arranged them in fluted vases and four-foot baskets. And the ovens had roared to life. Heavenly smells from the kitchens infused the whole Museum: capons, lamb, and whole sides of beef stewed with apples, plus fried onions, roasted nuts, chicken in cream and tarragon, gingered berries, and German sausage. All I could think of was my belly. I stole a loaf of bread and ate it all alone in the garden.

Contentedly, I tended to the birds in the Moral Lecture Room. I fed the Arboretum birds first, and each one greeted me as an old friend. Then I went about and dropped a thimbleful of seed into each of the songbirds' cages. They ate as though starving. Around four o'clock, a band struck up on the Broadway balcony, the music unusually pleasant, all horns and cymbals. The players swayed on their chairs, wine bottles at their feet. Thaddeus stood beyond, looking like a fool in a bright red suit and striped hat. He tilted over the railing, calling down to the crowds.

"Tonight, my friends, when the sun goes down, the great Phineas T. Barnum will light up your sky! Bring your children! Prepare to dance in the street!"

I thought about how Thaddeus had put the fear of God in me only a few weeks ago. What had he said? That there were always skinnier men waiting to take my place? Ha, I thought. After tonight it would no longer matter.

According to the schedule, all performers, visitors and regulars alike, were to meet for preparty instructions in the Green Room at seven o'clock. I was a bit worried about what would happen when I saw Alley and Matina again, but all I could do was take what came to me. Around six, I ate half a bowl of boiled pork and cabbage that I'd pilfered from the kitchen and sat in the window for a while with my nuthatch.

"Liberty," I said to her. "I am going to call you Liberty," and I held up the cage so she could see the sky. Then I bathed, put on my red tights and my best jacket, and went to the Green Room, hoping against the odds that I'd pass Iell on my way.

Only a few other performers wandered about the dressing room, most bedraggled and not yet dressed for the party. None of the headliners had shown up yet, and their mirrors were still dark. But soon a handful of thespians came in and crammed together in the corner near a large covered billboard, followed by the aerialists, the tumblers, and the musicians, until eventually at least fifty performers had stuffed themselves into the room, some spilling out the door into the hallway outside. I joined a group of actors bunched together by the Notice Board. They stunk of greasepaint but then so did I, my eye still covered with skin-colored paste, bits of it dried now and itching like mad.

At six-forty-five, Matina sauntered in on Alley's arm, his guard only two steps behind him. Alley didn't look my way, but when Matina nodded at me coolly from across the room, I smiled at her, despite the knot in the pit of my stomach. Was she going to let bygones be bygones? I hoped there could be peace between us someday, if not today. Next came Emma, accompanied by the giant Captain Bogardus and his brother. Then Zippy with Commodore Nutt, who was visiting from his Lilliputian tour of Europe, followed by Bridgett in a gold silk cape, her hair full of lace and pearls. I was surprised at how comfortable Bridgett had become, as if she'd been part of the troupe all her life.

At seven o'clock exactly, Iell strolled in. Barnum followed right behind her, and for a heart-stopping moment it looked like they were together. Barnum climbed on top of a soapbox near the door and banged his walking stick against the wall for silence; I threw him a challenging look, though if he saw me he paid me no mind. Iell moved into the shadows near the wall. I ached to go to her, to ask her if she'd really come in on Barnum's arm, but I didn't dare cross the room to her in front of everyone.

"Isn't this grand, folks?" Barnum pressed his chest out like a balloon about to burst. "Midnight tonight—my fifty-fifth birthday!" Barnum's statement was met by a rush of whispers. Ricardo's voice rose from somewhere in the room. "Bravo! All together now! Bravo!" His little cat—which he no longer bothered to hide—was draped across his shoulders like a stole. Barnum waved him back before continuing.

"In a few hours," he said, "guests from the finest families in this city will begin to arrive. When they do, you must treat them like royalty. I expect you to be on your best behavior and to carry yourselves with the dignity that the evening commands."

"Like they treat us?" I said, to no one in particular. Apparently, I'd spoken louder than I'd thought, because Barnum stopped and scowled down at me. I raised my hands in a gesture of apology.

"Thank you, Mr. Fortuno, for yielding the floor. Now," he continued, "we've brought in some wonderful visiting acts tonight, but before we get to the schedule, I want to remind you that if any of my guests wish to see a special talent of yours, you will accommodate and make them happy, yes?" No one spoke, so Barnum, assuming agreement, nodded his head to Ricardo. "Now please attend. Here is the final schedule for the night."

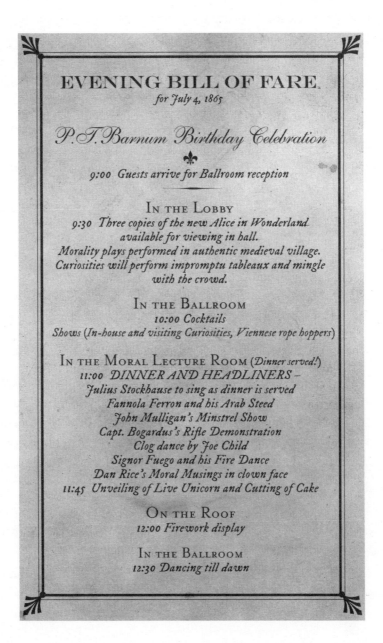

EVENING BILL OF FARE.
for July 4, 1865

P. T. Barnum Birthday Celebration
❖
9:00 Guests arrive for Ballroom reception

IN THE LOBBY
*9:30 Three copies of the new Alice in Wonderland
available for viewing in hall.
Morality plays performed in authentic medieval village.
Curiosities will perform impromptu tableaux and mingle
with the crowd.*

IN THE BALLROOM
*10:00 Cocktails
Shows (In-house and visiting Curiosities, Viennese rope hoppers)*

IN THE MORAL LECTURE ROOM (*Dinner served!*)
*11:00 DINNER AND HEADLINERS –
Julius Stockhause to sing as dinner is served
Fannola Ferron and his Arab Steed
John Mulligan's Minstrel Show
Capt. Bogardus's Rifle Demonstration
Clog dance by Joe Child
Signor Fuego and his Fire Dance
Dan Rice's Moral Musings in clown face
11:45 Unveiling of Live Unicorn and Cutting of Cake*

ON THE ROOF
12:00 Firework display

IN THE BALLROOM
12:30 Dancing till dawn

Ricardo dragged a cloth-covered board to the top of the table and flipped aside the cloth with a flourish.

A unicorn? Really! I would bet my life it was nothing more than an albino pony altered by the wizardry of Barnum's crew. The dishonesty infuriated me.

"Sir!" I yelled out, thrusting my hand in the air.

"A final reminder to my Curiosities," Barnum said, ignoring me. "Even when you are not performing, you are entertainment. As you mingle with guests, remember that they believe in the magic of you."

"*Sir!*" This time I yelled louder.

Barnum scowled down at me. "Fortuno? You have something else to add?"

"Unicorns, sir? Surely, our audiences don't believe in such drivel. I think this is a mistake."

Heads twisted toward me, but I kept my gaze on Barnum, ignoring the severity of his look.

"Mistake? No, son, no mistake. At least not on my part."

I reached into my pocket and touched the root, then looked briefly at Iell. "And why, with all due respect, did you first invite us to this party of yours as guests and then turn around and tell us to work?" I knew I should stop. Even if I planned to leave the Museum, it was stupid to rile him, but I could not help myself.

With thumbs hooking the pockets on either side of his vest, Barnum shook his head at me. "You seem to be having a little problem controlling yourself, Mr. Fortuno. And that eye of yours doesn't look too good. Perhaps it would be better if you didn't do the stage show this evening." He narrowed his eyes and looked down his nose at me. "In fact, don't even perform tableau. Take off that suit and wander about tonight in just those tights of yours. That should do it, I think."

Matina glanced over at me in alarm, and I was sure that everyone in the room was waiting for me to crumble.

I looked over to where Iell still stood but could not make out her face.

"Fine, sir. That's what I'll do."

Barnum ended our stalemate by turning to the room at large. "Our guests will begin to arrive at nine for cocktails," he said, "so please finish dressing now, and make sure you're in place exactly on time."

When Barnum released us, I elbowed my way through the players toward Iell, but by the time I made it to the door it was too late. She had slipped away.

✳ ✳ ✳

FROM MY parlor window, I watched a man on stilts carve through the horde in the street below. He blew a long-necked horn to clear the way, his wooden legs parting the crowd as he walked. Behind him, carriages heaved out overdressed passengers who chattered mindlessly as they scraped the horse manure from their shoes with the boot brushes near the doors. When the band broke into a hearty rendition of "Pop Goes the Weasel," the crowd started dancing.

I moved Liberty from the window to the top of my étagère. She seemed to like her new name and kept singing even after I covered her cage with a light tea towel. Already the street in front of the Museum teemed with jugglers and fire wheels, and a drunken crowd milled noisily about.

"He took me off the schedule," I said to the covered cage. "What do you think of that?" Liberty trilled once from beneath the towel, and I laughed despite my mood.

I slipped into my shirt and vest and the double padded suit, covering up my tights. If Barnum denied me my stage, I would deny him my talent. My stomach growled and I cringed. My talent—at least as long as it lasted. Well, tonight I would not be afraid. I would talk to Iell and we would choose. A stiff brush to the jacket shoulders, a final change of cravat, boots blackened to a high shine, and I was ready. The long mirror in my bedroom reflected a man quite thin of face and hands but otherwise normal. I tucked what was left of the Chinaman's root into my pocket and popped half an éclair into my mouth.

So many people were using the service stairs that it stank of sweat and filth. I held my breath as I pushed past the dancers and chattering servers to get to the second floor. As soon as I swung open the door, a new world opened up. The grand Atrium rang with the oompah of the brass band, the chiming of a hundred voices, the swishing of skirts and clicking of heels. Refracted shards of light bounced off a hundred hanging mirrors, and I lifted a hand to shield my eyes against the illumination.

"Can I serve you, sir?" A spry redheaded girl handed me a flute of champagne, the rest of the glasses on her tray teetering on napkins in the shape of elephants. I followed her all the way to the entrance of the Ballroom. Inside, the costumed animals threw down icy stares from their pedestal perches. Violins and cellos played a Bach concerto at the far end of the room.

The first thing I did was look for Iell. I wandered about in the big oval room, filled with the city's finest, but did not see her anywhere. Then Barnum and his wife entered and posted themselves near the Ballroom's main doors. As they welcomed guests, I did my best to keep out of their line of sight. Mrs. Barnum looked surprisingly elegant in a sand-colored evening dress.

Most of my fellow performers hung about on the sidelines in deference or in shyness, with the exception of Ricardo, who stood out front doing tumbling tricks and pulling faces at the women as they passed. Zippy sat off in a corner, sharing a flask with one of the waiters.

Alley, Emma, and the visiting giant, Captain Bogardus, were being presented in an action tableau. They'd mounted a low riser placed there for temporary acts and, with Colonel Nutt at their feet, took suggestions from the passing crowd.

"Diana and the Great Fox Hunt," a gentleman yelled out, and in response, the Colonel turned to the others. "Hunting," he reinterpreted, and Alley changed himself into a pot-bellied, slack-faced poacher with Emma next to him miming a bow and arrow in her hands as Captain Bogardus tumbled onto his behind like a dead elephant. This continued with suggestions of *war* and *drunken sailors*. When Colonel Nutt reinterpreted *Scarlet Letter* as "women of the night," the improvised tableau brought whoops from some of the male guests, especially after

Emma thrust out her mighty chest and a guest sporting a gray beard ran at her from the audience and threw his skinny arms around her waist. Alley seemed almost to be enjoying himself, maybe because this was the last tableau he would ever do.

The room grew warmer as the number of bodies increased, and I desperately wanted to slip off my heavy jacket. Instead, I sipped at my champagne and pushed through the crowd, spurred on by the need to find Iell.

Finally I saw her, enthroned on a plush, straight-back chair along the north wall. Her beard hung loose and sprawled out across her chest, and the silver of her dress shone through like a prize. From a distance, I watched her hold court, her head high but her attention clearly focused on some inner vista. She looked fatigued, as if she'd begun to tire of it all. I lifted a gloved hand toward her, but she didn't seem to see me.

"Are you putting on weight?" someone said behind me, and I jumped.

Matina wore a light pink dress, and when she lifted her arms to fix a stray ringlet, perspiration stains ran from her armpits to her waist like pools of spreading ink.

"Padded jacket," I answered, catching my breath, and then slipped the jacket off and folded it over my arm.

Matina regarded me, smiling.

"And that new bed of yours?"

I smiled. "Broken nearly in half."

Matina sighed. "I behaved horribly last night, didn't I? I'm sorry, Barthy, I really am."

"You did nothing wrong. I am a scoundrel. A coward. Any number of atrocious things. And what a cad, to have treated you as I have. I should have trusted you. I'm so sorry, my dear, I truly am."

Matina shrugged and flicked an invisible piece of lint from the front of her gown.

"Are you going to leave with Alley?" I asked.

"He likes me quite a lot, you know, and he's a good man. But I haven't made up my mind yet. You might be right. I'm not sure I belong out in the world."

"My dear, you will do well anywhere." Warmth spread through me when Matina smiled at me again, and in a final attempt to confide in her, I sputtered out, "Matina, please, there's something I want to show you." Reaching into my coat pocket, I brushed my fingers across the root.

"Mr. Fortuno. Join us, if you would!" Barnum, not twenty feet away, waved to me. He stood with his wife and another couple, a gentleman accompanied by a big-hatted lady, and beckoned imperiously.

"Looks like the old man wants to see you," Matina said. "Go ahead. Tell him about your broken bed." She winked. "After your unicorn remarks at the meeting, I'd like to see the look on his face." She stood on her toes and kissed me on the cheek, and I straightened my vest as she trundled into the crowd. "Goodbye, my dear," I whispered.

Before I made my way over to the Barnums, I slipped on my padded jacket.

"Fortuno, come meet some friends of mine. Margaret, Henry, this is Bartholomew Fortuno, performer extraordinaire." Barnum gave no indication of our recent spat in the Green Room. He presented only his public face, eager to entertain his friends. "Fortuno, may I present the Wallingtons."

"Sir. Madam." I kissed the hand of the big-hatted woman, and she giggled like a girl. But rather than shake hands with the gentleman, I took a step back and bowed curtly. The man wore a cutaway of the finest silk, but I could tell from his stiff carriage and his misshapen nose that he used to be a boxer. Had I been living in his world, I'd have been his superior. I resented having to play second fiddle at Barnum's behest.

"And of course you already know my charming wife," Barnum said, without an ounce of sarcasm. Mrs. Barnum nodded pleasantly. Ignoring my pounding heart, I kissed her hand. Obviously, Barnum had joined forces with his wife, and they were closing ranks against me. Fine. I waved a passing server to bring me more champagne. When I lifted the flute from the tray, the glass was surprisingly steady in my hands. I glanced at Mrs. Barnum. Her face was a pleasant mask.

"Fortuno, these folks were just asking about you," Barnum said. "Why don't you share something of your great philosophy with them." He turned to his friends. "Despite his current costume"—ah, he *had* noticed my padded jacket—"Fortuno here is a man who takes great pride in who he is. I can't help but appreciate a man who thinks so highly of himself."

I was filled with a reckless feeling, as if everything was on the table and I needed only to see my final card before knowing if I'd won or lost. A quick look over my shoulder told me that Iell had risen from her chair and was now chatting with a few admirers. Not far away, Matina twirled in front of a couple who'd stopped her for a quick demonstration.

The big-hatted woman gave me a mincing smile and brazenly opened the front of my jacket. "Aren't you starving, sir? I'd be absolutely famished if I weighed as little as you."

I imitated Barnum's smile. "If you were as thin as I, you wouldn't be hungry at all. Besides, I'm feasting my eyes on you as we speak."

The woman threw her hands in the air gleefully. "What a character, Phineas! Wherever did you find him?"

Barnum smiled in Mrs. Barnum's direction. "These people are easier to find than you'd imagine. Aren't they, my dear?"

Mrs. Barnum returned his smile. "They are, indeed, and Mr. Fortuno here would be hard-pressed to replace us."

"Talent always finds a home," I replied coldly.

"Phineas! Charity! Greetings." A ruddy-faced Mathew Brady approached us, his thick glasses reflecting the light. On his arm was a beautiful woman—Bridgett! "And is that you, Fortuno? Something about you seems different." Brady squinted through his thick glasses, and I instinctively pulled in my stomach.

"I was telling my friends here how lucky our performers are," Barnum said.

"Well, I'm the lucky fool around here," Brady answered, "escorting such a charming creature as this. An old man like me." He patted Bridgett's arm with his papery fingers and turned to the Wallingtons. "Let me introduce to you all the lovely Madame Zouve."

Bridgett held out a ring-laden hand and stuttered, "Mi Eenglesh no berry gud," and brandished her limp hand to one person and then the next. Brady patted her under her chin and laughed.

Mrs. Wallington smiled at Brady. "Very charming." She let her fan rest against her left cheek while Bridgett curtsied. Then she turned back to me. "But frankly, I'm interested in learning more about our thin friend here."

"Enough disguise. Take that jacket off, Fortuno. Let the woman see the real you." Barnum slapped me hard on the shoulder, and instinctively I complied, slipping off my padded jacket and gripping it in one hand. When Barnum saw that I wore a normal dress shirt over my tights, his expression changed.

The large-hatted woman fanned herself furiously. "Surely they object to being ogled all the time."

"Goodness, no, they love being stared at," Barnum said. "And, as my wife says, where else do they have to go? Pull up your shirt, Fortuno. Make the women squirm."

"No, sir. I'd rather not."

Both Barnums looked at me as if I'd dropped dead upon the floor, but whatever crisis my action might have initiated was momentarily postponed when Brady pointed toward Zippy, who was vomiting into the punch bowl at the far end of the room. I slipped back into my padded coat, tipping my hat to the guests. "If you will excuse me," I said, seizing upon the distraction as an opportunity to slip away.

✳ ✳ ✳

THE BALLROOM had grown more crowded. Although the attendants had thrown open the doors to draw in air from the balcony, the breeze did little more than sweep in the stink and the rumble of the city. I forged a path through the merrymaking toward where Iell now stood. When she saw me coming, she raised her hand above the teeming heads in greeting, but as I moved closer, she mouthed something to her admirers and walked off in the opposite direction.

I pushed harder past the guests, knocking into a serving girl and upsetting half her tray. Stopping to turn the spilled glasses upright, I almost lost Iell in the crowd, but I finally caught a glimpse of her gliding along the south wall. She stopped at the base of a stuffed bear dressed as a party guest. It was mounted on a mantel four feet above the floor and flanked by potted maple trees to create the illusion that it was walking into the party directly from the forest. Iell slipped behind one of the potted trees at floor level. It took many minutes to get through the crowd and reach her.

Iell's voice, sly and warm, floated out from the shadows. "You're a bit pale tonight, Bartholomew. How is your eye?"

I reached into the darkness, took Iell's hand, and brought it gently to my lips. Her skin tasted of oil and salt, and my mouth watered as I kissed her wrist. "Why did you walk away from me?"

Iell said nothing, so I let go her hand. Out of respect, I willed myself to be patient. My eyes fell level with the bear's feet. One of its nails, shriveled and carelessly attached, dangled from its foot. In front of us, the Ballroom churned with couples dancing to the orchestra's thin rendition of "The Tennessee Waltz." Across the room, Matina circled the floor surrounded by a pack of midgets, all eight of them grabbing the bottom of her skirts and twirling her about, like ants carting away a great morsel of food.

"We've so many things we need to discuss," I said, speaking into the shadows.

"Like what, Bartholomew?"

"Freedom. A new life. You promised me we would talk tonight. Please. Step into the light where I can see you."

Iell stepped forward, but her presence was like the flutter of a bird's wing—impossible to grasp—and I noted that her eyes were heavy-lidded. She'd probably just used opium. Even so, I fell beneath her spell. Did she love me? I had to know.

Raucous laughter broke out across the room. A man with a golden trumpet teetered wildly as he climbed on top of a dais along the south wall. He started to play a madcap song, and Zippy danced beside him like a monkey, hopping from foot to foot, his long arms hanging loose.

"I need to know what you want from me. We're running out of time."

Iell took my wrist and worked her index finger beneath the top of my glove. "Do you know what I most appreciate about you?"

I waited.

"Your patience. You are such a gentleman."

A single sour *ta-dah* spewed from the trumpet, and Barnum came barreling across the room, a wild grin plastered across his face. I desperately hoped he hadn't seen us, but he made a beeline straight toward me, the crowds parting as he came through. He stopped in front of Iell. His chest and neck looked massive. Clearly he'd seen us together, and he didn't like what he'd seen. But what did it matter? He was going to know everything soon enough.

Iell's face softened, and she smiled pleasantly at him. This seemed to endow Barnum with increased vigor. He loomed over her for a heartbreaking second and I tried to stand between them, but it was as if I didn't exist. Iell pushed past me and placed herself again in front of Barnum, her lovely beard spreading out like a fan. When Barnum took her face in his pawlike hand, rage nearly blinded me.

"I'm not interfering," Barnum said to Iell. "A promise is a promise."

"Interfering with what?" I demanded, fists clenched, mouth dry as the desert. Neither of them acknowledged me.

Barnum grinned ear to ear as he hopped up on the pedestal where the bear stood and, hanging on to the bear's neck, called out to the crowd: "Welcome to all of you and Happy Birthday to me!" Wild applause. All heads but Iell's twisted toward him.

"Interfering with what?" I demanded again, as Iell fussed absent-mindedly with her beard and gazed out over the crowd. My anger melted into confusion.

Barnum reached down and took a glass of champagne held up to him by one of serving girls. He lifted it high in the air, the liquor sloshing out and catching the light as it spilled to the Ballroom floor.

"It's not every day a man reaches his fifty-fifth year and finds himself surrounded by so many wonderful friends." A drunken whoop filled the room. "Our country is whole again! Our city thrives! And here we all are, together in the most magical place in the world. The home of the enchanted"—he looked straight down at Iell and winked—"*and* the grotesque. Both ends and in between."

I looked toward Iell and was horrified to find her gazing at Barnum as if he were the sun. My heart sank.

"So, tonight, I welcome you once more and hope you will have the most astonishing night of your lives!"

The crowd rose up, and the noise was deafening. Right on cue, the servers tossed ignitable powder over the candles so that the Ballroom popped and fizzed in luminescent colors. Then dozens of young boys dressed as cherubs poured through the Ballroom doors, each carrying a burning torch in one hand and a long silk banner in the other. The crowd began to stir, and Iell took a step forward. As the guests were herded out the Ballroom doors, Iell moved to join them.

"No. Wait," I sputtered behind her. "You promised we would talk tonight!"

"Meet me in the theater in five minutes," she called over her shoulder; then she slipped into the crowd and was gone.

chapter twenty seven

LAMING TORCHES IN FRONT OF THE MORAL Lecture Room doors redirected the partygoers from the Ballroom to the theater, and buckets of water had been discreetly placed a few feet from each torch. The guests, well into their cups, funneled through the doors, eager to see the opening act.

I was desperate to find Iell again. But just then, Bridgett moved past me.

"What happened to your 'Engleesh no berry gud'?" I asked, one eye on the lookout for Iell. "Faking it now in the name of love?"

Bridgett looked toward the far set of doors and waved at Brady, who waited for her, hat in hand. "It's a pity, Mr. Fortuno, that life ain't about love. Not in the end, anyways. Smart girls do what they need to do, and I ain't talking about Mr. Brady neither."

What in the world *was* she talking about? I tried to think as she wandered off, but a tingling up my neck made me turn around and look toward the outdoor balcony. Iell pushed through the heavy curtains separating the balcony from the Atrium and stood in the entrance alone, like a child abandoned by the side of a busy road. I all but ran to her.

"Finally," I said, catching her by the elbow and steering her toward the last set of open doors. "What were you doing out on the balcony? Are you all right?"

The heels of her shoes clicked as we hurried along the tile. "Of course. I'm fine."

"What did Barnum mean when he said he wasn't interfering?"

Iell put a finger to my lips. "Let's sit and talk like civilized people."

How rude of Iell to make me wait like this. But I could not force her to talk. She'd said she prized my patience. What were a few more minutes compared to the rest of our lives? I nodded with false amiability and led her through the theater doors.

Inside, the Moral Lecture Room radiated with excitement. Curls of smoke spiraled up from the great torches hanging on the walls, and the prisms reflected the flames, sending mad flashes of light bouncing everywhere one looked. Ahead of us, the stage heaved with tumblers and acrobats, and a huge bear ankle-chained to a metal bar swiped at a caged monkey an inch or two beyond its reach. Barnum sat on a throne to the right, watching the festivities and nodding in time to the orchestra's repeated choruses of "For He's a Jolly Good Fellow." And the new songbirds! In my absence, workers had tied the silver cages to the long streamers hanging from the ceiling, and now hundreds of little caged birds swung above our heads, catching the light and carving exquisite fan patterns in the air.

Iell and I stood in the rear of the theater for a time, staring into the sea of fancy hats, clinking glasses, and long white cigarettes. Then my stomach thundered to life again. I'd gotten a sudden whiff of roasted lamb coming from the food tables, and I had an overwhelming craving to fill myself up. Drawing my coat closed, I forced myself to remain in my place. I wasn't an animal. Hunger did not control me; I controlled it. As soon as I had regained my composure, I bent forward and whispered in Iell's ear.

"Are you hungry, my dear?"

Iell touched my arm with her fingertips, and without a word the two of us joined the procession of people snaking past the food tables along the far wall. My mouth watered madly as we slipped into line. Before us was a huge roasted pig, pheasants covered in rosemary sauce, sautéed baby spinach leaves, tournedos Rossini, apple and rhubarb turnovers, wonderfully browned corn soufflés, and lamb. Weak-kneed, I loaded up my plate. It was impossible to disguise the growling sounds coming from my stomach; at one point, the aroma of garlic and onions so overwhelmed me I had to bury my nose in my napkin. It took quite a few moments for me to regain my equilibrium, but finally I salvaged my plate and caught up to Iell, who had found us seats in the rear of the Lecture Room.

In front of us, guests sprawled across their own seats, plates balanced on their laps and flagons of burgundy on the floor near their feet. They applauded a group of harem dancers who swirled through the entrance doors behind us and sashayed down the aisles. Onstage, three jugglers, a singing dog, and a ballet dancer competed for the crowd's attention.

"What's that in your lap?" Iell asked me, after we'd sat down in our seats.

"Where?"

She frowned, nodding toward my overflowing plate.

"You mean the food?" Feigning innocence, I dropped my eyes to my lap. "I'm hungry," I said, glad for once to be the one in control of information. I bit into a chicken leg, its juices rolling down my chin, the taste of it overwhelmingly rich.

"What do you mean you're hungry?"

I looked over at Iell. She seemed disappointed. Wasn't this what she wanted?

"I do have a choice," I said, and Iell raised her wineglass to her lips. I needed to take command of the situation, so I put my hand over hers, bringing the glass down to rest.

"You never answered me about negotiating new contracts with Barnum, nor did you agree that I should write to Peale's in Philly. Is there something else you want?"

She studied my face intently.

"I have some money saved," I said. "Quite a lot, in fact. I have been quite disciplined in saving."

"What is it you are saying?"

"That I can take care of you. Of us. We can leave in the morning. If you don't want to work any longer, we can hire a little city house, one with a garden, and find other ways to earn a living, like regular people do."

"A normal life?"

"You said you believed in transformation. It doesn't matter what you promised Barnum. I can eat. I can take care of you."

Iell's eyes welled up.

Some performance on the stage in front of us elicited wild applause from the audience. I put my hand on Iell's knee. "You don't need any of this." I gestured to the theater in front of us. "Or Barnum." Then I reached up and gently touched her beard. "You don't even need this."

Iell furrowed her brow, her eyes shiny with tears.

"I love you, Iell," I spit out, dizzy with relief at finally telling her how I felt.

Iell bit her lip and moved my hand from her beard back to her lap. "Bartholomew, there's something I have to tell you." She squeezed my hand. "But tonight I have one more promise to fulfill. Meet me tomorrow morning in the Yellow Room. Nine o'clock. After that, I promise never to make you wait again."

She stood to leave.

"No." I struggled to my feet, nearly knocking my plate of food to the floor. "Please don't go. Don't leave me in the dark again." But Iell pushed past me and inched sideways down the row of seats.

As she hurried up the aisle, she glanced over her shoulder at me and smiled—gratefully, I thought, but I wasn't certain. I sat down full of self-reproach. Clearly, I'd overwhelmed her. It had been too soon to tell her that I loved her. And perhaps I'd been presumptuous about the future.

Miserable, I sat alone in the last aisle as the performers went on. Near the end of the show, Matina appeared atop a huge wooden horse pushed by six burly stagehands. She wore a pink body suit and a yellow wig long and thick enough to cover nearly all of her body. But the intent of the illusion was clear. She had decided to play the Menken role after all. Partygoers, women as well as men, yelled out, "Bravo!" "Delicious!" Applause and laughter came in equal measure as she rolled across the stage, face beaming, hand waving like a queen. Thaddeus stood at the front. "Like a holiday pudding, ain't she? Too tempting to leave alone and much too big to finish. Give her a hand, folks, give her a hand." I spotted Alley in the wings, watching over her, his escort still behind him.

Bridgett entered next, carried on from the other side in an open sedan chair, its glittery box tipping from side to side as the four men carrying its poles mismatched their steps. A poodle lounged in her lap, and two long-nosed Afghans tied to the back nipped at each other as they followed her to center stage. Bridgett's first "stage show" was visual only, but she got a rousing hand when Thaddeus blathered on about her mountain lineage and how she was the purest breed of Caucasian in the world.

On stomped the giants, who performed a mock wrestling match, and Zippy did a birthday dance inside a metal cage. I felt another stab of loss when Matina appeared after everyone else had finished, this time pushing a huge gong. She had thrown on a red satin cape with a sloping hat. A silver boa dangled carelessly around her neck, and she kept tossing it back as she rolled the gong to center stage.

"Mr. Barnum," Matina boomed across the heads of those not too drunk to sit upright. "In honor of you!" She bowed grandly and grabbed a mallet. With pink-faced flourish, she banged the gong until the room fell into a stunned hush. Gesturing toward the wings, she waved Barnum back onto the stage.

"Ain't she a honey of a gal," Barnum bellowed as he sauntered to the center, hat in hand, his broad grin like a spotlight beaming over the applauding crowd.

"For you, sir! Happy birthday from your loving friends here at the Museum!" Matina presented him with a blue tasseled pillow, a glass jar perched precariously on top.

"What is this?" Barnum lifted the jar and read the label. Laughing, he hoisted the jar aloft, the finger floating obscenely in the pale green water. "Look at this, folks. Blackbeard's finger! What a fine gift!"

Then Emma and Alley wheeled in a flatbed cart. On top of it was the largest birthday cake I had ever seen: over four feet high, and as

wide as Matina herself. They tilted the cake forward for everyone to
see the perfect marzipan rendition of the Museum, the carved doors
and balconies already dripping in the summer heat.

The audience let loose another round of hurrahs, and then, on cue,
in came the unicorn, followed by two aerialists who, in a smoldering
finale, flew across the stage on burning trapezes as the orchestra played
"Happy Birthday to You."

And finally, with everyone's attention riveted upward, the doors to
all the little birdcages popped open—they had been rigged with strings
pulled by lads running along beneath them—and a hundred frenzied
songbirds dashed out into the heights of the cavernous theater, a cockatoo and a conspicuous blue parrot among them as the boys released
all my birds as well.

The birds, set free, swooped about in fifty-foot drops, careening
over our heads and then dashing up again, as if they were trying to
make sense of a world without limits. I leaped to my feet with the rest
of the audience, bedazzled by the spectacle, hope and fear rising in me
in equal measure. Many of the birds settled on balconies or seatbacks
for a moment or two before taking off into the air again, and my heart
soared with them. But an unlucky few seemed to lose their way, and,
rather than fly with their brethren, they swooped too high or too low
and ended up smashing themselves against the walls, discovering the
hard way exactly what freedom meant.

✳ ✳ ✳

WITHOUT IELL, I couldn't bring myself to climb to the roof with the
rest of the guests for the party's fireworks finale. So as everyone
poured out of the theater and up the stairs, I went the other way. Fresh
air was what I needed, and the closest place to find it was on the large
balcony opposite the Ballroom. It felt good to part the musty curtains
and slide through them into the night.

The stars sparkled. On the far end of the balcony, the outdoor
band was finishing up, playing their final song at full tilt for the crowds
below. The musicians tipped side to side like windup toys, one player

teetering on top of his chair, his fiddle pressed low across his chest as he scrubbed across the front of it with an almost unstrung bow. Down in the middle of Broadway, a handful of bonfires raged, and the crowd, their upturned faces childlike and full of awe, clapped to the band's final flurry. Bravos went up to encourage an encore, but the musicians were done. They gathered their instruments and wandered past me, leaving me alone in the hot night air.

Above me, the sound of partygoers tramping out onto the roof made me sigh. What an evening it had been. What a week. What a summer. Fourth of July. A popping sound startled me into looking across the street as a multicolored whirl of light came charging forward. It was a pinwheel tied to a rope between the top spire of St. Paul and the street, a precursor to the fireworks. As it came whirling down like a falling star and burst into flame, a memory shook loose in my mind.

I was sitting in my mother's lap, watching a star shoot across the night sky.

"Can the sky fall, Mummy?" I clung to the bodice of her dress, and her lips moved, but I couldn't make out her words. The hour was late. We were waiting for my father to come home. We sat for what felt like hours, until finally we heard the whinny of a horse in the distance.

A hand clutching my upper arm drew me back to the present. It took a moment of looking around the balcony before I realized where I was. My head hurt.

"Slick ol' Stickman!"

Ricardo dangled by his legs from the upper balcony's railing, his fingers plowing into my arm as he stretched down toward me like a lumpy snake.

"Take your hands off me!" I swung at Ricardo and he grabbed my fist, but his grip slipped and his body snapped together with such force that he tumbled from above onto the stone balcony in front of me. I looked down at his inert body. "Ricardo?" I called loudly, worried that he'd knocked himself unawares. With a snap, his eyes slit open, and he coiled an arm around my leg. The weight of him rooted me to the spot, and I willed myself not to panic.

"Barnum's wife wants to see you one more time."

Above, lighting up the sky, a huge green-and-blue firework broke, and the crowd let loose a raucous cheer.

"You may tell Mrs. Barnum that I've no wish to be involved in her affairs. I am done with her." I shook my leg, and Ricardo's arm slid from me like an eel off a stick.

From the shadows came a voice. "I'm afraid you are already involved, Mr. Fortuno," Mrs. Barnum said.

She pushed through the curtains onto the semidark balcony, her figure backlit by the lights from inside the Museum. She looked small and glittering in her silk dress, one thin hand clasping her cane.

"Forgive my rudeness," I said, "but I really must go. I've got other obligations."

"Ah, yes, obligations. It's nice to see *someone* in this Museum thinks about such things." Mrs. Barnum moved toward me, the tip of her cane clinking against the stone floor. Another explosion of color: sky bursts of red and white tumbling into fragments, followed by a rotten egg smell that stung my nose and made my eyes tear up. For a moment, I worried that panic would overwhelm me, but I slipped my hand into my pocket and touched the root. I'd no reason to fear Mrs. Barnum anymore. I'd already decided to leave this place. What could the old woman threaten me with?

A boom of gunpowder shook the floor of the balcony, and a golden fireball illuminated the sky and outlined the empty chairs from the band a few feet away. Ricardo hopped up on one of the chairs and started to dance about as if he'd caught on fire.

Mrs. Barnum waited for a lull in the explosives before turning to Ricardo. "You may go now, young man, and if you wish to keep that mangy animal of yours, say nothing about this meeting to my husband."

Ricardo stopped. "So I can keep my little Poke, like you promised?"

"We'll talk about that later, lad."

"Not later. I helped you, and you said—"

Mrs. Barnum rapped her cane on the ground, dismissing him.

Ricardo's face fell, and for the second time, I caught sight of the little boy hiding beneath his arrogant façade. Had his gift hidden his true self instead of revealing it? I had a strong urge to tell him that he didn't have to stay in the Museum—that another life was possible—but out he went, a thin shaft of light from inside cutting across the balcony when he pushed through the balcony curtains.

When the curtain swung shut, the night swallowed us up again.

Mrs. Barnum turned to face me, her eyes now dulled and tired. "Let's sit for a moment, shall we?" She picked her way across the hard stone floor to where the brass band had played and sat down on a wooden chair, pulling her cane across her lap. I stood in front of her.

"You should understand, madam, that I take my commitments seriously, even when coerced into making them. For example, I did what you asked me to do the last time we met. I delivered your message to Iell. If she has declined your offer, it's not my doing."

Mrs. Barnum looked up into the sky, where wisps of smoke had already covered half the stars. "Who said she declined my offer?"

Her words jerked me back to reality like a fish on a hook.

"Mrs. Adams," Mrs. Barnum went on, "has all but accepted my offer, Mr. Fortuno. I thought you should know that. She has come to see me a number of times to work out the details. Only today, in fact, we shared tea and had a nice little chat. Rather a pleasant person, despite her peculiarities."

My heart tumbled. So that's why I'd been turned out into the street this morning. But it didn't make sense. Iell would have told me if she was negotiating with Mrs. Barnum. Maybe this was what Mr. Barnum had meant about not interfering. My head felt full of air.

"Where is she thinking of resettling?" I forced myself to ask.

"Have you heard of the Ivory Tower?"

"You mean the private club?" Again, I was taken aback. "It's not even a showplace."

"No, but its clientele is very, very wealthy." Mrs. Barnum slipped her hands around her cane and gripped it tight. "Although your Mrs. Adams is—how to say this—an acquired taste, I can see no limit to the fees she can garner as a private performer. I have all but convinced her to accept a place with them. But there's one small problem."

"What is that, madam?"

"You, Mr. Fortuno."

A hiss from above set off a Roman candle, which wheezed haphazardly into the crowd below, followed by howling.

"I don't understand."

"I've seen her type before, you know. Brave and self-possessed on the outside but without the kind of support that matters in the long run. And it's a callous world. You must know this. Especially for someone like her. If she's smart—and she's smart enough—she'd better find herself some security. I've offered her that possibility, and she will accept it for what it is: her salvation. Unless she thinks she has another way out." She paused for a moment, eyeing me skeptically. "Mr. Fortuno, she seems to think that you might be able to provide for her."

Of course I would provide for her. But if she'd already decided to be with me, why had she been putting me off all night?

Mrs. Barnum cleared her throat. "Iell will leave here tomorrow, Mr. Fortuno. She will join the Ivory Tower and be better off for it in the end. And if you try to dissuade her or help her in any way, I will not only see that her offer is withdrawn but will also make certain that no other establishment in our profession ever takes her on. Or you, Mr. Fortuno. I warn you. Step aside."

Using her cane to steady herself, Mrs. Barnum shifted and stood. I did not assist her. We both waited through another volley of thunderous color. Her self-assurance made me doubt myself.

"And what if I go to your husband. Tell him what you are doing?"

Mrs. Barnum's face softened. "Can't you see Phineas's hand behind all this? He thinks she'll run away with you. After you go, he can pretend that the problem has been solved. He'll wait on the sideline as the two of you try to manage, but it won't take long. You are no more able to care for yourself than she is, so the two of you will struggle, and she'll grow discontent. That is when Phineas will swoop in and make his own private arrangements for her. He thinks I don't understand this, but he's not the only one with a bit of foresight. I want her working in an establishment strong enough to take on her problems, and an establishment not connected with me. Stay out of it, Mr. Fortuno. Save her while you can."

"I think we will surprise you, madam."

Nothing else was said. Mrs. Barnum left me. For a moment I felt so light and inconsequential that I thought I might float away, but knowing I had the root in my pocket reassured me. What Mrs. Barnum didn't know was that I could change. That I had already begun to transform. The problem of Iell's opium still had to be solved, and I'd have to find new employment very soon. But I could find work. I could care for us both. All I needed to do was keep eating.

I pulled out the root and took the smallest bite, and as I chewed, I pictured myself full-bodied. Yes. All would be well. I'd go to the Chinaman next week and purchase another root, and then, for certain, I could see to Iell just fine.

"What are you eating?" Emma stood in the doorway, swinging a lantern in front of her.

"Nothing," I said, shocked to see her. I shoved the root into its bag and into my pocket.

Emma frowned, coming closer and lifting the lantern until its light shone in my face. I looked away. The sky burst open with a final flurry of fireworks, and try as I might to ignore it, again I saw that falling star. Then a darker memory from an earlier time. My mother's voice. "Hold the lantern still." There we were, my mother and me, hunched in the kitchen of our cottage, my arm shaking from the strain of holding a lantern over our heads as she ground mushroom-covered bark into powder and then poured it slowly into a glass jar she kept on the windowsill. "Watch the door," she said. "If he comes in, blow out the light."

"Fortuno?" Emma's voice pulled me back into our conversation. She eyeballed me. "Are you all right?"

I tried to shake my head clear. What was happening to me?

"Fortuno!" she said again.

"Yes, yes. What are you doing out here?"

She surprised me by chucking me gently under the chin. "I wanted to see how you fared with Mrs. Barnum." From the smell of Emma's breath, she'd been drinking something stronger than champagne.

"It might be a cruel world," I said, defiant now, "but I think I can manage without her help."

"You know," Emma said gruffly, "I didn't think you had it in you to stand up against her. What's different about you, Fortuno? I can't put my finger on it, but it suits you. It's too bad you're spoken for."

Emma held up the lantern again, and I shoved it away. "I didn't think men held much interest for you."

"Oh, no, I like men just fine." Emma leaned down, too close. "Unfortunately, so does Iell. I think she would have been better off with me in the long run, but she seems to think you understand her. That worries me a wee bit."

I could hear the racket of partygoers tumbling down the stairs toward the Ballroom, most likely windblown and starry-eyed.

"Whatever are you talking about?"

Emma narrowed her eyes and stayed silent for a moment. Then she said, "Maybe you should go and see for yourself. There's a special room downstairs, in the East Wing cellar. Why not go there right now and let *her* clarify things for you."

Lantern held high, Emma staggered away, mumbling, "He that walketh in darkness knoweth not whither he goeth."

chapter twenty~eight

I MADE MY WAY BACK INSIDE THE MUSEUM, walking through the revelers like a man in a dream. The orchestra had moved to the Ballroom, and I could hear them warming up. Birds that had escaped from the Moral Lecture Room flew above us in a world that now smelled of champagne and sweat and sulfur. I made it to the Grand Staircase and looked down the polished steps.

How simple it would be to stay in the light, to linger in the Ballroom until dawn with the rest of the guests, swaying to the sounds of the dusky waltzes. Perhaps I could laugh away my exchange with Emma. After all, she'd never shown any interest in my well-being before, and I knew she had aligned herself with Mrs. Barnum. Or I could go directly to Barnum and tell him about his wife's threats. It was possible that he didn't know about Mrs. Barnum's private arrangement with Iell and would be grateful to have such news. Whatever it was that Iell was doing in the cellars, it was her own business.

But no. If Iell and I were to be together, there could be no secrets between us. I took the stairs one step at a time, and the first floor rose to meet me. Now that the guests were up on the roof, the inner recesses of the Museum were all but deserted. My footsteps echoed through the quiet hallways. For a moment I swore I saw Iell far in front of me, her silver dress glimmering in the dim light like a lost star, but it was only the moonlight through the windows as it fell across the parquet floors. On I went, weaving through the statues in the Waxworks Room, then past the Arboretum, empty now of birds. The door to the

Yellow Room stood open, so I ducked in for a moment. Iell's pedestal looked less substantial in the darkened room, a shadow rather than a solid object.

As soon as I reached the door to the East Wing cellar, my hands began to sweat. A breeze drifted in from behind me, and I thought about turning around. But at the base of the door, a strip of light served as a beacon. I gave the door a good shove, and it creaked open onto a short stairway lined with candles, one on each step. Paraffin smoke curled up to greet me. Barnum would have a fit if he knew open candles burned in the cellars, what with the recent fires.

At the bottom of the stairs was another door, this one already open. Next to it sat an empty chair, a lit cigar smoldering in a tin ashtray on the floor beneath the seat. The guardian, whoever he was, seemed to have disappeared for a moment, so in I went, unimpeded, and followed the candlelit path along the wall to my left until it stopped in front of a third and final door, this one squat and tired.

"Tomorrow," I whispered to myself. "Find her tomorrow." But I'd come too far to walk away now. I stood at the final door, held my breath, and pushed.

The first thing I noticed was the music. Strange music. It wafted out from somewhere far away, the melodies of Eastern savages, weeping, low, provocative. I shut my eyes and listened for a moment, then opened my eyes again and tried to make sense of what was in front of me. Not that I could see much at first. The room was dark except for a small fire floating unsupported in the center of the room, giving off soft light. Waiting for my eyes to adjust, I leaned into the wall and, using it as a guide, inched deeper into the room. In front of me was a row of chairs, and in front of them another, and then another. I was in a makeshift theater. Nearly all the chairs were full. As my eyes adjusted, I could see from the looks of their well-made jackets that the audience members were highborn men. And the flame? It was not floating at all, but rather burning in an iron bowl balanced on top of a tall metal stem somewhere near the front of the room.

I edged my way farther along the wall, the men's backs obscuring whatever it was they were gawking at. Then I saw the edge of a low stage, the pale light washing over it, and smelled something sweetly familiar.

Someone coughed.

It is still not too late, I told myself.

And then it was.

Iell. Nearly naked on a deep purple divan.

The divan sat diagonally on a low riser surrounded by drapery of russet-colored silk. Patterned rugs from the Orient were layered about the floor. Iell lay draped along the divan, one arm stretched languidly behind her head, her upper body propped up on tasseled pillows. To the side sat an inlaid table, a crystal lamp, and baskets of lilies and camellias. Behind where Iell lay stood a large mirror like the one in my room. It reflected her unclad body, which was hidden beneath her loose beard and a few diaphanous scarves that trembled with the rise of her breath. In her free hand, she held her long bone pipe, the opium smoke curling above her head in patterns that begged the most lurid interpretations. My mouth grew dry as dust.

Try as I might to remember her as I'd seen her before—in her elegant show, in her apartment, in my arms—this new creature mesmerized me. Mesmerized us all. I half closed my eyes in a fight between decency and desire as I watched her release a torrent of smoke from her beautiful mouth. She moved her free hand into the air, playfully arching and rolling it through the smoke. Her aristocratic fingers cast a sorceress's spell. I had touched those hands less than an hour before, when she sat next to me in the Lecture Room.

The music shifted, its minor notes sinking into inscrutability. I tripped over a chair in the back and sank down on it, weak-kneed. I tried to will myself to look away but could not. Whatever sense I'd had of being a separate man disappeared, and I merged with the audience. We breathed in and out like a single animal, fixated on our prey.

Iell began to sing. In a slow and guttural voice, she crooned a nonsensical tune about heroes and brave lonely men, and the room went hot with fusty air. I swallowed hard. Praying for strength, I told myself to leave. To wait outside until this travesty was over, and then to whisk my love away and never mention this night. But then those visions came again—my mother's gaze through a little jar, falling stars, a river of mud—and despite the visions, or perhaps because of them, I decided to face the truth. I was not a little boy hiding behind his mama's petticoats. No manner of wishing would ever change what was in front of me.

And so I stayed.

In horror and fascination, I watched Iell curve her hand down toward a foreign-looking basket next to the divan, and I felt something coming loose in me. The basket was old, woven from black and brown fronds, the top of it pointed and held firmly in place by a worn leather binding. The small fire burned hotter and the flame flickered crimson across the basket's fronds as Iell's delicate fingers undid the straps. As she reached into its bowels, I smelled smoke.

Someone sighed as Iell pulled a long black snake from the basket and held it up high. The reptile corkscrewed around her fist, then slunk down and down along her arm. It slid its terrible way toward her thin white neck, and for a moment I worried that it might hurt her, but it stopped and nested for a time in the warmth and lusciousness of her beard. My breath left me. The snake stirred again. I marked the outline of its movement beneath the beard as it traveled in nearly perfect circles, round and round, a slow swell below the surface, a circular wave. It broke free just below her heavy bosom, and as it slithered down, traveling the road of her body beneath the silk scarves, moving in search of a place to hide, all I could hear was the low growl of men's breath as it rose and fell amid the occasional creak of a chair or a heavy boot pressed unthinkingly against the earthen floor. When Iell parted her perfect thighs, creating a furrowed escape route, the snake pushed out its blind, rounded head. The entire room inhaled, with no outward release at all. The snake slid from Iell's body onto the divan. It dropped with a thud onto the floor and curved its nasty way into the shadows. Each of us waited in a no-man's-land of tightening skin and unbelievable thirst.

Iell parted her knees, slowly, the silk scarves splitting, draping on either side of her long white thighs, the fire above her flaring, the smell of smoke more distinct now, cloying. And with all of the scarves parted, we saw the second beard, tied in ribbons. A devil's gift.

The sound of muffled feet from the floor above barely broke through my trance, and when the music began again—although I hadn't noticed that it had stopped—sights and sounds muddled in my head. A bewitching tune. Almost a chant. The smoke growing thicker, the clatter of boots outside on the stairs as Iell's fingers drew across the ribbons, unwinding, untying, her knees parting.

And then in that heartbreaking moment, the mirror behind her positioned perfectly to reflect it all, I came to understand the truth of Iell.

Her other sex, as real and as large as my own, eased out languidly from between her legs as she slipped a long slender finger into her orifice in proof that the he was also a she. I reeled with the fact of it. A gift like none I have ever seen. Magnificent. Utterly horrible. Not only woman, but man as well. My belly went hollow, lungs on fire, legs like broken weeds. My world cracked in half.

I slipped back in time. I fought the feeling. The experience of innocence melting away into some hideous truth. But then I was in my mother's lap. It was the middle of the night, and we were looking out the window at the sky as one star and then another fell toward the earth. I was afraid and trembling.

"Can the sky fall, Mummy?"

My mother's lips moved. This time, after all these years, I could finally hear her words.

"Everything must fall eventually, sweet boy, even your father." My mother gripped my hand and stared at me with eyes as dark as midnight. "But he brought himself down. I did not push him. You must remember that." Specks of sweat glinted across her brow, and her breathing was too low and too deep. "No matter what anyone says, you and I know it was his own doing. All that drinking and carrying on. A man with no control, Bartholomew, is no man at all."

She set me on the floor and handed me a lantern, its light flickering dimly. . . .

"Fire, fire!"

I startled awake. All around me in that cellar room, men had begun to rise and frantically look about, as if waking from a dream. Better the Museum burn to the ground and me along with it than face what was happening, I thought. But I'd no choice. Frantically, I pushed against the crowd and moved toward the stage. Smoke poured under the door. From above, gongs were clanging.

Iell looked up. Our eyes connected. She took in a sharp breath, as if from shock, and I reached down and touched the stark thinness of my own thighs and all but laughed aloud. The ultimate *Lusus naturae*. And then I could not move.

"Hold the lantern still." My mother reached for the glass bottle on the windowsill and carried it to where a kettle of mushroom soup had been set to boil. Without looking at me, my mother tipped the contents of that bottle into the soup. I heard my father stumble onto the porch outside. My mother blew the lantern out and took it from my hands. Cautioning me with a finger to her lips to stay silent, she set me down behind a potted tree, the smell of dirt comforting despite the pang of fear I felt at her leaving me alone like that.

Iell's face turned white with anger. "Bartholomew, how dare you!" I staggered toward her, the smoke thicker now.

My father stumbled into the room, and my mother seated him in the chair that was still warm from our bodies. I inched along the wall until I could see them. Humming still, my mother filled a bowl and sat by him. She dipped a silver spoon into the dark mushroom soup, then slid it between my father's lips. Even though he shook his head no, she coaxed him, and eventually he ate.

I watched as she lifted the spoon again and again. Some of the soup dribbled from the side of his mouth onto his chin, and, ever the dutiful wife, she dabbed it clean with the end of her apron. My father drifted into sleep. Night cicadas chirped in the meadow, and I wondered where the fallen stars had landed. My mother tucked a strand of hair behind her ear, and we waited until, with no warning, my father shot to his feet, his face gone purple, his eyes pushing out of his head. Shocked, I slid farther behind the potted tree as he lurched around the room, bellowing. Blindly, he came at my mother, knocking into the tree, a river of dirt spilling over me, and I turned away and wrapped my arms protectively around my head. Then I heard a thud. My father fell to the ground. Afraid, I ran for my mother. When she lifted her skirts, I dove beneath them without a thought, and, shivering beneath her pale yellow petticoats, I clung to her legs, which were covered in striped stockings traveling up and around like a barbershop pole.

Two men, handlers, I assumed, swooped in, covered Iell in a long robe, and hustled her past me and out the door. Somehow I lurched through the blackened air and up the cellar stairs, coming back to myself in the middle of the Atrium, where a herd of party guests stampeded by. Clouds of smoke billowed down the hallway, flames visibly licking the walls near Barnum's office and the Yellow Room and the closed door of the Arboretum. Bridgett was making her way down the hall by feel, one hand running along the wall, the other holding a handkerchief to her nose against the smoke. Then she stopped and calmly watched Fish hop about and scream orders to anyone who would listen, workers and partygoers alike running up and down the hallway with buckets of water, bells of the fire brigade banging in the distance. Litter from the departing party guests lay across the floor like refuse left after the retreat of a flood.

I made my way through the room, grabbing Bridgett by the elbow as I passed and dragging her with me. As soon as we hit the clean air of the Atrium, she yanked her arm away from me.

"Did you see Iell coming out?"

"We all saw her, Mr. Fortuno, no doubt about it."

"And where's Matina? Is she all right?"

"Why do you care? She's with Alley now."

I seized Bridgett by the shoulders and shook her hard.

"Oh, for God's sake, she's just outside."

I rushed out the big front doors and, sure enough, smack in the middle of Broadway stood Matina, next to Emma and a mass of distraught guests, wringing her hands but clearly fine. Panting with relief, I turned back to survey the Museum, looking up in dread. The upper windows showed no signs of flame or smoke. Thank God.

"Out of the way!" Alley barreled past me, his guard just behind; the two of them held up sloshing barrels of water above their heads and headed inside the Museum. I took off after them. Just before I reached the flames, I stopped. I could see the blaze slowly coming under control, and I doubted that whatever help I could offer would matter much. At least it was clear now that Alley was not the firebug. He'd been under constant guard for days, and it would have been impossible for him to set such a fire without discovery. I looked around for Matina, but she was gone.

My entire world was gone.

There was only one thing I had been right about: the capacity of true Prodigies to reflect what's hidden within us. Seeing the secret of the real Iell had shaken every one of my own secrets loose. She had shown me my true self. For years, I'd thought my thinness was a gift, a rare self-mastery set in motion by my mother and honed to perfection after the incident with Mary Louise in the barn. But now I knew the truth. What I'd seen as strength was actually weakness. I'd resisted physical gratification not because I was a purer soul but because I'd seen my mother poison my father, and I was terrified to eat! My body was not a gift at all. It never had been. I was no Prodigy. I was a Gaff, made by a madwoman. I was what I most despised.

✳ ✳ ✳

When the sun finally broke the horizon, its radiance poured over the rooftops and then flowed down the side of the Museum like a river of gold. I had been sitting on my windowsill all night, and I was almost sorry to see the darkness disappear. There was still a tinge of smoke in the air, but the fire brigade had left hours ago, and there was no outward sign of the fire in the street below. I pictured Cook making breakfast in the kitchens as always, pots and china clanging away.

Matina and the others would soon wander down to breakfast, most of them bleary-eyed from the champagne and the rich food and the excitement of the night before. Emma and Ricardo would chatter away, while Matina hunted down a loaf of bread or a fresh slice of ham to eat with her eggs. Business as usual. I sat and considered what to do next.

When the church bells struck nine, I rose and made my way down to the Yellow Room to meet Iell as planned. After the events of the previous evening, I wasn't sure whether she'd still be there to meet me, but I needed to know, one way or the other.

The nuthatch chirped at me as I pulled the sheet from her cage. "Soon, little one, soon," I said. I took out a pen, ink, and paper. I had two letters to write before I could leave.

I signed my resignation letter with a flourish, using my best red wax for the seal. Then I penned a longer letter to Matina, begging her forgiveness, telling her that she meant everything in the world to me and I hoped she would be happy with Alley.

After slipping that letter under Matina's door, I made my way downstairs. Despite the fire the night before, the Museum had already opened to the public, so I merged into the morning crowd, ignoring their stares and comments, knowing I'd not have to endure them much longer. The force of habit was strong, and I couldn't help but check the notice in the Green Room as I walked by. Emma and Bridgett's names were listed, but I saw no mention of Alley, Matina, or Iell. Shows were already in progress in the minor rooms. No one seemed to notice my absence.

I went down the Grand Staircase toward Barnum's office, or what was left of it. Someone, probably Thaddeus or Fish, had put up a screen to hide the mess at the back of the hall. I slipped past the screen onto a floor black with ash. The door to the Arboretum was dreadfully charred, but when I pressed it open, I was relieved to see that the inside had been untouched by flames. Farther on, I reached Barnum's door and found it burnt and black. I took out a handkerchief to protect my hand, and worked the doorknob to the right. The door creaked open, water dripping from the sill above. Inside, a few pieces of furniture had been singed, but the damage was not as bad as it could have been. I slipped into the room and set my resignation letter on Barnum's desk, aware that I'd tracked in black footprints from the hall.

The Yellow Room had gotten the worst of the fire. Somehow, a small sign posted at the entrance that read EXHIBIT CLOSED had survived, though it was curled at the edges, the paper half burnt. Inside, the floor was still so wet from the dousing it had received that my boots squished as I walked across the room. Iell's pedestal still stood, but everything else had been burned beyond recognition. Clearly the fire had started here.

There was no sign of Iell. Had she decided not to meet me after all? I didn't know if I was disappointed or relieved.

It wasn't until I made my way back through the main exhibit room—half full of visitors, since Barnum had decided to open his doors as usual—that I spotted her, half hidden next to a display of a two-headed calf whose little body floated in a sealed pickle jar. The plaque beside it read EVEN OUR LORD EXPERIMENTS. Morning light illuminated the cherrywood cases full of letters and leaflets, silver tea sets, and a grouping of stuffed owls, but Iell sat in the shadows, a bag and parasol on the floor at her side. She looked small and fragile in a plain black dress, her hands resting idly in her lap.

I took a step toward her. She smiled meekly but did rise to greet me.

I cleared my throat and waited for her to acknowledge her deceit or to ask for forgiveness, but all she gave me was a slow sensual sigh. When a group of boys came tromping down the hallway, she shifted her attention from me to them. One boy carried a large stick and banged the floor with it. Another mimicked birdcalls and then spit onto the floor.

"Nasty little animals, boys," Iell said finally. "So cruel. So fickle."

"When were you going to tell me?"

Iell rose. "When I first came here," she said, "all I wanted was to perform with dignity. To do my show in the Yellow Room—just my beard to keep their interest. But Barnum refused me. No matter how well I did as one of you, he wanted all of me." She paused and ran a slender finger down the side of her beard, taking a deep breath and letting it out slowly as she looked at me. "Now you've seen all of me, too. And I understand why you won't be leaving with me today."

It was true that I'd been doubting my decision, but I didn't appreciate Iell assuming she knew me best.

"You're not giving me a chance to make good on my word."

"Do you remember when I told you that I'd been married and that my husband died young?"

I nodded.

"Well, he didn't die. He found out my truth on our wedding night and was so horrified he left me, after beating me nearly to death with a horse whip." Iell's gaze dropped to the ground. "Have you any idea what it's like to see love warp into repulsion in the blink of an eye? But from the beginning, I saw how you looked at me, and I thought, Here is a man who will understand me. Here is a man who will accept me totally."

"I meant what I said about loving you."

"But that was before you knew my true nature. I saw the look on your face last night."

She was right that I'd been horrified to realize the true nature of her gift. But the truth was that I was drawn to her even now. I'd spent my whole life afraid of feeding my hungers. Perhaps this was my chance to see where my desires led me.

"I can live with your peculiarities, Iell. We can still make a decent life together. No one need know about . . . *that*. But you must promise never to keep secrets from me again."

"My *peculiarities*?" Iell's face went blank. "*That*?" She took a long breath. "I thought you, more than anyone else, would understand my specialness. I thought you would love all of me. Much as I want to live a normal life, you must see now that I can never do so. My differences run too deep. Your seeing me, all of me, has driven this home."

Before either of us could say anything else, the boys were upon us. They pushed the taller one forward and, in his awkwardness, he banged into me and sent me stumbling toward a wall of blackwood boxes. I righted myself and swung my cane at the boy's head, and all three ran laughing the other way down the hall.

Iell looked at me with guarded eyes. "I belong in this world, Bartholomew. Perhaps your place is somewhere outside the Museum walls."

My heart sank. There was a ruckus from somewhere upstairs, and I could hear the sound of pounding feet, then silence. She was right. Even though I was drawn to Iell, some part of me recoiled from who she really was. No matter that I offered to marry her and take her away, Iell understood the limits of my feelings, and so did I. She was calling an end to it.

Who knows what else either of us might have said that morning, but the boys came banging back up the hall, one of them with something stuffed beneath his shirt to make him look as if he had breasts. I shook my head in disgust, and while I was distracted, Iell turned and walked the other way.

✳ ✳ ✳

Suitcase in hand, Liberty in her cage tucked safely under my arm, I stepped onto the cobblestones of Ann Street and shut the service door behind me for the very last time. Earlier that afternoon, I'd taken a carriage and gone to see the Chinaman. I demanded a new root and wanted to know about its magic properties. He laughed at me. Told me the root was a restorative for sick people who couldn't eat, nothing more powerful than that, and if I was eating I didn't need it anymore. I would have panicked and perhaps been driven to unpleasantness, but for the look in the old man's eye. I knew he was right. The strength of the root had been my own all along. Now there was nothing left to do but move on.

Although dirt was blowing across the river from Hunters Point, clouding the horizon, I stood outside in the late-afternoon sun, knowing I'd made the right decision. I was a Gaff, but I was also a whole being, and I did not belong in Barnum's world.

I'd heard of a boardinghouse far uptown, near the city's new Central Park, and I hoped to secure a room there. What did I care if civilization didn't reach that high up the island? The city had cleared the area of squatters' shacks and pig farms, and I looked forward to the change of scenery. The new Central Park Arsenal already boasted an open-air aviary. I planned to write a letter to the caretaker, citing my credentials as an experienced bird feeder.

I walked up Ann Street to Broadway and waited in front of the Museum for a streetcar. Alley's voice came from somewhere behind me. I smiled.

"You look like you could use a drink. Just a quick nip before you go." He grabbed my bag and threw a beefy arm around my shoulder.

"What are you doing here?" I asked.

"Matina told me you left her a note saying you were leavin', and I thought I'd give you a hand. Can't say I'm sorry you quit, but I'm sure surprised, I'll give ya that."

Alley grabbed my bag and nodded toward the footbridge. Together, we walked in silence all the way to McNealy's. It was nearly empty inside, only Esmeralda and a few stragglers, who occupied the stools by the bar. Alley and I took a table away from the door and sat and drank beer, watching the sun burn through the grubby front windows. The tavern looked a little tired in the full light of day, its scarred oak tables and floors sticky with dried ale, the corners filled with dust and cobwebs never visible at night, but I was glad to be with my old friend.

At first, we talked about obvious things: the fire, the weather, the recent rumors that Barnum would be selling items from his collection to the new Museum of Science being opened uptown. I thought to apologize for doubting his word about setting the fires but said nothing, knowing Alley would prefer it that way. Eventually, I'd had enough to drink to drop my reserve and dared to bring up Matina.

"She's goin' with me," Alley said. "We leave tomorrow noon. She's a good woman." He shrugged, and my heart broke, and that was that.

One more beer, and I told him what I'd found out about Iell.

"Yeah, that's somethin', ain't it? We all saw last night when they dragged her out of the basement. Lots of talk before that, though none of us knew for sure, exceptin' Emma," Alley said. "And Matina. She suspected. She's got a nose for news."

My hand shook slightly, and I put down my beer. "I never thought . . . I never heard . . ."

"Oh, hell, Fortuno. Think of it as a case of a bird in the hand bein' worth two in the bush." Alley made a ferocious face, banging his long yellow teeth together and howling at his joke. Surprisingly, his comment made me laugh, too, and that seemed to please him even more than the joke itself. "There you go," he said, a smile puckering his grizzled chin. "In the end, most things are funny, Fortuno, and thank God for that."

The aroma of fried onions from McNealy's kitchen made me hungry, so I ordered a kidney pie. As it came to the table, Alley tipped up the end of his glass, draining the rest of his beer. He made no comment about my eating. Then his face lit up, and he nodded toward the front door. Matina walked in, a flustered cabdriver holding open the door for her as she scolded him. She moved toward us, her body rolling from side to side, a grand ship of a woman, built to endure.

Rising to his feet, Alley flushed red and pushed his dirty hair from his face. I stood, as one ought, in the presence of a lady.

I kissed Matina's hand. "How did you know where I'd be?"

"Alley promised me he would find you and bring you here, and he did, the dear boy."

Alley pulled a chair out for her, and Matina sat, grandly adjusting her bonnet, before she leaned over the table and pressed my hand between her plump palms. In an act of gentlemanly discretion, Alley excused himself and left us to talk alone.

"I simply had to see you before you left." Matina pressed my hand between her plump palms. Her eyes teared up, and she turned her face away until she'd regained control. "What will you do now?" she asked. "Where will you go?"

I told her about my new plans, ignoring the tug in my belly when she withdrew her hands from mine.

"My heart . . ." She lifted a hand and placed it on her chest, and my own heart hollowed out.

"I feel the same."

"Maybe a move to the country one day?" Matina asked, with a weak smile.

"You never know," I said. "Though I do like the bustle of the city."

"Well, you will be missed, Barthy. I hope you know that." She sighed, then looked about until she caught Alley's eye. "Enough said."

Alley ambled over and helped Matina to her feet, and when she pressed her lips against my forehead, my whole body mourned the loss of her, of Alley, of all of them. Then she patted her hair into place and let Alley take her arm and lead her out the door.

After that, I ate in silence, drinking my ale and watching the sun dim in the windows. I paid my bill with a final nod to Esmeralda, picked up my bag and my bird, and stepped out to the porch. The setting sun shone along the wall, illuminating the Plaques for the Dead. For the last time, I touched the bronze square of Grizzly Adams for luck. Maybe when I die? I thought fleetingly—but no, I'd never have a place on that wall.

A familiar squawk pulled my attention to the other side of the porch. The old oak had filled out with so many summer leaves that the top branches were invisible from where I stood. But if I tilted my head to the right, I saw them, nestled in the leaves like jewels: at least a dozen of my birds—the parakeets, the cockatoos, Arrow the parrot, one wing slightly ruffled, and the raven. After escaping from Barnum's Museum, they'd winged their way here to be near the river. Out of their natural element, but free.

I pulled the piece of bread I'd swiped from the Museum from my pocket. Leaning against the porch rail, I threw part of the crust to the birds and ate the rest myself.

Epilogue

September 23, 1865

Dearest Barthy,

I hope that this letter reaches you safely. I've just today received news from Emma, along with a clipping, about the demise of our Museum. It's hard to believe so many years of history could go up in smoke like that. The Lecture Room, the exhibits, our little dining room. It feels like the end of an era. But Emma tells me no person was harmed. Zippy and his nurse have moved on to Boston, and Ricardo and Emma have found new homes on the Bowery. No one seems to know what became of Bridgett. The rumor according to Emma is that the Copperheads recruited her months ago and that it was she who set the fires. I, for one, believe it. She was such an ambitious girl. But who knows what is true. She also said that Barnum told the newspapers that the fire started in the furnace room. He wanted no mention of arson or the Copperheads because bad news does not help attendance—I suppose he has a point.

Still, it brings joy to my heart to know that several of Barnum's treasures survived the disaster and are now in his new museum. And it brings even greater joy to know that you were safely settled into your new home before disaster hit, Barthy. Yes, Emma told me how you have made a new life for yourself outside of the business. As have we. Alley and I are happy here. There is much work to do, but the skies are wide, and there is space for people like us. And Alley and I are expecting our first child this spring. We are beside ourselves with joy.

So there is my news. Should you ever crave the country, there is always a room for you with us. And I look forward to telling our new child about Uncle Barthy, who tends to the birds in the big city back East.

All my love,

Matina

New York Times

THE NEW YORK TIMES - *July 14, 1865*

DISASTROUS FIRE

Total Destruction of Barnum's American Museum.

LOSS ESTIMATED AT $1,000,000.

GREAT EXCITEMENT IN THE CITY

The fire which yesterday destroyed BARNUM'S American Museum did a damage to this and the adjacent communities, which neither time nor money can replace. Birds of rarest plumage, fish of most exquisite tint, animals peculiar to every section, minerals characteristic of every region, and peculiarities of all portions of the earth, costly, beautiful, curious and strange were crowded on the dusty shelves of room after room, where they attracted the earnest attention and studious regard of the scholar and the connoisseur.

All this has gone.

The fire originated in a defective furnace in the cellar beneath the office of the MUSEUM and was first discovered by an employee of the Museum, at precisely thirty-five minutes past noon. The alarm was instantly given to the police and firemen and to the inmates of the Museum, of which latter, happily, there were few.

The firemen came clambering up the walls, and howling into the Lecture Room, dashing their axes through the floors and swinging their trumpets, as if to menace the multitude; and to the three or four spectators who preserved sufficient coolness to take sober note of the spectacle, it seemed wonderful that there was not enormous loss of life. The whales were, of course, burned alive. At an early stage of conflagration, the large panes of glass in the great "whale tank" were broken to allow the heavy mass of water to flow upon the floor of the main saloon. The large cage, in which were confined the anacondas and the pythons was capsized, and the tenants wandered whither their fancy led. Naturally enough, they took advantage of their new-found liberty, and soon were traveling down stairs, to the infinite astonishment and alarm of the multitude.

The "Man-Eater" alligator also suffered a cruel death amid the burning pile. True to his taciturn habits, the alligator failed to make the slightest attempt at escape.

The firemen, in their endeavors to save the property, exhibited a penchant for exhibits. One fireman was seen emerging from the building with a stuffed owl in his hands. Another fastened on one of the wax figures, and it is said that the wax figure of Mr. and Mrs. TOM THUMB and baby are among the things that were saved. A giantess made her way out without difficulty, but hastened to conceal herself from public exhibition, in a nearby hotel.

PROGRESS OF THE CONFLAGRATION.

At 1 o'clock the Museum was a mass of fire, and the flames had burst into the adjoining buildings in Fulton-street, Broadway and Ann-street. It seemed as though the entire block through to Nassau-street must be consumed but for the firemen, who had now arrived in force.

The heat had now become intense and unendurable. The crowd that thronged Park-row, Broadway and the Park were compelled to fall back. The throng that stood in Ann street were driven halfway to Nassau. The steam from the heated buildings and the dense smoke darkened the air.

At 1:30 the whole wall on the Ann-street side had fallen. At 1:45 o'clock the Broadway front of the Museum fell in three different sections, one after the other. The first to fall was the part parallel with Broadway, which went over in one mass, falling flat on the pavement of the street, and then — and not till then — breaking up into innumerable fragments.

At 2 o'clock, the section of the front wall facing on park-row still remained, and all eyes were turned in its direction. It was a very large, high portion, reaching to the uppermost story. About five minutes later this great facade careened gracefully over and slowly fell — not in among the burning ruins — but out on Broadway. It fell as a trap-door on a hinge and remained intact until it was smashed upon the pavement, sending up a frightful spray of bricks and mortar, and a vast cloud of smoke. This finished the old Museum.

At 3 o'clock the fire was wholly under control, but the building was totally destroyed.

Mr. BARNUM constantly labored to keep his museum up to the times, adding daily to the collections of curiosities, and varying and increasing the other attractions; and his efforts were rewarded by a constantly increasing popularity. People knew that there was a good deal of humbug about the place; but this they good-naturedly accepted and laughed at, while the intrinsic value of the museum, as a whole, was generally acknowledged.

There was no other place in the city where an equal amount of rational amusement would be obtained at a price which was within the reach of the poorest, and its destruction has occasioned almost universal regret.

Acknowledgments

THEY SAY IT TAKES A VILLAGE TO RAISE A CHILD. A FIRST BOOK isn't much different. Thanks to my early readers, especially Sue Loesburg, who believed, and Carrie Colburn, who was full of encouragement.

A writer needs good teachers, and I had two great ones: Mark Farrington and Elly Williams, both of the Johns Hopkins Advanced Academics Program's creative writing program in Washington, D.C.

Thanks also to the Circus World in Baraboo, Wisconsin, made possible by Douglas Jansson, president of the Milwaukee Community Foundation, for a wealth of source material. And to the various friends and readers who gave me great input: Ann Hood, Lisa Tucker, Alexia von Lipsey, Sharon Mazer, Claire Nelson, and Jeff Barry.

The lovely illustrations are the brainchild of Cecilia Sorochin.

Special thanks to Keith Donohue, who has been tremendously generous in time, wisdom, skill, and expertise, and again to Elly Williams, who walked the walk with me for many years. I have also been blessed with an awesome agent, Mollie Glick, and an equally talented editor, Helen Atsma.

Finally, what would I have done without my husband, Rick Jones: editor, proofreader, supporter, and very patient man.